THE
COLLECTED
ENCHANTMENTS

Also by Theodora Goss

Novels

The Extraordinary Adventures of the Athena Club
The Strange Case of the Alchemist's Daughter
European Travel for the Monstrous Gentlewoman
The Sinister Mystery of the Mesmerizing Girl

Novellas

The Thorn and the Blossom

Short Fiction Collections

In the Forest of Forgetting
The Rose in Twelve Petals & Other Stories
Snow White Learns Witchcraft

Poetry Collections

Songs for Ophelia

As Editor

Interfictions: An Anthology of Interstitial Writing
(with Delia Sherman)

Medusa's Daughters:
Magic and Monstrosity from Women Writers of the Fin-de-Siècle

Voices from Fairyland:
The Fantastical Poems of Mary Coleridge,
Charlotte Mew, and Sylvia Townsend Warner

THEODORA GOSS

THE COLLECTED ENCHANTMENTS

Mythic Delirium
BOOKS

mythicdelirium.com

The Collected Enchantments

Cover art © 2023 by Catrin Welz-Stein, catrinwelzstein.com.
All rights reserved.

Interior illustrations © 2023 by Paula Arwen Owen, arwendesigns.net.
All rights reserved.

Cover design © 2023 by Mike Allen, Brett Massé, and Sydney Macias.
All rights reserved

FIRST EDITION
February 14, 2023

Hardback ISBN: 978-1-7326440-7-6
Trade Paperback ISBN: 978-1-956522-02-0
E-Book ISBN: 978-1-7326440-8-3

Library of Congress Control Number: 2022950427

Published by Mythic Delirium Books
Roanoke, Virginia
mythicdelirium.com

Further copyright information begins on page 429.

Our gratitude goes out to the following who because of their generosity are from now on designated as supporters of Mythic Delirium Books: Saira Ali, Cora Anderson, Anonymous, Patricia M. Cryan, Steve Dempsey, Oz Drummond, Patrick Dugan, Matthew Farrer, C. R. Fowler, Mary J. Lewis, Paul T. Muse, Jr., Shyam Nunley, Finny Pendragon, Kenneth Schneyer, and Delia Sherman.

In Memoriam

To the women writers of fantasy and the fantastic who formed my literary imagination when I was growing up: Tanith Lee, Anne McCaffrey, Patricia McKillip, and Ursula K. Le Guin. I would not be the writer I am without you.

Contents

Introduction: Why I Write Fantasy

I magine a girl, about twelve years old. She is sitting on a bench under a tree, reading a book. It is recess—this is in the days when schools had still had a proper recess after lunch—and the other children in her class are engaged in a game of kickball, except three girls who are sitting on the hillside overlooking the field, talking about their favorite celebrity crushes. But this girl is not interested in kickball—she is incapable of kicking the red rubber ball in the correct direction, or of catching it once it has been kicked. When she is required to play, during gym class, she always goes out into the field, between second and third base, to get as far away from the ball as possible. She does not understand why anyone would play kickball for fun. And her most recent crush was on Robin Hood, not exactly the sort of figure one can gossip about. ("Robin who? Is he in a band?" most of the girls in her class would say.) When she grows up, she wants to be either a writer or a sorceress, preferably with a tame dragon, a small one that can sit on her shoulder, sort of like a winged, scaly cat. She will live in a tower deep in the forest, far away from anyone, and either write or whatever sorceresses do. Either of those seem like good life goals.

That was me in elementary school. What was I reading? Probably one of the Narnia books, or *The Hobbit*, or something by E. Nesbit, Edward Eager, Astrid Lindgren—*The Brothers Lionheart* was my favorite. Later I would graduate to Anne McCaffrey's Pern series, Tanith Lee's Flat Earth novels, Ursula K. Le Guin's Earthsea trilogy, Patricia McKillip's *The Forgotten Beasts of Eld*, Madeleine L'Engel's *A Wrinkle in Time* and its sequels. Some of the books I read were of higher quality than others, but I was not concerned with quality until much later. What I wanted was a magical secondary world—Pern, Earthsea, Narnia, Middle Earth. I did not realize until I was an adult why this particular aspect of fantasy was important for me: it spoke to my reality as an immigrant.

English was my third language. I was born in Budapest, Hungary, in the days of the Soviet Union, when there was still an Iron Curtain across Europe. The first books I read were collections of Hungarian and other European fairy tales. When I was five years old, my mother left Hungary, taking me with her, leaving behind the family and culture she had grown up in, for the hope of a better life in America. We moved first to Italy, then Belgium, and finally the United States, where I started school, speaking very little English—at that point I knew only Hungarian and French, and my Hungarian was fading fast. I remember the strangeness of encountering a new culture, with new food, new customs. Television taught me to ask for Wonder Bread and Campbell's Soup from a can, to watch Saturday morning cartoons. Hungary became a country I vaguely remembered. Soon, I could no longer speak its language. Its food was served ceremoniously on special occasions: madártej and beigli at Christmas, húsos palacsinta at the parties my mother would occasionally throw for colleagues from work. We observed its special customs, celebrating our name days and Mikulás, the day Szent Miklós left chocolates and small presents in my shoes. We painted eggs at Easter. My mother still cursed in Hungarian, so I came to associate the language with powerful, forbidden words. To me, Hungary was a magical land—one to which we could not return because of the political situation. It might as well have been Narnia.

As an adult, I read two essays that define for me what fantasy is and can be. The first was Le Guin's "A Citizen of Mondath" in her collection *The Language of the Night*. In it, she says that she first discovered the power of fantasy through reading Lord Dunsany's *A Dreamer's Tales*, in which he mentioned Mondath, one of the mysterious Inner Lands, "the lands whose sentinels upon their borders do not behold the sea." Le Guin calls that reading experience "decisive. I had discovered my native country." My native country is one of the Inner Lands. That is, Hungary is landlocked, bordered only by other countries, although it contains Lake Balaton, the largest freshwater lake in Europe, often called the Hungarian Sea. In Le Guin's first serious attempt at a fantasy novel, she created the country of Orsinia, from her own name, Ursula (meaning "little she-bear"). The Latin *ursinus*, meaning bearlike, gives us the surname Orsini. Orsinia, located somewhat vaguely in Central Europe, was Ursula Country, although she had never been to Central Europe herself—that part of the world was essentially Narnia to her as well. I loved Le Guin's *Orsinian Tales*, short stories set in her imaginary country. To me, they felt like home.

The second essay, actually the first chapter in an academic monograph, was by Katherine Hume. In *Fantasy and Mimesis: Responses to Reality in Western Literature*, Hume argues that "literature is the product of two impulses. These are *mimesis*, felt as the desire to imitate, to describe events, people, situations, and objects with such verisimilitude that others can share your experiences; and *fantasy*, the desire to change givens and alter reality." In this formulation, fantasy is not a genre but a mode, a way of approaching literature and the primary world it inevitably describes—because as J.R.R. Tolkien points out in "On Fairy-Stories," writing is always ultimately about our world, the one we inhabit. Fantasy approaches and examines that word in a different way, but there would be no Pegasus without the horse. Perhaps I should have added Tolkien's essay to my list of influences, and it certainly is, but I read it later than I read Le Guin and Hume, so by the time he told me that fantasy can give us three fundamental things we all need in our lives, escape, recovery, and consolation, I already agreed with his argument. Those are certainly three things fantasy gave the twelve-year-old girl avoiding a kickball game by traveling in Nangiyala. What Hume taught me, around the time I started writing fantasy professionally myself, was that fantasy is neither separate from the larger world of fiction, nor fundamentally different from it. Both fantasy and realism are approaches to the world we inhabit. Indeed, once enough time has passed, all realism becomes fantastical. To us, living in the twenty-first century, the characters in Jane Austen's novels are as unreal as Tolkien's elves, as bound by strange customs, as obsessed with rings.

In "A Citizen of Mondath," Le Guin writes that her Orsinian tales were not fantasy, exactly, but neither were they realistic. "Searching for a technique of distancing," she had placed them in Central Europe, which was, at the time to most Americans, a mysterious, exotic location—Mittel Europa was like Middle Earth. After her Orsinia novel failed to sell, she started writing more clearly categorizable fantasy and science fiction; she had found her distancing technique. But to me, Central Europe was not distant. It was as close as letters to my grandparents, as beigli at Christmas, as my mother cursing in Elvish (well, it may as well have been). My stories about the Central European country of Sylvania were inspired in part by Le Guin's Orsinian tales, but also in part by the fact that my grandmother's family comes from what Hungarians call Erdély—that is, Transylvania, often translated as "Land Beyond the Forest." Sylvania is not Transylvania; it inhabits the same vaguely Central European space as Orsinia. You can get to Vienna from there, but I can't tell you the train station, or what landscapes the train will pass through. It's a country of the imagination. Still, it's more real to me than, for example, Los Angeles. I have been to Los Angeles, I have driven up and down its highways, and I'm still not entirely convinced that it exists.

There is a sense in which my childhood was fantastical. The reality I read about in the teen novels we were sometimes assigned in school, or that I read on my own out of curiosity, was not my reality. I think this is a common experience for immigrants. Like many immigrant children, my literary education had started with the fairy tales of my native culture. A certain way of looking at the world had been passed on to me, one in which supposedly dimwitted third sons always prevailed and white cats could turn out to be cursed princesses in disguise. Snakes and wolves and bears spoke, if not in English, then in Hungarian. It was better to be lucky than clever, and even better to be kind, because it was the kind girl who was showered with gold, and her lazy sister who had to go home covered in pitch. In that world, the most important rule of all, always and forever, was "Be polite to old women," because they were inevitably fairies or witches, and both were equally dangerous.

It still seems to me that the world of fairy tales is more real than some of the supposedly realistic tales we tell ourselves. In "On Fairy-Stories," Tolkien makes the same argument: automobiles, he says, are not necessarily more real than dragons. Both are creatures of the human imagination, and dragons have been around a lot longer than automobiles. Who knows what automobiles will turn into—perhaps some day we will get flying cars, and we will have mechanical dragons in the sky. Our perception of reality is so conditioned by imagination that at some level, we are all fantasists. We see trees and dream of dryads or Ents. We make up countries, pretending that there are lines on maps, and sometimes we build walls to make those lines real—but eventually the walls come down. What is real, finally, when the world we see is created by rays of light passing through the lenses of our eyes, focused and projected back to our retinas and then interpreted by our individual brains? I have great respect for consensual reality and the fact that, as Zen masters tell us, when I kick a rock, my foot will hurt. But we live in a world in which the stock market operates on the same principle as Tinkerbell—if we stop believing, it winks out of existence. It's fairy gold.

In "Why are Americans Afraid of Dragons," Le Guin writes that fantasy involves the free play of the imagination, and when Americans fear it, what they really fear is freedom. I suppose as a hyphenated American, I am only half afraid of dragons. Tolkien has taught me to be wary of them, McCaffrey to want one of my own. Like most writers, I'll probably have to settle for a cat. Le Guin's central point is that fantasy may not paint an accurate picture of our consensual reality, but it can reveal fundamental truths—such as the need to throw certain rings into volcanoes and stand up to dictators. In "The Critics, the Monsters, and the Fantasists," she talks about another fundamental truth fantasy can reveal to us: it can move us beyond anthropocentrism. While literary realism is interested in the human—what we think, how we live—fantasy can show us the world from the perspective of a tree, or a laboratory rat, or an ant (all of which Le Guin has done). It seems to me that this is one of the most important functions of fantasy in our time. More than anything, in the twenty-first century, we humans need to get over ourselves, with our wars, our obsessive accumulation of money (itself an imaginary construct, as cryptocurrency has shown us), the fences we build to enforce those lines on the maps, to keep some of us in and some of us out. How different that territory would look from the point of view of a goose.

So why do I write fantasy? Perhaps because my experience of reality, as a Hungarian-American, was always fantastical, or perhaps because as an inhabitant of the twenty-first century, the world I see around me is more fantastical than most fiction. Tolkien wrote that literature comes from the great Cauldron of Story, into which have gone all the myths, legends, and fairy tales of human culture. What has gone into my particular cauldron of gulyás? The European tales I grew up on, certainly. My family history as well as the American suburbs I grew up in. Three language, the science fiction and fantasy I read growing up, the magical realism I studied in college, the English and American literary traditions I studied as a graduate student, from Chaucer to Toni Morrison. And my personal experiences growing up between two cultures, between Mikulás and kickball. Perhaps fantasy is simply my way of seeing and understanding the world, the shape those rays of light make on my retina. It took a long time for that twelve-year-old girl to become a writer. I'm still working on the sorcer-ess part. I don't yet have a tower in the depth of the forest, but I'm practicing my spells, and I'm sure at some point they'll summon an appropriate dragon (or cat) to sit on my keyboard as I write. In the meantime, I will keep writing stories about third sons and cat princesses and the fundamental importance of being polite to old women, because you just never know.

Why You Might Be a Witch

Because sometimes you dream of flying
the way you used to.

Because the traffic light always changes for you.

Because when you throw the crusts of your sandwich
to sparrows in the public park, they hop close
and closer, until they perch on your finger
and look at you sideways.

Because as you walk down the street,
the wind plays with the hem of your skirt
so it swings dramatically around your ankles.

Because as you walk, determined and sensible,
your shadow is dancing.

Because a lot of people talk to cats
but for you they answer.

Because the sweetgum trees along the sidewalk
love to show you their leaves, sometimes even tossing
them in front of you, yellow veined red,
brown shot with green and yellow,
like children showing off artwork.

Because when you look up,
the moon is always smiling.

Because sometimes darkness closes around you
and you remind yourself that it's all right,
you've worn this cloak before.

Because in winter you acknowledge
that snow is a blanket as well as a shroud,
and we must all sleep sometimes.

Because in spring you can hear the tinkling bell-sounds
that crocuses make, and the deeper gongs of the tulips.

Because the river waves to you in passing,
and you wave back.

Because even the brownstones of this ancient city
look at you with concern: they want to make sure you're well.
You belong to them as much as they to you.

Because witches know what they are
and if I asked, do you remember?
You would have to confess that yes,
you do.

The Rose in Twelve Petals

I. The Witch

THIS ROSE HAS twelve petals. Let the first one fall: Madeleine taps the glass bottle, and out tumbles a bit of pink silk that clinks on the table—a chip of tinted glass—no, look closer, a crystallized rose petal. She lifts it into a saucer and crushes it with the back of a spoon until it is reduced to lumpy powder and a puff of fragrance.

She looks at the book again. "Petal of one rose crushed, dung of small bat soaked in vinegar." Not enough light comes through the cottage's small-paned windows, and besides she is growing nearsighted, although she is only thirty-two. She leans closer to the page. He should have given her spectacles rather than pearls. She wrinkles her forehead to focus her eyes, which makes her look prematurely old, as in a few years she no doubt will be.

Bat dung has a dank, uncomfortable smell, like earth in caves that has never seen sunlight.

Can she trust it, this book? Two pounds ten shillings it cost her, including postage. She remembers the notice in *The Gentlewoman's Companion*: "Every lady her own magician. Confound your enemies, astonish your friends! As simple as a cookery manual." It looks magical enough, with *Compendium Magicarum* stamped on its spine and gilt pentagrams on its red leather cover. But the back pages advertise "a most miraculous lotion, that will make any lady's skin as smooth as an infant's bottom" and the collected works of Scott.

Not easy to spare ten shillings, not to mention two pounds, now that the King has cut off her income. Rather lucky, this cottage coming so cheap, although it has no proper plumbing, just a privy out back among the honey-suckle.

Madeleine crumbles a pair of dragonfly wings into the bowl, which is already half full: orris root; cat's bones found on the village dust heap; oak gall from a branch fallen into a fairy ring; madder, presumably for its color; crushed rose petal; bat dung.

And the magical words, are they quite correct? She knows a little Latin, learned from her brother. After her mother's death, when her father began spending days in his bedroom with a bottle of beer, she tended the shop, selling flour and printed cloth to the village women, scythes and tobacco to the men, sweets to children on their way to school. When her brother came home, he would sit at the counter beside her, saying his *amo, amas*. The silver cross

18

he earned by taking a Hibernian bayonet in the throat is the only necklace she now wears.

She binds the mixture with water from a hollow stone and her own saliva. Not pleasant this, she was brought up not to spit, but she imagines she is spitting into the King's face, that first time when he came into the shop, leaned on the counter, and smiled through his golden beard. "If I had known there was such a pretty shopkeeper in this village, I would have done my own shopping long ago."

She remembers: buttocks covered with golden hair among folds of white linen, like twin halves of a peach on a napkin. "Come here, Madeleine." The sounds of the palace, horses clopping, pageboys shouting to one another in the early morning air. "You'll never want for anything, haven't I told you that?" A string of pearls, each as large as her smallest fingernail, with a clasp of gold filigree. "Like it? That's Hibernian work, taken in the siege of London." Only later does she notice that between two pearls, the knotted silk is stained with blood.

She leaves the mixture under cheesecloth, to dry overnight.

Madeleine walks into the other room, the only other room of the cottage, and sits at the table that serves as her writing desk. She picks up a tin of throat lozenges. How it rattles. She knows, without opening it, that there are five pearls left, and that after next month's rent there will only be four.

Confound your enemies, she thinks, peering through the inadequate light, and the wrinkles on her forehead make her look prematurely old, as in a few years she certainly will be.

II. The Queen

PETALS FALL FROM the roses that hang over the stream, Empress Josephine and Gloire de Dijon, which dislike growing so close to the water. This corner of the garden has been planted to resemble a country landscape in miniature: artificial stream with ornamental fish, a pear tree that has never yet bloomed, bluebells that the gardener plants out every spring. This is the Queen's favorite part of the garden, although the roses dislike her as well, with her romantically diaphanous gowns, her lisping voice, her poetry.

Here she comes, reciting Tennyson.

She holds her arms out, allowing her sleeves to drift on the slight breeze, imagining she is Elaine the lovable, floating on a river down to Camelot. Hard, being a lily maid now her belly is swelling.

She remembers her belly reluctantly, not wanting to touch it, unwilling to acknowledge that it exists. Elaine the lily maid had no belly, surely, she thinks, forgetting that Galahad must have been born somehow. (Perhaps he rose out of the lake?) She imagines her belly as a sort of cavern, where something is growing in the darkness, something that is not hers, alien and unwelcome.

Only twelve months ago (fourteen, actually, but she is bad at numbers), she was Princess Elizabeth of Hibernia, dressed in pink satin, gossiping about the riding master with her friends, dancing with her brothers through the ruined arches of Westminster Cathedral, and eating too much cake at her seventeenth birthday party. Now, and she does not want to think about this so it remains at the edges of her mind, where unpleasant things, frogs and slugs, reside, she is a cavern with something growing inside her, something repugnant, something that is not hers, not the lily maid of Astolat's.

She reaches for a rose, an overblown Gloire de Dijon that, in a fit of temper, pierces her finger with its thorns. She cries out, sucks the blood from her finger, and flops down on the bank like a miserable child. The hem of her diaphanous dress begins to absorb the mud at the edge of the water.

III. The Magician

WOLFGANG MAGUS PLACES the rose he picked that morning in his buttonhole and looks at his reflection in the glass. He frowns, as his master Herr Doktor Ambrosius would have frowned, at the scarecrow in faded wool with a drooping gray mustache. A sad figure for a court magician.

"*Gott in Himmel*," he says to himself, a childhood habit he has kept from nostalgia, for Wolfgang Magus is a reluctant atheist. He knows it is not God's fault but the King's, who pays him so little. If the King were to pay him, say, another shilling per week—but no, that too he would send to his sister, dying of consumption at a spa in Berne. His mind turns, painfully, from the memory of her face, white and drained, which already haunts him like a ghost.

He picks up a volume of Goethe's poems that he has carefully tied with a bit of pink ribbon and sighs. What sort of present is this, for the Princess's christening?

He enters the chapel with shy, stooping movements. It is full, and noisy with court gossip. As he proceeds up the aisle, he is swept by a duchess's train of peau de soie, poked by a viscountess's aigrette. The sword of a marquis smelling of Napoleon-water tangles in his legs, and he almost falls on a baroness, who stares at him through her lorgnette. He sidles through the crush until he comes to a corner of the chapel wall, where he takes refuge.

The christening has begun, he supposes, for he can hear the Archbishop droning in bad Latin, although he can see nothing from his corner but taxidermied birds and heads slick with macassar oil. Ah, if the Archbishop could have learned from Herr Doktor Ambrosius! His mind wanders, as it often does, to a house in Berlin and a laboratory smelling of strong soap, filled with braziers and alembics, books whose covers have been half-eaten by moths, a stuffed basilisk. He remembers his bed in the attic, and his sister, who worked as the Herr Doktor's housemaid so he could learn to be a magician. He sees her face on her pillow at the spa in Berne and thinks of her expensive medications.

What has he missed? The crowd is moving forward, and presents are being given: a rocking horse with a red leather saddle, a silver tumbler, a cap embroidered by the nuns of Iona. He hides the volume of Goethe behind his back.

Suddenly, he sees a face he recognizes. One day she came and sat beside him in the garden, and asked him about his sister. Her brother had died, he remembers, not long before, and as he described his loneliness, her eyes glazed over with tears. Even he, who understands little about court politics, knew she was the King's mistress.

She disappears behind the scented Marquis, then appears again, close to the altar where the Queen, awkwardly holding a linen bundle, is receiving the Princess's presents. The King has seen her, and frowns through his golden beard. Wolfgang Magus, who knows nothing about the feelings of a king toward his former mistress, wonders why he is angry.

She lifts her hand in a gesture that reminds him of the Archbishop. What fragrance is this, so sweet, so dark, that makes the brain clear, that makes the nostrils water? He instinctively tabulates: orris-root, oak gall, rose petal, dung of bat with a hint of vinegar.

Conversations hush, until even the baronets, clustered in a rustic clump at the back of the chapel, are silent.

She speaks: "This is the gift I give the Princess. On her seventeenth birthday she will prick her finger on the spindle of a spinning wheel and die."

Needless to describe the confusion that follows. Wolfgang Magus watches from its edge, chewing his mustache, worried, unhappy. How her eyes glazed, that day in the garden. Someone treads on his toes.

Then, unexpectedly, he is summoned. "Where is that blasted magician!" Gloved hands push him forward. He stands before the King, whose face has turned unattractively red. The Queen has fainted and a bottle of salts is waved under her nose. The Archbishop is holding the Princess, like a sack of barley he has accidentally caught.

"Is this magic, Magus, or just some bloody trick?"

Wolfgang Magus rubs his hands together. He has not stuttered since he was a child, but he answers, "Y-yes, Your Majesty. Magic." Sweet, dark, utterly magic. He can smell its power.

"Then get rid of it. Un-magic it. Do whatever you bloody well have to. Make it not be!"

Wolfgang Magus already knows that he will not be able to do so, but he says, without realizing that he is chewing his mustache in front of the King, "O-of course, Your Majesty."

* * *

IV. The King

WHAT WOULD YOU do, if you were James IV of Britannia, pacing across your council chamber floor before your councilors: the Count of Edinburgh, whose estates are larger than yours and include hillsides of uncut wood for which the French Emperor, who needs to refurbish his navy after the disastrous Indian campaign, would pay handsomely; the Earl of York, who can trace descent, albeit in the female line, from the Tudors; and the Archbishop, who has preached against marital infidelity in his cathedral at Aberdeen? The banner over your head, embroidered with the twelve-petaled rose of Britannia, reminds you that your claim to the throne rests tenuously on a former James's dalliance. Edinburgh's thinning hair, York's hanging jowls, the seams, edged with gold thread, where the Archbishop's robe has been let out, warn you, young as you are, with a beard that shines like a tangle of golden wires in the afternoon light, of your gouty future.

Britannia's economy depends on the wool trade, and spun wool sells for twice as much as unspun. Your income depends on the wool tax. The Queen, whom you seldom think of as Elizabeth, is young. You calculate: three months before she recovers from the birth, nine months before she can deliver another child. You might have an heir by next autumn.

"Well?" Edinburgh leans back in his chair, and you wish you could strangle his wrinkled neck.

You say, "I see no reason to destroy a thousand spinning wheels for one madwoman." Madeleine, her face puffed with sleep, her neck covered with a line of red spots where she lay on the pearl necklace you gave her the night before, one black hair tickling your ear. Clever of her, to choose a spinning wheel. "I rely entirely on Wolfgang Magus," whom you believe is a fraud. "Gentlemen, your fairy tales will have taught you that magic must be met with magic. One cannot fight a spell by altering material conditions."

Guffaws from the Archbishop, who is amused to think that he once read fairy tales.

You are a selfish man, James IV, and this is essentially your fault, but you have spoken the truth. Which, I suppose, is why you are the King.

V. The Queen Dowager

WHAT IS THE GIRL doing? Playing at tug-of-war, evidently, and far too close to the stream. She'll tear her dress on the rosebushes. Careless, these young people, thinks the Queen Dowager. And who is she playing with? Young Lord Harry, who will one day be Count of Edinburgh. The Queen Dowager is proud of her keen eyesight and will not wear spectacles, although she is almost sixty-three.

What a pity the girl is so plain. The Queen Dowager jabs her needle into a black velvet slipper. Eyes like boiled gooseberries that always seem to be staring at you, and no discipline. Now in her day, thinks the Queen Dowager, remembering backboards and nuns who rapped your fingers with canes, in her day girls had discipline. Just look at the Queen: no discipline. Two miscarriages in ten years, and dead before her thirtieth birthday. Of course linen is so much cheaper now that the kingdoms are united. But if only her Jims (which is how she thinks of the King) could have married that nice German princess.

She jabs the needle again, pulls it out, jabs, knots. She holds up the slipper and then its pair, comparing the roses embroidered on each toe in stitches so even they seem to have been made by a machine. Quite perfect for her Jims, to keep his feet warm on the drafty palace floors.

A tearing sound, and a splash. The girl, of course, as the Queen Dowager could have warned you. Just look at her, with her skirt ripped up one side and her petticoat muddy to the knees.

"I do apologize, Madam. I assure you it's entirely my fault," says Lord Harry, bowing with the superfluous grace of a dancing master.

"It *is* all your fault," says the girl, trying to kick him.

"Alice!" says the Queen Dowager. Imagine the Queen wanting to name the girl Elaine. What a name, for a Princess of Britannia.

"But he took my book of poems and said he was going to throw it into the stream!"

"I'm perfectly sure he did no such thing. Go to your room at once. This is the sort of behavior I would expect from a chimney sweep."

"Then tell him to give my book back!"

Lord Harry bows again and holds out the battered volume. "It was always yours for the asking, Your Highness."

Alice turns away, and you see what the Queen Dowager cannot, despite her keen vision: Alice's eyes, slightly prominent, with irises that are indeed the color of gooseberries, have turned red at the corners, and her nose has begun to drip.

VI. The Spinning Wheel

It has never wanted to be an assassin. It remembers the cottage on the Isles where it was first made: the warmth of the hearth and the feel of its maker's hands, worn smooth from rubbing and lanolin.

It remembers the first words it heard: "And why are you carving roses on it, then?"

"This one's for a lady. Look how slender it is. It won't take your upland ram's wool. Yearling it'll have to be, for this one."

At night it heard the waves crashing on the rocks, and it listened as their sound mingled with the snoring of its maker and his wife. By day it heard the crying of the sea birds. But it remembered, as in a dream, the songs of inland birds and sunlight on a stone wall. Then the fishermen would come, and one would say, "What's that you're making there, Enoch? Is it for a midget, then?"

Its maker would stroke it with the tips of his fingers and answer, "Silent, lads. This one's for a lady. It'll spin yarn so fine that a shawl of it will slip through a wedding ring."

It has never wanted to be an assassin, and as it sits in a cottage to the south, listening as Madeleine mutters to herself, it remembers the sounds of seabirds and tries to forget that it was made, not to spin yarn so fine that a shawl of it will slip through a wedding ring, but to kill the King's daughter.

VII. The Princess

ALICE CLIMBS THE tower stairs. She could avoid this perhaps, disguise herself as a peasant woman and beg her way to the Highlands, like a heroine in Scott's novels. But she does not want to avoid this, so she is climbing up the tower stairs on the morning of her seventeenth birthday, still in her nightgown and clutching a battered copy of Goethe's poems whose binding is so torn that the book is tied with pink ribbon to keep the pages together. Her feet are bare, because opening the shoe closet might have woken the Baroness, who has slept in her room since she was a child. Barefoot, she has walked silently past the sleeping guards, who are supposed to guard her today with particular care. She has walked past the Queen Dowager's drawing room thinking: if anyone hears me, I will be in disgrace. She has spent a larger portion of her life in disgrace than out of it, and she remembers that she once thought of it as an imaginary country, Disgrace, with its own rivers and towns and trade routes. Would it be different if her mother were alive? She remembers a face creased from the folds of the pillow, and pale lips whispering to her about the lily maid of Astolat. It would, she supposes, have made no difference. She trips on a step and almost drops the book.

She has no reason to suppose, of course, that the Witch will be there, so early in the morning. But somehow, Alice hopes she will be.

She is, sitting on a low stool with a spinning wheel in front of her.

"Were you waiting for me?" asks Alice. It sounds silly—who else would the Witch be waiting for? But she can think of nothing else to say.

"I was." The Witch's voice is low and cadenced, and although she has wrinkles at the corners of her mouth and her hair has turned gray, she is still rather beautiful. She is not, exactly, what Alice expected.

"How did you know I was coming so early?"

The Witch smiles. "I've gotten rather good at magic. I sell fortunes for my living, you see. It's not much, just enough to buy bread and butter, and to rent a small cottage. But it amuses me, knowing things about people—their lives and their futures."

"Do you know anything—about me?" Alice looks down at the book. What idiotic questions to be asking. Surely a heroine from Scott's novels would think of better.

The Witch nods, and sunlight catches the silver cross suspended from a chain around her neck. She says, "I'm sorry."

Alice understands, and her face flushes. "You mean that you've been watching all along. That you've known what it's been like, being the cursed princess." She turns and walks to the tower window, so the Witch will not see how her hands are shaking. "You know the other girls wouldn't play with me or touch my toys, that the boys would spit over their shoulders, to break the curse they said. Even the chambermaids would make the sign of the cross when I wasn't looking." She can feel tears where they always begin, at the corners of her eyes, and she leans out the window to cool her face. Far below, a gardener is crossing the courtyard, carrying a pair of pruning shears. She says, "Why didn't you remove the curse, then?"

"Magic doesn't work that way." The Witch's voice is sad. Alice turns around and sees that her cheeks are wet with tears. Alice steps toward her, trips again, and drops the book, which falls under the spinning wheel.

The Witch picks it up and smiles as she examines the cover. "Of course, your Goethe. I always wondered what happened to Wolfgang Magus."

Alice thinks with relief: I'm not going to cry after all. "He went away, after his sister died. She had consumption, you know, for years and years. He was always sending her money for medicine. He wrote to me once after he left, from Berlin, to say that he had bought his old master's house. But I never heard from him again."

The Witch wipes her cheeks with the back of one hand. "I didn't know about his sister. I spoke to him once. He was a kind man."

Alice takes the book from her, then says, carefully, as though each word has to be placed in the correct order, "Do you think his spell will work? I mean, do you think I'll really sleep for a hundred years, rather than—you know?"

The Witch looks up, her cheeks still damp, but her face composed. "I can't answer that for you. You may simply be—preserved. In a pocket of time, as it were."

Alice tugs at the ribbon that binds the book together. "It doesn't matter, really. I don't think I care either way." She strokes the spinning wheel, which turns as she touches it. "How beautiful, as though it had been made just for me."

The Witch raises a hand, to stop her perhaps, or arrest time itself, but Alice places her finger on the spindle and presses until a drop of blood blossoms, as dark as the petal of a Cardinal de Richelieu, and runs into her palm.

Before she falls, she sees the Witch with her head bowed and her shoulders shaking. She thinks, for no reason she can remember, Elaine the fair, Elaine the lovable . . .

* * *

VIII. The Gardener

LONG AFTER, WHEN the gardener has grown into an old man, he will tell his grandchildren about that day: skittish horses being harnessed by panicked grooms, nobles struggling with boxes while their valets carry armchairs and even bedsteads through the palace halls, the King in a pair of black velvet slippers shouting directions. The cooks leave the kettles whistling in the kitchen, the Queen Dowager leaves her jewels lying where she has dropped them while tripping over the hem of her nightgown. Everyone runs to escape the spreading lethargy that has already caught a canary in his cage, who makes soft noises as he settles into his feathers. The flowers are closing in the garden, and even the lobsters that the chef was planning to serve with melted butter for lunch have lain down in a corner of their tank.

In a few hours, the palace is left to the canary, and the lobsters, and the Princess lying on the floor of the tower.

He will say, "I was pruning a rosebush at the bottom of the tower that day. Look what I took away with me!" Then he will display a rose of the variety called Britannia, with its twelve petals half-open, still fresh and moist with dew. His granddaughter will say, "Oh, grandpa, you picked that in the garden just this morning!" His grandson, who is practical and wants to be an engineer, will say, "Grandpa, people can't sleep for a hundred years."

IX. The Tower

LET US GET a historical perspective. When the tower was quite young, only a hovel really, a child knocked a stone out of its wall, and it gained an eye. With that eye it watched as the child's father, a chieftain, led his tribe against soldiers with metal breastplates and plumed helmets. Two lines met on the plain below: one regular, gleaming in the morning sun like the edge of a sword, the other ragged and blue like the crest of a wave. The wave washed over the sword, which splintered into a hundred pieces.

Time passed, and the tower gained a second story with a vertical eye as narrow as a staff. It watched a wooden structure grow beside it, in which men and cattle mingled indiscriminately. One morning it felt a prick, the point of an arrow. A bright flame blossomed from the beams of the wooden structure, men scattered, cattle screamed. One of its walls was singed, and it felt the wound as a distant heat. A castle rose, commanded by a man with eyebrows so blond that they were almost white, who caused the name Aelfric to be carved on the lintel of the tower. The castle's stone walls, pummelled with catapults, battered by rams, fell into fragments. From the hilltop a man watched, whose nose had been broken in childhood and remained perpetually crooked. When a palace rose from the broken rock, he caused the name D'Arblay to be carved on the lintel of the tower, beside a boar rampant.

Time passed, and a woman on a white horse rode through the village that had grown around the palace walls, followed by a retinue that stretched behind her like a scarf. At the palace gates, a Darbley grown rich on tobacco plantations in the New World presented her with the palace, in honor of her marriage to the Earl of Essex. The lintel of the tower was carved with the name Elizabeth I, and it gained a third story with a lead-paned window, through which it saw in facets like a fly. One morning it watched the Queen's son, who had been playing ball in the courtyard, fall to the ground with blood dripping from his nostrils. The windows of the palace were draped in black velvet, the Queen and her consort rode away with their retinue, and the village was deserted.

Time passed. Leaves turned red or gold, snow fell and melted into rivulets, young hawks took their first flight from the battlements. A rosebush grew at the foot of the tower: a hybrid, half wild rose, half Cuisse de Nymphe, with twelve petals and briary canes. One morning men rode up to the tower on horses whose hides were mottled with sweat. In its first story, where the chieftain's son had played, they talked of James III. Troops were coming from France, and the password was Britannia. As they left the tower, one of them plucked a flower from the rosebush. "Let this be our symbol," he said in the self-conscious voice of a man who thinks that his words will be recorded in history books. The tower thought it would be alone again, but by the time the leaves had turned, a procession rode up to the palace gates, waving banners embroidered with a twelve-petaled rose. Furniture arrived from France, fruit trees were planted, and the village streets were paved so that the hooves of cattle clopped on the stones.

It has stood a long time, that tower, watching the life around it shift and alter, like eddies in a stream. It looks down once again on a deserted village—but no, not entirely deserted. A woman still lives in a cottage at its edge. Her hair has turned white, but she works every day in her garden, gathering tomatoes and cutting back the mint. When the day is particularly warm, she brings out a spinning wheel and sits in the garden, spinning yarn so fine that a shawl of it will slip through a wedding ring. If the breezes come from the west, the tower can hear her humming, just above the humming that the wheel makes as it spins. Time passes, and she sits out in the garden less often, until one day it realizes that it has not seen her for many days, or perhaps years.

Sometimes at night it thinks it can hear the Princess breathing in her sleep.

X. The Hound

In a hundred years, only one creature comes to the palace: a hound whose coat is matted with dust. Along his back the hair has come out in tufts, exposing a mass of sores. He lopes unevenly: on one of his forepaws, the inner toes have been crushed.

He has run from a city reduced to stone skeletons and drifting piles of ash, dodging tanks, mortar fire, the rifles of farmers desperate for food. For weeks now, he has been loping along the dusty roads. When rain comes, he has curled himself under a tree. Afterward, he has drunk from puddles, then loped along again with mud drying in the hollows of his paws. Sometimes he has left the road and tried to catch rabbits in the fields, but his damaged paw prevents him from running quickly enough. He has smelled them in their burrows beneath the summer grasses, beneath the poppies and cornflowers, tantalizing, inaccessible.

This morning he has smelled something different, pungent, like spoiled meat: the smell of enchantment. He has left the road and entered the forest, finding his way through a tangle of briars. He has come to the village, loped up its cobbled streets and through the gates of the palace. His claws click on its stone floor.

What does he smell? A fragrance, drifting, indistinct, remembered from when he was a pup: bacon. There, through that doorway. He lopes into the Great Hall, where breakfast waits in chafing dishes. The eggs are still firm, their yolks plump and yellow, their whites delicately fried. Sausages sit in their own grease. The toast is crisp.

He leaves a streak of egg yolk and sausage grease on the tablecloth, which has remained pristine for half a century, and falls asleep in the Queen Dowager's drawing room, in a square of sunlight that has not faded the baroque carpet.

He lives happily ever after. Someone has to. As summer passes, he wanders through the palace gardens, digging in the flower beds and trying to catch the sleeping fish that float in the ornamental pools. One day he urinates on the side of the tower, from which the dark smell emanates, to show his disapproval. When he is hungry he eats from the side of beef hanging in the larder, the sausages and eggs remaining on the breakfast table, or the mice sleeping beneath the harpsichord. In autumn, he chases the leaves falling red and yellow over the lawns and manages to pull a lobster from the kitchen tank, although his teeth can barely crack its hard shell. He never figures out how to extract the canary from its cage. When winter comes, the stone floor sends an ache through his damaged paw, and he sleeps in the King's bed, under velvet covers.

When summer comes again, he is too old to run about the garden. He lies in the Queen Dowager's drawing room and dreams of being a pup, of warm hands and a voice that whispered "What a beautiful dog," and that magical thing called a ball. He dies, his stomach still full with the last of the poached eggs. A proper fairy tale should, perhaps, end here.

* * *

XI. The Prince

Here comes the Prince on a bulldozer. What did you expect? Things change in a hundred years.

Harry pulls back the break and wipes his forehead, which is glistening with sweat. He runs his fingers through blond hair that stands up like a shock of corn. It is just past noon, and the skin on his nose is already red and peeling.

Two acres, and he'll knock off for some beer and that liver and onion sandwich Madge made him this morning, whose grease, together with the juice of a large gherkin, is soaking its way through a brown paper wrapper and will soon stain the leather of his satchel. He leans back, looks at the tangle of briars that form the undergrowth in this part of the forest, and chews on the knuckle of his thumb.

Two acres in the middle of the forest, enough for some barley and a still. Hell of a good idea, he thinks, already imagining the bottles on their way to Amsterdam, already imagining his pals Mike and Steve watching football on a color telly. Linoleum on the kitchen floor, like Madge always wanted, and cigarettes from America. "Not that damn rationed stuff," he says out loud, then looks around startled. What kind of fool idiot talks to himself? He chews on the knuckle of his thumb again. Twenty pounds to make the Police Commissioner look the other way. Damn lucky Madge could lend them the money. The bulldozer starts up again with a roar and the smell of diesel.

You don't like where this is going. What sort of prince is this, with his liver and onion sandwich, his gherkin and beer? Forgive me. I give you the only prince I can find, a direct descendant of the Count of Edinburgh, himself descended from the Tudors, albeit in the female line. Of course, all such titles have been abolished. This is, after all, the Socialist Union of Britannia. If Harry knows he is a prince, he certainly isn't telling Mike or Steve, who might sell him out for a pack of American cigarettes. Even Madge can't be trusted, though they've been sharing a flat in the commune's apartment building for three years. Hell, she made a big enough fuss about the distillery business.

The bulldozer's roar grows louder, then turns into a whine. The front wheel is stuck in a ditch. Harry climbs down and looks at the wheel. Damn, he'll have to get Mike and Steve. He kicks the wheel, kicks a tree trunk and almost gets his foot caught in a briar, kicks the wheel again.

Something flashes in the forest. Now what the hell is that? (You and I know it is sunlight flashing from the faceted upper window of the tower.) Harry opens his beer and swallows a mouthful of its warm bitterness. Some damn poacher, walking around on his land. (You and I remember that it belongs to the Socialist Union of Britannia.) He takes a bite of his liver and onion sandwich. Madge shouldn't frown so much, he thinks, remembering her in her housecoat, standing by the kitchen sink. She's getting wrinkles on her forehead. Should he fetch Mike and Steve? But the beer in his stomach, warm, bitter, tells him that he doesn't need Mike and Steve, because he can damn well handle any damn poacher himself. He bites into the gherkin.

Stay away, Prince Harry. Stay away from the forest full of briars. The Princess is not for you. You will never stumble up the tower stairs, smelling of beer; never leave a smear of mingled grease and sweat on her mouth; never take her away (thinking, Madge's rump is getting too damn broad) to fry your liver and onions and empty your ashtray of cigarette butts and iron your briefs.

At least, I hope not.

XII. The Rose

LET US GO back to the beginning: petals fall. Unpruned for a hundred years, the rosebush has climbed to the top of the tower. A cane of it has found a chink in the tower window, and it has grown into the room where the Princess lies. It has formed a canopy over her, a network of canes now covered with blossoms, and their petals fall slowly in the still air. Her nightgown is covered with petals: this summer's, pink and fragrant, and those of summers past, like bits of torn parchment curling at the edges.

While everything in the palace has been suspended in a pool of time without ripples or eddies, it has responded to the seasons. Its roots go down to dark caverns which are the homes of moles and worms, and curl around a bronze helmet that is now little more than rust. More than two hundred years ago, it was rather carelessly chosen as the emblem of a nation. Almost a hundred years ago, Madeleine plucked a petal of it for her magic spell. Wolfgang Magus picked a blossom of it for his buttonhole, which fell in the chapel and was trampled under a succession of court heels and cavalry boots. A spindle was carved from its dead and hardened wood. Half a century ago, a dusty hound urinated on its roots. From its seeds, dispersed by birds who have eaten its orange hips, has grown the tangle of briars that surround the palace, which have already torn the Prince's work pants and left a gash on his right shoulder. If you listen, you can hear him cursing.

It can tell us how the story ends. Does the Prince emerge from the forest, his shirtsleeve stained with blood? The briars of the forest know. Does the Witch lie dead, or does she still sit by the small-paned window of her cottage, contemplating a solitary pearl that glows in the wrinkled palm of her hand like a miniature moon? The spinning wheel knows, and surely its wood will speak to the wood from which it was made. Is the Princess breathing? Perhaps she has been sleeping for a hundred years, and the petals that have settled under her nostrils flutter each time she exhales. Perhaps she has not been sleeping, perhaps she is an exquisitely preserved corpse, and the petals under her nostrils never quiver. The rose can tell us, but it will not. The wind sets its leaves stirring, and petals fall, and it whispers to us: you must find your own ending.

This is mine. The Prince trips over an oak log, falls into a fairy ring, and disappears. (He is forced to wash miniature clothes, and pinched when he complains.) Alice stretches and brushes the rose petals from her nightgown. She makes her way to the Great Hall and eats what is left in the breakfast dishes: porridge with brown sugar. She walks through the streets of the village, wondering at the silence, then hears a humming. Following it, she comes to a cottage at the village edge where Madeleine, her hair now completely white, sits and spins in her garden. Witches, you know, are extraordinarily long-lived. Alice says, "Good morning," and Madeleine asks, "Would you like some breakfast?" Alice says, "I've had some, thank you." Then the Witch spins while the Princess reads Goethe, and the spinning wheel produces yarn so fine that a shawl of it will slip through a wedding ring.

Will it come to pass? I do not know. I am waiting, like you, for the canary to lift its head from under its wing, for the Empress Josephine to open in the garden, for a sound that will tell us someone, somewhere, is awake.

The Ogress Queen

I can smell him: little Helios.
He smells of cinnamon
and sugar. I can smell him even though
he is down in the garden, playing with a ball
and his dog, whom he calls Pantoufle.
"Here, Pantoufle," he cries. "Here, catch!"
I would like to catch him by the collar,
lick the back of his neck, suck up
the beads of sweat between his shoulder blades
(for it is a hot day, and there is no shade
in the castle garden except under the lime trees).
He would taste like brioche, oozing butter.
(Oh, his cheeks! so fat! so brown!
as though toasted.)
He would taste like sugar and cinnamon
and ginger.

And then little Aurora. She, I am convinced,
would taste of vanilla and almonds,
like marzipan. Less robust, more delicate
than her brother. I would save her for after.
Look, there she is in her white dress,
all frills and laces, like a doll
covered with royal icing,
rolling her hoop.
If I dipped her in water,
she would melt.

And walking along the path, I see
her mother, reading a book.
Love poems, no doubt—she is so sentimental.
She has kept every letter from my husband,
the king. She has kept,
somehow, her virtue intact, despite
the violation, despite the rude awakening
by two children she does not recall conceiving.

She resembles a galette:
rich, filled with succulent peaches
and frangipane. I will eat her
slowly, savoring her caramel hair,
her toes like raisins
dried from muscat grapes.
I will particularly enjoy
her eyes, which stare at me
with such limpid placidity,
as though she had not stolen my husband.
They will taste like candied citrons.

Today, today I will go talk to the cook
while the king is away at war
and order him to serve them up, one by one,
slice by slice, with perhaps
a glass of Riesling. Then at last my hunger
for my husband beside me in the bed at night,
for a son to rule after him while I am regent,
for warm, fragrant flesh,
spiced and smelling of cinnamon,
may be appeased.

Rose Child

Wandering among the roses in my garden,
I found a child, only five inches tall,
under a Madam Hardy. She was standing
on mulch, leaning against one of the rose canes.
I bent down to look at her, and she looked back
fearlessly. She was lean and brown, dressed
in a dormouse skin, cleverly sewn together.
She raised one hand, and I saw that she was armed
with a long, sharp thorn. She was not threatening me,
just showing me that she was not defenseless.
She shook the cane, and rose petals fell down
around her like summer snow. What should I do?
She was a child, but clearly self-sufficient,
in no need of help from me. So I did nothing.

Every morning, when I went to check the roses
for blackspot or Japanese beetles, I would see her
or traces of her—aphids speared on a thorn,
a pile of raspberries pilfered from my garden.
I didn't mind—she could take what she wanted.
Would it be wrong of me to leave her something?
And what would be useful to her? String, I thought.
Toothpicks, pieces of felt, a cut-up apple.
I would leave them under the blossoming Cuisse de Nymphe
or Cardinal Richelieu. They were always taken.
One morning I found a Japanese beetle spitted
on a toothpick, and the next morning I found two.
I think it was her way of thanking me.
She must have noticed what they do to roses,
how they eat the leaves and petals, chewing through them
until they are only a series of ragged holes
held together by a spiderweb of veins.

I did not see her again for a long time,
just tiny footsteps where I had raked the soil.
But one day I found her lying under the birdbath.

Immediately, I could tell there was something wrong;
she was pale, her breathing irregular, in quick gasps.
She lay with her arms wrapped around her torso, the way
you do when you're trying to hold yourself together.
What should I have done? We are always told not to touch
the wild things: abandoned fawns aren't really abandoned,
mother birds may return for fallen fledglings.
But she was a girl—a wild girl, but still human.

I put her in a shoebox lined with batting
and carried her up to the porch, which had a screen
to keep out insects, but was not indoors, exactly.
I brought her the sorts of things I thought she ate
in the wilderness of my garden: raspberries,
sliced peaches, lettuce, peas, asparagus sprouts,
even a frog I had to spear myself,
but I had seen her thorn, so I knew she hunted.
She ate it raw, all except the skin and bones.
Nothing seemed to help. Each day she would eat
less, sleep more. Slowly, she grew sicker,
coughing and feverish, with the typical symptoms
of a respiratory infection, something viral
that even her strong system couldn't fight off.
One day, she stopped eating altogether.
She drank water from a thimble, that was all.

Next morning, I sat with her as she closed her eyes,
and then it was over, as quickly and peacefully
as a bird flies from its nest. I buried her
by the edge of the woods, under a stand of maples.
I put a stone there, gray with a vein of quartz.
Then winter came, and I was sick myself;
at my age, I don't get over these things as easily
as I used to. Meanwhile, the garden lay dormant, snowbound.
I mostly stared at it from the kitchen window.

When spring came again, and all the snow was melted,
I walked around to survey what had been damaged.
The rose canes were dry and brown. I'd have to prune them
so new green shoots could spring from above the graft
to form flowering mid-summer arches. The vegetable garden
was covered with burlap. I peeled it back to see
what had survived underneath: mostly beets and turnips.

Almost as an afterthought, I walked to her grave.
In front of the stone was heaped a strange assortment:
acorns, a piece of faded ribbon, the cap
from a soda bottle, several sharpened sticks,
a bright blue plastic button. I started to sweep
it away as rubbish, then suddenly realized
that no, these were grave goods. As ancient tribes would honor
their dead by burying them with weapons, supplies
for the afterlife. Later that day, I brought
the thimble she had drunk from and left it there,
like a chalice on a church altar. Every morning
I'd go and leave something: berries, and when the roses
had started blooming again, the finest blossom
I could find that morning, fragrant, still covered with dew.

It was mid-summer before I started to see them,
the wild children, no larger than she had been,
dressed in skins, with weapons just like hers.
Now, when I'm in the garden deadheading the lilies
or cutting back the mint, sometimes I'll see one,
sitting on the old stone wall, enjoying the sunshine,
never speaking, just being companionable.
Or one will be leaning on a tomato trellis,
arms crossed, watching the birds in the lilac bushes.
Sometimes I'll leave out something they might find useful,
a ragged handkerchief, a knitting needle
that would make a fine spear. But I try not to interfere
in their lives—some things should be left as they are;
at my age I've learned that. I hope eventually,
when I'm buried by the edge of the woods myself,
which is what I've arranged for, they will come and visit,
leaving bits of ribbon, or buttons, or maybe a rose
every once in a while. It makes the thought of death
easier, somehow, that they would still be climbing
up the branches of the apple tree, or fishing
in the pond, or maybe dancing under the moon
if indeed they do that—I've never seen them,
just tiny tracks in the newly prepared bed
where I was planning to sow the radish seeds.

If they could visit me, just once or twice,
even if there's nothing of me left
to know or care—I'd like that.

The Rapid Advance of Sorrow

I SIT IN one of the cafés in Szent Endre, writing this letter to you, István, not knowing if I will be alive tomorrow, not knowing if this café will be here, with its circular green chairs and cups of espresso. By the Danube, children are playing, their knees bare below school uniforms. Widows are knitting shapeless sweaters. A cat sleeps beside a geranium in the café window.

If you see her, will you tell me? I still remember how she appeared at the University, just off the train from Debrecen, a country girl with badly-cut hair and clothes sewn by her mother. That year, I was smoking French cigarettes and reading forbidden literature. "Have you read D. H. Lawrence?" I asked her. "He is the only modern writer who convincingly expresses the desires of the human body." She blushed and turned away. She probably still had her Young Pioneers badge, hidden among her underwear.

"Ilona is a beautiful name," I said. "It is the most beautiful name in our language." I saw her smile, although she was trying to avoid me. Her face was plump from country sausage and egg bread, and dimples formed at the corners of her mouth, two on each side.

She had dimples on her buttocks, as I found out later. I remember them, like craters on two moons, above the tops of her stockings.

SORROW: A FEELING of grief or melancholy. A mythical city generally located in northern Siberia, said to have been visited by Marco Polo. From Sorrow, he took back to Italy the secret of making ice.

THAT AUTUMN, INTELLECTUAL apathy was in fashion. I berated her for reading her textbooks, preparing for her examinations. "Don't you know the grades are predetermined?" I said. "The peasants receive ones, the bourgeoisie receive twos, the aristocrats, if they have been admitted under a special dispensation, always receive threes."

She persisted, telling me that she had discovered art, that she wanted to become cultured.

"You are a peasant," I said, slapping her rump. She looked at me with tears in her eyes.

THE PRINCIPAL EXPORT of Sorrow is the fur of the arctic fox, which is manufactured into cloaks, hats, the cuffs on gloves and boots. These foxes, which

37

live on the tundra in family groups, are hunted with falcons. The falcons of Sorrow, relatives of the kestrel, are trained to obey a series of commands blown on whistles carved of human bone.

She began going to museums. She spent hours at the Vármuzeum, in the galleries of art. Afterward, she would go to cafés, drink espressos, smoke cigarettes. Her weight dropped, and she became as lean as a wolfhound. She developed a look of perpetual hunger.

When winter came and ice floated on the Danube, I started to worry. Snow had been falling for days, and Budapest was trapped in a white silence. The air was cleaner than it had been for months, because the Trabants could not make it through the snow. It was very cold.

She entered the apartment carrying her textbooks. She was wearing a hat of white fur that I had never seen before. She threw it on the sofa.

"Communism is irrelevant," she said, lighting a cigarette.

"Where have you been?" I asked. "I made a paprikás. I stood in line for two hours to buy the chicken."

"There is to be a new manifesto." Ash dropped on the carpet. "It will not resemble the old manifesto. We are no longer interested in political and economic movements. All movements from now on will be purely aesthetic. Our actions will be beautiful and irrelevant."

"The paprikás has congealed," I said.

She looked at me for the first time since she had entered the apartment and shrugged. "You are not a poet."

The poetry of Sorrow may confuse anyone not accustomed to its intricacies. In Sorrow, poems are constructed on the principle of the maze. Once the reader enters the poem, he must find his way out by observing a series of clues. Readers failing to solve a poem have been known to go mad. Those who can appreciate its beauties say that the poetry of Sorrow is impersonal and ecstatic, and that it invariably speaks of death.

She began bringing home white flowers: crocuses, hyacinths, narcissi. I did not know where she found them, in the city, in winter. I eventually realized they were the emblems of her organization, worn at what passed for rallies, silent meetings where communication occurred with the touch of a hand, a glance from the corner of an eye. Such meetings took place in secret all over the city. Students would sit in the pews of the Mátyás Church, saying nothing, planning insurrection.

At this time we no longer made love. Her skin had grown cold, and when I touched it for too long, my fingers began to ache.

We seldom spoke. Her language had become impossibly complex, referential. I could no longer understand her subtle intricacies.

She painted the word ENTROPY on the wall of the apartment. The wall was white, the paint was white. I saw it only because soot had stained the wall to a dull gray, against which the word appeared like a ghost.

One morning I saw that her hair on the pillow had turned white. I called her name, desperate with panic. She looked at me and I saw that her eyes were the color of milk, like the eyes of the blind.

IT IS INSUFFICIENT to point out that the inhabitants of Sorrow are pale. Their skin has a particular translucence, like a layer of nacre. Their nails and hair are iridescent, as though unable to capture and hold light. Their eyes are, at best, disconcerting. Travelers who have stared at them too long have reported hallucinations, like mountaineers who have stared at fields of ice.

I EXPECTED TANKS. Tanks are required for all sensible invasions. But spring came, and the insurrection did nothing discernible.

Then flowers appeared in the public gardens: crocuses, hyacinths, narcissi, all white. The black branches of the trees began to sprout leaves of a delicate pallor. White pigeons strutted in the public squares, and soon they outnumbered the ordinary gray ones. Shops began to close: first the stores selling Russian electronics, then clothing stores with sweaters from Bulgaria, then pharmacies. Only stores selling food remained open, although the potatoes looked waxen and the pork acquired a peculiar transparency.

I had stopped going to classes. It was depressing, watching a classroom full of students, with their white hair and milky eyes, saying nothing. Many professors joined the insurrection, and they would stand at the front of the lecture hall, the word ENTROPY written on the board behind them, communicating in silent gestures.

She rarely came to the apartment, but once she brought me poppy seed strudel in a paper bag. She said, "Péter, you should eat." She rested her fingertips on the back of my hand. They were like ice. "You have not joined us," she said. "Those who have not joined us will be eliminated."

I caught her by the wrist. "Why?" I asked.

She said, "Beauty demands symmetry, uniformity."

My fingers began to ache with cold. I released her wrist. I could see her veins flowing through them, like strands of aquamarine.

SORROW IS RULED by the absolute will of its Empress, who is chosen for her position at the age of three and reigns until the age of thirteen. The Empress is chosen by the Brotherhood of the Cowl, a quasi-religious sect whose members hide their faces under hoods of white wool to maintain their anonymity. By tradition, the Empress never speaks in public. She delivers her commands in private audiences with the Brotherhood. The consistency of these commands, from one Empress to another, has been taken to prove the sanctity of the Imperial line. After their reigns, all Empresses retire to the Abbey of St. Alba, where they live in seclusion for the remainder of their lives, studying astronomy, mathematics, and the seven-stringed zither. During the history of Sorrow, remarkable observations, theorems, and musical arrangements have emerged from this Abbey.

No TANKS CAME, but one day, when the sun shone with a vague luminescence through the clouds that perpetually covered the city, the Empress of Sorrow rode along Váci Street on a white elephant. She was surrounded by courtiers, some in cloaks of white fox, some in jesters' uniforms sewn from white patches, some, principally unmarried women, in transparent gauze through which one could see their hairless flesh. The eyes of the elephant were outlined with henna, its feet were stained with henna. In its trunk it carried a silver bell, whose ringing was the only sound as the procession made its way to the Danube and across Erzsébet Bridge.

Crowds of people had come to greet the Empress: students waving white crocuses and hyacinths and narcissi, mothers holding the hands of children who failed to clap when the elephant strode by, nuns in ashen gray. Cowled figures moved among the crowd. I watched one standing ahead of me and recognized the set of her shoulders, narrower than they had been, still slightly crooked.

I sidled up to her and whispered, "Ilona."

She turned. The cowl was drawn down and I could not see her face, but her mouth was visible, too thin now for dimples.

"Péter," she said, in a voice like snow falling. "We have done what is necessary."

She touched my cheek with her fingers. A shudder went through me, as though I had been touched by something electric.

TRAVELLERS HAVE ATTEMPTED to characterize the city of Sorrow. Some have said it is a place of confusion, with impossible pinnacles rising to stars that cannot be seen from any observatory. Some have called it a place of beauty, where the winds, playing through the high buildings, produce a celestial music. Some have called it a place of death, and have said that the city, examined from above, exhibits the contours of a skull.

Some have said that the city of Sorrow does not exist. Some have insisted that it exists everywhere: that we are perpetually surrounded by its streets, which are covered by a thin layer of ice; by its gardens, in which albino peacocks wander; by its inhabitants, who pass us without attention or interest.

I BELIEVE NEITHER of these theories. I believe that Sorrow is an insurrection waged by a small cabal, with its signs and secrets; that it is run on purely aesthetic principles; that its goal is entropy, a perpetual stillness of the soul. But

I could be mistaken. My conclusions could be tainted by the confusion that spreads with the rapid advance of Sorrow.

So I have left Budapest, carrying only the mark of three fingertips on my left cheek. I sit here every morning, in a café in Szent Endre, not knowing how long I have to live, not knowing how long I can remain here, on a circular green chair drinking espresso.

Soon, the knees of the children will become as smooth and fragile as glass. The widows' knitting needles will click like bone, and geranium leaves will fall beside the blanched cat. The coffee will fade to the color of milk. I do not know what will happen to the chair. I do not know if I will be eliminated, or given another chance to join the faction of silence. But I am sending you this letter, István, so you can remember me when the snows come.

Lady Winter

My soul said, let us visit Lady Winter.

Why? I responded. Look, the leaves still lie
yellow and red and orange in the gutters.
The geese float on the river. On the sidewalks,
puddles continue to reflect the sky.

My soul said, the branches are bare.
And you can feel it, can't you, in your bones?
The chill that is a promise of her coming.
The year is growing older. Anyway,
you haven't seen her in so long: it's time.

We put on our visiting hats.
I stood admiring myself in the mirror
while my soul stood beside me looking pensive
and pale. Was she a little sick? I wondered.

Lady Winter lives on an ancient street
lined with elms that canker has not touched,
in a tall brownstone with lace curtain panels,
empty window boxes, two stone lions.
We rang the bell and heard it echoing.

A maid opened the door. Her name is Frost.

My lady looked the way she always does:
white hair, a string of pearls, rings on her fingers,
age somewhere between forty and four thousand,
a kind, implacable smile.

She said, my dear, what's wrong? You don't look well.
What, me? I'm fine. Perfectly fine, I said.
My soul just shook her head.

My lady has a parlor with a fireplace

in which I've never seen a fire. Instead,
it's filled with decorative branches. Doilies
lie like snowflakes on the tables, bookshelves,
over the backs of armchairs.

She's always wearing a gray cashmere sweater
and expensive shoes. She must have a closetful.

She usually serves us tea and ladyfingers.
But this time she said, I want you to go to bed.

Frost will take you upstairs, then I'll come up
to cover you in blankets of felted wool,
comforters stuffed with down from eider ducks
that nest by Norwegian fjords. I'll read you books
of fairytales about bears and princesses,
and stolen crowns, and castles beneath the sea,
and northern lights.
Grandmothers who grant wishes, talking reindeer,
a village in the clouds.

I'll talk to you until you fall asleep.
Your soul will sit and watch through the long night.
From time to time she'll take your temperature
to make sure you're all right.

So I lay down in Lady Winter's guest room:
reluctantly, but it looked so inviting,
a bed with draperies and a painted ceiling
from which the moon was hanging
by a silver chain.

My soul sat down beside me.
Don't worry, she said. There's plenty for me to do.
Poetry to embroider, plans to knit.
I'll wake you when the crocuses have broken
through the black soil, when warmth has come again.

Then Lady Winter put her soft, dry hand
like paper on my forehead
and she said
rest now.

Shoes of Bark

What would you think
if I told you that I was beautiful?
That I walked through the orchards in a white cotton dress,
wearing shoes of bark.

In early morning, when mist lingered over the grass,
and the apples, red and gold, were furred with dew,
I picked one, biting into its crisp, moist flesh,
then spread my arms and looked up at the clouds,
floating high above, and the clouds looked back at me.
By the edge of a pasture I opened milkweed pods,
watching the white fluff float away on the wind.

I held up my dress and danced among the chicory
under the horses' mild, incurious gaze
and followed the stream along its meandering ways.

What would you think
if I told you that I was magical?
That I had russet hair down to the backs of my knees
and the birds stole it for their nests
because it was stronger than horsehair and softer than down.
That when the storm winds roiled,
I could still them with a word.

That when I called, the gray geese would call back
come with us, sister, and I considered rising
on my own wings and following them south.
But if not me, who would make the winter come?
Who would breathe on the windows, creating landscapes of frost,
and hang icicles from the gutters?

What would you think, daughter, if I told you
that in a dress of white wool and deerhide boots
I danced the winter in? And that in spring,
dressed in white cotton lawn, wearing birchbark shoes,

I wandered among the deer and marked their fawns
with my fingertips? That I slept among the ferns?

Would you say, she is old, her mind is wandering?
Or would you say, I am beautiful, I am magical,
and go yourself to dance the seasons in?

(Look in my closet. You will find my shoes of bark.)

Miss Emily Gray

I. A Lane in Albion

IT WAS APRIL in Albion. To the south, in the civilized counties, farmers were already putting their lambs out to pasture, and lakeshores were covered with the daffodils beloved of the Poet. The daffodils were plucked by tourists, who photographed the lambs, or each other with bunches of daffodils, or the cottage of the Poet, who had not been particularly revered until after his death. But this was the north of Albion, where sea winds blew from one side of the island to the other, so that even in the pastures a farmer could smell salt, and in that place April was not the month of lambs or daffodils or tourists, but of rain.

In the north of Albion, it was raining. It was not raining steadily. The night before had wrung most of the water out of the sky, and morning was now scattering its last drops, like the final sobs after a fit of weeping. The wind blew the drops of water here and there, into a web that a spider had, earlier that morning, carefully arranged between two slats of a fence, and over the leaves, dried by the previous autumn, that still hung from the branches of an oak tree. The branches of the oak, which had stood on that spot since William the Conqueror had added words like mutton and testament to the language, stretched over the fence and the lane that ran beside it. The lane was still sodden from the night's rains, and covered by a low gray mist.

Along this lane came a sudden gust of wind, detaching an oak leaf from its branch, detaching the spiderweb from its fence, sweeping them along with puffs of mist so that they tumbled together, like something one might find under a bureau: a tattered collection of gray fluff, brown paper, and string. As this collection tumbled down the lane, it began to extend upward like a whirlwind, and then to solidify. Soon, where there had been a leaf and a spiderweb speckled with rain, there was now a plain but neat gray dress with white collar and cuffs, and brown hair pulled back in a neat but very plain bun, and a small white nose, and a pair of serious but very clear gray eyes. Beneath the dress, held up by small white hands so that its hem would not touch the sodden lane, were a pair of plain brown boots. And as they stepped carefully among the puddles, sending the mist swirling before them, they gathered not a single speck of mud.

* * *

46

II. Genevieve in a Mood

WHEN GENEVIEVE WAS in a "mood," she went to the nursery, to sulk among the rocking horses and decapitated dolls. That was where Nanny finally found her, sitting on a settee with broken springs, reading *Pilgrim's Progress*.

"There you are, Miss Genevieve," she said. She puffed and patted a hand against her ample bosom. She had been climbing up and down stairs for the last half hour, and she was a short, stout woman, with an untidy bun of hair held together by hairpins that dropped out at intervals, leaving a trail behind her.

"Evidently," said Genevieve. Nanny was the only person with authority who would not send her to her room for using "that" tone of voice. Therefore, she used it with Nanny as often as possible.

"Supper's almost over. Didn't you hear the bell? Sir Edward is having a fit. One of these days he'll fall down dead from apoplexy, and you'll be to blame."

Genevieve had no doubt he would. She could imagine her father's face growing red and redder, until it looked like a slice of rare roast beef. He would shout, "Where have you been, young lady?" followed by "Don't use that tone of voice with me!" followed by "Up to your room, Miss!" Then she would have brown bread and water for supper. Genevieve rather liked brown bread, and liked even better imagining herself as a prisoner, a modern Mary, Queen of Scots.

"And what will Miss Gray think?"

"I don't care," said Genevieve. "I didn't ask for a bloody governess."

"Genevieve!" said Nanny. She did not believe in girls cursing, riding bicycles, or—heaven forbid—smoking cigarettes.

"Do you know who's going away to school? Amelia Thwaite. You know, Farmer Thwaite's daughter. Who used to milk our cows. Whose grandfather was our butler. She's going to Paris, to study art!" Genevieve shut *Pilgrim's Progress* with a bang and tossed it on the settee, where it landed in a cloud of dust.

"I know, my dear," said Nanny, smoothing her skirt, which Genevieve and occasionally Roland had spotted with tears when their father had refused them something they particularly wanted: in Roland's case, a brown pony and riding crop that Farmer Thwaite was selling at what seemed a ridiculously low price. "Sir Edward doesn't believe in girls going away to school, and I quite agree with him. Now come down and make your apologies to Miss Gray. How do you think she feels, just arrived from—well, wherever she arrived from—without a pupil to greet her?"

Genevieve did not much care, but the habit of obedience was strong, particularly to Nanny's comfortable voice, so she rose from the settee, kicking aside *Pilgrim's Progress*. This, although unintentional, sufficiently expressed her attitude toward the book, which Old Thwaite had read to her and Roland every Sunday afternoon, after church, while her father slept on the sofa with a handkerchief over his face. When she read the book herself, which was not often, she imagined him snoring. More often, when she was in a "mood," she would simply hold it open on her lap at the picture of Christian in the Slough of Despont, imagining interesting ways to keep him from reaching the Celestial City, which she believed must be the most boring place in the universe.

As she clattered down the stairs after Nanny, speculating that her father would not shout or send her to her room in front of the new governess, she began to imagine a marsh with green weeds that looked like solid ground. From it would rise seven women, nude and strategically covered with mud, with names like Desire and Foolishness. They would twine their arms around Christian and drag him downward into the muddy depths, where they would subject him to unspeakable pleasures. She did not think he would escape their clutches.

III. The Book in the Chimney

It was not what she was, exactly. She was not anything, exactly. Genevieve could see her now, through the library window, sitting in a garden chair, embroidering something. Once, Genevieve had crept up behind her and seen that she was embroidering on white linen with white thread so fine that the pattern was barely perceptible.

Her gray dress was always neat, her white face was always solemn. Her irregular verbs, as far as Genevieve could judge, were always correct. She knew the principle exports of Byzantium. When Genevieve did particularly well on her botany or geography, she smiled a placid smile.

It was not, then, anything in particular, except that her hands were so small, and moved so quickly over the piano keys, like jumping spiders. She preferred to play Chopin.

No, it was something more mysterious, something missing. Genevieve reached into the back of the fireplace and carefully pulled out a loose brick. Behind it was an opening just large enough for a cigar box filled with dead beetles, which was what Roland had kept there, or a book, which was what she had kept there since Roland had left for Harrow and then the university. No fire had been lit in the library since her mother's death, when Genevieve was still young enough to be carried around in Nanny's arms. Her mother, who had liked books, had left her *Pilgrim's Progress* and a copy of *Clarissa* in one volume, which Genevieve read every night until she fell asleep. She never remembered what she had read the night before, so she always started again at the beginning. She had never made it past the first letter.

Out of the opening behind the brick, she pulled a book with a red leather cover, faded and sooty from its hiding place. On the cover, in gold lettering, Genevieve could still read the words *Practical Divination*. On the first page was written,

Practical Divination for the Adept or Amateur
By the Right Reverend Alice Widdicomb

Endorsed by the Theosophical Society

She brought the book to the library table, where she had set the basin and
a bottle of ink. She was out of black ink, so it would have to be purple. Her
father would shout at her when he discovered that she was out of ink again, but
this time she could blame it on Miss Gray and irregular verbs.

She poured purple ink into the basin, then blew on it and repeated the
words the Right Reverend Alice Widdicomb recommended, which sounded
so much like a nonsense rhyme that she always wondered if they were strictly
necessary. But she repeated them anyway. Then she stared at the purple ink
until her eyes crossed, and said to the basin, as solemnly as though she were
purchasing a railway ticket, "Miss Gray, please."

First, the purple ink showed her Miss Gray sitting in the garden, looking
faintly violet. Sir Edward came up from behind and leaned over her shoulder,
admiring her violet embroidery. Then it showed a lane covered with purple
mud, by a field whose fence needed considerable repair, over which grew a
purple oak tree. Rain came down from the lavender sky. Genevieve waited, but
the scene remained the same.

"Perfectly useless," she said with disgust. It was probably the purple ink.
Magic was like Bach. If you didn't play the right notes in the right order, it
never came out right. She turned to the back of the book, where she had tucked
in a piece of paper covered with spidery handwriting. On one side it said "To
Biddy, from Alice. A Sovereign Remedy for the Catarrh." On the other side was
"A Spell to Make Come True Your Heart's Desire." That had not worked either,
although Genevieve had gathered the ingredients carefully, even clipping the
whiskers from the taxidermed fox in the front hall. She read it over again, wondering where she had made a mistake. Perhaps it needed to be a live fox?

In the basin, Miss Gray was once again working on her violet embroidery.
Genevieve frowned, rubbing a streak of purple ink across her cheek. What was
it, exactly? She would have to find out another way.

IV. A Wedding on the Lawn

How, AND THIS was the important question, had she done it? The tulle, floating behind her over the clipped lawn like foam. The satin, like spilled milk. The
orange flowers brought from London.

Roland was drunk, which was only to be expected. He was standing beside
the tea table, itself set beside the yew hedge, looking glum. Genevieve found it
in her heart to sympathize.

"Oh, what a day," said Nanny, who was serving tea. She was upholstered in brown. A lace shawl that looked as though it had been yellowing in the attic was pinned to her bodice by a brooch hand-painted, entirely unnecessarily, thought Genevieve, with daffodils. Genevieve was "helping."

"The Romans," said Roland.

Genevieve waited for him to say something further, but he merely took another mouthful of punch.

"To think," said Nanny. "Like the woman who nursed a serpent, until it bit her bosom so that she died. My mother told me that story, and never did she say a truer word. And she so plain and respectable."

Miss Gray, the plain and respectable, was now walking around the garden in satin and tulle, on Sir Edward's arm, nodding placidly to the farmers and gentry. In spite of her finery, she looked as neat and ordinary as a pin.

"The Romans," said Roland, "had a special room where they could go to vomit. It was called the vomitorium." He lurched forward and almost fell on the tea table.

"Take him away, won't you, Nanny," said Genevieve. "Lay him down before he gives his best imitation of a Roman." That would get rid of them both, leaving her to ponder the mystery that was Miss Gray, holding orange blossoms.

When Nanny had taken Roland into the library—she could hear through the window that he had developed a case of hiccups—Genevieve circled behind the hedge, to an overgrown holly that she had once discovered in a game of hide and seek with Roland. From the outside, the tree looked like a mass of leaves edged with needles that would prick anyone who ventured too close. If you pushed your way carefully inside, however, you found that the inner branches were sparse and bare. It was the perfect place to hide. And if you pushed a branch aside just slightly, you could see through the outer leaves without being seen. Roland had never found her, and in a fit of anger had decapitated her dolls. But she had never liked dolls anyway.

Miss Gray was listening to Farmer Thwaite, who was addressing her as Lady Trefusis. She was nodding and giving him one of her placid smiles. Sir Edward was looking particularly satisfied, which turned his face particularly red.

The old fool, thought Genevieve. She wondered what Miss Gray had up those capacious sleeves, which were in the latest fashion. Was it money she wanted?

That did not, to Genevieve's disappointment, seem to fit the Miss Gray who knew the parts of the flower and the principle rivers of Cathay.

Security? thought Genevieve. People often married for security. Nanny had said so, and in this at least she was willing to concede that Nanny might be right. The security of never again having to teach irregular verbs.

Genevieve pushed the holly leaves farther to one side. Miss Gray turned her head, with yards of tulle floating behind it. She looked directly at Genevieve, as though she could see through the holly leaves, and—she winked.

I must have imagined it, thought Genevieve a moment later. Miss Gray was smiling placidly at Amelia Thwaite, who looked like she had stepped out of a French fashion magazine.

She couldn't have seen me, thought Genevieve. And then, I wonder if she will expect me to call her mother?

V. A Meeting by Moonlight

GENEVIEVE WAS ON page four of *Clarissa* when she heard the voices.

First voice: "Angel, darling, you can't mean it."

Second voice: Inaudible murmur.

First voice, which obviously and unfortunately belonged to Roland: "If you only knew how I felt. Put your hand on my heart. Can you feel it? Beating and burning for you."

How embarrassing, having one's brother under one's bedroom window, mouthing banalities to a kitchenmaid.

Second voice, presumably the maid: Inaudible murmur.

Roland: "But you can't, you just can't. I would die without you. Don't you see what you've done to me? Emily, my own. Let me kiss this white neck, these little hands. Tell me you don't love him, tell me you'll run away with me. Tell me anything, but don't tell me to leave you. I can't do it any more than a moth can leave a flame." A convincing sob.

How was she supposed to read *Clarissa*? At this rate, she would never finish the first letter. Of course, she had never finished it on any other night, but it was the principle that mattered.

Genevieve put *Clarissa* down on the coverlet, open in a way that would eventually crack the spine, and picked up the pitcher, still full of tepid water, from her nightstand. She walked to the window. It was lucky that Nanny insisted on fresh air. She leaned out over the sill. Below, she could see the top of Roland's head. Beside him, her neck and shoulders white in the moonlight, stood Emily the kitchenmaid.

Except, thought Genevieve suddenly, that none of the maids was named Emily. The woman with the white shoulders looked up.

This time it was unmistakable. Miss Gray had winked at her. Genevieve lay on her bed for a long time, with *Clarissa* at an uncomfortable angle beneath her, staring at the ceiling.

* * *

VI. The Burial of the Dead

"I am the resurrection and the life, saith the Lord."

"He was so handsome," whispered Amelia Thwaite to the farmer's daughter standing beside her, whose attention was absorbed in studying the pattern of the clocks on Amelia's stockings. "I let him kiss me once, before he went to Oxford. He asked me not to fall in love with anyone else while he was away, and I wouldn't promise, and he must have been so angry because when I saw him again this summer, he would barely speak to me. And I'm just sick with guilt. Because I really did think, in my heart, that I could love only him, and now I will never, ever have the chance to tell him so."

"Blessed are the dead who die in the Lord; even so saith the Spirit, for they rest from their labors."

"There's something behind it," whispered Farmer Thwaite to the farmer standing beside him, who had been up the night before with a sick ewe and was trying, with some success, not to fall asleep. "You mark my words." His neighbor marked them with a stifled yawn. "A gun doesn't go off, not just like that, not by itself. They say he was drunk, but he must of been pointing it at the old man for a reason. A strict enough landlord he was, and I'm not sorry to be rid of him, I tell you. The question is, whether our Ladyship will hold the reins as tightly. She's a pretty little thing in black satin, like a cat that's got into the pantry and is sitting looking at you, all innocent with the cream on its chin. But there's something behind it, you mark my words." His neighbor dutifully marked them.

"Why art thou so full of heaviness, O my soul? and why art thou so disquiet within me?"

It was inexplicable. Genevieve could hear the rustle of dresses, the shuffle of boots, the drone of the minister filling the chapel. Each window with its stained-glass saint was dedicated to a Trefusis. A Trefusis lay under each stone knight in his stone armor, each stone lady folding her hands over stone drapery. A plaque beside the altar commemorated Sir Roland Trefusis, who had come across the channel with William the Conqueror—some ungenerously whispered, as his cook.

"We must believe it was an accident," Mr. Herbert had said. "In that moment of confusion, he must have turned the pistol toward himself, examining it, unable to imagine how it could have gone off in his hands. And we have evidence, gentlemen," this to the constable and the magistrate of the county, "that the young man was intoxicated. What is the use, I put it to you, of calling it suicide under these circumstances? You have a son yourself," to the magistrate. "Would you want any earthly power denying him the right to rest in sacred ground?"

Nanny sniffed loudly into her handkerchief, which had a broad black border. "If it wasn't for that woman, that wicked, wicked woman, your dear father and that dear, dear boy would still be alive. I don't know how she done it, but she done it somehow, and if the good Lord don't smite her like he smote the witch of Endor, I'll become a Mahometan."

"By his last will and testament, signed and witnessed two weeks before the unfortunate—accident," Mr. Herbert had said, "your father left you to the guardianship of your stepmother, Lady Emily Trefusis. You will, of course, come into your own money when you reach the age of majority—or marry, with your guardian's permission. I don't suppose, Genevieve, that you've discussed any of this with your stepmother?"

Miss Gray turned, as though she had heard Nanny's angry whisper. For a moment she looked at Genevieve and then, inexplicably, she smiled, as though the two of them shared an amusing secret.

"There is a river, the streams whereof make glad the city of God, the holy place of the tabernacle of the Most High."

"I am quite certain it was an accident," the minister had said, patting Genevieve's hand. His palm was damp. "I knew young Roland when he was a boy. Oh, he would steal eggs from under a chicken for mischief, but there was no malice in his heart. Be comforted, my dear. They are in the Celestial City, singing hymns with the angels of the Lord."

Genevieve wondered. She was inclined, herself, to believe that Roland at least was most likely in Hell. It seemed, remembering Old Thwaite's Sunday lessons, an appropriate penalty for patricide.

She sniffed. She could not help it, fiercely as she was trying to hold whatever it was inside her so that it would not come out, like a wail. Because, as often as she thought of Mary, Queen of Scots, who had gone to her execution without hesitation or tears, she had to admit that she was very much afraid. "For so thou didst ordain when thou createdst me, saying, dust thou art, and unto dust shalt thou return. All we go down to the dust; yet even at the grave we make our song: Alleluia."

It must, of course, be explicable. But she had hidden and watched and followed, and she was no closer to an explanation than that day on which, in a bowl of purple ink, she had watched violet clouds floating against a lavender sky.

For a moment she leaned her head against Nanny's arm, but found no comfort there. She would have, she realized, to confront the spider in its web. She would have to talk with Miss Gray.

VII. A Conversation with Miss Gray

" . . . and this prayer I make,
Knowing that Nature never did betray
The heart that loved her; 'tis her privilege,
Through all the years of this our life, to lead

From joy to joy: for she can so inform
The mind that is within us, so impress
With quietness and beauty, and so feed
With lofty thoughts, that neither evil tongues,
Rash judgements, nor the sneers of selfish men,
Nor greetings where no kindness is, nor all
The dreary intercourse of daily life,
Shall e'er prevail against us, or disturb
Our cheerful faith, that all which we behold
Is full of blessings."

MISS GRAY SHUT her book. "Hello, Genevieve. Can you tell me what I have been reading?"

"Wordsworth," said Genevieve. Miss Gray always read Wordsworth.

She was sitting on a stone bench beside the yew hedge, dressed in black with a white collar and cuffs, looking plain but very neat. The holly was now covered with red berries.

"In these lines, the Poet is telling us that if we pray to Nature, our great mother, she will answer us, not by transporting us to a literal heaven, but by making a heaven for us here upon earth, in our minds and hearts. I'm afraid, my dear, that you don't read enough poetry."

Genevieve stood, not knowing what to say. It had rained the night before, and she could feel a dampness around her ankles, where her stockings had brushed against wet grass.

"Have you been studying your irregular verbs?"

Genevieve said, in a voice that to her dismay sounded hoarse and uncertain, "This won't do, you know. Talking about irregular verbs. We must have it out sometime." How, if Miss Gray said whatever do you mean Genevieve, would she respond? Her hands trembled, and she clasped them in front of her.

But Miss Gray said only, "I do apologize. I assumed it was perfectly clear."

Genevieve spread her hands in a silent question.

"I was sent to make come true your heart's desire."

"That's impossible," said Genevieve, and "I don't understand."

Miss Gray smiled placidly, mysteriously, like a respectable Mona Lisa. "You wanted to go to school, like Amelia Thwaite, and wear fine clothes, and be rid of your father."

"You're lying," said Genevieve. "It's not true," and "I didn't mean it." Then she fell on her knees, in the wet grass. Her head fell forward, until it almost, but not quite, touched Miss Gray's unwrinkled lap.

"Hush, my dear," said Miss Gray, stroking Genevieve's hair and brushing away the tears that were beginning to fall on her dress. "You will go to school in Paris, and we will go together to Worth's, to find you an appropriate wardrobe. And we will go to the galleries and the Academy of Art . . ."

There was sobbing now, and tears soaking through to her knees, but she continued to stroke Genevieve's hair and said, in the soothing voice of a hospital nurse, "And my dear, although you have suffered a great loss, I hope you will someday come to think of me as your mother."

In the north of Albion, rain once again began to fall, which was no surprise, since it was autumn.

The Witch

Sometimes in the morning, the mist curled into the corners
of the house like a cat, and Grimalkin, she would cry,
come to me, my Grimalkin. She would gather
the mist to her, and stroke it, and it would settle
in her lap, and lick itself.

                              Sometimes, she wove
cobwebs and out of the cloth, thin, gray, luminescent,
she would cut the pattern for a dress. But for what purpose?
Where could she wear it? Where could she go, except
to the pond, where she would kneel and dip her fingers
into the water, and stir, and out would jump
a trout, thick, silver, luminescent, and splashing
water onto her dress, whose hem was already
soaked and covered with mud.

                              She would make it speak,
recite Shakespearean sonnets, sing old songs,
before she put it into the pot. Witches
are lonely, but also hungry, and practical
in their impracticality. She had learned
how from her mother, the old witch, now dead
if witches are ever entirely dead, which is doubtful.

She never wondered who her father had been,
a peasant gathering wood, perhaps a hunter,
perhaps even a prince, on his way to the country
where a princess had been promised for dispatching
a dragon or something similar, and had seen
a light through the trees, and found her mother waiting,
and perhaps gone on the next morning, and perhaps not.

Her mother had built the house by the edge of the pond,
out of gray stone and branches of white birch,
birds' nests and moss, and spit to hold it together.
That is how witches build what they call houses.

What they are not: sturdy, comfortable.
What they are: cold.

There was still a row of bottles
in the cupboard, holding martens' eyes, dried frogs,
robins' eggs, random feathers, balls of string,
oak galls. She had forgotten what they were for.
From the rafters hung a fox's skeleton.

Once, village girls had come to visit her mother
for charms to attract the schoolmaster's attention,
make their rivals' hair fall out, abortions.

Afterward, they would say, Did you see her? Standing
by the door? In her ragged dress, with her tangled hair,
I tell you, she creeps me out. But they stopped coming
after the old witch disappeared and her daughter
was left alone. Sometimes she would remember
the smell of the bread in their pockets, the clink of coins,
their dresses covered with embroidery,
their whispering, and look at her reflection
in the pond, floating on the water like a ghost.
Sometimes she made the frogs at the edge of the pond,
calling to one another, speak to her.
"Pretty one," they would say, "in your spider silk,
in your birchbark shoes, like a princess lost in the woods,
kiss us." But she knew that was not her story.

Sometimes she would make the birds perch on her fingers
and sing to her: warblers, thrushes, chickadees,
and sing to them out of tune, then break their necks
and roast them.

Sometimes she would gather the stones
that had fallen from her house, and think of making
a dog, a stone dog. Then, she would forget.
It was the forgetting that made her what she was,
her mother's daughter. Witches never remember
important things: that fire burns, and that bottles
labeled poison are not to be drunk. Witches
are always doing what they should not, dancing
at midnight with the Gentleman, kicking their skirts
over the tops of their stockings, kissing frogs

they know perfectly well won't turn into princes.

She makes no magic. Although the stories won't tell you,
witches are magic. They do not need the props
of a magician, the costumes or the cards,
the scarves, the rabbits. They came down from the moon
originally, and it still calls to them,
so they go out at night, when the moon is shining,
and make no magic, but magic happens around them.

Sometimes at night she would look up at the moon
and call Mother? Mother? but never got an answer.

I want you to imagine: her ragged dress,
her hair like cobwebs, her luminescent eyes,
mad as all witches are, stirring the pond
like a cauldron (witches need no cauldrons, whatever
the stories tell you) while above her the clouds
are roiling and a storm is about to gather.

Binnorie

What is it about being made into a harp,
your bones as smooth as poplar, about being strung
with your own hair, golden or black or brown,
that presents such an appropriate allegory
for being a woman, and therefore an instrument
of fathers, husbands, or sons? Or is it rather
an allegory for being a poet, which is
a different thing altogether, I like to think,
although poetry can command you like a father,
berate you like a husband, and abandon
you like any number of sons?

The Wings of Meister Wilhelm

MY MOTHER WANTED me to play the piano. She had grown up in Boston, among the brownstones and the cobbled streets, in the hush of rooms where dust settled slowly, in the sunlight filtering through lace curtains, over the leaves of spider-plants and aspidistras. She had learned to play the piano sitting on a mahogany stool with a rotating top, her back straight, hair braided into decorous loops, knees covered by layers of summer gauze. Her fingers had moved with elegant patience over the keys. A lady, she told me, always looked graceful on a piano stool.

I did try. But my knees, covered mostly by scars from wading in the river by the Beauforts' and then falling into the blackberry bushes, sprawled and banged—into the bench, into the piano, into Mr. Henry, the Episcopal Church organist, who drew in the corners of his mouth when he saw me, forming a pink oval of distaste. No matter how often my mother brushed my hair, I ran my fingers through it so that I looked like an animated mop, and to her dismay I never sat up straight, stooping over the keys until I resembled, she said, "that dreadful creature from Victor Hugo—the hunchback of Notre Dame."

I suppose she took my failure as a sign of her own. When she married my father, the son of a North Carolina tobacco farmer, she left Boston and the house by the Common that the Winslows had inhabited since the Revolution. She arrived as a bride in Ashton expecting to be welcomed into a red brick mansion fronted by white columns and shaded by magnolias, perhaps a bit singed from the war her grandfather the General had won for the Union. Instead, she found herself in a house with only a front parlor, its white paint flaking, flanked by a set of ragged tulip poplars. My father rode off every morning to the tobacco fields that lay around the foundations of the red brick mansion, its remaining bricks still blackened from the fires of the Union army and covered through the summer with twining purple vetch.

A MONTH AFTER my first piano lesson with Mr. Henry, we were invited to a dinner party at the Beauforts'. At the bottom left corner of the invitation was written, "Violin Recital."

"Adeline Beaufort is so original," said my mother over her toast and eggs, the morning we received the invitation. "Imagine. Who in Balfour County plays the violin?" Her voice indicated the amused tolerance extended to Adeline Beaufort, who had once been Adeline Ashton, of the Ashtons who had given their name to the town.

Hannah began to disassemble the chafing dish. "I hear she's paying some foreign man to play for her. He arrived from Raleigh last week. He's staying at Slater's."

"Real-ly?" said my mother, lengthening the word as she said it to express the notion that Adeline Beaufort, who lived in the one red brick mansion in Ashton, fronted by white columns and shaded by magnolias, should know better than to allow some paid performer staying at Slater's, with its sagging porch and mixed-color clientele, to play at her dinner party.

My father pushed back his chair. "Well, it'll be a nice change from that damned organist." He was already in his work shirt and jodhpurs.

"Language, Cullen," said my mother.

"Rose doesn't mind my damns, does she?" He stopped as he passed and leaned down to kiss the top of my head.

I decided then that I would grow up just like my father. I would wear a blue shirt and leather boots up to my knees, and damn anything I pleased. I looked like him already, although the sandy hair so thick that no brush could tame it, the strong jaw and freckled nose that made him a handsome man made me a very plain girl indeed. I did not need to look in a mirror to realize my plainness. It was there, in my mother's perpetual look of disappointment, as though I were, to her, a symbol of the town with its unpaved streets where passing carriages kicked up dust in the summer, and the dull green of the tobacco fields stretching away to the mountains.

After breakfast I ran to the Beauforts' to find Emma. The two of us had been friends since our first year at the Ashton Ladies' Academy. Together we had broken our dolls in intentional accidents, smuggled books like *Gulliver's Travels* out of the Ashton library, and devised secret codes that revealed exactly what we thought of the older girls at our school, who were already putting their hair up and chattering about beaux. I found her in the orchard below the house, stealing green apples. It was only the middle of June, and they were just beginning to be tinged with their eventual red.

"Aren't you bad," I said when I saw her. "You know those will only make you sick."

"I can't help it," she said, looking doleful. The expression did not suit her. Emma reminded me of the china doll Aunt Winslow had given me two summers ago, on my twelfth birthday. She had chestnut hair and blue eyes that always looked newly painted, above cheeks as smooth and white as porcelain, now round with the apple pieces she had stuffed into them. "Mama thinks I've grown too plump, so Callie won't let me have more than toast and an egg for breakfast, and no sugar for my coffee. I get so hungry afterward!"

"Well, I'll steal you some bread and jam later if you'll tell me about the violin player from Slater's."

We walked to the cottage below the orchard, so close to the river at the bottom of the Beauforts' back garden that it flooded each spring. Emma felt above the low doorway, found the key we always kept there, and let us both in. The cottage had been used, as long as we could remember, for storing old furniture. It was filled with dressers gaping where their drawers had once been and chairs whose caned seats had long ago rotted through. We sat on a sofa whose springs sagged under its faded green upholstery, Emma munching her apple and me munching another although I knew it would give me a stomachache that afternoon.

"His name is Johann Wilhelm," she finally said through a mouthful of apple. "He's German, I think. He played the violin in Raleigh, and Aunt Otway heard him there, and said he was coming down here, and that we might want him to play for us. That's all I know."

"So why is he staying at Slater's?"

"I dunno. I guess he must be poor."

"My mother said your mother was original for having someone from Slater's play at her house."

"Yeah? Well, your mother's a snobby Yankee."

I kicked Emma, and she kicked back, and then we had a regular kicking battle. Finally, I had to thump her on the back when she choked on an apple from laughing too hard. I was laughing too hard as well. We were only fourteen, but we were old enough to understand certain truths about the universe, and we both knew that mothers were ridiculous.

IN THE WEEK that followed, I almost forgot about the scandalous violinist. I was too busy protesting against the dress Hannah was sewing for me to wear at the party, which was as uncomfortable as dresses were in those days of boning and horsehair.

"I'll tear it to bits before I wear it to the party," I said.

"Then you'll go in your nightgown, Miss Rose, because I'm not sewing you another party dress, that's for sure. And don't you sass your mother about it, either." Hannah put a pin in her mouth and muttered, "She's a good woman, who's done more for the colored folk in this town than some I could name. Now stand still or I'll stick you with this pin, see if I don't."

I shrugged to show my displeasure, and was stuck.

On the night of the party, after dinner off the Sèvres service that Judge Beaufort had ordered from Raleigh, we gathered in the back parlor, where chairs had been arranged in a circle around the piano. In front of the piano stood a man, not much taller than I was. Gray hair hung down to his collar, and his face seemed to be covered with wrinkles, which made him look like a dried-apple doll I had played with one autumn until its head was stolen by a squirrel. In his left hand he carried a violin.

"Come on, girl, sit by your Papa," said my father. We sat beside him although it placed Emma by Mr. Henry, who was complaining to Amelia Ashton, the town beauty, about the new custom of hiring paid performers.

The violinist waited while the dinner guests told each other to hush and be quiet. Then, when even the hushing had stopped, he said "Ladies and Gentlemen," bowed to the audience, and lifted his violin.

He began with a simple melody, like a bird singing on a tree branch in spring. Then came a series of notes, and then another, and I imagined the tree branch swaying in a rising wind, with the bird clinging to it. Then clouds rolled in, gray and filled with rain, and wind lashed the tree branch, so that the bird launched itself into the storm. It soared through turbulence, among the roiling clouds, sometimes enveloped in mist, sometimes with sunlight flashing on its wings, singing in fear of the storm, in defiance of it, in triumph. As this frenzy rose from the strings of the violin, which I thought must snap at any moment, the violinist began to sway, twisting with the force of the music as though he were the bird itself. Then, just as the music seemed almost unbearable, rain fell in a shower of notes, and the storm subsided. The bird returned to the branch and resumed its melody, then even it grew still. The violinist lifted his bow, and we sat in silence.

I sagged against my father, wondering if I had breathed since the music had started.

The violinist said "Thank you, ladies and gentlemen." The dinner guests clapped. He bowed again, drank from a glass of water Callie had placed for him on the piano, and walked out of the room.

"Papa," I whispered, "Can I learn to play the violin?"

"Sure, sweetheart," he whispered back. "As long as your mother says you can."

It took an absolute refusal to touch the piano, and a hunger strike lasting through breakfast and dinner, to secure my violin lessons.

"You really are the most obstinate girl, Rose," said my mother. "If I had been anything like you, my father would have made me stay in my room all day."

"I'll stay in my room all day, but I won't eat, not even if you bring me moldy bread that's been gnawed by rats," I said.

"As though we had rats! And there's no need for that. You'll have your lessons with Meister Wilhelm."

"With what?"

"Johann Wilhelm studied music at a European university. In Berlin, I think, or was it Paris? You'll call him Meister Wilhelm. That means Master, in German. And don't expect him to put up with your willfulness. I'm sure he's accustomed to European children, who are polite and always do as they're told."

"I'm not a child."

"Real–ly?" she said with an unpleasant smile, stretching the word out as long as she had when questioning Adeline Beaufort's social arrangements. "Then stop behaving like one."

"Well," I said, nervous under that smile, "should I go down to Slater's for my lessons?" The thought of entering the disreputable boarding house was as attractive as it was frightening.

"Certainly not. The Beauforts are going to rent him their cottage while he stays in Ashton. You'll have your lessons there."

MEISTER WILHELM LOOKED even smaller than I remembered, when he opened the cottage door in answer to my knock. He wore a white smock covered with smudges where he had rubbed up against something dusty. From its hem hung a cobweb.

"Ah, come in, Fraulein," he said. "You must forgive me. This is no place to receive a young lady, with the dust and the dirt everywhere—and on myself also."

I looked around the cottage. It had changed little since the day Emma and I had eaten green apples on the sagging sofa, although a folded blanket now lay on the sofa, and I realized with surprise that the violinist must sleep there, on the broken springs. The furniture had been pushed farther toward the wall, leaving space in the center of the room for a large table cracked down the middle that had been banished from the Beauforts' dining room for at least a generation. On it were scattered pieces of bamboo, yards of unbleached canvas, tools I did not recognize, a roll of twine, a pot of glue with the handle of a brush sticking out of it, and a stack of papers written over in faded ink.

I did not know what to say, so I twisted the apron Hannah had made me wear between my fingers. My palms felt unpleasantly damp.

Meister Wilhelm peered at me from beneath gray eyebrows that seemed too thick for his face. "Your mother tells me you would like to play the violin?"

I nodded.

"And why the violin? It is not a graceful instrument. A young lady will not look attractive, playing Bach or Corelli. Would you not prefer the piano, or perhaps the harp?"

I shook my head, twisting the apron more tightly.

"No?" He frowned and leaned forward, as though to look at me more close-ly. "Then perhaps you are not one of those young ladies who cares only what the gentlemen think of her figure? Perhaps you truly wish to be a musician."

I scrunched damp fabric between my palms. I scarcely understood my motives for wanting to play the violin, but I wanted to be as honest with him as I could. "I don't think so. Mr. Henry says I have no musical talent at all. It's just that when I saw you playing the violin—at the Beauforts' dinner party, you know—it sounded, well, like you'd gone somewhere else while you were play-ing. Somewhere with a bird on a tree, and then a storm came. And I wanted to go there too." What a stupid thing to have said. He was going to think I was a complete idiot.

Meister Wilhelm leaned back against the table and rubbed the side of his nose with one finger. "It is perceptive of you to see a bird on a tree and a storm in my music. I call it *Der Sturmvogel*, the Stormbird. So you want to go somewhere else, Fraulein Rose. Where exactly is it you want to go?"

"I don't know." My words sounded angry. He did think I was an idiot, then. "Are you going to teach me to play the violin or not?"

He smiled, as though enjoying my discomfiture. "Of course I will teach you. Are not your kind parents paying me? Paying me well, so that I can buy food for myself, and pay for this bamboo, which has been brought from California, and glue, for the pot there, she is empty? But I am glad to hear, Fraulein, that you have a good reason for wanting to learn the violin. In this world, we all of us need somewhere else to go." From the top of one of the dressers, Meister Wilhelm lifted a violin. "Come," he said. "I will show you how to hold the instrument between your chin and shoulder."

"Is this your violin?" I asked.

"No, Fraulein. My violin, she was made by a man named Antonio Stradivari. Some day, if you are diligent, perhaps you shall play her."

I learned, that day, how to hold the violin and the bow, like holding a bird in your hands, with delicate firmness. The first time I put the bow to the strings I was startled by the sound, like a crow with a head cold, nothing like the tones Meister Wilhelm had drawn out of his instrument in the Beauforts' parlor.

"That will get better with time," he told me. "I think we have had enough for today, no?"

I nodded and put the violin down on the sofa. The fingers of my right hand were cramped, and the fingers of my left hand were crisscrossed with red lines where I had been holding the strings.

On a table by the sofa stood a photograph of a man with a beard and mustache, in a silver frame. "Who is this?" I asked.

"That is—was—a very good friend of mine, Herr Otto Lilienthal."

"Is he dead?" The question was rude, but my curiosity was stronger than any scruples I had with regard to politeness.

"Yes. He died last year." Meister Wilhelm lifted the violin from the sofa and put it back on top of the dresser.

"Was he ill?" This was ruder yet, and I dared to ask only because Meister Wilhelm now had his back to me, and I could not see his face.

"Nein. He fell from the sky, from a glider."

"A glider!" I sounded like a squawking violin myself. "That's what you're making with all that bamboo and twine and stuff. But this can't be all of it. Where do you keep the longer pieces? I know—in Slater's barn. From there you can take it to Slocumb's Bluff, where you can jump off the big rock." Then I frowned. "You know that's awfully dangerous."

Meister Wilhelm turned to face me. His smile was at once amused and sad.

"You are an excellent detective, kleine Rose. Someday you will learn that everything worth doing is dangerous."

NEAR THE END of July, Emma left for Raleigh, escorted by her father, to spend a month with her Aunt Otway. Since I had no one to play with, I spent more time at the cottage with Meister Wilhelm, scraping away at the violin with ineffective ardor and bothering him while he built intricate structures of bamboo and twine.

One morning, as I was preparing to leave the house, still at least an hour before my scheduled lesson with the violinist, I heard two voices in the parlor. I crept down the hall to the doorway and listened.

"You're so fortunate to have a child like Emma," said my mother. "I really don't know what to do with Elizabeth Rose."

"Well, Eleanor, she's an obstinate girl, I won't deny that," said a voice I recognized as belonging to Adeline Beaufort. "It's a pity Cullen's so lax with her. You ought to send her to Boston for a year or two. Your sister Winslow would know how to improve a young girl's manners."

"I suppose you're right, Adeline. If she were pretty, that might be some excuse, but as it is . . . Well, you're lucky with your Emma, that's all."

I had heard enough. I ran out of the house, and ran stumbling down the street to the cottage by the river. I pounded on the door. No answer. Meister Wilhelm must still be at Slater's barn. I tried the doorknob, but the cottage was locked. I reached to the top of the door frame, pulled down the key, and let myself in. I banged the door shut behind me, threw myself onto the sagging sofa, and pressed my face into its faded upholstery.

Emma and I had discussed the possibility that our mothers did not love us. We had never expected it to be true.

The broken springs of the sofa creaked beneath me as I sobbed. I was the bird clinging to the tree branch, the tree bending and shaking in the storm Meister Wilhelm had played on his violin, and the storm itself, wanting to break things apart, to tear up roots and crack branches. At last my sobs subsided, and I lay with my cheek on the damp upholstery, staring at the maimed furniture standing against the cottage walls.

Slowly I realized that my left hip was lying on a hard edge. I pushed myself up and, looking under me, saw a book with a green leather cover. I opened it. The frontispiece was a photograph of a tired-looking man labeled "Lord Rutherford, Mountaineer." On the title page was written, "*The Island of Orillion: Its History and Inhabitants*, by Lord Rutherford." I turned the page. Beneath the words "A Brief History of Orillion" I read, "The Island of Orillion achieved levitation on the twenty-third day of June, the year of our Lord one thousand seven hundred and thirty-six."

I do not know how long I read. I did not hear when Meister Wilhelm entered the cottage.

"I see you have come early today," he said.

I looked up from a corner of the sofa, into which I had curled myself. Since I felt ashamed of having entered the cottage while he was away, ashamed of having read his book without asking, what I said sounded accusatory. "So that's why you're building a glider. You want to go to Orillion."

He sat down on the other end of the sofa. "And how much have you learned of Orillion, liebling?"

He was not angry with me then. This time, my voice sounded penitent. "Well, I know about the painters and musicians and poets who were kicked out of Spain by that Inquisition person, Torquesomething, when Columbus left to discover America. How did they find the island in that storm, after everyone thought they had drowned? And when the pirate came—Blackbeard or Bluebeard or whatever—how did they make it fly? Was it magic?"

"Magic, or a science we do not yet understand, which to us resembles magic," said Meister Wilhelm.

"Is that why they built all those towers on the tops of the houses, and put bells in them—to warn everyone if another pirate was coming?"

Meister Wilhelm smiled. "I see you've read the first chapter."

"I was just starting the second when you came in. About how Lord Rutherford fell and broke his leg on a mountain in the Alps, and he thought he was going to die when he heard the bells, all ringing together. I thought they were warning bells?"

"Orillion has not been attacked in so long that the bells are only rung once a day, when the sun rises."

"All of them together? That must make an awful racket."

"Ah, no, liebling. Remember that the citizens of Orillion are artists, the children and grandchildren of artists. Those bells are tuned by the greatest musicians of Orillion, so that when they are rung, no matter in what order, the sound produced is a great harmony. From possible disorder, the bells of Orillion create musical order. But I think one chapter is enough for you today."

At that moment I realized something. "That's how Otto Lilienwhatever died, didn't he? He was trying to get to Orillion."

Meister Wilhelm looked down at the dusty floor of the cottage. "You are right, in a sense, Rose. Otto was trying to test a new theory of flight that he thought would someday allow him to reach Orillion. He knew there was risk—it was the highest flight he had yet attempted. Before he went into the sky for the last time, he sent me that book, and all of his papers. 'If I do not reach Orillion, Johann,' he wrote to me, 'I depend upon you to reach it.' It had been our dream since he discovered Lord Rutherford's book at university. That is why I have come to America. During the three years he lived on Orillion, Lord Rutherford charted the island's movements. In July, it would have been to the north, over your city of Raleigh. I tried to finish my glider there, but was not able to complete it in time. So I came here, following the island—or rather, Lord Rutherford's charts."

"Will you complete it in time now?"

"I do not know. The island moves slowly, but it will remain over this area only during the first two weeks of August." He stood and walked to the table, then touched the yards of canvas scattered over it. "I have completed the frame of the glider, but the cloth for the wings—there is much sewing still to be done."

"I'll help you."

"You, liebling?" He looked at me with amusement. "You are very generous. But for this cloth, the stitches must be very small, like so." He brought over a piece of canvas and showed me his handiwork.

I smiled a superior smile. "Oh, I can make them even smaller than that, don't worry." When Aunt Winslow had visited two summers ago, she had insisted on teaching me to sew. "A lady always looks elegant holding a needle," she had said. I had spent hours sitting in the parlor making a set of clothes for the china doll she had given me, which I had broken as soon as she left. In consequence, I could make stitches a spider would be proud of.

"Very well," said Meister Wilhelm, handing me two pieces of canvas that had been half-joined with an intricate, overlapping seam. "Show me how you would finish this, and I will tell you if it is good enough."

I crossed my legs and settled back into the sofa with the pieces of canvas, waxed thread and a needle, and a pair of scissors. He took *The Island of Orillion* from where I had left it on the sofa and placed it back on the shelf where he kept the few books he owned, between *The Empire of the Air* and *Maimonides: Seine Philosophie*. Then he sat on a chair with a broken back, one of his knees crossed over the other. Draping another piece of canvas over the raised knee, he leaned down so he could see the seam he was sewing in the dim light that came through the dirty windows. I stared at him sewing like that, as though he were now the hunchback of Notre Dame.

"You know," I said, "if you're nearsighted you ought to buy a pair of spectacles."

"Ah, I had a very good pair from Germany," he answered without looking up from his work. "They were broken just before I left Raleigh. Since then, I have not been able to afford another."

I sewed in silence for a moment. Then I said, "Why do you want to go to Orillion, anyway? Do you think—things will be better there?"

His fingers continued to swoop down to the canvas, up from the canvas, like birds. "The citizens of Orillion are artists. I would like to play my *Sturmvogel* for them. I think they would understand it, as you do." Then he looked up and stared at the windows of the cottage, as though seeing beyond them to the hills around Ashton, to the mountains rising blue behind the hills. "I do not know if human beings are better anywhere. But I like to think, liebling, that in this sad world of ours, those who create do not destroy so often."

* * *

AFTER THE DAY on which I had discovered *The Island of Orillion*, when my lessons had been forgotten, Meister Wilhelm insisted that I continue practicing the violin, in spite of my protest that it took time away from constructing the glider. "If no learning, then no sewing—and no reading," he would say. After an hour of valiant effort on the instrument, I was allowed to sit with him, stitching triangles of canvas into bat-shaped wings. And then, if any time remained before dinner, I was allowed to read one, and never more than one, chapter of Lord Rutherford's book.

In spite of our sewing, the glider was not ready to be launched until the first week of August was nearly over. Once the pieces of canvas were sewn together, they had to be stretched over and attached to the bamboo frame, and then covered with three layers of wax, each of which required a day and a night to dry.

But finally, one morning before dawn, I crept down our creaking stairs and then out through the kitchen door, which was never locked. I ran through the silent streets of Ashton to Slater's barn and helped Meister Wilhelm carry the glider up the slope of the back pasture to Slocumb's Bluff, whose rock face rose above the waving grass. I had assumed we would carry the glider to the top of the bluff, where the winds from the rock face were strongest. But Meister Wilhelm called for me to halt halfway up, at a plateau formed by large, flat slabs of granite. There we set down the glider. In the gray light, it looked like a great black moth against the stones.

"Why aren't we going to the top?" I asked.

He looked over the edge of the plateau. Beyond the slope of the pasture lay the streets and houses of Ashton, as small as a dolls' town. Beyond them, a strip of yellow had appeared on the hilltops to the east. "That rock, he is high. I will die if the glider falls from such a height. Here we are not so high."

I stared at him in astonishment. "Do you think you could fall?" Such a possibility had never occurred to me.

"Others have," he answered, adjusting the strap that held a wooden case to his chest. He was taking his violin with him.

"Oh," I said, remembering the picture of Otto Lilienthal. Of course what had happened to Lilienthal could happen to him. I had simply never associated the idea of death with anyone I knew. I clenched and unclenched my hands.

"Help me to put on the glider," said Meister Wilhelm.

I held the glider at an angle as he crouched under it, fastened its strap over his chest, above the strap that held the violin case, and fitted his arms into the armrests.

"Rose," he said suddenly, "listen."

I listened, and heard nothing but the wind as it blew against the face of the bluff.

"You mean the wind?" I said.

"No, no," he answered, his voice high with excitement. "Not the wind. Don't you hear them? The bells, first one, then ten, and now a hundred, playing together."

I turned my head from side to side, trying to hear what he was hearing. I looked up at the sky, where the growing yellow was pushing away the gray. Nothing.

"Rose." He looked at me, his face both kind and solemn. In the horizontal light, his wrinkles seemed carved into his face, so that he looked like a part of the bluff. "I would like you to have my books, and my picture of Otto, and the violin on which you learned to play. I have nothing else to leave anyone in the world. And I leave you my gratitude, liebling. You have been to me a good friend."

He smiled at me, but turned away as he smiled. He walked back from the edge of the plateau and stood, poised with one foot behind the other, like a runner on a track. Then he sprang forward and began to sprint, more swiftly than I thought he could have, the great wings of the glider flapping awkwardly with each step.

He took one final leap, over the edge of the plateau, into the air. The great wings caught the sunlight, and the contraption of waxed canvas fastened on a bamboo frame became a moth covered with gold dust. It soared, wings outstretched, on the winds that blew up from the face of the bluff, and then out over the pasture, higher and farther into the golden regions of the sky.

My heart lifted within me, as when I had first heard Meister Wilhelm play the violin. What if I had heard no bells? Surely Orillion was there, and he would fly up above its houses of white stucco with their belltowers. The citizens of Orillion would watch this miracle, a man like a bird, soaring over them, and welcome him with glad shouts.

The right wing of the glider dipped. Suddenly it was spiraling down, at first slowly and then faster, like a maple seed falling, falling, to the pasture.

I heard a thin shriek, and realized it had come from my own throat. I ran as quickly as I could down the side of the bluff.

When I reached the glider, it was lying in an area of broken grass, the tip of its right wing twisted like an injured bird. Meister Wilhelm's legs stuck out from beneath it.

I lifted one side of the glider, afraid of what I might see underneath. How had Otto Lilienthal looked when he was found, crushed by his fall from the sky?

But I saw no blood, no intestines splattered over the grass—just Meister Wilhelm, with his right arm tangled in a broken armrest and twisted under him at an uncomfortable angle.

"Rose," he said in a weak voice. "Rose, is my violin safe?"

I lifted the glider off him, reaching under him to undo the strap across his chest. He rolled over on his back, the broken armrest still dangling from his arm. The violin case was intact.

"Are you going to die?" I asked, kneeling beside him, grass tickling my legs through my stockings. I could feel tears running down my nose, down to my neck, and wetting the collar of my dress.

"No, Rose," he said with a sigh, his fingers caressing the case as though making absolutely sure it was unbroken. "I think my arm is sprained, that is all. The glider acted like a helicopter and brought me down slowly. It saved my life." He pushed himself up with his left arm. "Is it much damaged?"

I rubbed the back of my hands over my face to wipe away tears.

"No. Just one corner of the wing."

"Good," he said. "Then it can be fixed quickly."

"You mean you're going to try this again?" I stared at him as though he had told me he was about to hang himself from the beam of Slater's barn.

With his left hand, he brushed back his hair, which had blown over his cheeks and forehead. "I have only one more week, Rose. And then the island will be gone."

Together we managed to carry the glider back to Slater's barn, and I snuck back into the house for breakfast.

Later that day, I sat on the broken chair in the cottage while Meister Wilhelm lay on the sofa with a bandage around his right wrist.

"So, what's wrong with your arm?" I asked.

"I think the wrist, it is broken. And there is much pain. But no more breaks."

His face looked pale and old against the green upholstery. I crossed my arms and looked at him accusingly. "I didn't hear any bells."

He tried to smile, but grimaced instead, as though the effort were painful. "I have been a musician for many years. It is natural for me to hear things that you are not yet capable of hearing."

"Well, I didn't see anything either."

"No, Rose. You would see nothing. Through the science—or the magic— of its inhabitants, the bottom of the island always appears the same color as the sky."

Was that true? Or was he just a crazy old man, trying to kill himself in an especially crazy way? I kicked the chair leg, wishing that he had never come to Ashton, wishing that I had never heard of Orillion, if it was going to be a lie. I stood up and walked over to the photograph of Otto Lilienthal.

"You know," I said, my voice sounding angry, "it would be safer to go up in a balloon instead of a glider. At a fair in Brickleford last year, I saw an acrobat go up under a balloon and perform all kinds of tricks hanging from a wooden bar."

"Yes, you are right, it would be safer. I spent many years in my own country studying with Count Von Zeppelin, the great balloonist. But your acrobat, he cannot tell the balloon where to go, can he?"

"No." I turned to face him again. "But at least he doesn't fall out of the sky and almost kill himself."

He turned away from me and stared up at the ceiling. "But your idea is a good one, Rose. I must consider what it is I did wrong. Will you bring me those papers upon the table?"

I walked over to the table, lifted the stack of papers, and brought it over to the sofa. "What is this, anyway?" I asked.

Meister Wilhelm took the stack from me with his left hand. "These are the papers my friend Otto left me." He looked at the paper on top of the stack. "And this is the letter he wrote to me before he died." Awkwardly, he placed the stack beside him on the sofa and lifted the letter to his nearsighted eyes.

"Let me read it to you," I said. "You'll make yourself blind doing that."

"You are generous, Rose," he said, "but I do not think you read German, eh?"

I shook my head.

"Then I will read it to you, or rather translate. Perhaps you will see in it another idea, like she of the balloon, that might help us. Or perhaps I will see in it something that I have not seen before."

He read the letter slowly, translating as he went, sometimes stumbling over words for which he did not know the English equivalent. It was nothing like the letters Emma and I were writing to each other while she stayed in Raleigh. There was no discussion of daily events, of the doings of family.

Instead, Otto Lilienthal had written about the papers he was leaving for his friend, which discussed his theories. He wrote admiringly of Besnier, the first to create a functional glider. He discussed the mistakes of Mouillard and Le Bris, and the difficulties of controlling a glider's flight. He praised Cayley, whose glider had achieved lift, and lamented Pénaud, who became so dispirited by his failures that he locked his papers into a coffin and committed suicide. Finally he wrote of his own ideas, their merits and drawbacks, and of how he had attempted to solve the two challenges of the glider, lift and lateral stability. He had solved the problem of lift early in his career. Now he would try to solve the other.

The letter ended, "My dear Johann, remember how we dreamed of gliding through the air, like the storks in our native Pomerania. I expect to succeed. But if I fail, do you continue my efforts. Surely one with your gifts will succeed, where I cannot. Always remember that you are a violinist." When he had finished the letter, Meister Wilhelm passed his hand, still holding a sheet of paper, over his eyes.

I looked away, out of the dirty window of the cottage. Then I asked, because curiosity had once again triumphed over politeness, "Why did he tell you to remember that you're a violinist?"

Meister Wilhelm answered in a tired voice, "He wanted to encourage me. To tell me, remember that you are worthy to mingle with the citizens of Orillion, to make music for them before the Monument of the Muse at the center of the city. He wanted—"

Suddenly he sat up, inadvertently putting his weight on his right hand. His face creased in pain, and he crumpled back against the seat of the sofa. But he said, in a voice filled with wonder, "No. I have been stupid. Always remember, Rose, that we cannot find the right answers until we ask the right questions. Tell me, what did the glider do just before it fell?"

I stared at him, puzzled. "It dipped to the right."

He waved his left forefinger in the air, as though to punctuate his point. "Because it lacked lateral stability!"

I continued to look puzzled.

He waved his finger again, at me this time. "That is the problem Otto was trying to solve."

I sat back down. "Yes, well he didn't solve it, did he?"

The finger waved once again, more frantically this time. "He solved it in principle. He knew that lateral stability is created with the legs, just as lift is controlled with the position of the body in the armrests. His final flight must have been intended to test which position would provide the greatest amount of control." Meister Wilhelm sat, pulling himself up this time with his left hand. "After his death, I lamented that Otto could never tell me his theory. But he has told me, and I was too stupid to see it!" He rose and began pacing, back and forth as he spoke, over the floor of the cottage. "I have been keeping my legs still, trying not to upset the glider's balance. Otto was telling me that I must use my body like a violinist, that I must not stay still, but respond to the rhythm of the wind, as I respond to the rhythm of music. He thought I would understand."

He turned to me. "Rose, we must begin to repair the glider tomorrow. And then, I will fly it again. But this time I will fly from the top of Slocumb's Bluff, where the winds are strongest. And I will become one with the winds, with the great music that they will play through me."

"Like the Stormbird," I said.

His face, so recently filled with pain, was now filled with hope. "Yes, Rose. Like der Sturmvogel."

SEVERAL DAYS LATER, when I returned for dinner after a morning spent with Meister Wilhelm, Hannah handed me a letter from Emma.

"Did the post come early?" I asked.

"No, child. Judge Beaufort came back from Raleigh and brought it himself. He was smoking in the parlor with your Papa, and I'm gonna have to shake out them parlor curtains. So you get along, and don't bother me, hear?"

I walked up the stairs to my room and lay on top of the counterpane to read Emma's letter. "Dear Rose," it began. "Aunt Otway, who's been showing me an embroidery stitch, asks what I'm going to write." That meant her letter would be read. "Father is returning suddenly to Ashton, but I will remain here until school begins in September." She had told me she was returning at the end of August. And Emma never called Judge Beaufort "Father." Was she trying to show off for Aunt Otway? Under the F in "Father" was a spot of ink, and I noticed that Emma's handwriting was unusually spotty. Under the b and second e in "embroidery," for instance. "Be" what? The letters over the remaining spots spelled "careful." What did Emma mean? The rest of her letter described a visit to the Museum of Art.

Just then, my mother entered the room. "Rose," she said. Her voice was gentler than I had ever heard it. She sat down on the edge of my bed. "I'm afraid you can't continue your lessons with Meister Wilhelm."

I stared at her in disbelief. "You don't want me to have anything I care about, do you? Because you hate me. You've hated me since I was born. I'll tell Papa, and he'll let me have my violin lessons, you'll see!"

She rose, and her voice was no longer gentle. "Very well, Elizabeth. Tell your father, exactly as you wish. Until he comes home from the Beauforts', however, you are to remain in this room." She walked out, closing the door with an implacable click behind her.

Was this what Emma had been trying to warn me about? Had she known that my mother would forbid me from continuing my lessons? But how could she have known, in Raleigh?

As the hours crept by, I stared at the ceiling and thought about what I had read in Lord Rutherford's book. I imagined the slave ship that had been wrecked in a storm, and the cries of the drowning slaves. How they must have wondered, to see Orillion descending from the sky, to walk through its city of stucco houses surrounded by rose gardens. How the captain must have cursed when he was imprisoned by the citizens of Orillion, and later imprisoned by the English as a madman. He had raved until the end of his life about an island in the clouds.

Hannah brought my dinner, saying to me as she set it down, "Ham sandwiches, Miss Rose. You always liked them, didn't you?" I didn't answer. I imagined myself walking between the belltowers of the city, to the Academy of Art. I would sit on the steps, beneath a frieze of the great poets from Sappho to Shakespeare, and listen to Meister Wilhelm playing his violin by the Monument of the Muse, the strains of his *Sturmvogel* drifting over the surface of the lake.

After it had grown dark, I heard the bang of the front door and the sound of voices. They came up the stairs, and as they passed my door I heard one word—"violin." Then the voices receded down the hall.

I opened my door, cautiously looking down the hall and then toward the staircase. I saw a light under the door of my father's study and no signs of my mother or Hannah.

Closing my bedroom door carefully behind me, I crept down the hall, stepping close to the wall where the floorboards were less likely to creak. I stopped by the door of the study and listened. The voices inside were raised, and I could hear them easily.

"To think that I let a damned Jew put his dirty fingers on my daughter." That was my father's voice. My knees suddenly felt strange, and I had to steady them with my hands. The hallway seemed to sway around me.

"We took care of him pretty good in Raleigh." That was a voice I did not recognize. "After Reverend Yancey made sure he was sacked from the orchestra,

Mr. Empie and I visited him to get the money for all that bamboo he'd ordered on credit. He told us he hadn't got the money. So we reminded him of what was due to decent Christian folk, didn't we, Mr. Empie?"

"All right, Mr. Biggs," said another voice I had not heard before. "There was no need to break the man's spectacles."

"So I shook him a little," said Mr. Biggs. "Serves him right, I say."

"What's done is done," said a voice I knew to be Judge Beaufort's. "The issue before us is, what are we to do now? He has been living on my property, in close proximity to my family, for more than a month. He has been educating Mr. Caldwell's daughter, filling her head with who knows what dangerous ideas. Clearly he must be taken care of. Gentlemen, I'm open for suggestions."

"Burn his house down," said Mr. Biggs. "That's what we do when negroes get uppity in Raleigh."

"You forget, Mr. Biggs," said Judge Beaufort, "that his house is my house. And as the elected judge of this town, I will allow no violence that is not condoned by law."

"Than act like a damned judge, Edward," said my father, with anger in his voice. "He's defaulted on a debt. Let him practice his mumbo jumbo in the courthouse jail for a few days. Then you can send him on to Raleigh with Mr. Biggs and Mr. Empie. Just get him away from my daughter!"

There was silence, then the sound of footsteps, as though someone were pacing back and forth over the floor, and then a clink and gurgle, as though a decanter had been opened and liquid were tumbling into a glass.

"All right, gentlemen," said Judge Beaufort. I leaned closer to the door even though I could hear his voice perfectly well. "First thing tomorrow morning, we get this Wilhelm and take him to the courthouse. Mr. Empie, Mr. Biggs, I depend on you to assist us."

"Oh, I'll be there all right," said Mr. Biggs. "Me and Bessie." I heard a metallic click.

My father spoke again. "Put that away, sir. I'll have no loaded firearms in my home."

"He'll put it away," said Mr. Empie. "Come on, Biggs, be sensible, man. Judge Beaufort, if I could have a touch more of that whiskey?"

I crept back down the hall with a sick feeling in my stomach, as though I had eaten a dozen green apples. So this was what Emma had warned me about. I wanted to lie down on my bed and sob, with the counterpane pulled over my head to muffle the sounds. I wanted to punch the pillows until feathers floated around the room. But as I reached my door, I realized there was something else I must do. I must warn Meister Wilhelm.

I crept down the stairs. As I entered the kitchen, lit only by the embers in the stove, I saw a figure sitting at the kitchen table. It was my mother, writing a note, with a leather wallet on the table beside her.

She looked up as I entered, and I could see, even in the dim light from the stove, that her face was puffed with crying. We stared at each other for a moment. Then she rose. "What are you doing down here?" she asked.

I was so startled that all I could say was, "I heard them in the study."

My mother stuffed the note she had been writing into the wallet, and held it toward me.

"I was waiting until they were drunk, and would not miss me," she said. "But they think you're already asleep, Rose. Run and give this to Meister Wilhelm."

I took the wallet from her. She reached out, hesitantly, to smooth down my mop of hair, but I turned and opened the kitchen door. I walked through the back garden, picking my way through the tomato plants, and ran down the streets of Ashton, trying not to twist my ankles on invisible stones.

When I reached the cottage, I knocked quietly but persistently on the door. After a few minutes I heard a muffled grumbling, and then a bang and a word that sounded like an oath. The door opened, and there stood Meister Wilhelm, in a white nightshirt and nightcap, like a ghost floating in the darkness. I slipped past him into the cabin, tossed the wallet on the table, where it landed with a clink of coins, and said, "You have to get out of here, as soon as you can. And there's a note from my mother."

He lit a candle, and by its light I saw his face, half-asleep and half-incredulous, as though he believed I were part of some strange dream. But he read the note. Then he turned to me and said, "Rose, I hesitate to ask of you, but will you help me one final time?"

I nodded eagerly. "You go south to Brickleford, and I'll tell them you've gone north to Raleigh."

He smiled at me. "Very heroic of you, but I cannot leave my glider, can I? Mr. Empie would find it and take it apart for its fine bamboo, and then I would be left with what? An oddly shaped parachute. No, Rose, I am asking you to help me carry the glider to Slocumb's Bluff."

"What do you mean?" I asked. "Are you going to fly it again?"

"My final flight, in which I either succeed, or— But have no fear, liebling. This time I will succeed."

"But what about the wing?" I asked.

"I finished the repairs this afternoon, and would have told you about it tomorrow, or rather today, since my pocket watch on the table here, she tells me it is after midnight. Well, Rose, will you help me?"

I nodded. "We'd better go now though, in case that Mr. Biggs decides to burn down the cottage after all."

"Burn down—? There are human beings in this world, Rose, who do not deserve the name. Come, then. Let us go."

The wind tugged at the glider as we carried it up past the plateau where it had begun its last flight, toward the top of Slocumb's Bluff. In the darkness it seemed an animated thing, as though it wanted to fly over the edge of the bluff, away into the night. A little below the top of the bluff, we set it down beneath a grove of pine trees, where no wind came. We sat down on a carpet of needles to wait for dawn.

Through the long, dark hours, Meister Wilhelm told me about his childhood in Pomerania and his days at the university. Although it was August, the top of the bluff was chilly, and I often wished for a coat to pull over my dress. At last, however, the edges of the sky looked brighter, and we stood, shaking out our cold, cramped legs.

"This morning I am an old man, liebling," said Meister Wilhelm, buckling the strap of the violin case around his chest. "I do not remember feeling this stiff, even after a night in the Black Forest. Perhaps I am too old, now, to fly as Otto would have me."

I looked at the town. In the brightening stillness, four small shapes were moving toward Judge Beaufort's house. "Well then, you'd better go down to the courthouse and give yourself up, because they're about to find out that you're not at the cottage."

Meister Wilhelm put his hand on my shoulder. "It is good that you have clear eyes, Rose. Help me to put on the glider."

I helped him lift the glider to his back and strap it around his chest, as I had done the week before. The four shapes below us were now moving from Judge Beaufort's house toward Slater's barn.

Meister Wilhelm looked at me sadly. "We have already said our goodbye, have we not? Perhaps we do not need to say it again." He smiled. "Or perhaps we will meet, someday, in Orillion."

I said, suddenly feeling lonelier than I had ever felt before, "I don't have a glider."

But he had already turned away, as though he were no longer thinking of me. He walked out from under the shelter of the trees and to the top of the bluff, where the wind lifted his gray hair into a nimbus around his head.

"Well, what are you waiting for?" I asked, raising my voice so he could hear it over the wind. Four shapes were making their way toward us, up the slope above Slater's barn.

"The sun, Rose," he answered. "She is not yet risen." He paused, as though listening, then added, "Do you know what day this is? It is the ninth of August, the day that my friend Otto died, exactly one year ago."

And then the edge of the sun rose over the horizon. As I had seen him do once before, Meister Wilhelm crouched into the stance of a runner. Then he sprang forward and sprinted toward the edge of the bluff. With a leap over the edge, he was riding on the wind, up, up, the wings of the glider outspread like the wings of a moth. But this time those wings did not rise stiffly. They turned and soared, as thought the wind were their natural element. Beneath them, Meister Wilhelm was twisting in intricate contortions, as though playing an invisible violin. Then the first rays of the sun were upon him, and he seemed a man of gold, flying on golden wings.

And then, I heard them. First one, then ten, then a hundred—the bells of Orillion, sounding in wild cacophony, in celestial harmony. I stood at the top of Slocumb's Bluff, the wind blowing cold through my dress, my chin lifted to the sky, where the bells of Orillion were ringing and ringing, and a golden man flying on golden wings was a speck rapidly disappearing into the blue.

"Rose! What in heaven's name are you doing here?" I turned to see my father climbing over the top of the bluff, with Judge Beaufort and two men, no doubt Mr. Biggs and Mr. Empie, puffing behind. I looked into his handsome face, which in its contours so closely resembled mine, so that looking at him was like looking into a mirror. And I answered, "Watching the dawn."

I MANAGED TO remove *The Island of Orillion* and the wallet containing my mother's note from the cottage before Mr. Empie returned to claim Meister Wilhelm's possessions in payment for his bamboo. They lie beside me now on my desk, as I write.

After my father died from what the Episcopal minister called "the demon Drink," I was sent to school in Boston because, as Aunt Winslow told my mother, "Rose may never marry, so she might as well do something useful." When I returned for Emma's wedding to James Balfour, who had joined his uncle's law practice in Raleigh, I read in the Herald that the Wrights had flown an airplane among the dunes near Kitty Hawk, on the winds rising from the Atlantic. As I arranged her veil, which had been handed down through generations of Ashton women and made her look even more like a china doll, except for the caramel in her right cheek, I wondered if they had been searching for Orillion.

And then, I did not leave Ashton again for a long time. One day, as I set the beef tea and toast that were all my mother could eat, with the cancer eating her from the inside like a serpent, on her bedside table, she opened her eyes and said, "I've left you all the money." I took her hand, which had grown so thin that blue veins seemed to cover it like a net, and said, "I'm going to buy an airplane. There's a man in Brickleford who can teach me how to fly." She looked at me as though I had just come home from the river by the Beauforts', my mouth stained with blackberries and my stockings covered with mud. She said, "You always were a troublesome child." Then she closed her eyes for the last time.

I have stored the airplane in Slocumb's barn, which still stands behind the remains of the boarding house. Sometimes I think, perhaps Orillion has changed its course since Lord Rutherford heard its bells echoing from the mountains. Perhaps now that airplanes are becoming common, it has found a way of disguising itself completely and can no longer be found. I do not know. I read Emma's letters from Washington, in which she complains about the tedium of being a congressman's wife and warns about a war in Europe. Even without a code, they transmit the words "be careful" to the world. Then I pick up the wallet, still filled with a crumbling note and a handful of coins. And I consult Lord Rutherford's charts.

The Egg in Twelve Scenes

I.

The egg was immaculate.
I made certain to keep the egg immaculate.

He could not fault me for being a bad housekeeper.

II.

He said, I'm going to marry one of your sisters.
He said, I'm going to marry the other of your sisters.
I said, What happened to my first sister?

He said, I don't know. Maybe she joined the circus.

III.

My oldest sister was named Doris.
She resented this.
My father had named her.
Beware the wizard Fitcher, he had told us
when we were, respectively, three, five, and seven.

Doris was seven.
Why, what will he do to me? she asked.
She was always practical and curious,
a typical first-born, a brunette,
sometimes a bit too bossy.

My father answered, He will eat your heart.

IV.

My middle sister was named Eglantine.
My mother had given her that name,
together with her blessing.

She had golden hair, and hazel eyes,
and a laugh like water
falling over small stones.
She was the sensitive, artistic one.
It was no wonder
Fitcher came for her, after
Doris disappeared.

V.

My name was Mag
or Maggie, or Come-here-Margaret,
or What-did-you-do-this-time?
I was not the cause of my mother's death,
they assured me. But I
knew better.

I carried guilt like a seamed and
faded letter in my pocket.

VI.

When Fitcher came for me,
I said, What have you done with Eglantine?
He said, She left to go find herself.
Maybe in India, maybe in Indiana, who knows.
She could be anywhere.

I said, I didn't know she was lost.

VII.

I said, I will not be like my sisters.
I will not run off to become an acrobat
or meditate on a yoga mat. Instead, I will be content.
I will learn to cook. Let's start with breakfast:
how do you like your eggs?

But Fitcher was already gone.
I was talking to myself.

VIII.

He said to keep the egg clean,
so I kept the egg clean by putting it on a shelf.
He said not to open the door
with the smallest key on the ring heavy
with all the keys, from cellar to butler's pantry.
So I cut off my little finger and used the bone instead.

My mother could not read me fairy tales,
so I had to read them myself.

IX.

Doris had taught me to sew.
Carefully, I stitched them together again,
trying to remember which was her arm,
which Eglantine's.
I'm not entirely sure I got it right,
because Doris has started painting,
and Eglantine is a much better seamstress.

When I was done, my sisters said,
Maggie, you know he's coming back.
We need to get out of here double-quick.

So I put them in the basket
and covered them with feathers.

X.

Where is the key? said Fitcher.
I showed him the key, unspotted
on its heavy ring.

Where is the egg? he said.
I showed him the egg, as white
as a lily. He smiled at me.
Good girl, Maggie, he said.

My name, I whispered, is Margaret.
Then I asked him to carry the basket
to my father's house.

XI.

They say I am clever for saving my sisters.
They say Fitcher deserved what he got
when my sisters climbed out of the basket
and explained everything.

My father roared and lunged toward him.
Fitcher stepped back, tumbled down the porch steps,
and broke his head on the concrete,
like in a children's rhyme.
The yoke spilled out.
They could not put him together again.

It was an accident, they said. Anyway,
that's what he gets for being an evil wizard.
Your Maggie is a clever girl, they said.

XII.

I didn't want the house.
The blood would never come out
of that floor.

But I took the insurance money.
After all, every girl
needs a nest egg.

Now I'm with the circus, wearing yellow tights
and a silver cape that looks like wings
when I spread my arms under the Big Top.
I always fancied myself
on the flying trapeze.

Vivian to Merlin

I called you, and you would not answer me.
What power was it that trapped you in the oak?
They blame me, saying I have cast a spell,
but even if I had that sort of knowledge,
I would not hold you.

When I was young, a girl in Lyonesse,
a prince's daughter running through the fields,
where all the peasants greeted me, or forests,
where I could call the birds down from their nests,
my two braids swinging,

I found a wounded raven, lifted him,
carried him back into my father's castle,
placed him inside a basket on the hay
I'd stolen from the horses. There he sat,
regarding me

with his black eyes, eating the worms and insects
I brought him. And eventually the wing,
which had been wounded by a dog perhaps,
holding the raven in its mouth, was healed.
At first he flew

around my room and perched upon the chest,
the windowsill. You know this story ends
the day he flung himself into the air
and flew over the fields, back to his forest.
Its moral is

you can't hold what you love. Not for a moment,
not for a century. It must have been
another magician, as powerful as yourself,
or a giant who just happened to have a curse
handy. It must have.

I sit here with my back against the oak,
hoping it was a curse and not your choice.
(But who could trap Merlin himself? I could not,
despite the magic you have taught me.) Love,
if you can hear me,

as you sit curled inside the oak tree's bole,
just tell me this: that it was not by choice
you left me, weary of our days and nights,
by daylight casting spells, by night lying
entwined, together.

You can't hold what you love. I would not hold you—
but I had hoped that you would choose, yourself,
to stay with me. And yet you sit there, curled
in silence, Merlin of the silver tongue,
and I wait, hoping . . .

In Autumn

S HE WAITED UNTIL autumn.

She wanted to wait until the children were home and back in school. Bobby had been at soccer camp—Robert, he wanted to be called now, which was confusing because his father was Robert too, so when she called either of them, they both answered. He started tenth grade and slipped right back into his usual routine of school, soccer, and hanging out with friends, like a fish sliding through a pond without making a ripple. It was Eleanor she was worried about. At the end of seventh grade she'd quarreled with her best friend, or her best friend had quarreled with her, and Eleanor had said they were never speaking again, then had run up to her room and cried with the sort of passionate intensity best left to itself. That summer she had gone to riding camp, and then visited her grandparents, Robert's parents, who lived in a large house surrounded by pastures and forest, where her grandmother had made all her favorite foods. Somehow, over Facebook or Snapchat or whatever teenagers were using at the moment, a reconciliation had been effected, and Eleanor and Emily were once again inseparable. But Eleanor was the sensitive one, the one who secretly wrote poetry, so it was Eleanor she was worried about.

She put it off as long as she could, methodically doing everything she thought was necessary. She had lunch with her best friends, women she'd met in art school: Elsa, who was a sculptress and older, and Amelia, who was a graphic designer and younger. They had started going out for coffee after the required *Introduction to Aesthetic Theory* class. That had been in the early days of her marriage, when she was still learning the language, how to walk and talk and dress the right way as the wife of Robert Foster, Esq. They had helped her navigate the complexities of registration and the school's computer system. At the time, she thought she might become an artist, have a career of her own. But Bobby had been born, and then Eleanor. Over the living room sofa hung one of her first paintings: swirls of white and gray in an abstract pattern. Well, at least the friendships had lasted. She and Amelia had taken care of Elsa's cats in the weeks after her mastectomy. She and Elsa had been attendants at Amelia's wedding. Elsa or Amelia had babysat the children so she could have date nights with Robert. The three of them met at the new restaurant downtown that Amelia recommended. She and Elsa ordered wine, Elsa ordered the salad because she was dieting, Amelia ordered dessert because she was eating for two now. Afterward she held their hands. "You've been my best friends here," she said. Amelia cried a little, saying it was the hormones, and Elsa asked, "What's going on? You don't sound like yourself." But she didn't answer.

After lunch, she met with the bank manager and set up trusts for the children. Although she had never worked full time, she's saved some money from her part-time job at the art studio. Once Eleanor had started school, she'd wanted to work, even though Robert had told her it wasn't necessary, that she should prioritize the children. She knew Robert would give them more than enough, but she wanted them to have a little something from her, to spend as they wished. For Eleanor, she also left a box and letter, to be delivered on her eighteenth birthday. In the following weeks, she had the rugs cleaned, the armchair that the cat had scratched reupholstered. She made sure the dog was current on his shots. There always seemed to be something more that needed doing, so she kept putting it off.

By the end of September, she could not wait any longer. It was still warm, but winter was coming—she had seen a flock of geese by the river, stopping for a few days on its way from Canada to Mexico. The last of the tomatoes were cracking on the vine. She thought of canning them, but really what did it matter? The garden had been planted to teach the children where food came from; what it produced could be bought cheaper at the supermarket. And anyway, this had to end at some point. There was only so much she could do.

That day, she made waffles for breakfast, with coffee for Robert and a kiss as he rushed out the door, on the way to a client meeting. She sent Bobby and Eleanor off to school, hugging them both tightly. Bobby sighed and said "Mooooom" in protest, but she was surprised when Eleanor hugged her back just as tight. Then she picked up the drycleaning, went to the grocery store and stocked up on toilet paper, paid the family cell phone bill. What else? The breakfast dishes were in the dishwasher. Really there was nothing more for her to do.

She was out of excuses.

She sat down at the desk in the kitchen, the one where she paid bills, and opened the drawer. It was just as she had left it, and for a moment she wished that someone, anyone, had opened that drawer—but no one else had a reason to use it. Scissors, stamps, checks, spare keys, and a bundle of gray feathers the roofer had found, when he had replaced the roof tiles damaged in last winter's ice storm. "Looks like some bird made a nest in your roof," he had said, showing her the feathers, tucked behind a rafter. She had laughed and pulled them down, saying she would throw them out. Now she put them on the desk: they were long and gray, iridescent in the light. She spread them out. They were attached to an integument that looked, more than anything, like a hood. She remembered vaguely that Robert had been up there, soon after she first arrived—patching a hole, he said. So that's where he had put it. No one had worked on the roof since. She stroked the feathers. It had been so long.

Should she take her raincoat? It looked like rain. And then she laughed at herself, aloud in the empty house.

The flock was still there, six gray geese by the river. They eyed her warily, the lead goose standing up and craning his neck. He hissed. At the last moment, she realized she had forgotten to tell Robert there was frozen lasagna for dinner—all he had to do was put it in the microwave. But for goodness' sake, he was a grown man and a lawyer. He could figure it out for himself.

She pulled the feathers out of the plastic bag she was carrying, all the feathers the roofer had found except one she had put in a box, with a note for Eleanor. It was a long note, but the most important part was short and at the end: *When you call, I will come for you. Love, Mom.* She held the bundle of feathers in front of her, like a talisman, then shook it out. The lead goose stopped hissing and bobbed his head once, twice. If he had been human, he would have been nodding. One by one, the flock of geese stood up in their absurd, elegant way. She could feel the air: moist, cold, with a wind blowing from the east—the ocean smell was in it. She drew the feathered hood over her head. It was time.

She stretched out her wings, and scooped the air, and then she was airborne.

SEVEN GEESE ROSE into the autumn sky, through swirls of white and gray, until they were only a V-formation high above, winging their way south.

Seven Shoes

The witch said, "I will give you what you want.
All you have to do is wear through seven
pairs of shoes." "Which shoes?" she asked. "Oh, any.
But the number is important."

The first pair, she was wearing that day in the woods:
red Keds. In them, she would ride her bike down the road,
hike along the top of the ridge to a tree
where an owl was nesting, wade through the rocky stream,
until her mother declared they were beyond help.
But each time, they revived in the washing machine.
She would wear them to go hunting for dragonflies
and minnows, or up to the attic where she kept
her favorite books. Finally, the soles split
while she was climbing over slick, wet rocks.
She almost fell into the muddy water,
not that she would have minded.
By then, they had faded to a dusty pink.

The second was a pair of flip-flops bought
for a dollar at the bait and tackle shop
next to the lake while visiting her father.
By the end of summer, they were getting moldy
from all the times she had worn them in the canoe,
rowing along the banks through lotus flowers,
leaving a path of dark water in her wake.
Finally, on a fishing trip, the strap
broke, and she walked back barefoot,
carrying the trout in a basket, almost sorry
it would be her dinner that night,
with butter and parsley.

The third was a pair of silver sandals, worn
to the spring formal with a long blue dress
the color of the sky that reminded her
of both Amelia Earhart and a princess.

They only lasted an hour: the buckle snapped.
After that, she danced barefoot in the gym,
holding hands with her friends under basketball hoops
decorated with paper streamers.

The fourth was a pair of black patent pumps she wore
to her law firm internship, running up and down
the internal staircase, taking notes at meetings,
sitting in on conference calls, making copies.
One day, while she was hurrying to the deli
to pick up sandwiches, her left heel caught
between two bricks of an ancient city sidewalk.
She twisted her ankle and laddered her pantyhose.
The patent leather cracked.

The fifth was a pair of sensible boots that lasted
through four New England winters while she trudged
along a familiar track from dorm to classrooms
to library, and back.
By the time she graduated, the leather tops
had separated from the rubber soles,
so water seeped through and soaked both layers of socks.
But the degree was worth wet feet.

The sixth pair were white satin and cost as much
as her dress, which she had found in a second-hand store,
real silk, probably from the 1950s.
She danced in them carefully, they felt so delicate,
and made her feel delicate too. Later, she wrapped them
in tissue paper and stored them beside the veil
of antique lace, the bouquet of silk roses.
They were shoes for just one day. As in a fairy tale,
they had served their purpose.

The seventh was a pair of bedroom slippers.
She wore through the soles by walking back and forth
in the apartment until her daughter was sleeping.
Then she would sit at her desk beside the crib
and work on her dissertation while the words
swam in front of her eyes, she was so tired.
Like minnows in a stream . . . She wondered where
that image had come from. One day, she realized the slippers
had worn right through: there were holes under her toes.

She had not even noticed.

By then, she had forgotten the witch in the woods.

One day, as she was walking through the campus
where she was now a professor, she met a woman
who asked, "So, have you started writing your stories?"
"Sort of," she said, wondering how this person,
dressed in a raincoat, with a colorful kerchief
over her head, very Eastern European,
knew that late at night when the papers were graded
and her daughter had gone to bed after finishing homework,
she would sit at her computer, trying to write.
That morning she had put on a pair of red Keds
that for some reason always made her happy,
even though the weather channel had forecast rain.
"I'm working on a novel," she replied.
"I've always wanted to be a writer, since
I was a little girl." "Good," said the woman,
patting her on the arm. "You're ready now."

The Clever Serving-Maid

Here are the things your mother did not give you:
a chest filled with linens for your marriage bed,
a casket of jewels to wear on your wedding day,
a handkerchief spotted with her own red blood,
a talking horse named Falada.

Here are the things she did: your life, of course,
a tendency to get in and out of trouble
since you were a scullion. And now here you are,
so grand, a lady's maid, but you are thinking
you could be grander still. So you tell the princess
to put on your plain brown linen while you dress
yourself in her sky-blue silk. It suits you better
anyway. And then you get on Falada.

The prince doesn't even notice the substitution.
Why should he? You've been in service since you were twelve.
You can sound as articulate as a duchess,
or more so, the way the butler is somehow always
more impressive than the king.

But you have to shake your head when you look out the window
and see her in the courtyard—the princess is hopeless
at tending geese. She'd make a terrible queen.
If she can't control a flock of geese, how can she
control a household, a diplomatic mission,
troops sent into battle? Queens have to know
these sorts of things, not just embroidery.

And look at the stable-boy pestering her! You would stick
your knife into him—then he'd stop being obnoxious!

You're sad when Falada dies, which wasn't your doing.
He was an old horse—what did anyone expect?
But the princess is inconsolable, cries all day,
her soft white hands are developing blisters, her nose

is getting freckled. All right you say, let's end
this charade. I'm not the princess.

The problem is, the prince has already fallen
in love with you, but he has a weak chin and eyes
like gooseberries. So you decide there's adventure
out there somewhere, countries you have not heard of,
seas that have not been sailed, another future
than either the one reserved for serving-maids
or princesses. As you walk through the castle gates
(the king is threatening to put you in a barrel
filled with nails and have you dragged through the streets
as punishment, the prince is begging you
to stay, the princess is looking confused, as always),
the head of Falada calls from above the gates,
"Where will you go, false maid?" You answer, "Anywhere
I please, and nowhere in particular."

The air is cool, the way it usually is
after a night of rain, the birds cacophonous.
The road winds through the town, then into forest.
Where should you go? East, you decide, where ahead of you
the sun has risen and shines on the dusty road,
making it seem, just for a moment, golden.

Princess Lucinda and the Hound of the Moon

W HEN THE QUEEN learned that she could not have a child, she cried for three days. She cried in the clinic in Switzerland, on the shoulder of the doctor, an expert on women's complaints, leaving tear stains on his white coat. She cried on the train through Austria, while the Alps slipped past the window of her compartment, their white peaks covered with snow. She cried when the children from the Primary School met her at the station, bringing her bouquets of snowdrops, the first of the season. And after the French teacher presented her with the bouquets, and the children sang the Sylvanian national anthem, their breaths forming a mist on the cold air—she cried especially then.

"It doesn't matter, Margarethe," said King Karel. "My nephew Radomir will make a fine king. Look at how well he's doing at the Primary School. Look at how much he likes building bridges, and if any country needs bridges, it's Sylvania." For the Danube and its tributaries ran through the country, so that wherever you went in Sylvania was over a river, or perhaps two.

And then Queen Margarethe stopped crying, because it was time to greet the French ambassador, and she was after all the youngest daughter of the King of Greece. She had been trained to restrain her emotions, at least at state functions. And the blue satin of her dress would stain.

But that night, when the French ambassador was discussing business with the bankers of Sylvania, and her other guests were discussing French innovations in art (for although Sylvania was a small country, it had a fashionable court) or losing at cards in a cloud of cigarette smoke, the Queen walked out to the terrace.

It was a cold night, and she pulled the blue satin wrap more closely about her shoulders. The full moon above her was wearing a wrap of gray clouds. In its light, she walked down the steps of the terrace, between the topiaries designed by Radomir IV, boxwood swans swimming in a pool of grass, a boxwood stag running from overgrown boxwood hounds. She shivered because her wrap was not particularly warm, but walked on through the rose garden, which was a tangle of canes. She did not want to go back to the castle, or face her guests.

She reached the croquet lawn, beyond which began the forest that surrounded Karelstad, where croquet balls were routinely lost during tournaments between the ministers and the ladies-in-waiting. Suddenly, she heard laughter. She looked around, frightened, and said, "Is anyone there?"

No one answered. But under a chestnut tree that would be covered with white flowers in spring, she saw a basket. She knelt beside it, although the frost on the grass would stain her dress more certainly than tears, and saw a child. It was so young that the laugh she had heard might have been its first, and it waved its fist, either at the moon above or at the Queen, whose face looked like a second moon in the darkness.

She lifted the child from its basket. Surely it must be cold, left out on a night like this, when winter still covered Sylvania. Surely whoever had left it here did not deserve a child. She picked it up, with the blanket it was wrapped in, and carried it over the croquet lawn, through the rose garden, between the boxwood swans and the boxwood stag, up the terrace steps, to the castle.

"Surely she has a mother," said the King. "I know this has been difficult for you, Margarethe, but we can't just keep her."

"If you could send the Chamberlain out for diapers," said the Queen. "And tell Countess Agata to warm a bottle."

"We'll have to advertise in the Karelstad Gazette. And when her mother replies, we'll have to return her."

"Look," said the Queen, holding the child up to the window, for the cook had scattered cake crumbs on the terrace, and pigeons were battling over them. "Look, embroidered on the corner of her blanket. It must be her name: Lucinda."

No one answered the advertisement, although it ran for four weeks, with a description of the child and where she had been found. And when the King himself went to look beneath the chestnut tree, even the basket was gone.

PRINCESS LUCINDA WAS an ordinary child. She liked to read books, not the sort that princesses were supposed to like, but books about airplanes, and mountain climbing, and birds. She liked to play with her dolls, so long as she could make parachutes for them and toss them down from the branches of the chestnut tree. The Queen was afraid that someday Lucinda would fall, but she could not stop her from climbing trees, or putting breadcrumbs on her windowsill for the pigeons, or dropping various objects, including the King's scepter, out of the palace window, to see if they would fly.

Lucinda also liked the gardener's daughter, Bertila, who could climb trees, although not so well as the Princess. She did not like receptions, or formal dresses, or narrow shoes, and she particularly disliked Jaromila, her lady-in-waiting and Countess Agata's daughter.

But there were two unusual things about Princess Lucinda. Although her hair was brown, it had a silver sheen, and in summer it became so pale that it seemed purely silver. And the Princess walked in her sleep. When the doctor noticed that it happened only on moonlit nights, the Queen ordered shutters to be placed on Lucinda's windows, and moonlight was never allowed into her room.

For the Princess' sixteenth birthday, the Queen planned a party. Of course she did not know when the Princess had been born, so she chose a day in summer, when the roses would be at their best and her guests could smoke on the terrace.

Everyone of importance in Sylvania was invited, from the Prime Minister to the French teacher at the Primary School. (Education was considered important in Sylvania, and King Karel had said on several occasions that education would determine Sylvania's success in the new century.) The Queen hired an orchestra that had been the fashion that winter in Prague, although she confessed to the Chamberlain that she could not understand modern music. And Prince Radomir came home from Oxford.

"They ought to be engaged," said the Queen at breakfast. "Look at what an attractive couple they make, and what good friends they are already." Princess Lucinda and Prince Radomir were walking below the morning room windows, along the terrace. The Queen might have been less optimistic if she had known that they were discussing airplane engines. "And then she would be Queen."

She looked steadily at the King, and raised her eyebrows.

"But I can't help it, Margarethe," said King Karel, moving his scrambled eggs nervously around on his plate with a fork. "When the first King Karel was crowned by the Pope himself, he decreed that the throne must always pass to a male heir."

"Then it's about time that women got the vote," said the Queen, and drank her coffee. Which was usually how she left it. King Karel imagined suffragettes crashing through the castle windows and writing "Votes for Women" on the portraits of Radomir IV and his queen, Olga.

"How can you not like him?" asked Bertila later, as she and Lucinda sat on the grass, beneath the chestnut tree.

"Oh, I like him well enough," said Lucinda. "But I don't want to marry him. And I'd make a terrible queen. You should have seen me yesterday, during all those speeches. My shoes were hurting so badly that I kept shifting from foot to foot, and Mother kept raising her eyebrows at me. You don't know how frightening it is, when she raises her eyebrows. It makes me feel like going to live in the dungeon. But I don't want to stand for hours shaking hands with ambassadors, or listen to speeches, even if they are in my honor. I want —"

What did she want? That was the problem, really. She did not know.

"But he's so handsome, with those long eyelashes, and you know he's smart." Bertila lay back on the grass and stared at the chestnut leaves.

"Then you should marry him yourself. Honestly, I don't know what's gotten into you lately. You used to be so sensible, and now you're worse than Jaromila."

"Beast. As though a prince could marry a gardener's daughter." Bertila threw a chestnut, rejected by a squirrel the previous autumn because a worm had eaten through its center, at the Princess.

"Ouch. Stop it, or I'll start throwing them back at you. And not only do I have more chestnuts, I have much better aim. But seriously, Bertie, you'd make a better queen than I would. You're so beautifully patient and polite. And since you're already in love with his eyelashes . . ."

"There you are," said Jaromila. "Lying in the dirt as usual, and talking with servants." She tapped one shoe, as pointed and uncomfortable as fashion demanded, on the grass.

"You're not wanted here," said Lucinda.

"But you're wanted at the reception, half an hour ago."

"You see?" said Lucinda to Bertila, in dismay. "You'd make a much better queen than I would!"

"And she'd be just as entitled to it," said Jaromila. She had also seen Lucinda walking with Radomir on the terrace, but she had reacted quite differently than the Queen. She could not tell you the length of Radomir's eyelashes, but she knew that one day he would be king.

"What do you mean?" asked Lucinda.

"Yes, what *do* you mean?" asked Bertila. She was usually patient, just as Lucinda had said, but today she would have liked to pull Jaromila's hair.

"Well, it's time someone told you," said Jaromila, shifting her feet, because it was difficult to stand on the grass, and because she was nervous. "But you can't tell anyone it was me." From the day the Princess had been found, Queen Margarethe had implied that Lucinda was her own child, born in Switzerland. No one at court had dared to question the Queen, and the Chamberlain and Countess Agata liked their positions too well to contradict her. But Jaromila had heard them discussing it one night, over glasses of sherry. If anyone found out that Jaromila had told the Princess, she would be sent to her grandmother's house in Dobromir, which had no electric lights or telephone, not even a phonograph.

"Told what?" asked Lucinda. "You'd better tell me quickly. I have a whole pile of chestnuts, and you can't run in those shoes."

"That you're not a princess at all. You were found in a basket under this chestnut tree, like a peasant's child."

That afternoon, the Queen had to tell Lucinda three times not to fidget in front of the French ambassador.

As soon as the reception was over, Lucinda ran up to her room and lay on her bed, staring up at the ceiling. Who was she, if she was not the Princess Lucinda? After a while, she got up and took off the dress she had worn to the reception, which had been itching all afternoon. She put on her pajamas. But she could not sleep. For the first time in her life, she opened the shutters on her bedroom windows and looked out. There was the moon, as full as a silver krona, casting the shadows of boxwood swans and hounds on the lawn.

In her slippers, she crept down the stairs and out the French doors to the terrace. She walked between the topiaries and the rose bushes, over the croquet lawn, to edge of the forest. There, she lay on the grass and stared up at the moon, through the branches of the chestnut tree. "Who am I?" she asked. It seemed to smile at her, but gave no answer.

* * *

LUCINDA WOKE SHIVERING, with dew on her pajamas. She had to sneak back into the castle without being seen by the footmen, who were already preparing for the party.

Jaromila had forgotten to set out the dress she was supposed to wear, a white dress the Queen had chosen, with a train she would probably trip over on the stairs. With a sigh, Lucinda opened the door of her dressing room and started looking through the dresses that hung there, all the dresses she had worn since her christening, for although Lucinda did not care about dresses, Queen Margarethe cared a great deal.

That was why she missed the excitement.

Jaromila had been afraid to go to the Princess's room that morning. Lucinda would certainly tell the Queen what she had said, and when the Queen found out—Jaromila remembered Dobromir. So she stayed in the ballroom, where Queen Margarethe was preparing for the party by changing her mind several times about who should sit where. Countess Agata was writing place cards, and the footmen were setting out the glasses for champagne.

King Karel, still in his slippers, wandered into the ballroom and said, "Margarethe, have you seen my crown? I thought I left it next to my pocket watch on the bureau—"

That was when the shaking started. The ballroom shook as though the earth were opening beneath it. Jaromila, who was standing by the French doors, clutched at the curtains to stay upright. The Queen fell on Countess Agata's lap, which made a relatively comfortable cushion. The King, less fortunate, stumbled into the footmen, who toppled like dominoes. Most of the champagne glasses crashed to the floor.

A voice resounded through the ballroom. "Bring me the Princess Lucinda!"

The King, recovering his breath, said, "Whatever was that?"

Prince Radomir ran into the room and said, "Was it an earthquake?"

One of the footmen, who had fallen by the French doors, said, "By Saint Benedek, that's the biggest dog I've ever seen."

The King went to the French doors, leaving Prince Radomir to pick up the Queen and the Countess. There, on the terrace, stood a hound, as white as milk and as large as a pony.

"Bring me the Princess Lucinda!" he said again, in a voice like thunder. Then he shook himself, and the ballroom shook with him, so the King had to hold on to a curtain, like Jaromila, to stay upright. The remaining champagne glasses crashed to the floor, and the footmen fell down again in a heap.

Nothing in King Karel's training had prepared him for an enormous hound on his terrace, a hound who evidently had the ability to shake his castle to its foundations (his training having focused on international diplomacy and the Viennese waltz). But he was a practical man. So he said, from behind the curtain, "Who are you, and what do you want with the Princess?"

"I am the Hound of the Moon. If you don't bring me the Princess Lucinda, I will bite the head off the statue of King Karel in front of the cathedral, and the steeple off the cathedral itself, and the turrets off the castle. And if I'm still hungry, I'll bite the roofs off all the houses in Karelstad—"

"Here she is, here is the Princess Lucinda!" said the Queen, pushing Jaromila out the French doors. Jaromila, surprised and frightened, screamed. The Countess, who was leaning on Radomir, also screamed and fainted.

But the hound grabbed Jaromila by the sash around her waist, leaped from the terrace and landed among the topiaries, then leaped through the rose garden and over the forest, into the clouds.

Lucinda never noticed. When the castle had shaken, all the dresses on the shelves of the dressing room had fallen on top of her, along with most of the shoes, and when she had crawled out from beneath them, she imagined that she had somehow shaken them down herself. And still the dress for the ball was nowhere to be found.

THE HOUND DROPPED Jaromila on the floor of a cave whose walls were covered with crystals.

The first thing she said when she had regained her breath was, "I'm not the Princess Lucinda."

"We shall see," said the hound. "Get up, whoever you are, and take a seat."

At the center of the cave, arranged around a table, Jaromila saw three chairs. The first was an obvious example of Opulentism, which had been introduced at the Exposition Universelle in Paris. Its arms were carved to resemble griffins, with garnets for eyes, and it was elaborately gilded. The second was a chair any Sylvanian farmer could have carved on a winter night as he sat by his fireside. The third was simply a stool of white wood.

Surely he didn't expect her to sit on *that*. And as for the second chair, she wasn't a peasant. Jaromila sat in the first chair, on its cushion of crimson velvet, and put her arms on the griffins.

"Can I offer you something to drink?" asked the hound.

On the table, she saw three cups. The first was certainly gold, and probably Lalique. The others were unimportant, a silver cup like those common in Dobromir, which had a silver mine, and a cup of horn that a shepherd might have drunk from. Of course she would drink from the first. She took a careful sip. The wine it contained, as red as the griffins' eyes, gave her courage.

"I'm not the Princess Lucinda. You will take me home at once!"

"As you wish," said the hound. "But the journey might be cold. Can I offer you a coat?"

In his mouth he held three coats. The first was a crimson brocade embroidered with gold thread, which she had seen just that week in a catalog from Worth's. That was the coat she would wear, not the plain green wool, or the dingy white thing that the hound must have drooled on.

But as soon as she reached to take it, the hound opened his mouth, dropped the coats, and once again grabbed her sash. And then they were off, over the forests of Sylvania, over Karelstad and the croquet lawn, to the castle terrace.

The King was still trying to soothe the Queen, who was crying, "What have I done?" Prince Radomir was waving smelling salts under the Countess' nose. The footmen were trying to sweep up the shattered glasses.

Upstairs, Lucinda had finally found her dress. It was in the Queen's own dressing room, behind an ermine cape. She sighed with relief. Now at last she could go to the party.

Just as the hound landed, Jaromila's sash ripped, and she dropped to the terrace.

"Bring me the Princess Lucinda!" said the hound. "If you don't bring me the Princess, I will drink up the fountain in front of King Karel's statue, and the pond by the secondary school where children go skating in winter, and the river Morek, whose waters run through all the faucets of Karelstad. And if I'm still thirsty, I'll drink up the Danube itself—"

"I am the Princess Lucinda," said a voice from the garden. Bertila walked up the terrace steps. She had woken early to see the preparations for the party, and had been watching all this time from behind the topiary stag.

"Isn't that the gardener's daughter?" asked Prince Radomir. But at that moment the Queen screamed (it seemed her turn), and nobody heard him.

Under ordinary circumstances, no one would have mistaken Bertila for a princess. Her dresses were often patched, and because her mother had died when she was born, she sewed on the patches herself, so they were usually crooked. But today all the servants not needed for the party had been given a holiday, and she was wearing an old dress of Lucinda's. Lucinda had been allowed to give it away because it had torn on a tree branch. Bertila had mended it (with the wrong color thread), but the rip was toward the back, so she hoped it would not be noticed.

"Climb on my back then," said the hound, and climb she did. She twisted her fingers into the hair at his neck, and held on as well as she could when he leaped from the terrace over the forests of Sylvania.

"Mama!" cried Jaromila, at which the Countess revived. But the Queen went into hysterics. And that was when Lucinda finally came down the stairs, holding her train, and stared about her, at the footmen sweeping the floor and the sobbing Queen.

"What in the world is going on?" she asked. King Karel tried to tell her, as did the Queen between broken sobs, and even the Countess, who clutched Prince Radomir's arm so hard that he could not answer. Jaromila tried to powder her nose in the mirror, because after all Prince Radomir was present.

"Radomir?" said Lucinda. And then Radomir explained about the hound and Bertila's deception.

"Well," said Lucinda, when the explanation was over. She turned to the King and Queen. "I think it's time you told me everything."

Bertila looked about the cave.

"Will you take a seat?" asked the hound.

"Thank you," said Bertila. Which chair should she choose? Or rather, which chair would Lucinda choose, since she must convince the hound? She had read Lucinda's copy of the Brothers Grimm, which Lucinda had left on the croquet lawn. This was surely a test. Her hands were shaking, and she could scarcely believe that she had spoken in the garden. But here she was, and the deception must continue. Whatever danger Lucinda was in, she must try to save her friend.

Surely Lucinda would never choose a chair so gaudy as the gold one. And a stool did not seem appropriate for a princess. But the wooden chair looked like the one her father had carved for her mother. Lucinda had sat in it often, when she came to the gardener's cottage. The wood had been sanded smooth by a careful hand, and ivy leaves had been painted over the arms and back. That was a chair fit for a princess of Sylvania. She sat down.

"Would you care for something to drink?" asked the hound.

"Thank you," said Bertila. "I really am thirsty."

Lucinda would make fun of the gold cup, and the cup of white horn was like the stool, too plain. But the silver cup, with the snowdrops in enamel, might have been made by the silversmiths of Dobromir, who were the finest in Sylvania. It was a cup fit for the Pope himself. She paused before taking a sip, but surely the hound would not harm her. He had treated her well so far. The cup was filled with a delicate cider, which smelled like peaches.

"Thank you," she said. "And now I think I'm ready." Although she did not know what she was ready for.

"Very well," said the hound. "You must choose a coat for the journey."

Lucinda would never wear the crimson brocade. But the coat of green wool, with its silver buttons and tasseled hood, looked warm and regal enough for a princess. There was another coat beneath, but it looked tattered and worn.

"I'll wear this one," said Bertila.

"You're not the Princess Lucinda," said the hound.

Bertila stood silently, twisting the coat in her hands. "No" she said finally. "I'm sorry. I hope you don't blame me."

"It was brave of you," said the hound. "But you must return to the castle."

When he landed on the terrace with Bertila, Lucinda was waiting.

"You don't have to threaten anyone this time, or break any glasses," she said. "I'm Princess Lucinda, and I'm ready to go with you."

The Queen was sent to bed with a dose of laudanum. The King cancelled the invitations for the party. Countess Agata had a lunch of poached eggs with the Chamberlain and asked what the monarchy was coming to. Jaromila tried to find Prince Radomir. But he was sitting under the chestnut tree with Bertila, asking if she was all right, and if she was sure. Bertila was blushing and admiring his eyelashes.

"Will you take a seat?" asked the hound.

"What a strange stool," said Lucinda. She had never read the Brothers Grimm, although Bertila had handed her the book with a reproachful glance. "The wood seems to glow. I wonder where it comes from?"

"From the mountains of the moon," said the hound. "Down the slopes of those mountains flow rivers as clear as glass, and on the banks of those rivers grow willow trees, with leaves as white as paper. When the wind blows, they whisper secrets about what is past and what is to come. This stool is made from the wood of those willow trees."

"This is where I'll sit," said Lucinda.

"Can I offer you something to drink?" asked the hound.

"What a curious cup," said Lucinda, picking up the cup of horn. "It's so delicate that the light shines right through it."

"On the slopes of the mountains of the moon," said the hound, "wander herds of sheep, whose wool is as soft and white as thistledown. This cup is carved from the horn of a ram who roamed those mountains for a hundred years."

Lucinda drank from the cup. The water in it was cold, and tasted of snow.

"And now," said the hound, "you must choose a coat for our journey."

"Where are we going?" asked Lucinda. "Oh, how lovely!" She held up a coat that had been lying beneath the coats of crimson brocade and green wool. "Why, it's covered with feathers!"

"The rivers of the moon flow into lakes," said the hound, "and on those lakes live flocks of herons. They build their nests beneath the willow branches, and line them with feathers. There, they lay their eggs and raise their children through the summer. When winter comes, they return to Africa, leaving their nests behind. This coat is made from the feathers of those herons. As for your question, Princess—to meet your mother."

"My mother?" said Lucinda, sitting abruptly back down on the stool. "Oh, I don't know. I mean, until yesterday I thought Queen Margarethe — What is my mother like? Do you think she'll like me?"

The hound seemed to smile, or at least showed his teeth. "She's my mother also. I'm your brother, Lucinda, although we have different fathers. Mine was Sirius, the Dog Star. Yours was a science teacher at the secondary school."

"And my mother—our mother?" asked Lucinda.

"Our mother is the Moon, and she's the one who sent me for you. Put on your coat, Lucinda. Its feathers will warm you in the darkness we must pass through. Now climb on my back. Mother is eager to see you, and we have waited long enough."

As though in a dream, for nothing in her life, not even the books on airplanes and mountain climbing, had prepared her for such an event, Lucinda put on the coat of white feathers and climbed on the back of the hound. He leaped to the edge of the cave, and then into the sky itself. She was surrounded at first by clouds, and then by stars. All the stars were visible to her, and the Pleiades waved to her as she flew past, calling out, "She's been waiting for you, Lucinda!" Sirius barked and wagged his tail, and the hound barked back. Then they were landing in a valley covered with grass as white as a handkerchief, by a lake whose waters shone like silver.

"Lucinda! Is that really you?"

The woman standing by the side of the lake had silver hair so long that it swept the grasses at her feet, but her face looked not much older than Lucinda's. She seemed at once very young and very old, and at the moment very anxious.

"It is," said the hound. "Go on," he said to Lucinda, nudging her with his nose. "Don't you want to meet her?"

Lucinda walked forward, awkwardly. "It's nice to meet you . . ."

"Oh, my dear," said the Moon, laughing and taking Lucinda in her arms. "I'm so happy to have found you at last!"

THE MOON LIVED in a stone house surrounded by a garden of white roses. A white cat sat on the windowsill, watching Lucinda with eyes like silver kroner.

"The soup will be ready in a moment," said the Moon. "I find that the journey between the earth and my home always makes me hungry."

"Do you travel to the earth?" asked Lucinda.

The Moon laughed again. Her laughter sounded like a silver bell, clear and sweet. "You would not have been born, otherwise! In a shed at the back of the house live my bats. Whenever I want to travel to the earth, I harness them and they pull me through the darkness. Perhaps later you'll help me feed them. They like the nectar of my roses. Here, blow on this if you think it's too hot."

She put a bowl of soup in front of Lucinda. It was the color of milk but smelled like chicken, and Lucinda suddenly realized that she had forgotten to eat breakfast.

"Tell me about that," said Lucinda. "I mean, how I was born. If you don't mind," she added. There was so much she wanted to know. How did one ask a mother one had just met?

"Well," said the Moon, sitting down at the table and clasping her hands. "Your father's name was Havel Kronborg. When he was a child, he would lie at night in his father's fields, in Dobromir, and look at the stars. But even then, I think, he loved me better than any of them. How glad I was when he received a scholarship to study astronomy in Berlin! And how proud when his first paper was published in a scientific journal. It was about me, of course, about my mountains and lakes. But when his father died, the farm had to be sold to pay the mortgage, so he worked as a science teacher at the secondary school. Each night he wandered on the slopes of the mountains about Karelstad, observing the stars. And one night, I met him in the forest.

"How well I remember those months. I could only visit him when the moon was dark—even for love, I could not neglect my work. But each month that we met, our child—that was you, Lucinda—was closer to being born, and his book, *Observations on the Topography of the Moon*, closer to being completed.

"When you were born, I wrapped you in a blanket I had woven from the wool of my sheep, and laid you in a basket of willow branches. Your brother slept beside you and guarded you, and all the stars sang you lullabies."

"Was it this blanket?" asked Lucinda. Out of her pocket she pulled a blanket as fine as silk, which the King had given her in the course of his explanation. Her name was embroidered on one corner. She had been carrying it with her since, but had almost forgotten it. How far away Karelstad seemed, and the Queen, and her life as a princess.

The Moon reached out to touch it, and her eyes filled with silver tears. "Your father asked me to leave you with him for a month. How could I refuse? But I told him to set you in the moonlight every night, so I could see you. One night, while he was gathering mushrooms in the forest for a botany lesson, he placed your basket beneath a tree. I watched you lying there, laughing up at me. But suddenly a cloud came between us, and when it had passed, you were gone.

"You can't imagine his grief. He searched all that night through the forest around the castle. When the gardener found him in the morning, he was coughing, and could not speak. The doctor told him he had caught pneumonia. He died a week later. I found the basket by his bedside. It's the only thing I've had of yours, all these years."

Silver tears trickled down her cheeks. She wiped them away with the blanket.

Lucinda reached out her hand, not knowing what to say. The Moon took it in her own, and smiled through her tears. "But now we've found each other. How like him you look, so practical and solemn. I searched the world for years, but never saw you until last night, lying beneath the tree where he had left you. I knew who you were at once, although you've grown so tall. Will you walk with me, Lucinda? I want to show you the country where you were born."

THE STRANGEST THING about being on the moon was how familiar it seemed. Lucinda learned to feed the bats, gathering white roses from the garden, tying them together in bundles, and hanging them upside down from the rafters where the bats slept through the night, while the moon was shining. She learned to call the sheep that roamed the mountains, and to comb their fleece. The Moon spun the long hairs caught in the comb on a spinning wheel that sang as it whirled. She learned to gather branches from the willow trees and weave them into baskets, like the one the Moon had shown her, saying, "This is where you slept, as a child."

Sometimes, after the night's work was done, she would sit with the Moon beside the lake, watching the herons teach their children to fly. They would talk about Lucinda's childhood in Karelstad, or the Moon's childhood, long ago, and the things she had seen, when elephants roamed through Sylvania, and the Romans built their roads through its forests, and Morek drove out the Romans, claiming its fertile valleys for his tribe. Then they would lie on the grass and look at the stars dancing above them.

"Their dances were ancient before I was born," said the Moon. "Look at Alcyone! She always wears diamonds in her hair. And Sirius capering among them. We were in love, when I was young. But we each had our work to do, and it could not last. Ah, here is your brother."

The white hound lay down next to Lucinda. She put her arm around him, and the three of them watched the stars in their ancient dances.

One day, the Moon showed Lucinda her observatory, on a slope above the lake. "This is where I watch what happens on the earth," she said.

Lucinda put her eye to the telescope. "I can see the castle at Karelstad."

"That was where I last looked," said the Moon. "Since you've been here, I've had no wish to look at the earth. It reminds me of the years before I found you."

"There's Bertila, walking in the garden with Radomir. I can see Jaromila. She's looking in her mirror. And King Karel is talking to the French ambassador. Why do they look so sad? Well, except Jaromila. And there's the Queen. Why, she seems to be crying. And I've never seen her wearing a black dress. Oh!" said Lucinda. "Is it me? Do they think I'm dead?"

The Moon looked at her sadly.

"I'm so sorry," said Lucinda. "It's just—I grew up with them all. And Queen Margarethe was my mother. I mean, I thought she was."

"She was, my dear," said the Moon. "She was the best mother she could be, and so I forgive her, although she has caused me much grief. I knew that eventually you'd want to return to the earth. It's where your father belonged, and you belong there also. But you will come to visit me, won't you?"

"Of course I will, Mother," said Lucinda.

THAT NIGHT, WHILE the moon was shining, they harnessed the bats. Lucinda put on her coat of heron feathers and took the reins.

"Before you go," said the Moon, "I have something to give you. This is the book your father wrote. I've kept it for many years, but I would like you to have it. After all, I have my memories of him." For a moment, she held Lucinda, then said to the bats, "Fly swiftly!"

The bats lifted Lucinda above the white roses in the garden, and above the stone house. The Moon called, "Goodbye, my dear," and then she was flying over the mountains of the moon and toward the earth, which lay wrapped in darkness.

She landed on the castle terrace, just as the sun was rising over the forest around Karelstad. Lucinda released the reins, then ran into the castle and up the stairs, to the Queen's bedroom.

Queen Margarethe was sitting by the window. She had not slept all night, and her eyes were red with weeping. She thought she must be dreaming when she saw Lucinda enter the room and say, "Good morning, Mother."

Lucinda's sixteenth birthday party took place a month late, but was perhaps all the merrier. The orchestra from Prague played, the champagne flowed freely, and the footmen danced with one another in the hall. Under a glittering chandelier, the French ambassador asked Jaromila to marry him, and on the terrace, beneath a full moon, Radomir asked Bertila the same question.

When Lucinda went to her room that night, her head spinning from champagne and her feet aching from the narrow shoes, she found a white stool on which sat a white cup. In the cup was a silver necklace. From it hung a moonstone, which glowed like the moon itself, and next to the cup was a card on which was written, in silver ink, "Happy Birthday, my dear."

The next morning, Lucinda went to the graveyard behind the cathedral. There, by the grave of a forgotten science teacher, she laid a bouquet of white roses.

Observations on the Topography of the Moon received an enthusiastic reception among astronomers in London, Paris, and New York, and was widely quoted in the scientific journals. It was eventually included in the secondary school curriculum, and the author's portrait appeared on the two zlata stamp.

After her husband's death, Jaromila opened a couture house in Paris and became famous as the inventor of the stiletto heel. When Radomir finished his degree in engineering, King Karel retired. He and Queen Margarethe lived to a contented old age in the country. King Radomir and Queen Bertila guided Sylvania through the Great War. During their reign, Karelstad became a center of international banking, where even the streets were said to be paved with kroner. They sat together, listening to the radio, on the night Lucinda won the Nobel prize for her theories on astrophysics.

But no one, except the white hound that was occasionally seen wandering around the garden of her house in Dobromir, ever found out that she had been the first person on the moon.

The Cinder Girl Burns Brightly

Each night, her mother speaks to her out of the fire:
come to me, my daughter. Come into the flames.
And the Cinder Girl, the one they call Dirty Ella,
even the housekeeper, even the kitchen maid,
steps into the fireplace. She burns
brightly, hair flaring upward,
skin as white as the heart of the sun itself.
When she emerges, she is as clean as though
she had bathed in lavender water with castile soap.
She must rub soot again all over her body
to disguise herself as the Cinder Girl.

The fire is her mother's arms, it is the love
in her mother's breast, as hot as a train furnace.
If you have that kind of love, not even death
can defeat it.

When her stepmother says, sort these peas
from these lentils, the fire says
put them on the hearth, daughter.
She does, and out of the fire
fly two birds, one red, one yellow.
The red one picks out the peas,
the yellow one picks out the lentils,
until they are all sorted.
The Cinder Girl sits there, watching
with flames flickering in her eyes.

When her stepsisters say, mend these gowns,
the fire says again, put them on the hearthstone,
and out of the flames come small white mice,
squeaking, squealing, swarming over the kitchen.
They stitch the ripped hems, the torn bodices,
so neatly and evenly that the seams
are almost invisible.

On the first night of the ball, the fire says,
wear this—it is a dress
as red as passion. If you wear this, the prince
will want to dance with you all night.
The Cinder Girl puts it on, and now she is
a forest fire. She burns through the ballroom.
The prince dances with no one else. But at midnight
she runs back home to her mother.

On the second night, the fire says,
wear this—a dress as yellow as jealousy.
If you wear this, the prince will ask you to marry him.
He does, in the moonlit garden, but once again
the Cinder Girl flees. She does not know
if she wants to spend all night in the arms
of a man she has just met
who likes to play with matches.

On the third night, the fire says,
daughter, you know what to do. This dress
is as white as innocence. The Cinder Girl will shine
like no one else, not that the prince has eyes
for any other woman. Since he was a boy,
he has been attracted to danger and sharp objects:
swords and knives, court gossip,
the game of politics, like his father before him,
who preferred to imprison recalcitrant noblemen,
including the Cinder Girl's grandfather,
in the castle dungeon. She herself
intrigues him—she is the greatest secret of all.
Who is she? Tonight he calls her
Princess Diamond. In the rose garden,
she accepts his proposal.

She leaves her shoe, covered with diamonds,
under a rosebush.

In three days, the prince and his retinue will ride
up to her door, where her stepmother
will laugh at the idea that Dirty Ella, imagine!
could be the mysterious Princess Diamond. But Cinder
will produce the other shoe out of her pocket.
Miraculously, she will be clean

under her rags, her skin as white as frostbite.
The prince will put her in his carriage, and the household—
stepmother, stepsisters, housekeeper, kitchenmaid—
will gape as they drive off.

She will be married in the white dress. That night,
while the prince is sleeping in a mahogany four-poster
with brocade hangings, she will kneel before the fireplace
of their cavernous bedroom, cold despite the tapestries
on which hunters trap a unicorn with the help
of a virgin, innocent, complicit. She will say, mother,
I am here. Out of the fire will fly two birds,
one red, one yellow, and perch on the carved bedposts,
above the snoring prince. Out will come
a swarm of white mice to scamper around the room,
over the oriental carpets.

The fire will hold out its arms, saying, daughter,
come into my embrace, and the Cinder Girl
will hold out her arms in turn, saying mother, come to me.
She will wrap the fire around her
like a shawl, red, orange, yellow, safe in its warmth,
and burn the palace down.

The Stepsister's Tale

It isn't easy, cutting into your feet.

Years later, when I had become a podiatrist,
I learned the parts of the feet. Did you know your feet
contain a quarter of your bones? Calcaneus, talus, cuboid, navicular.
Lateral, intermediate, and medial cuneiform.
Metatarsals and then the phalanges, proximal, middle, distal.
They're beautiful on the tongue, these words from a foreign language.

My sister cut into her heels, which are in the hindfoot.
I cut into my big toes, called the halluces.
She cut into flesh and tendon and sinew.
I cut into bone, between the phalanges,
through the interphalangeal joint.
That's in the forefoot, which bears half the body's weight.
To this day, both of us walk with a slight limp.

The problem is you do desperate things for love.
We loved her, the woman who wanted us to be perfect:
unblemished skin, waist like a corsetier's dream,
feet that would fit even the tiniest slipper.
And so we played the aristocratic game
of identify-the-princess.

Sometimes it's a slipper, sometimes a ring.
Oh mother, love me without asking me to scrape
my fingers like carrots, cut off my heels and toes.
Eventually, she became your favorite daughter,
the cinder-girl, the princess-designate.
She was the best at being perfect, but abuse
will do that to you.

A woman comes into my office, asking me
to cut off her little toes so she can wear
the latest fashion. I sit her down and say
did you know your feet provide the body

with balance, mobility, support?
Come, let me show you a model: here's the toe,
metatarsal and phalanges. You can see
how elegantly they move, as in a waltz,
surrounded by your blood vessels and nerves,
the ball gown of your soft tissue,
a protective coat of skin, the delicate nail.

Look, underneath, how beautiful you are . . .

Lily, With Clouds

E LEANOR TOLLIVER'S HEELS clicked on the sidewalk—click click, click click, like a cantering horse, if a horse could canter in size 7½ shoes. It was odd, this lopsided step, in a woman whose lavender suit had been bought last week at Lord & Taylor. Really, she admitted to herself as she clicked down Elm Street, she should not have bought the narrows. The left shoe, in particular, pressed against her corn and produced the cantering gait we have noticed. And this was fitting because Eleanor, in spite of her lavender suit and matching handbag, looked like nothing so much as a horse.

The Eliots had always been horsy. The men had ridden hard, shot straight, and drunk whiskey. Their women had ruled the social world of Ashton, North Carolina. Any of them could show you the foundations of a house destroyed in what they still privately referred to as The War. If you looked carefully, you could see the stump of a column among the lilac bushes. When a daughter of the house, in the irresponsible twenties, had run off with a black chauffeur, her name in the family Bible had been scratched over with ink. The Eliots were rich and respectable. On Sundays, they took up the first two pews of the Methodist church.

Eleanor had been a quintessential Eliot. Although her face had the approximate dimensions of a shoe box, its length fitted her particular type of beauty, which was angular and expensive. Charles Tolliver had felt himself lucky to catch the oldest Eliot girl, when he was only a junior partner at her father's law office. The youngest, now, he wouldn't have touched with a ten foot pole, in spite of her father's money.

Poor Lily, thought Eleanor, clicking past the hardware store that was going out of business now a Walmart had opened fifteen miles down the interstate. She had been an inadequate Eliot, an unsatisfying sister. Instead of being angular, she had been round, with startled brown eyes and a figure that Eleanor in her less generous moments described as chubby. Instead of Sweet Briar, which had matriculated three generations of Eliot women, she had gone to an art school in New York. There, she had met and presumably married an artist. Presumably was the word Eleanor used to her friends. After all, no one had been invited to her wedding with András Horvath, and although Lily wrote a letter about it afterward, since when was Lily to be trusted? Look at how she had burned Eleanor's school uniform by leaving a hot iron on it, in ninth grade. The artist had died in an airplane crash. He had been flying alone and probably, Eleanor told her friends, drunk. Afterward, Eleanor had assumed Lily would move back to Ashton. But she had stayed in New York.

This thought brought Eleanor to a gate that was half off its hinges, which anyway were attached to a fence that was half fallen over from the masses of honeysuckle climbing over it. Just like Lily, to come back not to Eleanor's house, where she and Charles had lived since her father's death, but to this shack with its peeling paint and its gutters hanging down from the roof. Everyone would think Eleanor had refused to take her sister in. How perfectly unfair. She would have put Lily in the guest bedroom, which had lavender-scented liners in all of the drawers. Lily could have shared a bathroom with Jane.

Eleanor smiled at this reminder of her evolutionary success. Jane had the sandy Eliot hair, the angular Eliot features. Everyone said she would grow up to be as attractive as her mother. On her last report card from Saint Catherine's, Sister Michael had written, "Jane is a bright girl, who could accomplish a great deal if she would only apply herself." Catholics were so good at educating girls.

As if she had unconsciously internalized her clicking, Eleanor repeated its pattern on the door: knock knock, knock knock. After an impatient moment, which she spent inspecting her fingernails, manicured a week ago and painted in Chanel Pink Fantasy, someone opened the door.

Someone might have been a housekeeper or a hospital nurse, but she held out her hand and, in a voice Eleanor would later describe to everyone as "New York, you know, though I'm sure she's a very nice woman," invited Eleanor into the house. "I'm Sarah Goldstein. Lily probably wrote about me."

Eleanor refrained from mentioning that Lily had rarely written, and that even her last postcard, with a picture of the Statue of Liberty on it, has said only, "Dying of cancer. Coming home June 7, 2:30 p.m. Charlotte. Could you send Charles to pick me up? Lots of baggage. Love, Lil." Charles had talked about her baggage all through dinner. "You know what she had?" He spooned more mashed potatoes onto his plate. In the last two years, his waist had expanded. If he didn't stop eating so much, he would have hips like a woman. But he refused to exercise, except for golf. "Cardboard boxes. Hell of a lot of cardboard boxes. I think I sprained my back carrying them to the car." Eleanor had said "Charles," because you didn't say "Hell" at the dinner table. Jane had looked superior, because everyone nowadays said "Hell." Even Sister Michael had said it once, when her chalk broke on the blackboard.

"Let me make sure she's awake," said Sarah. She stepped around the cardboard boxes on the living room floor and opened a door on the far wall. She said something Eleanor couldn't hear, then closed the door again. "She needs a minute to get herself together. She's still tired from travelling." She gestured around at the boxes. "We had some time getting these through airport security. You'd think we were carrying automatic weapons. Would you like some tea?" Eleanor said that would be fine. Charles hadn't mentioned that Lily was travelling with someone. But Charles never noticed unattractive women, she thought, looking at Sarah's bottom, retreating through what was presumably the kitchen door. Why did anyone wear puce?

Eleanor walked around the living room, her shoes sounding hollow on the
wooden floor. No furniture, just boxes. Lily would have to come live with her.
Jane could probably lend Lily her television, at least while she was in school.
Eleanor looked out the window, at the overgrown honeysuckle. Charles kept
the grass in their yard trimmed short enough that he could practice golf swings.
On Jane's seventh birthday, they had installed a pool so she could have friends
over for swimming parties. In summer, there were always young people in
swimsuits lying on the deck chairs, smelling like coconuts. Jane was one of the
most popular girls in school.

Eleanor looked at the boxes again. The tape on one had been torn off and
balled into a sticky brown tangle on the floor. She reached down to open it,
more out of boredom than curiosity, when Sarah walked back into the room.
"I've put the water on. It took me a while, figuring out the stove. Lily hated
leaving that apartment. She said she had spent the happiest years of her life
there. I don't mind that, but I do miss the dishwasher. We had everything
there—and a toaster just for bagels. But don't mind me, I'm a little homesick
for New York. I think she's ready to see you now. Go on in. I'll bring the tea
when it's ready."

Lily had changed. She was lying in a double bed, the only piece of furniture
Eleanor had seen so far in the house, with a blanket pulled over her breasts.
Her cheeks, which had always been round and slightly red from rosacea, were
yellow and sagged toward the pillow. She seemed to have melted, all but her
small, sharp nose. Even her hands, lying on the blanket, looked like puddles of
flesh. And she was bald.

"Ellie," she said. Her voice sounded like an echo, as though she were
speaking from the bottom of a well. "Do you have a cigarette? Sarah won't
let me have one." From the living room, Eleanor could hear the sound of
ripping tape. "She thinks they make my throat worse, but they help me, Ellie.
I can't think without them." On Lily's bedside table were orange plastic bottles,
with varying levels of pills. Eleanor counted them twice, and got two different
numbers.

So this was Lily. The same old Lily, who couldn't take care of herself, who
made wrong decisions. The same old Lily, but wrinkled and unattractive—and
dying.

There was no chair. Eleanor sat down on the side of the bed, which sagged
under her. "I think Sarah's quite right. Look where smoking has gotten you."

"Sarah's always right." Lily shook her head from side to side, fretfully. "I
was so mad when I found out András had been sleeping with her, almost from
the day we got married. But he said she was the best manager he ever had. She
found him galleries, you know. Really good galleries. And when she moved in,
she managed the apartment for us. She's a wonderful manager." Lily's voice
faded. She lay with one cheek on the pillow, her eyes closed, like a piece of
parchment that had been folded many times, then smoothed out again.

Eleanor sat up straighter and put her handbag on her lap. So this was her sister's marriage to the great artist. Poor, stupid Lily. "I don't understand why you're staying here with that woman, instead of coming home to your family." Eleanor spoke calmly, as though to a horse that wouldn't jump over a hedge. One always had to be calm around Lily when she was unreasonable. Like when she had refused to come downstairs at Eleanor's debutante ball. "A woman your husband—well. If this were my house, I'd turn her out at once."

Lily opened her eyes and put one hand on Eleanor's knee. "Ellie, it wasn't like that. I was mad at first, but then I realized it didn't matter. I invited her to move in with us. She had such a small apartment in Brooklyn, and we had that huge loft. She cleaned and paid the bills. She would have cooked, but I wanted to do it. They liked my cooking, you know. They never minded when I burned anything."

Ellie put her manicured hand on Lily's. It felt cold and flabby. "Did he continue sleeping with her, after she moved in?" It was best to know these things, distasteful as they were.

Lily pulled her hand out from under her sister's, as though it had grown too hot. "But he painted me. He slept with her, but he painted me. He never painted her, not once. Such wonderful paintings. Oh Ellie, you have to see the paintings."

"Chamomile tea," said Sarah, opening the door. "Am I interrupting?"

"Sarah, you have to show Ellie the paintings." Lily tossed her head again, from side to side.

"Calm down, you," said Sarah, "or you'll lose the benefits of your beauty sleep. I put a little honey in it," she said to Eleanor, handing her a pottery mug decorated with yellow bees.

"See, isn't she a good manager?" said Lily. "I don't know what I would have done without her after András died. I had run out of money, you know. She sold his paintings to all the right galleries, and paid for my treatments." She raised her hand, then dropped it again over the edge of the bed. Sarah took it, put it back on the blanket, and stroked it for a moment. Lily closed her eyes. Without those spots of brown, she looked curiously colorless, as though already a corpse.

"I think we'd better leave her," Sarah said in a low voice. "She's worn out. Maybe she'll have more energy tomorrow."

Eleanor followed her out of the room, wondering what András Horvath had seen in this woman, with her puce bottom and her gray hair, which looked like it had been cropped by a barber. Artists, she thought, had peculiar tastes in women.

In the living room, Sarah said, "I'm glad you came to see Lily today. I don't think she'll hold on much longer. You'll want to bring your husband, and Lily said you had a daughter?"

Ellie nodded and tapped her fingernails on the mug. What did you say to your sister's husband's mistress? "Maybe I'll bring Jane. My daughter, Jane."

Of course she wouldn't bring Jane. And Charles never liked being around sick people. He hadn't visited his own mother in the nursing home before she died.

Sarah looked at her for a moment, then looked toward the window, where the honeysuckle was growing over the fence. "Lily wanted you to see the paintings." She leaned down and opened one of the cardboard boxes. Many more of them were untaped, now. Out of it, she pulled an unframed canvas.

It was a painting of Lily. But Lily as she had never appeared in real life. Lily elongated and white as a sheet of paper. Lily with forget-me-nots for eyes. In the painting behind it, Lily had horns: short, curving spirals like seashells. Behind that, Lily held a pomegranate in her left hand. Lily, her head covered with butterflies. A lily that was also, improbably, Lily. Lily blue like the sky, with clouds moving over her breasts. Endless Lilies, all different, all—Eleanor caught herself before she said the word—beautiful.

Sarah pointed to the painting with the clouds. "He painted all sorts of things, of course, but before his death he only painted Lily. He did a larger one of those, with the sun as her left eye. I gave it to the Guggenheim."

"Gave it? You gave it?" Lily had said something about spending all her money. What, Eleanor suddenly wondered, were András Horvath's paintings worth?

Sarah looked at her, and continued to look at her until Eleanor shuffled her feet. "András left his paintings to me. Just like he left Lily to me. He knew I would manage everything." She put down the paintings she had been holding. "András could see things. He once told me his great-grandfather had married a witch or a woman who lived in a tree or something like that. Back in his own country." She smiled, and shrugged. "Hell, I don't know. But you can see it in the paintings. If he painted a rock, it looked like a snake, and every time you looked at that rock afterward, it would look like a snake to you, because he was right. It was a snake, even though it was also a rock. Then maybe every rock would start looking like a snake, or a flower, or a piece of bread. Sometimes I wonder if that's how he died. There he was, flying a plane. What if he saw something—really saw it? He wouldn't have cared that he was about to crash. It's frightening, if you think about it too hard. Maybe art always is." Sarah turned to the window again. "He saw people, too. He saw me so well. One day he said, 'I'll never paint you, Sarah. I don't need to paint you, because you're exactly yourself.' But he saw Lily better than he saw anyone else in the world."

CLICK CLICK, WENT the heels of Eleanor's shoes on the sidewalk. She clicked homeward because Charles would need his dinner. She would make mashed potatoes. What did she care about his weight? Men always looked more dignified with a little extra padding. She would make mashed potatoes and peas, and she would ask Jane about school, and Jane would look superior, and maybe afterward they would all play monopoly.

Was it already five-thirty? Eleanor looked up at the sky, and there was Lily, with clouds moving over her breasts. Her left eye was the sun. She tried to imagine Lily with her yellow skin sagging, her bald head sinking into the pillow. But Lily's head was covered with butterflies, and she was holding a pomegranate in her left hand.

Click click went her heels, faster and faster, and finally in spite of her corn Ellie began to canter in earnest through a world that was Lily, endlessly Lily, her handbag swinging like an irregular pendulum and her hair, which had been permed only last week, shedding hairpins behind her.

The Gold-Spinner

There was a little man, I told him.

I gave the little man my rosary,
I gave the little man my ring,
my mother's ring, which she had given me
as she lay dying. A thin circlet of gold
with a garnet, fit for a commoner.

As I was a commoner, I reminded him.
Nothing magical about me.

Very well, he said. You may go
back to your father's mill. I have no use
for a miller's daughter without magic in her fingers.
I'll keep the three roomfuls of gold.

I walked away from the palace, still barefoot,
still dressed in rags, looking behind me
surreptitiously, afraid he would change his mind.
Afraid he would realize he'd been tricked.
I mean, what kind of name
is Rumpelstiltskin?

But he would have kept me spinning
in a succession of rooms, forever.

I passed my father's mill without entering,
either to greet or berate. I wanted you to be queen,
he had told me, after I said how could you
betray me like this?
You deserve that, you deserve better
than your mother. What kind of life
did I give her?

No, I wasn't going back there.

By mid-afternoon I had left the town,
I had forded the river, I had come
to unfamiliar fields. I sat me down
by a hedge on which a few late roses bloomed
and from a thorn I plucked a tuft of wool
left by a passing sheep. I spun,
twisting it between my fingers
as my mother had taught me.
She, too, had the gift.

I coiled the resulting thread
of thin, soft gold
around my wrist. Somewhere along the road
it would buy me bread.

Until then, there were crabapples
and blackberries to share with the birds.
And the road ahead of me,
leading I knew not where, but somewhere different
than the road behind.

Rumpelstiltskin

The little man
tore himself in two.
What did the two halves do
after that?
Fairy folk don't die
from such simple operations.

And no, they didn't hop about,
each on a single leg.
Each half was a complete
facsimile of the original,
except that one was reversed:
a mirror image of the other.
One was left-handed, the other right.

The two halves stared at each other.
Brother, said one,
I shall go into the forest:
I'm done with humanity.
Let millers' daughters ever after
suffer the consequences of their own folly.
I shall live alone, with only the birds and squirrels,
the occasional deer, for company.
I shall live off mushrooms, acorns, ferns,
eggs fallen from the nest, rose hips
and blackberries in summer: the forest's bounty.
Dress myself in moss, breathe slowly,
become like the rocks.
I shall call myself Rumpel,
if you've no objection.

None at all, said the other half.
I, however, want to see the world,
live as you have never dared to.
Start as a thief, steal coins from the rich,
food from the poor. Visit whorehouses.

Build my fortune, gamble with it—
win, lose, end up in debtor's prison.
Drink dirty water, and a year later
fine Burgundy, when I have regained my fortune
and more. I shall have estates
in Germany, in France. My mills will spew black smoke
over the countryside, manufacturing
fabric for elegant ladies, so they can wear
the latest fashions, my great looms
clacking and whirring like mechanical spiders.
That is the way to spin gold, brother.
When I am richer than the king,
he will offer me his daughter.
By then, I shall be Lord Stiltskin.

The two halves parted, with every sign
of mutual respect. Neither
chastised the other.
There were no recriminations.

In each of us
there is a thief and a saint.
The trouble of it is,
we cannot part them.

Singing of Mount Abora

A HUNDRED YEARS ago, the blind instrument-maker known as Alem Das, or Alem the Master, made a dulcimer whose sound was sweeter, more passionate, and more filled with longing than any instrument that had ever been made. It was carved entirely from the wood of an almond tree that had grown in the garden of Al Meseret, that palace with a thousand rooms where the Empress Nasren had chosen to spend her widowhood. The doors of the palace were shaped like moons, its windows like stars. It was a palace of night, and every night the Empress walked through its thousand rooms, wearing the veil she had worn for her wedding to the Great Khan. If the cooks, who sometimes saw her wandering through the kitchen, had not known who she was, they would have mistaken her for a ghost. The dulcimer was strung with the whiskers of the Cloud Dragon, who wreaths his body around the slopes of Mount Abora. He can always be found there in the early morning, and that is when Alem Das approached him, walking up the path on the arm of his niece Kamora.

"What do you want?" asked the dragon.

"Your whiskers, luminous one," said Alem Das.

"My whiskers! You must be that instrument maker. I've heard of you. You're the reason my cousin, the River Dragon, no longer has spines along his back, and why my other cousin, the Phoenix, no longer has tail-feathers. Why should I give you my whiskers?"

"Because when I have made my dulcimer, my niece Kamora will come and play for you, and sing to you the secrets of your soul," said Alem Das.

"We dragons have no souls," said the Cloud Dragon, wreathing himself around and around, like a cat.

"You dragons are souls," said Alem Das, and he asked his niece to sing one of the songs that she sang at night, to sooth the Empress Nasren. Kamora sang, and the Cloud Dragon stopped wreathing himself around and around. Instead, he lay at her feet, which disappeared into mist. When she was done, he said, "All right, instrument maker. You may have my whiskers, but on one condition. First, your niece Kamora must marry me. And when you have made your dulcimer, she must sing to me every night the secrets of my soul."

Kamora knew how the Cloud Dragon looked at night, when he took the form of a man, so she said, "I will marry you, if my Empress allows it." And that is my first song.

* * *

You can't imagine how cold Boston is in winter, not for someone from a considerably warmer climate. In my apartment, I sat as close as I could to the radiator, sometimes with my back against it. The library at the university was warmer, but the chairs were wooden and hard, so it was a compromise: the comforts of my apartment, where I had to wrap my fingers around incessant cups of chamomile tea to warm them, or the warmth and discomfort of the library. I had been born in Abyssinia, which is now Ethiopia, and had been brought up in so many places that they seemed no place at all, Italy and France and Spain. Finally, I had come to cold, shining North America, where the universities, I told my mother, were the best in the world. And the best of the best universities were in Boston.

My mother was beautiful. I should say rather that she was a beauty, for to her, beauty was not a quality but a state of being. Beauty was her art, her profession. I don't mean that she was anything as vulgar as a model, or even an actress. No, she was simply beautiful, and so life gave her what it gives the beautiful: apartments in Italy, France, and Spain, and an airplane to travel between them, and a diamond called the Robin's Egg, because it was as big as a robin's egg, and as blue.

"Oh, Sabra," she would say to me, "what will we do about you? You look exactly like your father." And it was true. In old photographs, I saw my nose, the bones of my cheeks and jaws on a man who had not needed to be handsome, because he was rich. But his riches had not saved his life. Although he could have bought his way out of the revolution, he had remained loyal to the Emperor. He had died when his airplane was shot down, with the Emperor in it, just before crossing the border. This was after the Generals had taken power and the border had been closed. My mother and I were already on our way to Italy, with the Robin's Egg in her brassiere. "Loyalty is nothing," my mother would say. "If your father had been more sensible, he would still be with us. Loyalty is a breath. It is not worth the ring on my finger."

"But he had courage," I said. "Did he not have courage?"

"Courage, of course. He was, after all, my husband. But it is better to have diamonds."

Her beauty gave her ruthless practicality, an indescribable charm.

"You are like him, Sabra. Always with your head in the clouds. When are you going to get married? When are you going to live properly?" She thought it was foolish that I insisted on living on my stipend, but she approved of my studying literature, which was a decorative discipline. "That Samuel Coleridge whose poem you read to me," she would say. "I am convinced he must have been a handsome man."

I insisted on providing for myself, and living in a city that was too cold for her, because it kept me from feeling the enchantment that she threw over everything around her. She was an enchantress without intention, as a spider gathers flies by instinct. One longed to be in her web. In her presence, one could not help loving her, without judgement. And I was proud of my independence, if of nothing else.

Let me sing about the marriage of Kamora and the Cloud Dragon. Among all the maidens of the Empress Nasren, there was none so clever as Kamora. She knew every song that had ever been sung, since the world was made. When she sang, she could draw the nightingales into the Empress's garden, where they would sit on the branches of the almond trees and sing accompaniment. Each night she followed the Empress through the thousand rooms of the palace, singing her songs. Only Kamora could soothe the Empress when Nasren sank down on the courtyard stones and wept into her hands with the wild abandon of a storm.

On the night after Alem Das had visited the Cloud Dragon, Kamora said to the Empress, "Lady, whose face is as bright as the moon, there is nothing more wonderful in the world than serving you, except for marrying the one I love. And you know this is true, because you have known the delights of such a marriage."

The Empress, who sat in a chair that Alem Das had carved for her from the horns of Leviathan, stood suddenly, so that the chair fell back, and a figure of Noah broke off from one corner. "Kamora, would you too leave me, as the Great Khan left me to wander among the stars? Some night, it may be this night, he will come back to me. But until that night, you must not leave me!" And she stared at Kamora with eyes that were apprehensive, and a little mad.

"Lady, whose eyes are as dark as the night," said Kamora, in her most soothing voice, "you know that the Great Khan lies in his tomb on Mount Abora. You built it yourself of white marble, stone on stone, and before you placed the last stone, you kissed his lips. Do you think that your husband would leave the bed you made for him? You would not keep me from marrying the one I love."

The Empress turned and walked, out of that room and into another, and another, and through all the thousand rooms of the palace. Kamora followed her, not singing tonight, but silent. When the Empress had reached the last room of the palace, a pantry in which the head cook kept her rose-petal jam, she said, "Very well. You may marry your Cloud Dragon. Do not look surprised that I know whom you love. I am not so insensible as all that. But first, you must complete one task for me. When you have completed it, then you may marry whom you please."

"What is that task?" asked Kamora.

"You must find me someone who amuses me more than you do."

It was Michael who introduced me to Coleridge. "Listen to this," he said.

> "In Xanadu did Kubla Khan
> A stately pleasure-dome decree:
> Where Alph, the sacred river, ran

Through caverns measureless to man
Down to a sunless sea.

"I can't believe you've never read it before. I mean, I learned that in high school."

"Who is this Michael Cavuto you keep talking about?" asked my mother over the telephone. "Where does he come from?"

"Ohio," I said.

She was as silent as though I had said, "The surface of the moon."

We were teaching assistants together, for a class on the Romantics. We read sentences to each other from our students' papers. "A nightingale is a bird that comes out at night to which Keats has written an ode." "William and his wife Dorothy lived together for many years until she died and left him lamenting." "Coleridge smoked a lot of opium, which explains a lot." We laughed, and marked our papers together, and one day, when we were both sitting in the library, making up essay questions for the final exam, we started talking about our families.

"Yours is much more interesting than mine," he told me. "I'd like to meet your mother."

You never will, I told myself. I liked him, with his spiky hair that stood up although he was always trying to gel it down, the angular bones that made him look graceless, as though his joints were not quite knit together, and his humor. I did not want him, too, to fall hopelessly in love. For goodness' sake, the woman was fifty-four. She was in Italy again, with a British rock star. He was twenty-seven. They had been together for two years. I could tell that she was already beginning to get bored.

"There's no one like Coleridge," Michael had said. "You'll see."

I HAVE TOLD you that Kamora was clever. Listen to how clever she was. She said to the Empress, "I will bring you what you ask for, but you must give me a month to find it, and a knapsack filled with bread and cheese and dried apricots, and a jar of honey."

"Very well," said the Empress. "You shall have all these things, although I will miss you, Kamora. But at the end of that month you will return to me, won't you?"

"If at the end of that month I have not found someone who amuses you more than I do, then I will return to you, and remain with you as long as you wish," said Kamora.

The Empress said, "Now I can sleep, because I know you will remain with me forever."

The next day, Kamora put her knapsack on her back. "I wish you luck, I do," said the head cook. "It can't be easy, spending every night with Her Craziness upstairs. Though why you would want to marry a dragon is beyond me."

Kamora smiled but did not answer. Then she turned and walked through the palace gates, chewing a dried apricot.

First, Kamora went to the house of her uncle Alem Das, which was built against the wall that surrounded the palace. She found him sitting on the stone floor, carving a bird for the youngest daughter of the River Dragon. When you wound it with a key, it could sing by itself. "Uncle," she said, "They call me clever, but I know that you are more clever than I am. You talked the horns off Leviathan, and once Bilkis, the sun herself, gave you three of her shining hairs. Who can amuse the Empress more than I can?"

Alem Das sat and thought. Kamora was his favorite niece, and he did not want to disappoint her. "You might bring her the Laughing Hound, who dances on his hind legs, and rides a donkey, and tells jokes all day long, or the Tree of Tales, whose leaves whisper all the secrets that men do not wish to reveal. But she would eventually tire of these. You, my dear, can sing all the songs that were ever sung. If she tires of a song, you can sing her another. If she is sad, you can comb her hair with the comb I gave you for your fourteenth birthday, and cover her with a blanket, and sit by her until she has fallen asleep. It will be difficult to find anyone as amusing as you are."

Kamora sighed. "I hoped that you could help me. Oh, uncle," and for the first time she did not sound perfectly confident, "I do love him, you know."

"I'm not clever enough to help you," said Alem Das, "but I know who is. Kamora, I will tell you a secret. If you climb to the top of Mount Abora, even higher than the Cloud Dragon, you will find the Stone Woman. She is the oldest of all things, and I think she will be able to help you. But you must tell no one where she lives, and allow no one to follow you, because she values her privacy. If it grows dark, take out the tail-feather of the Phoenix, which I gave you for your twelfth birthday. It will light your way up the mountain."

Kamora said, "But uncle, why should the Stone Woman help me?"

"Take this drum," said Alem Das. "I made it from the skin that the Sea Serpent sheds once a year. The Stone Woman is old, and the old always like a present."

"Thank you, uncle," said Kamora, kissing him on both cheeks. "There truly is no one in the world as clever as you."

Kamora walked through the village, chewing a dried apricot. She walked over the hills, to the foot of Mount Abora. At the foot of the mountain, where the climb begins in earnest, she picked a handful of lilies, which grow by the streams that flow down the mountain to become the Alph. She left them at the tomb of the Great Khan, who had given her sugared almonds when she was a girl. Then she began to climb the path up the mountain. Halfway up, Kamora ate her lunch, bread and cheese and dried apricots. She washed her hands in one of the streams, put her knapsack on her back, and continued to climb. Near the top, she stopped to see the Cloud Dragon and tell him the Empress's condition.

"Well, good luck to you," he said. "If you were anyone else, I would be certain that you would fail, but I've been told that you're almost as clever as your uncle."

"I will not fail," said Kamora, and she gave him a look that made him break into puffs that flew every which way over the mountain. *And this is the woman I'm going to marry*, he thought. *What have I gotten myself into?*

In his house by the palace wall, Alem Das thought about his niece and smiled. He said to himself, "Sometimes she is too clever, that girl. First she asked for one of the Phoenix's tail-feathers, then for a comb carved from the shell of the Great Turtle. And now I've given her my drum. Does she really think she's tricked me? Oh, Kamora! It's certainly time you got married."

I'M NOT SURE when we started dating. There was a gradual progression between friend and boyfriend. We were comfortable together; we seemed to fit together like two pieces of a puzzle. But a puzzle that showed what picture? I did not know.

It was a Friday. I remember because we had just turned back a set of graded papers. I was still taking classes, and for my own class on the Romantics, taught by the same professor for whom I was TAing, I had decided to write a final paper on Coleridge. This will be easy, I thought. Michael and I have talked about him so often.

I was in my apartment. It was cold. It felt like a cave of ice.

And suddenly, I was there.

The Kubla Khan of Coleridge's poem is not the historical Kubla Khan, founder of the Yuan Dynasty, and Xanadu is not Shangdu. Both are dreams or hallucinations. Indeed, if we examine Coleridge's description of the palace itself, we notice that it does not make sense. Here, the river Alph, fed by the streams that flow down Mount Abora, does something strange: it disappears into a series of fissures in the ground, flowing through them until it comes to an underground lake. Coleridge's identification of this lake as a "sunless sea" or "lifeless ocean" is certainly poetic exaggeration, as my experience will show. The palace itself is situated where the river disappears, so that seen from one side, it seems to sit on the river itself. Seen from the other, it is surrounded by an extensive garden, where the Khan has collected specimens from all of the fantastical countries, plants from lost Atlantis and Hyperborea and Thule. The palace is built of stone, and rises out of the stone beneath it, so that an outcropping will suddenly turn into a wall. Although Coleridge describes "caves of ice," this is again a poetic exaggeration. He means that since the palace is built of stone, even in summer the rooms are cold, so cold. I was always cold in that palace, as long as I was there.

It was empty. There were silk cushions on the floor, embroidered with dragons and orange trees, but no one to sit on them. There were tables inlaid with tulips and gazelles and chessboards, but no one to play. The curtains that hung in the doorways, filtering the sunlight, rose and fell with the breath of the river. But there was no other breath, and no noise other than a ceaseless rushing as the river swept through the caves below. As I walked, my steps sounded hollow, and I knew that the floors hung over rushing water and empty space. As an architectural feat, the Khan's palace is impossible.

There was water everywhere, in pools where ornamental fish swam, dappled white and orange and black, and basins in which the inhabitants, if there were any, would have washed their hands. The air had the clean, curiously empty smell of sunlight and water.

"I have looked. There is no one but ourselves."

He was dressed as you might expect, in breeches and a waistcoat over a linen shirt that seemed too large for him. He had thick brown hair and a thin, inquisitive face, and his hands moved nervously. The young poet, already an addict.

I was not sure how to respond. "Have you been here long?"

"Several hours, and I confess that I'm beginning to feel hungry. Surely there is a kitchen? Shall we attempt to find it?"

The kitchen was empty as well, but the pantry was full. We ate sugared almonds, and a sweet cheese studded with raisins, and dried fish that was better than it looked. We drank a wine that tasted like honey.

"Sabra is a pretty name," he said. "Mine is Samuel, not so pretty, you see, but then I'm not as pretty as you." He wiped the corner of his mouth with a handkerchief. "Here we are, Samuel and Sabra, in the palace of the Khan. Where is the Khan, I wonder? Is he out hunting, or in another of his palaces? Perhaps when he returns he will execute us for being here. Have you thought of that, Sabra? We are, after all, trespassers."

"I don't know," I said. "I don't feel like a trespasser. And anyway, he isn't here now."

"That is true," he said. "Would you like the last of the almonds? I've never much cared for almonds." He leaned back against a cushion, his hair spread out over an apricot tree in bloom, with a phoenix in its boughs. "Will you sing to me, Sabra? I am tired, and I feel that I have been speaking inanities. There is an instrument on that table. Can you play it, do you think?"

"Yes," I said, and picked up the instrument: a dulcimer. While my friends in school were at soccer practice, I was learning to play the dulcimer. It was another of my mother's charming impracticalities.

"Then sing me something, won't you, pretty Sabra? I'm so tired, and my head aches, I don't know why."

So I put away the last of the sugared almonds, picked up the dulcimer, and began to sing.

KAMORA COULD FEEL blisters forming where her sandals rubbed against her feet, but she climbed steadily. It was late afternoon, and the sun was already sinking into the west, when she reached the summit. The Stone Woman was waiting for her. She was wrapped in a gray shawl and hunched over with age, so that she looked like a part of the mountain itself.

"Back again, are you? And did you ever find your own true love, the one whose face you saw in my mirror?"

"I found him, lady who is wiser than the stars," said Kamora. "But now I have to win him."

"None of your flattery for me, girl," said the Stone Woman. "I know exactly how wise I am. What are you going to give me for my help?"

Kamora took the drum out of her knapsack.

The Stone Woman looked at it appreciatively. "Ah, this is better than the other stuff you gave me. Although the tail-feather of the Phoenix, which you gave me for teaching you all the songs that have ever been sung, burns all night long, so I can weave my tapestries. And every morning I use the comb made from the shell of the Great Turtle, which you gave me for showing you the Cloud Dragon in my mirror, so my hair never tangles." She ran one hand over her braid of gray hair, which was so long that it touched the ground. "But this!" She tapped the drum once with her finger, and Kamora heard a reverberation, not only from the drum itself, but from the stones around her; the scrubby cedars, bent by the wind; and even the air. It seemed to echo over the forested slopes of the mountain, and the hills below, on which she could see the tomb of the Great Khan, as white as the rising moon, and the plains stretching away into the distance.

"What is it?" asked Kamora.

"You uncle didn't tell you? That sound is the beat of the world, which governs everything, even the beating of your heart, and on this drum I can play it slower or faster, more sadly or more joyfully. No one can make an instrument like your uncle Alem, but I think this is his masterpiece. No wonder he wanted you to bring it to me. I'm the only one in whose hands it is perfectly safe. Think, girl, what would a man do who could alter the beat of the world? And by getting you to carry it, he saved himself a trip up the mountain! He is a clever man, your uncle. Now, it's dinnertime, and I'm hungry. Have you brought me any food?"

Kamora took out the honey, of which she knew the Stone Woman was inordinately fond.

"Good girl. Well, come inside, then, and tell me what you want this time."

The walls of the Stone Woman's cave were covered with tapestries. On one you could see the creation of the world by Lilit, and her marriage to the Sea Serpent, for which she wore a veil of stars. On another you could see the flood that resulted from their thrashing when they lay together, so that many of the first creatures she had created, the great dragons with horns like Leviathan's and eyes like rubies and emeralds, and the great turtles that carried mountains and even small lakes on their backs, were drowned. The whole history of the world was there, and on a panel that Kamora had not seen before, she saw Mount Abora, and the marriage of the Empress Nasren, the oldest daughter of the River Dragon, to the Great Khan, with the apricot trees on the mountain blooming around them.

The Stone Woman sat on a cushion and opened the honey-pot. She dipped a wooden spoon into it, tasted the honey, and licked her lips. "Very good, very good. Well, what do you want this time?"

Kamora knew that it was time to be, not clever, but direct. "The Empress, whose hands move like doves, will not let me marry until I have brought her someone who amuses her more than I do."

"So that's how it is," said the Stone Woman. "You can't marry your Cloud Dragon until she lets you, and she won't let you until she has found a substitute. You have been too clever, Kamora. When you asked me to teach you all the songs that have ever been sung, so the Empress would choose you as one of her maidens, to serve her and live in the palace, did you consider that she might want to keep you forever? Getting what you wish for isn't always a good thing, you know."

"If I had not learned all the songs that have ever been sung," said Kamora, "the Cloud Dragon would not have wanted to marry me. And I love him, I can't help loving him, since I saw how he looks at night, when he is a man. Perhaps I should not have looked in your mirror and asked to see my own true love, but when I saw how happy the Empress was with the Great Khan . . ." A tear slid down her cheek, and she wiped it away with her hand.

"Ah, clever Kamora! So you wanted to love and be loved. You have a heart after all," said the Stone Woman. "Just remember that cleverness is not enough to keep a husband, not even the Cloud Dragon, who is less clever than you are. You must show him your heart as well. I warned him about choosing such a clever wife! But how do you expect me to help you?"

Kamora said, "I thought about that, when I walked through the thousand rooms of the palace at night with the Empress. What is more amusing than a person who knows all the songs that have ever been sung? Only a person who can create new songs. Only a poet."

"If you know the answer yourself," said the Stone Woman, "why do you need me?"

"Because I need you to make me a poet. Not one of those poets who sit in the marketplace, selling rhymes so that soldiers, and anyone with a silver coin, can sing them to the Empress's maidens—out of tune! I need a true poet, who can write what has never been sung before."

"A poet?" asked the Stone Woman. "And how do you expect me to make you a poet?"

"In the same way you made the world, Lilit."

Kamora and the Stone Woman stared at each other. Finally the Stone Woman said, "You are as clever as your uncle. How did you know who I am?"

Kamora smiled. "Who else would know all the songs that have ever been sung? Who else would keep the Mirror of Truth in a cave on Mount

Abora? And when the Great Khan was laid in his tomb, the Empress put honey on his lips so you would kiss them when he entered the land of the dead. Even songs from the making of the world mention how fond you are of honey. You have created the Sea Serpent; the Lion of the Sun who carries Bilkis on his back, and whose walk across the sky warms the earth; the Silver Stag who summons men to the land of the dead . . . Only you can make a poet."

"Very well," said the Stone Woman. "I will make you a poet, Kamora. But only because I like you. And this is my wedding gift, and the last thing I will do for you. You have had two gifts from me already, and three is enough for anyone." She stood and considered. "But I haven't made a poet for a long time. I wonder if I remember how?"

HAVE YOU SEEN the stone caves beneath the palace of Kubla Khan, called the Lesser Khan because for all his palaces, he could not match the conquests of his grandfather, the Great Khan? Where the stone is thin, it is translucent, so that the caves are filled with a strange, ghostly light. In the dark water, which is still and no longer rushing, since the river has mingled into the underground lake, there are luminescent fish. When they swim to the surface, they shine like moving stars.

Samuel took off his breeches and swam in the dark water, in just his shirt. I sat on the bank, striking the dulcimer, thinking of songs that he might like. He floated on his back, his hair spreading around his face like seaweed. "There seems to be no time here," he said. "At home, I was expecting a person from Porlock. But here, I feel that no person from Porlock will ever come. Time has stopped, and nothing will ever happen. Except that you will keep singing, Sabra. You will keep singing, won't you? Sing to me about how the Stone Woman made a poet." But I did not finish my song, then.

Later, we walked in the garden that surrounded the palace.

"They go on for ten miles," I said.

"How do you know that?" he asked, but I did not answer. It was hot, even in the shade of the almond trees, and the roses, which had been transported at great expense from Nineveh, were releasing their fragrance into the evening. "I think I could stay here forever," he said. "Forget my damned debts. Forget my . . . marriage. Never write again, never write anything else. I'm no good at it anyway. I never finish anything."

"That's not what Lilit said, when she made you."

"What do you mean?"

"Lilit created the poet out of clay. Kamora watched her mold the figure, the height and shape of a man. It was late now. Outside, the moon had risen, and it shone in through the opening of the cave, its pale light meeting the light of the Phoenix's tail-feather. Kamora sat on the floor and watched, but she was so tired that her eyes kept closing, and somehow, between one blink of her eyes and another, the man was complete. He was tall, well-formed, and gray, the color of the clay at the bottom of the river Alph. His mouth was open, as though already speaking a poem.

"'Now we must awaken him,' said Lilit. 'I will walk around him three times one way, and you must walk around him three times the other. Then I will spread honey on his lips, and you must put honey into his mouth, so that his words will be both nourishing and sweet.'

"Kamora rose. She was so tired that she stumbled as she walked, but three times she stumbled around the poet, and when she had done so, she took the jar from Lilit and put honey into the poet's open mouth.

"'There,' said Lilit. 'And I really think that this time I have outdone myself. He will be the greatest poet that ever lived, and every night he will write a poem that has never been heard before for the Empress Nasren. He will be like the river Alph, endlessly replenished by the streams that flow down Mount Abora.' The poet was no longer the color of clay. Now he had brown hair hanging down to his shoulders, and his skin was as white as milk and covered, irregularly, with brown hair. Lilit took off her gray shawl and wrapped it around his hipbones. 'Speak, poet. Give us the gift of your first poem.'

"The poet turned to her and said,

> 'A damsel with a dulcimer
> In a vision once I saw:
> It was an Abyssinian maid,
> And on her dulcimer she played,
> Singing of Mount Abora.'

"'That's enough for now,' said Lilit. 'You see, Kamora, your poet works. Now take him to your Empress, and marry your Cloud Dragon. But don't visit me again, because the next time you come I won't be here.'"

"And was he the greatest poet that ever lived?" asked Samuel. We were sitting on the riverbank, where the Alph begins to disappear into the fissures below, surrounded by the scent of roses. The sun was setting, and the walls of the palace had changed from white to gold, and then to indigo. I could not see his face, but his voice sounded sad.

"He was, in the palace of the Empress Nasren," I said. "He wrote a different poem for her every night, and she gathered scribes around her to make copies so they could be taken to every village. They were set to music, as poems were in those days, and sung at every village fair. And when her ambassadors traveled to other countries, they carried the volumes of his poems, fourteen of them, the number of the constellations, on the back of a white elephant, so they could be presented to foreign sultans and caliphs and tzars."

"But elsewhere, in the country of daffodils and mutton and rain? Because I think, Sabra, that you come from outside this dream, as I do."

"In that country, he was a poet who could not finish his poems, and who, for many years, did not write poetry at all. How could he, when every night in the palace of the Empress, he wrote a new poem entirely for her? What was left over, after that?"

"Perhaps. Yes, perhaps that is true."

We heard it then: lightning, crashing over the palace, turning the walls again from indigo to white. Once, twice, three times.

"He has come," said Samuel. "He has come, the person from Porlock." And then, suddenly, he was gone.

I WAS STARING at my computer screen, on which I had written, "The Kubla Khan of Coleridge's poem is not the historical Kubla Khan, founder of the Yuan Dynasty, and Xanadu is not Shangdu."

Again, I heard three knocks on the apartment door. "Sabra, are you there? It's Michael."

I rose and went to open the door. "You people!" I said, as Michael walked in, carrying two bags of groceries.

"What do you mean?" he asked, startled.

"You people from Porlock, always interrupting."

He kissed me and put the bags he had been carrying on the table. "I was thinking of making a curry, but—you've had better curry than I can make. Are you going to laugh at my curry?"

"I would never laugh at your curry."

He began unpacking the grocery bags. "So, what were you thinking about so hard that you didn't hear me knock?"

"Coleridge. About how he never finished anything. And about how I'm not sure I want to finish this PhD. Michael, what would you think if I became a writer?"

"Fine by me, as long as you become famous—and rich, so you can keep me in a style to which I am not accustomed."

Later, after dinner, which was not as disastrous as I had expected, I called my mother. "Nasren Makeda, please."

"Just a moment. Madame Makeda, it's your daughter."

"Sabra! How good it is to hear your voice. I'm in Vienna with Ronnie. Darling, I'm so bored. Won't you come visit your poor mother? You can't imagine these rock and roll people. They have no culture whatsoever. One can't talk to them about anything."

"Mom, I'd like you to come to Boston and meet Michael."

"The one from Ohio? Oh, Sabra. Well, I suppose we can't control whom we fall in love with. It was like that with your father. He was the only man I ever loved, and yet he was shorter than I am by three inches, and that nose—such a pity you inherited it, although you have my ears, thank goodness. But I tell you the truth, I would have married him even if he had not been rich. He was that sort of man. So, I will come and meet your Michael. I can fly over in Ronnie's plane. Is there a month when Boston is warm? I can come then."

Perhaps he would fall in love with her. But sometimes one has to take chances.

FOR KAMORA'S MARRIAGE to the Cloud Dragon, the Empress's poet Samuel wrote a new poem, one that no one had heard before. It began,

> Do you ask what the birds say? The sparrow, the dove,
> The linnet and thrush say, "I love and I love."

Alem Das himself sang it, playing a dulcimer strung with the whiskers of the Cloud Dragon, whose sound was sweeter, more passionate, and more filled with longing than any instrument that had ever been made. When he was finished, the Empress Nasren clapped, and Kamora, in the Empress's wedding veil, turned to her husband and blushed.

Later that night, in the cave of the Cloud Dragon, he said to her, "It may be that you are too clever to be my wife."

She stroked his silver hair and looked with wonder at his pale shoulders, shy for once before his human form. "And perhaps you are too beautiful to be my husband."

"Then we are well-matched," he said, "for together there is none in the world more clever or more beautiful than we. And now, my clever wife, are you going to kiss your husband?"

That night, the top of Mount Abora was wreathed in clouds. The Empress Nasren saw it as she walked in the garden of her palace, and she told it to blind Alem Das, who was walking with her. "Did you know, my friend, that it would end like this?" she asked.

Alem Das laughed in the darkness. "I suspected, from the moment Kamora insisted that my dulcimer should be strung with the whiskers of the Cloud Dragon. She always was a clever girl, although not as clever, I like to think, as her uncle."

"So, your niece is happy," said the Empress. "It is good that she is happy, although we who are old, Alem, know that happiness is fleeing." And she sighed her soft, mad sigh.

"Yes, lady," said Alem Das. "But tonight your roses are blooming, and I can hear the splashing of fountains. Somewhere inside the palace, your poet is reciting to the wedding guests, who are drunk on honey wine. And we who are old can remember what it was like to be young and foolish and happy, and be content." And they walked on in the moonlight, the instrument-maker and the Empress.

The Dragons

One day, the dragons came.

It was on a Tuesday, she remembers. It was
the sort of thing that would happen on a Tuesday,
which is an unsatisfying sort of day,
not the beginning of the week, nor the middle,
without the anticipation of a Thursday.
A troublesome sort of day.

And there they were, sitting on the back porch railing,
where she had hung boxes for geraniums
that summer. But now, since it was November,
there were no geraniums—only dragons, quite small,
the size of a Pomeranian or Toy Poodle,
but of course with scales, which shone with a dim sheen
in the gray light of a rainy Tuesday morning.
Seven of them—green, blue, red, orange, another orange,
a sort of purple, and a white one that seemed smaller
than the others, the runt of the litter. It shone opalescent.
They were damp with rain, and obviously
too young to be out on their own. Had someone abandoned them,
the way people sometimes leave dogs at the edge of the woods?
Or were they feral, born to a wild mother?

She couldn't just leave them there. As soon as they saw her,
the white one started a piteous baby roaring
and the green one joined in, showing the interior
of its pink mouth, like a geranium with teeth.
But when she opened the porch door, they just sat there,
staring at her with iridescent eyes.
What did dragons eat? She had no idea,
so she put half of last night's Chinese takeout
in a bowl outside the porch door.
The rest she put into another bowl, inside
the open door, then went to get ready for work.
By the time she returned, in her suit and sensible pumps,

they were curled up on the sofa, already asleep,
except for the blue one, which hissed at her, not in anger,
she thought, but simply to let her know it was there.
The bowls were empty.

They continued to be trouble.
The orange one burned a hole in the carpet, or was it
the other orange one? They were so similar,
initially she could not tell them apart.
But eventually she learned to distinguish them
by their quirks and personalities—
one was just playful, the other more mischievous.
She gave them all names: Hyacinth (that was the purple),
Orlando, Alexander (after her brother,
who was a software designer in San Francisco
and sent her pictures at Christmas of his apartment
decorated with plastic poinsettia).
Ruby (a little too obvious, but it suited her),
Dolores and Delilah (the orange ones),
and little Cordelia, the runt, who affectionately
clawed apart her favorite afghan
while trying to climb the armchair into her lap.
She tried calling the ASPCA
and the local veterinary clinics, but no one was missing
a clutch of dragons. The receptionist at one clinic
thought she meant geckos.
What in the world was she supposed to do with them?
The nearest shelter said it had no facilities
for dragons, sounding a little incredulous
over the phone. Meanwhile, they scratched the furniture,
got tangled in the hangers while creating
a nest in her closet of scarves and pantyhose.
She could not leave out a pair of earrings, or coins
in a jar for laundry and parking—anything shiny.
They would begin to hoard it, hissing at her
when she approached to take back her watch or car keys.
Her bills for Chinese takeout
were astronomical.

She took sick leave when Orlando and Alexander
both caught pneumonia and had to be nursed back to health.
(She finally found a vet who would treat dragons,
a younger guy trying to establish a practice.)

"I'm not sure about dosage," he said, as he gave her
a prescription for antibiotics. "About the same
as for a golden retriever? But it's just a guess.
Aren't they getting a little big, for a place
of this size?" And she had to admit he was right.
Now when Ruby curled up next to her
as she watched *Casablanca*, the red dragon
took up half the sofa. Her sort-of-boyfriend,
Paul, who worked in the tax and bankruptcy group,
started complaining. She understood his perspective—
the dragons had never liked him. Hyacinth
always bellowed when he came over, Delilah
peed on his baseball cap, and Dolores chewed
a corner of his briefcase. "They're dragons," he told her.
"They're dangerous—what if they bite someone? You'd have
a lawsuit on your hands. I really don't know
why you keep them around."
Probably because they were warm at night,
piled on her bed, with Cordelia's silky muzzle
tucked under her chin. Whenever she got home
after a long day at the office, they greeted her,
trilling in unison. They never told her
that her hairstyle didn't fit the shape of her face,
or she really should lose a few pounds, unlike her mother.
They never asked her to file incorporation
documents yesterday, or talked to her
for an hour about baseball while she was trying to listen
to NPR. Anyway, who would take them,
all seven of them? Dragons don't make good pets,
and she hated the thought of separating them.
They needed each other.

Finally, she moved to a lighthouse in New England.
She saw the advertisement—*Lighthouse keeper
wanted. Must be willing to live on an island
off the coast of Maine, near Portland. Competitive salary.*

The ferry comes twice a week. She can take it to Portland
if she wants to, but it brings everything she needs,
from lightbulbs to chocolate chip cookies to art supplies.
Sometimes she goes, just to get Chinese takeout.
The dragons have learned to fish and fend for themselves.
She watches them flying up in the sky like kites

when she goes on her morning walk, collecting shells
and bits of seaglass. Mostly they stay outdoors,
but Cordelia still sleeps in the bed beside her at night,
stretched out on the blanket. She has not grown much larger
than a Great Dane, although Alexander is now
the size of a Volkswagen Beetle. On sunny mornings
she finds them lying on the rocky shore, like seals,
shining in the sunlight. On rainy days, there's a cave
on the other side of the island, although Dolores
curls up in the lighthouse itself, around the beacon.
On stormy nights, she's seen them guide a ship
to shore, which seems an unusual behavior, but dolphins
do it, so why not dragons?
She's started painting again, the way she used to
when she was a teenager, before her father
told her to focus on something more practical.
Her canvases sell in a gallery and on her website.
Mostly, she paints the dragons—rolling around
in the waves, lying on the shore, cavorting above
in intricate arabesques, as if they knew
she was sketching below, showing off for her.

She doesn't make as much money
as she did at the law firm. But then, on the other hand,
she has dragons.

Thumbelina

Sometimes I would like to be very small
so I could curl into a snail's shell
or a seashell: abalone, nautilus,
even an oyster shell. I would let the oyster
cover me with layer on layer of nacre,
come out shining.

Sometimes I would like to be very small
so I could hide myself inside a flower,
between the petals of a tulip or crocus,
inside purple or crimson walls, like a genie
in her bottle. I would emerge covered
with pollen, riding a bee.

Sometimes I would like to be small enough
to live in the hollow of a tree, like a bird
or squirrel. I would dress in leaves, eat acorns,
make a coat of felted fur. I would live alone,
hiding, hiding, always hiding,
because the world is full of large things
that are too large, too loud.
Over them, I can't hear the sea
whispering, the beat of a sparrow's wings,
the annoyed chuff of a robin.

I would like to be small enough
to hear the dawn breaking, the tulip opening,
the sand as it shifts under each tide,
the long dream of rocks.

In the Forest of Forgetting

S HE STOOD AT the edge of the forest. She knew it was the edge because behind her the path disappeared into undergrowth. She could see rhododendrons, covered with flowers like cotton candy. There were bushes without flowers, which she could not name: *shrubus leafiana*. Ahead of her, the path was shadowed by oaks, poplars, maples with leaves like Canadian flags. In the shadow of the trees, the air was cool and smelled of toothpaste.

"Welcome," said the Witch. She was standing beneath an oak tree whose branches were covered with green acorns. The Witch was wearing a white coat. Around her neck was a silver chain, with a silver disk hanging from it. Just what a Witch should look like, she thought. It was comforting when things looked as they should. The forest, for instance.

"Where am I?" she asked.

"In the Forest of Forgetting," said the Witch. "Hence the forgetting. Let me check your heart."

"Why am I here?"

The Witch placed the silver disk on her chest. It felt cold against her bare skin. "Heart normal. You're here because you have lumps."

She looked down at her chest, where the silver disk had been placed. There they were, the only lumps she could see, above the slight bulge of her stomach.

"What's wrong with them?" They were small and a bit crooked, but they looked all right.

The Witch put her hands in her pockets. "Your lumps have metastasized. They must be removed."

"Well," she said. And again, "Well." Even in the stillness under the trees, which made her feel calm and a bit sleepy, this seemed unnecessarily repetitive. "How—"

"With this," said the Witch, pulling a silver wand from one pocket. It looked harmless enough. The Witch muttered something under her breath and waved her wand.

Before she had time to close her eyes or prepare herself for whatever might happen, two moths rose from her chest, white with flecks of gray on their wings. They fluttered along the path, looping and twisting around one another, as though making invisible macrame.

She looked down at her chest. The lumps were gone.

"That went quite well," said the Witch, replacing the wand in her pocket.

The moths fluttered upward, spiraling into the treetops until she could no longer see them. The clouds overhead were white and fluffy, like sheep. No, she thought. Like pillows, like unrolled toilet paper left in heaps on the floor. She liked creating unusual similes.

"Don't go too far into the forest," said the Witch. "You'll have to come back, eventually." The Witch began walking toward the rhododendrons and nameless bushes.

"Wait," she said. Something had been bothering her. She had almost forgotten it, watching the moths rise upward. "What is my name?"

The Witch turned back for a moment. Her silver disk winked in the shifting light under the trees. "Your name is Patient."

She looked down at the path: her feet were bare, and her toenails needed clipping. That didn't sound right at all. She wasn't particularly patient, was in fact generally impatient. She looked up, wanting to ask the Witch if she was certain, but the Witch was gone.

There was nothing to do but go farther into the forest. It was silent, except for the occasional rustle high among the treetops.

WHEN SHE HEARD laughter, she looked up. In the branches of a laurel, spiders had woven their webs, like a giant game of cat's cradle. They were brown, and about the size of her hand.

"What sort of web? What web? What web?" The words came down to her in clacking sing-song, as though she were being questioned by a collection of sewing machines. One spider spun itself down from a branch and hung by its thread in front of her. "What web?" It went into paroxysms of laughter, shaking on its thread like a brown yo-yo.

She looked around her, trying to see what the spiders were laughing about, and saw that the path behind her was littered with brown string. She knelt down, picked up a handful, and suddenly realized what she was holding

"Not a web," she said to the spiders. "My hair. See?" She put her hand on her head. It was bare. Her arms and legs were bare. Even the place under her belly was bare. "It's fallen out. I won't have to buy shampoo or disposable razors." She said this to show it was probably for the best. Perhaps they believed her, because their laughter stopped and the dangling spider rose again to his branch. But she sat on the path and cried, wiping her eyes with a handful of hair.

When she was finished, she blew her nose on an oak leaf and went on. It was no use, she told herself, crying over spilt hair. Perhaps she would grow a winter coat. Perhaps it would come in white, like an arctic hare's.

SHE WAS SO focused on planning for winter, when her coat would come in and she would live on acorns, that she almost tripped over the coffin.

"Be careful," said the first Apprentice. He was dressed in a blue coat, and wore a blue showercap on his head. Around his neck was a silver chain, with a silver disk hanging from it.

"You'll trip over the Queen," said the second Apprentice, who was dressed just like him.

"If you tripped, she would blame us," said the third Apprentice. Her showercap was pushed back to show her bangs.

"Who?" she asked. "The Queen?" The Queen looked incapable of blaming anybody.

"The Witch. We're her Apprentices," said the Apprentices together. "Obviously," muttered the third Apprentice. She wondered if they had practiced beforehand.

"Let us check your heart," said the first Apprentice. All three came together and put their silver disks on her chest.

"Heart normal."

"Too slow."

"Too fast."

They glared at each other and began arguing among themselves.

She looked down at the Queen. The glass of the coffin was perfectly clear. Through it she could see the Queen's robe, a deep blue, and her blue turban. Her face was a little blue as well.

"She died of lumps," said the Apprentices.

"They metastasized."

"The Witch could not remove them in time."

"Magic is much more advanced, nowadays."

She put her hands on the coffin and, not knowing what else to do, tapped her fingers on the glass. Her cuticles were ragged. What would the Queen think?

"She left you gifts," said the Apprentices.

"A dress." It was made of paper, and tied in back. She could not reach the strings, so the first Apprentice tied it for her. She had never liked floral patterns, she thought, looking down at herself. But it would have to do until her winter coat came in.

"A mirror." The second Apprentice held it for her. She realized, with surprise, that she had no eyebrows. She should have expected that. It made her look surprised, which seemed appropriate.

The third Apprentice smiled and said, "You look a little like her, only not so blue."

She did, indeed, look a little like the Queen. "Thank you," she said. The Queen approved of politeness. "Did she, by any chance, leave me a name?" She did not want to seem ungrateful, but this was, after all, important to her. You needed a name, if someone was going to, for example, ask you to lunch. She had not eaten since breakfast, and she was beginning to feel hungry.

"Your name is Daughter," they said. "Now it's time to turn back."

"Why?" Surely she was too old for a name like Daughter.

They looked at each other, then muttered among themselves. "Because," they said decisively.

She frowned, wondering what it looked like without eyebrows, wondering if she should look in the mirror again to find out. Instead, she turned and walked farther along the path, deeper into the forest.

"Wait!" they shouted behind her.

"You're going too far!"

"Your heart can't take it!"

"Do you want to end up like the Queen?"

Eventually, it was silent again.

THE FOREST BEGAN to grow darker. Maples and poplars were replaced by pines. Needles prickled her feet as she walked on the path. She tried to eat a pinecone, but it left her hands sticky and tasted like gasoline. Not that she had tasted gasoline, but she imagined it would taste exactly like that. If she could wash her hands in the river—

"No one may cross the river," said the Knight.

"I don't want to cross. I just want to wash my hands and have a drink."

"No," said the Knight. Above the knees, he was dressed in a suit of armor. Below, he wore a pair of galoshes. "Ouyay aymay otnay inkdray oray ashway. Onay Oneway." He lifted his visor. His mustache looked like it had been cut with nail clippers. It was turning gray.

"Why?" It was the question she had been asking since she entered the forest. The Knight looked puzzled. "I don't know. I think it's a rule or something." He had a nice voice. The Witch and her Apprentices had sounded like subway conductors. And the Queen hadn't spoken at all. "I think you're supposed to go back."

"That's just it," she said. "Who is you? I mean, who is me?" She sounded impatient, and she realized that she must be: hungry, tired, impatient. No one in this forest answered questions directly. Would anyone tell her what she wanted to know?

"Well," he said. He tugged at his mustache, although his armored hands were clumsy. "You like blackberry pie. You overwater houseplants, feed stray cats on the back porch, sleep through your alarm clock." He began counting on his fingers. It must help him remember, she thought. "You write stories for children: *A Camembert Moon, Priscilla's Flying Pig, The Train to Nowhereton.* You complain about your knees, and you hate wearing glasses. Once, you went on a diet where you ate nothing but cucumbers for a week. You can't mend socks, play tennis, or sing. You hate scrubbing toilets." He reached ten and looked at her, fingers outspread. "How am I doing?"

"Well," she said. She did like blackberry pie, although she didn't need glasses. Her eyesight was perfectly clear. She could see, for instance, that the Knight had wrinkles under his eyes. They made him look rather handsome.

"But what is my name?"

"I think," said the Knight, looking at his fingers as though trying to remember. "I think your name is Wife."

It was a nice name, whispery, like "wish" and "whinny" and "willow." It was the nicest name she had heard so far. But it wasn't quite right.

"I'm sorry," she said, because the Knight was looking at her with an anxious smile. She stepped into the river.

"Wait!" said the Knight.

The river was cold and clear and shallow. Although there were stepping stones, she walked on the muddy bottom, letting the water curl around her ankles, then around her knees. In the middle of the river, she bent down to wash her hands and frightened a brown fish under a rock. Once her hands were no longer sticky, she drank from them and splashed water on her face, scattering drops of water on her paper dress.

"Won't you reconsider?" shouted the Knight. He was standing in the water, up to the buckles of his galoshes. She wondered if he would follow her into the river, but he did not. Perhaps, she thought, he was afraid that his armor would rust. Instead, he stood near the riverbank, arms held out like an airplane. He was standing there each time she turned back to look. Finally, the path bent and she could no longer see him.

ONCE, A FAMILY of squirrels scrambled down from an oak tree and asked for her autograph. The squirrel children had copies of *A Camembert Moon*. When she told them she had no pen, they brought her berries. She signed each one "With regards, Author." She wondered where they kept books, whether there were shelves in the oak tree. When she had signed copies for Jumpy, Squirmy, Tailless, Nuthunter, and Squawk, they shared their dinner with her: an acorn mash that would have made a good meal, if she had been a squirrel. She was still hungry, although less hungry than before.

FINALLY, THE TREES grew farther apart. She saw undergrowth, including a bush with berries. They looked like the berries the squirrels had used for ink. She wondered if they were safe to eat, and thought of trying a few. Surely if they were poisonous she would feel sick or throw up. A few would not kill her. But she was too nervous to try.

The trees ended at the edge of a meadow filled with Queen Anne's lace, poppies, cornflowers. And beyond the meadow—

"Are you going to the mountains?" asked the Princess. She wore pajamas with feet and a necklace of paperclips.

Was she? They were blue with pines, and probably farther away than they appeared.

"Look at what I have," said the Princess. She was holding a wicker cage. In it were two moths, white with gray markings on their wings.

"I wondered where they had gone," she said. She was sorry, now, to have lost them. They were pretty, like sheets of newspaper turned into kites.

"I'll give them water in the teacups my dolls use. Do you know my dolls?"

"No," she said. It was an important question: was she going to the mountains?

"Their names are Octavia, because she only has eight toes, and Puddle. Because you know." The Princess raised her hand to her mouth, as though speaking through a trumpet. "She's just a baby."

"Do you like making dresses for your dolls?" she asked the Princess.

"Yes," said the Princess. "I make them from leaves and toilet paper."

"If you help me untie it," she said, "you can have my dress." It had been itching for some time, and anyway she would not need it in the mountains. When the strings were untied, she slipped the dress off and handed it to the Princess.

Someone was moving in the meadow, someone in a blue coat, with a blue shower cap on his head. He was holding an enormous butterfly net. And another someone, and another.

"We'll catch her!" shouted the Apprentices, jumping and turning as though chasing enormous butterflies.

"She shouldn't have crossed the river!"

"Her heart can't take the strain!"

"But we'll catch her here, never worry!"

Had she made her final decision? Was she going to the mountains? The Apprentices began stalking away from each other, like detectives.

"You're good at names, aren't you?" she said to the Princess.

The Princess nodded. "I once named seventeen caterpillars. They were named one, two, three, four, five, and so on, up to seventeen."

"What would you name me?" Every few minutes, one Apprentice would run up to another, shouting "Boo!" and making the other jump. The mountains looked mysterious and inviting.

The Princess considered. "I think I would name you Mother."

"An excellent name." But not her name, not quite. She would find her name in the mountains. It would be unexpected and inevitable, a name she could never have imagined, like Rumpelstiltskin. In the mountains she would learn about berries. Her winter coat would come in.

She leaned down and kissed the Princess, then put one hand on the wicker cage. "Goodbye," she said. "Take good care of them. I think they once belonged to the Queen."

She stepped into the sunlight. It was warm on her body. Bees circled around her, visiting the Queen Anne's lace. The Apprentices were stalking away from each other, butterfly nets raised and fluttering in the breeze. She hoped they would not notice her.

She held out her hands so they brushed the tops of the grasses, and started across the meadow.

Autumn's Song

You are not alone.

If they could, the oaks would bend down to take your hands,
bowing and saying, Lady, come dance with us.
The elder bushes would offer their berries to hang
from your ears or around your neck.
The wild clematis known as Traveler's Joy
would give you its star-shaped blossoms for your crown.
And the maples would offer their leaves,
russet and amber and gold,
for your ball gown.

The wild geese flying south would call to you, Lady,
we will tell your sister, Summer, that you are well.
You would reply, *Yes, bring her this news—*
the world is old, old, yet we have friends.
The squirrels gathering nuts, the garnet hips
of the wild roses, the birches with their white bark.

You would dress yourself in mist and early frost
to tread the autumn dances—the dance of fire
and fallen leaves, the expectation of snow.
And when your sister Winter pays a visit,
You would give her tea in a ceramic cup,
bread and honey on a wooden plate.

You would nod, as women do, and tell each other,
The world is more magical than we know.

You are not alone.

Listen: the pines are whispering their love,
and the sky herself, gray and low, bends down
to kiss you on both cheeks. *Daughter, she says,*
I am always with you. Listen: my winds are singing
autumn's song.

Green Man

Come to me out of the forest, man of leaves,
whose arms are branches, whose legs are twin trunks,
rough bark covered with lichen. Come and take
my hands in yours, and lead me in this dance:

In spring, green buds will sprout upon your head;
in summer they will lengthen into leaves.
Oak man, willow man, linden man, which are you?
In autumn, they will fall, and through the winter
you will be bare, with only clumps of snow
or birds upon your branches.

Come and love me,
my man of leaves, my forest man. For you,
I'll be an alder woman, birch woman.
In spring I'll wear pink blossoms like the cherry;
in summer ripening fruit will bend my boughs;
in autumn I will bear, distributing
a hundred seeds, our children. And the birds
will sing my praises. Let us learn to love
the sun and wind together; let us twine
our bodies, filled with sap, until we make
a single tree on which two different kinds
of leaves are growing, where birds build their nests,
among whose roots the squirrels hide their nuts,
storing them for winter.

A hundred years from now, we will still stand,
crooked perhaps, the sap running more slowly,
our two hearts beating, separately and together,
under the summer skies, in autumn rains.

Sleeping With Bears

I. The Invitation

Dr. and Mrs. Elwood Barlow
request the honor of your presence
at the marriage of their daughter Rosalie
to Mr. T. C. Ursus
on Saturday the thirteenth of June
at one o'clock
at the First Methodist Church

Reception to follow in the Church Hall

II. The Bride

THEY ARE WEALTHY, these bears. Their friends come to the wedding in fur coats.

Rosie is wearing Mom's dress, let out at the waist. When Mom married, she was Miss Buckingham County. She shows us the tape measure. "That's what I was, twenty-two inches around the waist: can you imagine?" My sister, after years of jazzercize and Jane Fonda, is considerably thicker. When, I wonder, were women's waists replaced by abdominals? When cheerleaders started competing for state championships, I guess. Rosie was a cheerleader. Her senior year, our squad was fourth in state. That year she wore the class ring of the student council president, who was also the captain of the football team. She was in the homecoming court. She was furious when Lisa Callahan was elected queen.

After she graduated from Sweet Briar and began working as a legal secretary, she met a lawyer who was making sixty thousand a year. They started talking about having children, buying a Mercedes.

So I don't understand why she decided to marry a bear.

III. The Groom

OF COURSE HE comes from old money. *Ursus Americanus* has been in Virginia since before John Smith founded the Jamestown Colony. The family has gone down in the social scale. It doesn't own as much land as it used to, and what it

148

does own is in the mountains, no good for livestock, no good for tobacco. No good for anything but timber. But there sure is a lot of timber.

Anyway, that's how Southern families are. Look at the Carters or Randolphs. If you haven't degenerated, you're not really old. If you want to join the First Families of Richmond, you'd better be able to produce an insane uncle, an aunt who lives on whiskey, to prove you're qualified.

We don't come from that kind of family. Mom is the daughter of a Baptist preacher from Arvonia. There was no whiskey in her house. She didn't even see a movie until she was seventeen. Dad was a step up, the son of the town's doctor. Grandpa Barlow didn't believe in evolution. I don't think he ever got over learning, in medical school, that men don't have a missing rib. Mom and Dad met in third grade. They went to the sock hop and held hands in church while sharing a hymnal. You can see their pictures in the Arvonia High School yearbook. Dad lists his future career as astronaut, Mom as homemaker. They were voted Most Likely to Get Married. They look clean, as though they just stepped out of a television show from the 1950s.

So maybe that's it, maybe Rosie's still mad that we didn't belong to the Richmond Country Club, that Dad didn't send her to Saint Gertrude's, where the daughters of the First Families learn geometry and which fork to use with the fish. That he didn't think of giving her a debutante ball. Mom's friends would have looked at her and said, with raised eyebrows, "My, isn't Rosie the society lady?"

And when I see them, the bears sitting on the groom's side of the church, I have to admit that they are aristocratic, like the Bear Kings of Norway, who sat on thrones carved from ice and ruled the Arctic tundra. (Nevertheless, they look perfectly comfortable in the heat, even in their fur coats.)

IV. The Procession

"WHAT DO YOU call him in private?" I ask Rosie. I've never dared call him anything other than Mr. Ursus. When a man—or bear—is six feet tall and over two hundred pounds, he commands respect.

"Catcher," she says. "That's his middle name, or maybe part of his first name. Trout Catcher. That's what his family calls him."

"How much do you really know about bears?" I ask. "Like, do you know what to cook him for dinner?"

"For goodness' sake, Blanche," she says. "Put the brush down, you're tangling my hair. Some of his relatives eat garbage, all right? I'll figure it out as I go along."

I wonder. In the library, I found a book about bears. *Ursus Americanus* eats acorns, melons, honey (including the bees), and gut piles left by hunters. I don't know what Rosie's going to do with gut piles.

I help her with the veil, which comes down to her fingernails, manicured yesterday and painted bubble gum pink. I wonder if bears like bubble gum? I hold her train as she walks along the gravel path from the minister's house, where she's been applying a final coat of mascara, to the church. I'm careful not to let her skirt trail on the gravel.

Mom's and Dad's friends are standing, the women in dresses from Lord & Taylor, the men in linen suits. The bears are standing, black and brown and the toffee color called gold. "Black bear" is a misnomer, really. They look like a forest of tree trunks, without leaves.

The organist plays the wedding march. This is Rosie's choice. She has no originality. Which again makes me wonder: why is she marrying a bear?

V. The Ceremony

OR PERHAPS I should ask, why is he marrying her?

When she first brought him home, Mom hid in the bathroom. Dad had to tell her repeatedly that bears don't eat people. That they're really quite gentle, except when their cubs are threatened. That they're probably more afraid of you than you are of them.

Still, Mom sat at the edge of her chair, moving the roast beef around on her plate, not reassured to see Catcher eating only peas and carrots, mashed potatoes.

"What do you do, Mr. Ursus?" asked Dad.

He managed the family property. Conservation land, most of it, in trust for future generations. You could call him a sort of glorified forest ranger. He laughed, or perhaps growled, showing incisors of a startling whiteness.

"Your children will never need dental work," said Dad.

Rosie was mortified. They hadn't gotten to that stage yet. I don't think she'd even kissed him good night.

She'll kiss him now, certainly, and I wait to see how it will happen: whether she will be swallowed by that enormous and powerful jaw. But he kisses her on the cheek. I can see his whiskers tickling her ear. I suppose the devouring will begin later.

VI. The Photographs

DON'T GET ME wrong, I don't think he's going to eat her. Bears don't eat people, remember?

But I know the facts of life. When Mom married at eighteen, Grandma told her, "Just close your eyes and pray for children." When I was fifteen, Mom taught me what happens between men and women. Though I have to admit, she never said anything about bears.

When our photographs are taken, I stand next to the best man—or bear, Catcher's younger brother. He looks at me and grins, unless he's just showing his teeth. He's not as tall as his brother and only a few inches taller than me, so maybe he's not fully grown. Bears take five years to grow to maturity. I wonder where he goes to school, then decide he probably doesn't go anywhere. Bears probably homeschool. Otherwise, they'd have to go through several grades in a year, to make it come out right. I wonder how old I am in bear years, and if he's older than me.

VII. The Reception

BEFORE SHE MET with the caterer, Mom asked me, "For goodness' sake, what do bears eat?"

There are ham biscuits for the people and honey biscuits for the bears, melon soup for everybody. Trout with sauce and *au naturale*, as they say in French class. Raspberries. She didn't take my suggestion to serve the honey biscuits with dead bees. I'm sure the bears would have appreciated that.

The bears drink mead, which is made from honey. I try some. It feels like fire going down my throat, and burns like fire in my stomach. Like a fire on the altar of the Bear Goddess. Her name is Callisto. Once, by accident when she was hunting in the forest, she killed her son, Arcas. So she put him in a cave for the winter, and when spring came again, he emerged healed. That's why bears sleep through the winter.

This isn't what it says in *Bullfinch's Mythology*. But Catcher says Bullfinch got it all wrong. He says Bullfinch is a bunch of bull—. You know what I mean. He doesn't curse often, but when he does, Mom clutches the hem of her dress, as though trying to hold it against a wind that will lift it over her knees.

VIII. The Dancing

DAD DOESN'T REMEMBER how to dance, so he and Rosie sway back and forth, like teenagers at prom. The bears know how to dance, of course. They begin a Virginia Reel, whirling down the line in each other's arms, then go into figures I don't recognize. To punctuate the rhythm, they growl and stamp their feet.

Frog Biter asks me to dance. I guess he was checking me out, too, when the photographs were taken. I'm worried about following the bear dances, but he swings me out in a waltz. I never knew anyone could be so strong.

Yeah, he tells me. And I'm only four and a half. Wait until I'm fully grown. I'll be taller than Catcher.

Hearing this makes something burn in the pit of my stomach, which may be the mead.

IX. The Cake

CATCHER CUTS THE cake, which is shaped like a beehive.

"What a charming couple they make," says Mrs. Ashby.

"I'm surprised she wore white," says Mrs. Coates. "I heard her relationship with the lawyer was pretty hot and heavy."

He feeds a slice to Rosie, then licks frosting from the corner of her mouth. His tongue is the color of raspberry ice cream.

"Do you think their children will be black?" asks Mrs. Mason, the minister's wife. She walks with a cane and must be over eighty.

"There are bears in the ladies' room," says Mrs. Partlow. "Do you know they go just like a man?"

"I think he's sexy, with all that fur," says Alison Coates. She's in my French class.

"I don't know how she caught him," says Mrs. Sutton. "All that real estate, and I never thought she was pretty in the first place."

She feeds him a slice. Her hand disappears into the darkness between his teeth.

X. The Honeymoon

BITER PROMISES TO stop whenever I want to.

When Rosie left on her honeymoon, everyone threw rose petals. They stuck to Catcher's fur. I could see her brushing them off through the limousine window.

It's nothing like when Eddie Tyler felt me up under the bleachers. His fur smells like rain, his mouth tastes like honey. I run my tongue over his incisors, and he laughs—or growls, I don't know which. And suddenly we're rolling around in the vestry, my fingers gripping his fur, trying to pull out brown tufts. It doesn't hurt him a bit.

I want to sleep with you, I say, and I mean through the winter, with the snow above us and branches covered with ice, creaking in the wind. While the deer are starving, searching for grasses under the snow, we'll lie next to each other, living off our fat, sharing body heat. I'll even cook him deer guts.

But he takes it another way, and that's all right too. His curved claws are good at climbing trees, and unbuttoning dresses. And I finally understand why my sister is marrying a bear. Maybe if Eddie Tyler had been a bear, I would have let him get to third base.

* * *

XI. The Announcement

Our June brides include Miss Rosalie Barlow, who was married in the First Methodist Church to Mr. T.C. Ursus. The new Mrs. Ursus has a B.A. from Sweet Briar College. Mr. Ursus manages his family's extensive property in the Blue Ridge Mountains. The maid of honor was Miss Blanche Barlow, the bride's sister. The best man was the groom's brother, Mr. F.B. Ursus. The bride carried white lilies and wore her mother's wedding dress of *peau de soie* decorated with seed pearls. The bride's mother, Mrs. Elwood Barlow, is the former Miss Buckingham County, 1965.

Goldilocks and the Bear

They met when they were children.

She was a thief,
yellow-haired, small for her age,
only twelve years old, already hardened
by poverty, already a noted pickpocket,
stealing into the bears' house.

He was a rube, a rustic,
or so she said then. A mark
is what she called him—
to his face, no less.

He was the one who found her in his bedroom,
trying to climb out the window,
and hid her in his closet
while his father raged:
who had stolen the carved wooden box
filled with gold coins, the profits
of their honey business?

He would not let her keep the coins.
He was not that much of a rube.

But while his father was talking to the constable,
a comical fellow straight out of Shakespeare,
he returned the box, saying he had found it
by the kitchen door, where the thief must have dropped it
on his way out. They should look in the forest—
he could be a mile away by now.

That night, he told her the coast was clear
and let her out the window.
At the last moment, before she made her escape,
she kissed him on the cheek
and laughed. That's the way she was
back then, fearless.

He got on with his life,
finishing school, then going into the business,
learning how to care for the bees,
how to keep them healthy,
taking extension classes on bee diseases:
mites and spores that endanger bees directly,
hive beetles that infect their homes,
wax moths that feed on honeycombs,
damaging the larvae.
He learned what to plant in the fields,
how to prune the trees in the orchard:
to produce lavender honey, and clover,
and linden-flower.

He learned how to mold the wax sculptures
sold in the gift shop.
His mother was particularly good at those.

Meanwhile, she worked with a gang
of child thieves out of a Dickens novel:
ragged clothes, solidarity pacts,
the possibility of incarceration.
She ended up in jail once, was broken out,
continued to steal until she was fifteen
and their leader suggested prostitution.
It was, he said, an honorable profession,
as old as thieving. And she such a pretty girl,
with that yellow hair: she was sure to do well.
He would, of course, take a small percentage.
The suggestion was punctuated
by his fist on the table, and a grin
she did not like the look of.

That night she climbed up to the bear's window—
she had not forgotten the location—
and knocked on the pane.
"Help me," she said when he opened it.
"I need help, and you're the only one
who's helped me before."

He listened patiently, then angrily:
three years' worth of exploits
and exploitation. She showed him her wrist

where the gang leader had once broken it.
She was still small and pale from malnutrition.

They dyed her hair brown with walnuts.
He got her a job in the honey business,
first in the gift shop, then because she showed interest,
taking care of the bees.

She had never seen anything so fascinating:
like a city of soft, furry bodies
moving in a mass, then in individual flight,
seemingly wild, erratic, but purposeful.
She loved to watch them among the lavender,
the dusting of yellow pollen on their fur.
There was something purely joyful about them,
and they were always making, making—
thieves, like her, taking the nectar,
but making wax catacombs, the golden honey
more precious, she thought, than coins.

He showed her how to work among the bees,
wearing thick cotton and a hat veiled with muslin,
which he did not need, protected by his pelt.
Eventually, he asked her to dinner
with his parents.

His mother said she was charming.
His father had a serious talk
with him: you can't trust humans, he said.
They're not like bears. Think of that thief, long ago,
who tried to take our gold.
They don't even sleep in winter,
which is unnatural, unbearlike.
If you have to fall for someone, can't it be
another bear from a good family,
like ours?

The bear explained that love
doesn't work like that.

When he asked her to marry him
beneath the linden branches,
she said, aren't you afraid

I might still be that girl?
That I might become a thief again?
You are, and you might, he said.
But I'm not my father. I've always been willing
to take risks, like letting you go that day
or trying new honey flavors. Look how well
the rhubarb honey turned out.

I'm not rhubarb honey, she said, laughing.
Close enough, he said, and kissed her.

Goldilocks and the bear lived to a grand old age
together. Their children could turn
into bears at will. One married a princess,
one joined the circus,
one took over the honey business.
They have five grandchildren.
Her hair is silver now.

Look how well her thievery turned out.
She got the gold, she got the bear,
she got the fields of clover,
the flowering orchard, the house filled with sunlight
and sweetness, like a jar of honey. The life
of a happy woman.

The Bear's Wife

I went to the bear's house
reluctantly: my father would have a pension
for his old age, my mother a pantry filled
with food for winter. My brothers would go to school,
my little sister—all she wanted, she said,
was a dolly of her very own. I went
dutifully. Like a good daughter.

In the bear's house there were carpets with dim, rich colors
from Isfahan, and mahogany furniture,
and brocade curtains. More bedrooms than I could count,
a ballroom in which I was the only dancer,
a library filled with books. And electric lights!
But I chose a candle to see him by—the bear,
my husband. The wax dripped.

He woke, reproaching me, and it was gone—
house, carpets, furniture, curtains, books,
even the emptiness of empty rooms.
I was alone in the forest.

If I returned to my father's house, they would greet me
with cakes and wine. My mother would draw me aside.
This is what comes of marrying a bear, she would say,
but now it's over. You can live a normal life,
marry again, have children that are not bears,
become a respectable woman.

There was the path back to my father's house.
Instead I turned toward the pathless forest,
knowing already what the choice entailed:
walking up glass mountains in iron shoes,
riding winds to the corners of the earth,
answering ogres' riddles. And at the end
the bear, my husband, whom I barely knew.
And yet, I walked into the dangerous trees,

knowing it was my life, knowing I chose it
over safety, maybe over sanity. Because it was mine,
because it was life.

Professor Berkowitz Stands on the Threshold

I. the sun rises in an ecstasy of brightness

WHEN THE SUN rose, Alistair Berkowitz realized that he was standing on a beach. His slippers were covered with sand, and cold water was seeping up the bottoms of his pajamas. He could smell the sea, and as the mist began to dissipate he could see it, a line of gray motion closer than he had imagined. He stood beside a tidal pool, which was probably responsible for the uncomfortable feeling of wet fabric around his ankles. In it, iridescent snails crawled over a rock. In the distance, he heard the scream of a gull. He shivered. The wind off the water was cold.

Then the sun shone on the water, creating a gold pathway, and he said without thinking,

> the sun rises in an ecstasy of brightness,
> like a lion shaking its mane, like a chrysanthemum
> discovering itself

"Ah, you speak English."

Berkowitz turned so quickly that he lost a slipper and had to find it again in the sand. The man behind him was dressed in a suit of purple velvet. Dark hair hung over his eyes. It looked as though he had combed it with his fingers.

"Myself, I speak English also. My mother, when she was sober, told me my father was an English duke. When she was drunk, she told me he was a Russian sailor. Unfortunately I speak no Russian."

Berkowitz stared at him, then looked down at his slippers and shifted his feet. Why was he wearing pajamas? He rubbed his hands in an effort to warm them. "I'm assuming," he said, "that this is a dream. Sorry to imply that you're a figment of my imagination."

"Pas du tout," said the man in the purple suit, smiling. His teeth were crooked, which gave his smile the charm of imperfection. "Although as for that, perhaps you are a—how you say? Figment of my imagination. Perhaps I am lying with my head on the table of a café in Montmartre, and Céline is drawing a mustache over my mouth with charcoal, while that scoundrel Baudelaire is laughing into his absinthe. Perhaps all of this," he extended his arms in a gesture that took in the rocks behind them, and the sand stretching down to the water, and the sun that was rising and covering the gray sky with a wash of gold, "is all in my head. Including you, mon ami. Although why I should dream of an Englishman . . ."

"American," said Berkowitz. "I'm American. From Vermont." Then, putting his hands in his pajama pockets, he said, "I'm a professor. At a university."

"Ah," said the man in the purple suit. "If my father were an English duke, I might have travelled to the land of Edgar Poe. It is a difficult question. Did my mother lie when she was drunk, or when she was sober?"

"I mean," Berkowitz continued, annoyed at the interruption. It was what he habitually said when students interrupted his lectures with ringing cell phones. "I mean, I'm not an art historian. But Baudelaire. 'Le Visage Vert,' about the death of the painter Eugène Valentin, poisoned by his mistress Céline la Creole. At a café in Montmartre. It makes sense for a professor of comparative literature to dream of Eugène Valentin. Not the other way around."

Valentin looked up at the sky. "Citron, with blanc de chine and strips of gris payne. Ah, Céline. Did you love me enough to poison me?"

Berkowitz shifted his feet again, trying to knock sand off his slippers. A gull flew over them, its wings flashing black and silver in the sunlight. How much longer would he remain a professor of comparative literature? Next week was his tenure evaluation. The department chairman had never believed in his research, never recognized the importance of Marie de la Roche. No wonder he was talking to a man in a purple suit, on a beach, in pajamas.

"And is she a figment of your imagination as well?" asked Valentin.

A woman was walking toward them, along the edge of the water. Her skin had the sheen of metal, and she was entirely hairless, from her bald head to her bare genitals. She had no breasts. Berkowitz would have assumed she was a boy, except that she lacked the usual masculine accoutrements.

Berkowitz stared at her and rubbed the bridge of his nose.

"If I imagined a female form," Valentin added, "it would look like Venus, not Ganymede."

The woman stopped a few feet away from them and, without speaking, turned and looked at the water. The two men turned as well. Between the sky and the sea, both of which were rapidly beginning to turn blue, a black speck was moving toward them.

"What is it?" he asked Valentin. He really should get glasses.

Valentin brushed his hair back from his eyes. "A ship. At last, I believe something is beginning to happen."

II. seashells, whose curves are as intricate as madness

THE HARBOR WAS built of stone blocks, so large that Berkowitz wondered how they had been moved. Like those statues on Easter Island. He looked over the side of the ship, at the waves below. If he were in someone else's dream, he would disappear when the dreamer woke up. What did that remind him of? Humpty Dumpty, he thought, and realized that he had answered in Helen's voice. Once, they had gone to Nantucket together. He remembered her sitting on the beach under a straw hat, taking notes for her article on the feminist implications of the Oz books. He wondered how she liked Princeton, and tenure.

He stumbled as the ship pitched and rolled.

Valentin opened his eyes. "You have kicked my elbow." He had been asleep for the last hour, with his head on a coil of rope.

"Sorry," said Berkowitz. The metallic woman was sitting on the other side of the deck, legs crossed and eyes closed. She seemed to be meditating. About noon, Berkowitz had decided to call her Metallica.

Valentin sat up and combed his fingers through his hair. "Have you considered that perhaps we are dead? If, as you say, I am poisoned . . ."

Berkowitz looked around the deck and up at the sails. "This isn't exactly my idea of death."

"Ah," said Valentin. "Are they still dancing, les petits grotesques?"

They were not dancing, exactly. But they moved over the deck and among the rigging, women with the calves of soccer players below gossamer tunics, like the workings of an intricate machine.

Berkowitz said, "At first I thought they were wearing masks."

One had the head of a cat as blue as a robin's egg, with fins for ears. Another, the head of a parrot covered with scales, the green and yellow and orange of an angelfish. Another, a pig's head with the beak of a toucan. This one had taken Berkowitz's hand and said in a hoarse voice, as though just getting over the flu, "The Luminous Vessel. The Endless Sea." Then he had realized they were not wearing masks after all. Now, they seemed to be taking down the sails.

"You know," he said to Valentin, "I think we've arrived."

Metallica rose and walked to their part of the ship. She looked over the side, at the harbor and the water below.

Berkowitz whispered, "I wonder if she's a robot?"

"Look at their legs," said Valentin, rising. "So firm. I wonder . . ."

The path from the harbor was covered with stone chips. Berkowitz felt them through his slippers, edged and uncomfortable. They walked through a thicket of bushes with small white flowers.

Ahead of him, Valentin was trying to put his arm around Catwoman's waist. Berkowitz touched him on the shoulder. "Feathers," he said. "Not flowers. See, on the bushes. They're growing feathers."

"Yes?" said Valentin. "I have made a discovery also, mon ami." Catwoman took the opportunity to walk ahead. "She is a flirt, that one. But look, you see our silver-plated friend?" Ahead of them, Metallica and Pigwoman walked together. They were gesturing rapidly to one another.

"Are they playing a game?" asked Berkowitz.

"I think," said Valentin, "it is a conversation."

They emerged from the bushes. Ahead of them was a castle. At least, thought Berkowitz, it looks more like a castle than anything else. It was built of the same stone blocks as the harbor, but on one side it seemed to have grown spines. On the other, metal beams extended like a spider's legs. Towers rose, narrowing as they spiraled upward. What did they remind him of? Something from under the sea—probably seashells. He suddenly understood why Marie de la Roche had compared seashells to madness. The castle glittered in the sunlight, as though carved from sugar.

They passed through a courtyard carpeted with moss and randomly studded with rocks, like a Zen landscape. They passed under a doorway shaped, thought Berkowitz, like the jawbone of a whale. He felt as though he were being swallowed.

The room they entered seemed to confirm that impression. It was large, with a ceiling ribbed like a whale's skeleton. Pale light filled the room, from windows with panes like layers of milk glass. Valentin's footsteps echoed. Berkowitz could even hear the shuffle of his slippers reverberating.

At the other end of the room, he saw robed figures, huddled together. They looked like professors in academic robes. In the moment it took for his eyes to adjust to the light, he imagined they were discussing his tenure evaluation. But when they turned, he clutched Valentin's arm. They were not wearing masks either. One had the head of a stag, its horns tipped with inquisitive eyes. Another was a boar, with bristles like butterfly wings. Another seemed to be a serpent with spotted fur. Their robes were a random patchwork of satin, burlap, and what looked like plastic bags, held together with gold thread and bits of straw.

They moved apart to reveal an ordinary kitchen chair, painted a chipped and fading green. On it was sitting a girl in a white dress, sewn at the sleeves and hem with bleached twigs, coral beads, pieces of bone. Her hair was held back by a gold net. She looked like she had been dressed for a school play.

Pigwoman curtsied. "The Endless Sea," she said. "The August Visitors."

The girl rose from her chair. "Bienvenu, Monsieur Valentin. Welcome, Professor Berkowitz." She turned toward Metallica and bowed. Metallica answered with a movement of her fingers.

"I understand you have been communicating in English," she continued. "I shall do the same. Aeiou, of course, requires no verbal interpretation."

The collection of vowels, Berkowitz assumed, was Metallica's name. He stared at the girl. What had Helen told him? "Look at Alice, and Ozma. Literature, at least imaginative literature, is ruled by adolescent girls." Then she had leaned across the library table, with her elbows on a biography of Verlaine, and asked him on their first date.

"Of course you have already learned one another's qualifications?" She looked at them, as though expecting confirmation. "No? Well then. Eugène Valentin, perhaps most celebrated for your *Narcisse à l'Enfer*. Although *L'Orchidée*

Noire, your painting of the dancer Céline la Creole, is equally magnificent, Monsieur. Professor Alistair Berkowitz, translator of the fragmentary poems of Marie de la Roche. I am, of course, addressing you chronologically. Aeiou, follower of Vasarana, the goddess of wisdom, once temple singer for the goddess." She turned to Valentin and Berkowitz. "Her name, as you may have guessed, is a chanted prayer. I have not pronounced it correctly. Her vocal chords were surgically removed during incarceration, to prevent her from spreading the teachings of her sect. Professor, I believe you have heard of American Sign Language? She has asked me to tell you that she wishes you the blessings of wisdom."

She looked at them, as though waiting for a response.

They looked at each other. Valentin shrugged. Then, simultaneously, Valentin said, "We are pleased to make her acquaintance," and Berkowitz blurted, "I don't understand. Who are you? Where are we? What kind of dream is this, anyway?"

She raised her eyebrows. "I am the Questioner. Haven't you discussed this at all among yourselves? Surely you must have realized that you have come to the Threshold."

III. the sea is as deep as death, and as filled with whispers

VALENTIN AND BERKOWITZ stared at the mossy courtyard.

"This garden was planted to represent the known world," said the Questioner. "The mosses, of course, represent the Endless Sea, with darker varieties for the depths, lighter for the relative shallows. And there," she pointed to a central area where rocks were clustered, "are the Inner Islands. That gray one is your island."

"I still don't understand," Berkowitz whispered to Valentin.

Valentin looked back at the doorway, where Pigwoman stood as though on guard. "I wonder if she is so firm everywhere, mon ami?" he whispered.

Berkowitz edged away from him. Did he have to share his dream with a lecherous Frenchman?

"Around the Inner Islands lies the Endless Sea," said the Questioner, "unnavigable except in the Luminous Vessel. Anyone sailing to the Outer Islands must stop here, at the Threshold."

She turned to them and smiled as though she had explained everything.

"I still don't understand," he said.

The Questioner frowned. She looked, thought Berkowitz, as though she were trying to solve an algebra problem. "Professor Berkowitz, I have tried to suit my explanation to your understanding. But you are a man of the space age. Perhaps if I call those central rocks the Inner Planets, and the mosses an Endless Space, and tell you that you can only reach the Outer Planets in the Luminous

Rocketship. To a tribesmen I might speak of the Inner Huts. Aeiou, who needs no explanation, understands them as representations of Inner Consciousness. The result is the same. Tomorrow I will ask you the Question, and based on your answer you will either return to the Inner Islands, or proceed onward."

"But I still don't . . ." said Berkowitz.

"Excellent," said Valentin. "Look, mon ami. We are from there." He pointed to the central cluster of rocks. "But we have qualifications, as she said. You have your book, I have my paintings, and our companion of the vowels has evidently been singing. If we answer her question correctly, we will be allowed to go on."

"But to where?" asked Berkowitz, with exasperation. He was coming to the uncomfortable conviction that, rather than dreaming, he was probably going mad. Perhaps he was at that moment being strapped into a straitjacket.

"Out, out!" said Valentin. "Have you never wanted to go out and away?"

He suddenly remembered a story he had told Helen, when they had been together for almost a year. One morning in high school, the captain of the wrestling team had locked him into the boys' bathroom, shouting, "Man, if my name were Alistair, I would have drowned myself at birth!" He had wanted, more than anything, to go out and away. Away from the small town in New Jersey, away from his father, a small town lawyer who could not understand why he had wanted to study something as useless as literature. Helen had smiled at him across the scrambled eggs and said, "Lucky for me you had a lousy childhood."

Perhaps that was why he had become interested in Marie de la Roche. She had wanted to go out and away. Away from her parents' olive trees, away from the convent. He imagined her, on her cliff beside the sea, in a hut made of driftwood lashed together with rope. Each morning she climbed down its nearly perpendicular face to gather seaweed and whatever the sea had left in tidal pools: crabs, mussels, snails. Fishermen claimed her broth could revive drowned men. Each afternoon she sat on her cliff and wrote, on driftwood with sharp rocks, on scraps of her habit with cuttlefish ink, and sent the fragments flying. Fishermen believed they brought a good catch. He thought of the year he had spent studying her fragments, now in a case at the Musée National. How many had been lost, buried by sand or floating out to sea? She had found her way out, through madness and suicide. Fishermen had built a church in her honor, and in certain parts of Brittany she was still considered a saint. Was that what had fascinated him, her willingness to toss everything—her poems, herself—over a cliff?

Valentin and the Questioner were staring at him. How long had he been standing there, lost in thought?

"Perhaps," said the Questioner, "if I showed you the Repository?"

It looked like a museum. Where the walls were not covered with shelves, they were covered with tapestries, paintings, photographs. Metal staircases twisted upward to balconies, containing more shelves. They were filled with books and scrolls, disappearing upward into the shadows of the ceiling. Toward the center of the room were glass cases filled with manuscripts, small statues, things he did not recognize. One looked like a collection of sea sponges. They passed a sculpture that looked suspiciously like the *Nike of Samothrace*, and the skeleton of a rhinoceros painted blue. "Not bad, that," said Valentin, examining it with admiration.

"By those who have come to the Threshold," said the Questioner. "I believe my collection is fairly complete." At the end of the room was a fireplace. Over it hung Van Gogh's *Irises*. She walked to a long table that looked like it belonged in a public school library. "Ah," she said, "the collected works of Keats. I wondered where I had left it." She opened a box on the table, which began to play music, low and melancholy, that Berkowitz faintly recognized. "Lady Day," she said. "And of course Elihu's *Lamia*." She tapped her index finger on one of the glass cases. A green glow levitated and stretched elegant tendrils toward her, like an art nouveau octopus. "So simple, yet so satisfying."

"My *Narcisse*, is it here?" asked Valentin.

"I will show it to you," said the Questioner. "But I believe Professor Berkowitz would like to see this." She opened a glass case and took out a scrap of fabric. "When Marie de a Roche leaped into the sea, she held this in her hand. It was the last piece of her habit. She gave it to me, when she passed through the Threshold."

Berkowitz took the linen, which looked fresh although worn, as though it had never touched sea water. He recognized her angled writing. Mentally, he translated into rough iambs and anapests:

> the sea is as deep as death, and as filled with whispers
> of the past

She had been here. She had walked through the Threshold. He wondered what sort of question he would be asked, and whether he would pass the test.

IV. my mind crawls, like a snail, around one thought

Berkowitz drank through a course of tangerine fish and fish-shaped tangerines, through a course of translucent jellies. The liquid in his glass was the color of amber, and shards of gold leaf floated in it. It tasted like peaches and burned his throat going down. Every once in a while he had to peel gold leaf from his teeth.

He looked down the table and felt a throbbing start in his left temple. A woman with what looked like a flamingo on her head winked at him. The flamingo winked as well. Too much fur, too many wings, and not a single nose was the correct shape or size. The Abominable Snowman jogged his elbow.

He stared at his soup, which tasted like celery.

The Questioner leaned over to him and said, "Aeiou is a neighbor of yours. She comes from Connecticut."

"Oh," said Berkowitz. She smiled encouragingly, as though waiting for him to respond with something clever. He said, "Connecticut isn't really that close to Vermont." He tried to laugh and knocked over his bowl, which looked like a sea urchin. Soup spilled over the table.

She turned to Stagman, who was sitting on her other side.

Damn, thought Berkowitz. I've already failed. Who made up the rules of this game anyway?

The Questioner rose. "I believe it's time for a quadrille. Are the musicians ready?"

They evidently were, because the music began.

The Questioner led with Stagman. Valentin, who was learning the steps as he went along, capered behind Pigwoman.

Berkowitz drank, and despised them all. He despised the musicians, playing citoles, lyres, pipes that curled like the necks of swans, and what looked like the lid of a trash can. He despised the dancers, gliding or shuffling or hopping in complicated figures he could not understand. He despised Aeiou, weaving through them in a dance of her own, and Valentin, who kept treading on Pigwoman's toes. He despised himself, which had never been difficult for him. The department would never give him tenure. The chairman had told him that Marie de la Roche was marginal. Hell, how much more marginal could you get than an insane nun living on a cliff? He should have written a book on Baudelaire. He should have stayed in New Jersey and become a lawyer. By the time he began to despise Marie de la Roche, on her damn rock, with her damn poetry, the room was beginning to look distinctly lopsided. "Enough," said the Questioner. The music, which had been drifting from a waltz to cacophony, ceased. Valentin stopped abruptly and would have fallen, except that his arm was wrapped around Pigwoman's waist. "It is time for your questions."

Already? thought Berkowitz. I didn't even have a chance to study.

"Tomorrow morning, as you know, I will ask each of you the Question that will determine whether you step through the Threshold." There she went again with her "as you know." As though they knew anything. "Tonight, however, you may each ask me a question of your own."

Stagman brought her green chair, and she sat in the middle of the room. Light flickered from candles and oil lamps and fluorescent bulbs. That explained why the room was beginning to blur. Berkowitz pinched the bridge of his nose. Helen had been right—he should get glasses.

Valentin, who had been trying to kiss Pigwoman's neck, stumbled and kissed the air. He must be drunk, thought Berkowitz.

"Aeiou will begin," said the Questioner. Aeiou gestured. The pain spread to Berkowitz's right temple. God, he needed an aspirin.

She smiled and nodded. "Your songs will be sung for a thousand years, until the factories and prisons of the Imperium return to dust, and pomegranates grow on Manhattan Island."

Aeiou bowed her head, and metallic tears ran down her cheeks. The audience clapped.

Damn, thought Berkowitz. This must be part of the test. The Questioner looked at him. Not me, he thought. Not yet. I need time to think.

"Monsieur Valentin," she said. "What would you like to ask me?"

Valentin looked down at the floor, then said, "Did she poison me? Céline."

The Questioner looked amused. "Yes, in the absinthe. If you choose not to return, she will wear black orchids in your memory." The audience clapped. The Abominable Snowman giggled, and Catwoman nudged whoever was standing beside her.

What a stupid question, thought Berkowitz. That won't get him any brownie points. He tried to think of something profound.

The Questioner said, "And finally, Professor Berkowitz."

Profound. What was the most profound question he could think of? He needed a hundred aspirins. She was leaning toward him, waiting for his question. Berkowitz said, "Is there a God?"

She leaned back in her chair. She seemed disappointed, or perhaps just tired. "Yes," she said. "Once, she would visit our island. We would work in the garden together, tying back the roses. But she has grown old, and sleeps a great deal now. I do not know what will happen when—but that wasn't your question."

There was a moment of silence. Then the audience clapped, without enthusiasm. A thousand aspirins, that's what he needed. Berkowitz took another drink and despised the universe.

Later, lying in bed and trying to keep the room from spinning, he thought about the test. Clearly, he had already failed. All the failures of his life gathered around him. Failing to make the soccer team because he couldn't kick worth a damn. Failing calculus. Failing to get into Yale. Failing with Helen, who had waited for him in the kitchen, under a lightbulb he had forgotten to replace, with the letter from Princeton in her hand. "Tell me," she had said. "How am I supposed to compete with a dead nun?" Failing his tenure evaluation, because he already knew he would fail.

Marie de la Roche had not failed. She had succeeded at going mad, at committing suicide, at becoming a saint. She had stepped through the Threshold.

The question. His mind crawled around it like a snail.

Valentin would get through, because the Questioner liked him. Look at the way she had answered him tonight. She didn't like Berkowitz. The question. His mind crawled around and around it, in the darkness.

V. faith, like a seagull hanging in mid-air

Berkowitz woke with the sun shining on his face and a headache that made him long for swift decapitation. Seeing no sign of breakfast, he walked to the moss garden. Valentin was standing with his hands in his pockets, staring at the central rocks.

"Sleep well?" asked Berkowitz. His voice sounded unnaturally loud, and his tongue was a piece of lead covered with felt.

"No," said Valentin. "That is, I did not sleep. She was very firm, the petit cochon." He smiled to himself.

"What do you think the question will be?" asked Berkowitz. He had no desire to learn the details of Pigwoman's anatomy.

Valentin shrugged and touched a rock with the tip of his shoe. "A little gray stone. Just what one would expect, no?"

Stagman walked into the courtyard. He looked at Valentin and said, "The Ambiguous Threshold."

"My turn," said Valentin. "The one of the vowels has already gone."

"Good luck," said Berkowitz.

"Mon ami," said Valentin, "I suspect luck has nothing to do with it."

When Valentin had gone, Berkowitz walked around the garden, looking at the Outer Islands. Rocks, no different than the ones in the central cluster. Rocks scattered across a carpet of moss.

He looked down at his pajamas. They were badly wrinkled, and one sleeve was spotted with soup. Didn't that prove this was a dream? Showing up for an exam in pajamas. One of the classic scenarios. Lucky he wasn't naked. He wondered if Marie de la Roche had been.

"The Ambiguous Threshold." Stagman was waiting for him. Berkowitz felt a sudden impulse to shake him by the shoulders and beg him to say something, anything, else—to get one real answer in this place. His stomach gave a queasy rumble. They could at least have fed him breakfast.

Instead, he followed Stagman into the garden. They passed between rose-bushes that seemed to whisper as he walked by. Berkowitz looked closely and realized, with distaste, that the petals on the roses were pink tongues. They passed a fountain, in which waterlilies croaked like frogs. In alcoves on either side of the path, ornamental cherries were weeping on the heads of stone nymphs that were evidently turning into foxes, owls, rabbits—or all of them at once. He brushed against a poppy, which fluttered sepals that looked like lashes.

Beyond the fountain was a hedge of Featherbushes, with an opening cut into it, like an arch. Berkowitz followed Stagman through the archway.

The hedge grew in a circle, its only opening the one they had passed through. Grass grew over the ground, so soft under his slippers that Berkowitz wanted to take them off and walk barefoot. He had often gone barefoot as a child, but he could not remember what it felt like, walking on grass. The grass was spotted with daisies that were, for once, actually daisies.

At the center of the circle was a stone arch, shaped like the arch in the hedge, but built of the same blocks as the harbor and the castle. Its top and sides were irregular, and broken blocks lay scattered on the grass beside it, as though it were the final remnant of some monumental architecture. Sitting on one of those blocks was the Questioner.

"Good morning, Professor," she said. Today she was wearing a blue dress decorated with bits of glass. Her hair hung in two braids tied with blue ribbons.

"Good morning," said Berkowitz, trying to put as much irony into his voice as he could with a felted tongue. The silence in the circle made him uncomfortable. Even the sound of the fountain was muted.

The Questioner rose and asked, "Are you ready for the Question?"

"I guess," he said. He looked at Stagman, waiting with his hands folded together, like the Dalai Lama. This had to be a dream.

"Would you like to step through the Threshold?"

"What," said Berkowitz, "you mean now?"

"That is the Question, Professor. The only Question there is. Would you like to step through the Threshold?"

Berkowitz stared at her, and then at the arch. "You mean that thing?" Through it he could see the hedge, and grass spotted with daisies.

The Questioner sighed. "That thing is the Threshold. Everything you see around you, including myself, is what you might call an emanation of it. If you step through it, you will proceed to the Outer Islands."

"So that's the whole test?"

"There is no test," said the Questioner. "There is only the Question. Would you like to step through the Threshold?"

"What if I don't?" asked Berkowitz.

"You will, of course, return to the Inner Islands."

"You mean I'll be back at the university?"

"Yes," said the Questioner. "You will return to your life, as though you had never left it. You will forget that you once stood on the Threshold, or you will think of it as a dream whose details you can never quite remember."

"And if I do?"

The Questioner tugged at one of her braids. For the first time, she looked like an impatient child. "You will, of course, proceed to the Outer Islands." She added, slowly and with emphasis, "As I have previously explained."

"What about the university?"

"You will appear to have died. Probably of a heart attack. Your diet, Professor, is particularly conducive." She gave him a lopsided smile, which looked almost sympathetic. "Unless you would prefer suicide?"

"Died?" said Berkowitz. "No one said anything about dying. If I go back to the Inner Islands, whatever they are, will I ever come here again?"

"No one gets more than one chance to stand on the Threshold."

"Why?" asked Berkowitz. "Look, here are the things I want to know. What exactly are the Outer Islands? What will I be if I go there? Will I be me or something else, like a chicken man with daisies growing out of my head?"

"Enough," said the Questioner. She was no longer smiling. "I am a questioner, not an answerer. When Marie de la Roche stepped through the Threshold, she said,

> *la foi, une mouette suspendue*
> *au milieu de l'air*

Professor Berkowitz, will you step through the Threshold?"

Berkowitz looked at her, standing beside the archway. He looked at the arch itself, and through it at the hedge. A breeze ruffled the feathers on the bushes.

He thought of returning to the house they had rented, without Helen. Without the smell of her vegetarian lasagna, without her voice, which would suddenly, even while reading the newspaper, begin reciting "Jabberwocky." To his bookshelves, now relatively bare. He thought of gray rocks scattered across a moss courtyard. Of the collected works of Keats, a woman with a flamingo on her head, roses whispering as he walked by. Of the university, and his students with their ringing cell phones. Perhaps Helen would call. He did not think so.

Then he looked at Stagman, who was rubbing the side of one furred cheek. This was a dream, and next week was his tenure evaluation.

"No," he said. The Questioner nodded with finality. He looked at her for an excruciating moment, then put his hands over his eyes. He waited to wake up.

Persephone in Hades

Poppies have never been my favorite flowers.
Here they bloom all year long, if one can say
a year in Hades, where no seasons pass,
where summer never fades. Ironic, that—
a land of death where nothing ever dies.

I have almost forgotten how it feels
when snowflakes fall and melt against my cheeks,
when frost spreads her white veil across the landscape,
covering the hills, decorating the leaves
that rattle on the trees with intricate lace.
I miss that time of year when autumn fires
bloom in the household hearths. Here, no fires burn.
Instead, among the wheat, the poppies sway:
an endless field to drug men into sleep,
relieve their pains or worries for a while,
here, in this silent land where all are welcome.

As silent as my husband, Hades himself,
who sits all day in his library reading scrolls
lost to the world above us. "Why did you bring me
to this stagnant country," I ask him, "if not to talk?
To sit and brood in a chair made out of bones,
or stare out the window at the unchanging garden,
in which only yew trees grow, and never speak?
Why abduct the daughter of Demeter?
Why not some other girl?" He shakes his head
and sighs. He would be handsome, if not so lost
in his own dreams. Or if he would trim his beard.
"I saw your hair lift in the wind," he says,
"and thought of it blowing back against my face,
but there is no wind down here. I saw your mouth
and thought perhaps it would kiss me, or whisper poems
into my ears. Perhaps then I'd wake up
from this endless sleep, this abyss of timelessness.
I thought you might love me in time, forgetting that love

cannot live in this land." He looks at me, frowning.
"You'll never love me, will you, Persephone?"
"Not," I say, "as long as you keep me here,
while above us frost and snow blanket the earth—
away from death, among the endless dead."
"Yet how can I let you go?" His eyes plead with me,
I suppose to be forgiven or understood,
but I turn away, unsympathetic. He should
know better: you cannot have love on such terms.
Even the gods, selfish as children, know that.

It is useless, here, to count the days, and yet
a day will come, a day without a dawn,
when I will feel that ache within my chest,
as though a string were tied around my heart,
and know, with crocuses and hyacinths,
it's time to push my way through the dark soil
into the sunlight, into my mother's arms.
It's time to blossom like the olive trees,
be born again into mortality
for a little while, laugh and shake water drops
from my hair, dance across the sunlit meadows
sprinkled with daisies and cornflowers, forget the land
of death and poppies, at least for a little while.

To forget, for a little while, the silent husband
who waits implacably at summer's end.

The Princess and the Peas

It was raining.
It had been raining for four days
and you were as wet
as a wet pig, as your mother would say.
Water was dripping from your hair
down to your collarbones
and to your dress, already sopping,
rags, really—regulation wear for a pig girl.
At first you didn't realize
it was a castle, and when you did,
what of it? A castle was as good
shelter as any other.

When you knocked on the door, the footman,
to your surprise, said, "Are you a princess?
They're looking for princesses in here."
His smirk, you realized, was not for you,
but them in there, intent
on a princess hunt.

"Sure," you said. Why not?
What is a princess anyway?
You were the princess of a hovel,
a field of mud, a pigsty, a herd of porkers,
daughter of the pig-queen of a village
too small to have its own name,
Lesser Something.

What is a princess, anyway?
Someone who sleeps on a feather bed, evidently.
Make that fourteen feather beds.
The queen looked at you askance
of course, with your rags and hair dripping,
bare feed muddy from trudging
through what the rain had made of the roads.
But royalty, once they've given their word,

seldom go back on it, seemingly.
You said you were a princess, so
you got the feather beds.

Of course it was a test. What isn't, in this life?
You had known that
as soon as the footman looked at you sideways.
You knew it twice as surely
when the prince looked at you sideways.
He was a scrawny kid. The pigs would
have made quick work of him.
But what was the test?
It had to be about the feather beds.
That was the only strange thing
in the room, which was otherwise
perfectly ordinary—for royalty, that is.
Bigger than your hovel, about as big
as your hovel and the pig field,
but with no pigs in it. You didn't miss them.

The water in the bath was hot and scented.
You emerged from it hot, scented, and as pink
as a newborn piglet. You were surprised to find
that your hair was blonde, and actually rather pretty.
It was nice not to be quite so muddy, for once.
The nightgown was soft and white, pure linen.
You had never felt anything like it
before, never having had a nightgown.
You quite liked it. So what was the test?
It took you a while to find the peas,
but not too long. You were used to finding
bits of carrot under muddy straw,
turnip ends, cabbage leaves,
any other vegetables that had not rotted,
trodden on by the pigs.
You would put them back in the troughs.
No use wasting good food.
You could root out anything the pigs could.
They would have found the peas, easy.

It was not until the next morning, when the queen
asked, "How did you sleep, my dear,
were you comfortable?" with a certain

look in her eyes, a *significance*,
that you figure it out.
"Terribly," you said. "Excuse me,
your majesty, but I thinking someone
accidentally left rocks in my bed.
I am of course grateful
for your hospitality, but I could not
sleep a wink."
There was something in the way
she looked at you, a small, satisfied smile,
that clued you in to what was going on.
The weak prince, the queen
who was looking for, not a princess,
but someone clever enough to solve her riddle.
The right girl for her son, the right girl for her throne.
What is a princess, anyway?
A girl that people bow to and call princess.

They gave you fine clothes, silk of course, and ermine.
They gave you a crown with a pair of matching earrings,
diamonds and pearls. You considered, for a while,
whether to stay or abscond with the jewelry.
But the queen, looking at you approvingly,
after the ladies in waiting had finished their labors,
said, "You know, my dear, before I was queen,
I was a shopkeeper's daughter.
That's why my son insisted, in his wisdom,
on a *true* princess."
"Of course, your majesty," you said in your best
princess voice. "I understand completely."

Anyway, why shouldn't you be queen?
Ruling a kingdom
was probably no more difficult than ruling a pigsty,
keeping the peace among a bunch of hogs,
keeping the sows from sleeping on their young.
By and by, you would inform your mother
that she was now the queen of a faraway kingdom
called something like Porcinia.
You would bring her to court, give her the comforts
she'd never had. Yes, Ma would like that,
especially the baths.
Your children would be heirs to the throne,

and by the look of the prince, you would be the power
behind it, eventually regent.
Not bad for a pig-keeper's daughter
who had out into the world
to make something of herself, saying to her mother,
give me your blessing, Ma. I'll be somebody
someday. Watch me.

Blanchefleur

T HEY CALLED HIM Idiot.

He was the miller's son, and he had never been good for much. At least
not since his mother's death, when he was twelve years old. He had found her
floating, face-down, in the millpond, and his cries had brought his father's
men. When they had turned her over, he had seen her face, pale and bloated,
before someone had said, "Not in front of the child!" and they had hurried
him away. He had never seen her again, just the wooden coffin going into the
ground, and after that, the gray stone in the churchyard where, every Sunday,
he and his father left whatever was in season—a bunch of violets, sprays of the
wild roses that grew by the forest edge, tall lilies from beside the mill stream. In
winter, they left holly branches red with berries.

Before her death, he had been a laughing, affectionate child. After her
death, he became solitary. He would no longer play with his friends from
school, and eventually they began to ignore him. He would no longer speak
even to his father, and anyway the miller was a quiet man who, after his wife's
death, grew more silent. He was so broken, so bereft, by the loss of his wife
that he could barely look at the son who had her golden hair, her eyes the color
of spring leaves. Often they would go a whole day, saying no more than a few
sentences to each other.

He went to school, but he never seemed to learn—he would stare out
the window or, if called upon, shake his head and refuse to answer. Once, the
teacher rapped his knuckles for it, but he simply looked at her with those eyes,
which were so much like his mother's. The teacher turned away, ashamed of
herself, and after that she left him alone, telling herself that at least he was sitting in the schoolroom rather than loafing about the fields.

He learned nothing, he did nothing. When his father told him to do the
work of the mill, he did it so badly that the water flowing through the sluice
gates was either too fast or slow, or the large millstones that grind the grain
were too close together or far apart, or he took the wrong amount of grain in
payment from the farmers who came to grind their wheat. Finally, the miller
hired another man, and his son wandered about the countryside, sometimes
sleeping under the stars, eating berries from the hedges when he could find
them. He would come home dirty, with scratches on his arms and brambles in
his hair. And his father, rather than scolding him, would look away.

If anyone had looked closely, they would have seen that he was clever at
carving pieces of wood into whistles and seemed to know how to call all the

178

birds. Also, he knew the paths through the countryside and could tell the time by the position of the sun and moon on each day of the year, his direction by the stars. He knew the track and spoor of every animal, what tree each leaf came from by its shape. He knew which mushrooms were poisonous and how to find water under the ground. But no one did look closely.

It was the other schoolboys, most of whom had once been his friends, who started calling him Idiot. At first it was Idiot Ivan, but soon it was simply Idiot, and it spread through the village until people forgot he had ever been called Ivan. Farmers would call to him, cheerfully enough, "Good morning, Idiot!" They meant no insult by it. In villages, people like knowing who you are. The boy was clearly an idiot, so let him be called that. And so he was.

No one noticed that under the dirt, and despite the rags he wore, he had grown into a large, handsome boy. He should have had sweethearts, but the village girls assumed he was slow and had no prospects, even though he was the miller's son. So he was always alone, and the truth was, he seemed to prefer it.

The miller was the only one who still called him Ivan, although he had given his son up as hopeless, and even he secretly believed that the boy was slow and stupid.

This was how things stood when the miller rode to market to buy a new horse. The market was held in the nearest town, on a fine summer day that was also the feast-day of Saint Ivan, so the town was filled with stalls selling live-stock, vegetables from the local farms, leather and rope harnesses, embroidered linen, woven baskets. Men and women in smocks lined up to hire themselves for the coming harvest. There were strolling players with fiddles or pipes, danc-ers on a wooden platform, and a great deal of beer—which the miller drank from a tankard.

The market went well for him. He found a horse for less money than he thought he would have to spend, and while he was paying for his beer, one of the maids from the tavern winked at him. She was plump, with sunburnt cheeks, and she poured his beer neatly, leaving a head of foam that just reached the top of the tankard. He had not thought of women, not in that way, since his wife had drowned. She had been one of those magical women, beautiful as the dawn, as slight as a willow-bough and with a voice like birds singing, that are perhaps too delicate for this world. That kind of woman gets into a man's blood. But lately he had started to notice once again that other women existed, and there were other things in the world than running a mill. Like his son, who was a great worry to him. What would the idiot—Ivan, he reminded himself— what would he do when his father was gone, as we must all go someday? Would he be able to take care of himself?

He had saddled his horse and was fastening a rope to his saddle so the new horse could be led, when he heard a voice he recognized from many years ago. "Hello, Stephen Miller," it said.

He turned around and bowed. "Hello, Lady."

She was tall and pale, with long gray hair that hung to the backs of her knees, although she did not look older than when he had last seen her, at his wedding. She wore a gray linen dress that, although it was midsummer, reminded him of winter.

"How is my nephew? This is his name day, is it not?"

"It is, Lady. As to how he is—" The miller told her. He might not have, if the beer had not loosened his tongue, for he was a proud man and he did not want his sister-in-law to think that his son was doing badly. But with the beer and his worries, it all came out—the days Ivan spent staring out of windows or walking through the countryside, how the local farmers thought of him, even that name—Idiot.

"I warned you that no good comes of a mortal marrying a fairy woman," said the Lady. "But those in love never listen. Send my nephew to me. I will make him my apprentice for three years, and at the end of that time we shall see. For his wages, you may take this."

She handed him a purse. He bowed in acknowledgment, saying, "I thank you for your generosity—" but when he straightened again, she was already walking away from him. Just before leaving the inn yard, she turned back for a moment and said, "The Castle in the Forest, remember. I will expect him in three days' time."

The miller nodded, although she had already turned away again. As he rode home, he looked into the purse she had given him—in it was a handful of leaves. He wondered how he was going to tell his son about the bargain he had made. But when he reached home, the boy was sitting at the kitchen table whittling something out of wood, and he simply said, "I have apprenticed you for three years to your aunt, the Lady of the Forest. She expects you in three days' time."

The boy did not say a word. But the next morning, he put all of his possessions—they were few enough—into a satchel, which he slung over his shoulder. And he set out.

In three days' time, Ivan walked through the forest, blowing on the whistle he had carved. He could hear birds calling to each other in the forest. He whistled to them, and they whistled back. He did not know how long his journey would take—if you set out for the Castle in the Forest, it can take you a day, or a week, or the rest of your life. But the Lady had said she expected him in three days, so he thought he would reach the Castle by the end of the day at the latest.

Before he left, his father had looked again in the purse that the Lady had given him. In it was a pile of gold coins—as the miller had expected, for that is the way fairy money works. "I will keep this for you," his father had said. "When you come back, you will be old enough to marry, and with such a fortune, any of the local girls will take you. I do not know what you will do as the Lady's apprentice, but I hope you will come back fit to run a mill."

Ivan had simply nodded, slung his satchel over his shoulder, and gone.

Just as he was wondering if he would indeed find the castle that day, for the sun was beginning to set, he saw it through the trees, its turrets rising above a high stone wall.

He went up to the wall and knocked at the wooden door that was the only way in. It opened, seemingly by itself. In the doorway stood a white cat.

"Are you the Idiot?" she asked.

"I suppose so," he said, speaking for the first time in three days.

"That's what I thought," she said. "You certainly look the part. Well, come in then, and follow me."

He followed her through the doorway and along a path that led through the castle gardens. He had never seen such gardens, although in school his teacher had once described the gardens that surrounded the King's castle, which she had visited on holiday. There were fountains set in green lawns, with stone fish spouting water. There were box hedges, and topiaries carved into the shapes of birds, rabbits, mice. There were pools filled with waterlilies, in which he could see real fish, silver and orange. There were arched trellises from which roses hung down in profusion, and an orchard with fruit trees. He could even see a kitchen garden, with vegetables in neat rows. And all through the gardens, he could see cats, pruning the hedges, tying back the roses, raking the earth in the flower beds.

It was the strangest sight he had ever seen, and for the first time it occurred to him that being the Lady's apprentice would be an adventure—the first of his life.

The path took them to the door of the castle, which swung open as they approached. An orange tabby walked out and stood waiting at the top of the steps.

"Hello, Marmalade," said the white cat.

"Good evening, Miss Blanchefleur," he replied. "Is this the young man Her Ladyship is expecting?"

"As far as I can tell," she said. "Although what my mother would want with such an unprepossessing specimen, I don't know."

Marmalade bowed to Ivan and said, "Welcome, Ivan Miller. Her Ladyship is waiting in the solar."

Ivan expected the white cat, whose name seemed to be Blanchefleur, to leave him with Marmalade, but instead she followed them through the doorway, then through a great hall whose walls were hung with tapestries showing cats sitting in gardens, climbing trees, hunting rabbits, catching fish. Here too there were cats, setting out bowls on two long wooden tables, and on a shorter table set on a dais at the end of the room. As Marmalade passed, they nodded, and a gray cat who seemed to be directing their activities said, "We're almost ready, Mr. Marmalade. The birds are nicely roasted, and the mint sauce is really a treat if I say so myself."

"Excellent, Mrs. Pebbles. I can't tell you how much I'm looking forward to those birds. Tailcatcher said he caught them himself."

"Well, with a little help!" said Mrs. Pebbles, acerbically. "He doesn't go on the hunt alone, does he now, Mr. Marmalade? Oh, begging your pardon, Miss," she said when she saw Blanchefleur. "I didn't know you were there."

"I couldn't care less what you say about him," said Blanchefleur, with a sniff and a twitch of her tail. "He's nothing to me."

"As you say, Miss," said Mrs. Pebbles, not sounding particularly convinced.

At the back of the great hall was another, smaller door that led to a long hallway. Ivan was startled when, at the end of the hallway, which had been rather dark, they emerged into a room filled with sunlight. It had several windows looking out onto a green lawn, and scattered around the room were low cushions, on which cats sat engaged in various tasks. Some were carding wool, some were spinning it on drop spindles, some were plying the yarn or winding it into skeins. In a chair by one of the windows sat the Lady, with a piece of embroidery in her lap. One of the cats was reading a book aloud, but stopped when they entered.

"My Lady, this is Ivan Miller, your new apprentice," said Marmalade.

"Otherwise known as the Idiot," said Blanchefleur. "And he seems to deserve the name. He's said nothing for himself all this time."

"My dear, you should be polite to your cousin," said the Lady. "Ivan, you've already met my daughter, Blanchefleur, and Marmalade, who takes such marvelous care of us all. These are my ladies-in-waiting: Elderberry, Twilight, Snowy, Whiskers, and Fluff. My daughter tells me you have nothing to say for yourself. Is that true?"

Ivan stared at her, sitting in her chair, surrounded by cats. She had green eyes, and although her gray hair hung down to the floor, she reminded him of his mother. "Yes, ma'am," he said.

She looked at him for a moment, appraisingly. Then she said, "Very well. I will send you where you need not say anything. Just this morning I received a letter from an old friend of mine, Professor Owl. He is compiling an Encyclopedia of All Knowledge, but he is old and feels arthritis terribly in his legs. He can no longer write the entries himself. For the first year of your apprenticeship, you will go to Professor Owl in the Eastern Waste and help him with his Encyclopedia. Do you think you can do that, nephew?"

"It's all the same to me," said Ivan. It was obvious that no one wanted him here, just as no one had wanted him at the mill. What did it matter where he went?

"Then you shall set out tomorrow morning," said the Lady. "Tonight you shall join us for dinner. Are the preparations ready, Marmalade?"

"Almost, My Lady," said the orange cat.

"How will I find this Professor Owl?" asked Ivan.

"Blanchefleur will take you," said the Lady.

"You can't be serious!" said Blanchefleur. "He's an idiot, and he stinks like a pigsty."

"Then show him the bathroom, where he can draw himself a bath," said the Lady. "And give him new clothes to wear. Those are too ragged even for Professor Owl, I think."

"Come on, you," said Blanchefleur, clearly disgusted. He followed her out of the room and up a flight of stairs, to a bathroom with a large tub on four clawed legs. He had never seen anything quite like it before. At the mill, he had often washed under the kitchen spigot. After she had left, he filled it with hot water that came out of a tap and slipped into it until the water was up to his chin.

What a strange day it had been. Three days ago he had left his father's house and the life he had always lived, a life that required almost nothing of him: no thought, no effort. And now here he was, in a castle filled with talking cats. And tomorrow he would start for another place, one that might be even stranger. When Blanchefleur had taunted him by telling the Lady that he had nothing to say for himself, he had wanted to say—what? Something that would have made her less disdainful. But what could he say for himself, after all?

With the piece of soap, he washed himself more carefully than he had ever before in his life. She had said that he smelled like a pigsty, and he had spent the night before last sleeping on a haystack that was, indeed, near a pen where several pigs had grunted in their dreams. Last night, he had slept in the forest, but he supposed the smell still lingered—particularly to a cat's nose. For the first time in years, he felt a sense of shame.

He dried himself and put on the clothes she had left for him. He went back down the stairs, toward the sound of music, and found his way to the great hall. It was lit with torches, and sitting at the two long tables were cats of all colors: black and brindled and tortoiseshell and piebald, with short hair and long. Sitting on the dais were the Lady, with Blanchefleur beside her, and a large yellow and brown cat who was striped like a tiger. He stood in the doorway, feeling self-conscious.

The Lady saw him across the room and motioned for him to come over. He walked to the dais and bowed before it, because that seemed the appropriate thing to do. She said, "That was courteous, nephew. Now come sit with us. Tailcatcher, you will not mind giving your seat to Ivan, will you?"

"Of course not, My Lady," said the striped cat in a tone that indicated he did indeed mind, very much.

Ivan took his place, and Marmalade brought him a dish of roast starlings, with a green sauce that smelled like catmint. It was good, although relatively flavorless. The cats, evidently, did not use salt in their cooking. Halfway through the meal, he was startled to realize that the cats were conversing with one another and nodding politely, as though they were a roomful of ordinary people. He was probably the only silent one in the entire room. Several times he noticed Blanchefleur giving him exasperated looks.

When he had finished eating, the Lady said, "I think it's time to dance." She clapped her hands, and suddenly Ivan heard music. He wondered where it was coming from, then noticed a group of cats at the far end of the room playing, more skillfully than he had supposed possible, a fife, a viol, a tabor, and other instruments he could not identify, one of which curved like a long snake. The cats that had been sitting at the long tables moved them to the sides of the room, then formed two lines in the center. He had seen a line dance before, at one of the village fairs, but he had never seen one danced as gracefully as it was by the cats. They wove in and out, each line breaking and reforming in intricate patterns.

"Aren't you going to ask your cousin to dance?" said the Lady, leaning over to him.

"What? Oh," he said, feeling foolish. How could he dance with a cat? But the Lady was looking at him, waiting. "Would you like to dance?" he asked Blanchefleur.

"Not particularly," she said, looking at him with disdain. "Oh, all right, Mother! You don't have to pull my tail."

He wiped his mouth and hands on a napkin, then followed Blanchefleur to the dance floor and joined at the end of the line, feeling large and clumsy, trying to follow the steps and not tread on any paws. It did not help that, just when he was beginning to feel as though he was learning the steps, he saw Tailcatcher glaring at him from across the room. He danced several times, once with Blanchefleur, once with Mrs. Pebbles, who must have taken pity on him, and once with Fluff, who told him that it was a pleasure to dance with such a handsome young man and seemed to mean it. He managed to step on only one set of paws, belonging to a tabby tomcat who said, "Do that again, Sir, and I'll send you my second in the morning," but was mollified when Ivan apologized sincerely and at length. After that, he insisted on sitting down until the feast was over and he could go to bed.

The next morning, he woke and wondered if it was all a dream, but no—there he was, lying in a curtained bed in the Lady's castle. And there was Blanchefleur, sitting in a nearby chair, saying, "About time you woke up. We need to get started if we're going to make the Eastern Waste by nightfall."

Ivan got out of bed, vaguely embarrassed to be seen in his nightshirt, then reminded himself that she was just a cat. He put on the clothes he had been given last night, then found his satchel on a dresser. All of his old clothes were gone, replaced by new ones. In the satchel he also found a loaf of bread, a hunk of cheese, a flask of wine, and a shiny new knife with a horn handle.

"I should thank the Lady for all these things," he said.

"That's the first sensible thing you've said since you got here," said Blanchefleur. "But she's gone to see my father, and won't be back for three days. And we have to get going. So hurry up already!"

* * *

THE LADY'S CASTLE was located in a forest called the Wolfwald. To the north, it stretched for miles, and parts of it were so thick that almost no sunlight reached the forest floor. At the foot of the northern mountains, wolves still roamed. But around the castle it was less dense. Ivan and Blanchefleur walked along a path strewn with oak leaves, through filtered sunlight. Ivan was silent, in part because he was accustomed to silence, in part because he did not know what to say to the white cat. Blanchefleur seemed much more interested in chasing insects, and even dead leaves, than in talking to him.

They stopped to rest when the sun was directly overhead. The forest had changed: the trees were shorter and spaced more widely apart, mostly pines rather than the oaks and beeches around the Lady's castle. Ahead of him, Ivan could see a different sort of landscape: bare, except for the occasional twisted trees and clumps of grass. It was dry, rocky, strewn with boulders.

"That's the Eastern Waste," said Blanchefleur.

"The ground will be too hard for your paws," said Ivan. "I can carry you."

"I'll do just fine, thank you," she said with a sniff. But after an hour of walking over the rocky ground, Ivan saw that she was limping. "Come on," he said. "If you hate the thought of me carrying you so much, pretend I'm a horse."

"A jackass is more like it," she said. But she let him pick her up and carry her, with her paws on his shoulder so she could look around. Occasionally, her whiskers tickled his ear.

The sun traveled across the sky, and hours passed, and still he walked though that rocky landscape, until his feet hurt. But he would not admit he was in pain, not with Blanchefleur perched on his shoulder. At last, after a region of low cliffs and defiles, they came to a broad plain that was nothing but stones. In the middle of the plain rose a stone tower.

"That's it," said Blanchefleur. "That's Professor Owl's home."

"Finally," said Ivan under his breath. He had been feeling as though he would fall over from sheer tiredness. He took a deep breath and started for the tower. But before he reached it, he asked the question he had been wanting to ask all day, but had not dared to. "Blanchefleur, who is your father?"

"The man who lives in the moon," she said. "Can you hurry up? I haven't had a meal since that mouse at lunch, and I'm getting hungry."

"HE'S AN OWL," said Ivan.

"Of course he's an owl," said Blanchefleur. "What did you think he would be?"

Professor Owl was in fact an owl, the largest Ivan has ever seen, with brown and white feathers. When they entered the tower, which was round and had one room on each level, with stairs curling around the outer wall, he said, "Welcome, welcome. Blanchefleur, I haven't seen you since you were a kitten.

And this must be the assistant the Lady has so graciously sent me. Welcome, boy. I hope you know how to write a good, clear hand."

"His name is Idiot," said Blanchefleur.

"My name is Ivan," said Ivan.

"Yes, yes," said Professor Owl, paying no attention to them whatsoever. "Here, then, is my life's work. The Encyclopedia."

It was an enormous book, taller than Ivan himself, resting on a large stand at the far end of the room. In the middle of the room was a wooden table, and around the circular walls were file cabinets, all the way up to the ceiling.

"It's much too heavy to open by hand—or foot," said Professor Owl. "But if you tell the Encyclopedia what you're looking for, it will open to that entry."

"Mouse," said Blanchefleur. And sure enough, as she spoke, the pages of the Encyclopedia turned as though by magic (*although it probably is magic*, thought Ivan) to a page with an entry titled *Mouse*.

"Let's see, let's see," said Professor Owl, peering at the page. "'The bright and active, although mischievous, little animal known to us by the name of Mouse and its close relative the Rat are the most familiar and also the most typical members of the Murinae, a sub-family containing about two hundred and fifty species assignable to no less than eighteen distinct genera, all of which, however, are so superficially alike that the English names rat or mouse would be fairly appropriate to any of them.' Well, that seems accurate, doesn't it?"

"Does it say how they taste?" asked Blanchefleur.

"The Encyclopedia is connected to five others," said Professor Owl, turning to Ivan. "One is in the Library of Alexandria, one in the Hagia Sophia in Constantinople, one in the Sorbonne, one in the British Museum, and one in the New York Public Library. It is the only Encyclopedia of All Knowledge, and as you can imagine, it takes all my time to keep it up to date. I've devoted my life to it. But since I've developed arthritis in my legs (and Ivan could see that indeed, the owl's legs looked more knobby than they ought to), it's been difficult for me to write my updates. So I'm grateful to the Lady for sending you. Here is where you will work." He pointed to the table with his clawed foot. On it was a large pile of paper, each page filled with scribbled notes.

"These are the notes I've made indicating what should be updated and how. If you'll look at the page on top of the pile, for instance, you'll see that the entry on Justice needs to be updated. There have been, in the last month alone, five important examples of injustice, from the imprisonment of a priest who criticized the Generalissimo to a boy who was deprived of his supper when his mother wrongly accused him of stealing a mince pie. You must add each example to the entry under Justice—Injustice—Examples. The entry itself can be found in one of the cabinets along the wall—I believe it's the twenty-sixth row from the door, eight cabinets up. Of course I can't possibly include every example of injustice—there are hundreds every hour. I only include the ones that most clearly illustrated the concept. And here are my notes on a species of wild rose newly discovered in the mountains of Cathay. That will go under Rose—Wild—Species. Do you understand, boy? You are to look at my notes and add whatever information is necessary to update the entry, writing directly on the file. The Encyclopedia itself will incorporate your update, turning it into typescript, but you must make your letters clearly. And no spelling errors! Now, it's almost nightfall, and I understand that humans have defective vision, so I suggest you sleep until dawn, when you can get up and start working on these notes as well as the ones I'll be writing overnight."

"Professor," said Blanchefleur, "we haven't had dinner."

"Dinner?" said Professor Owl. "Of course, of course. I wouldn't want you to go hungry. There are some mice and birds in the cupboard. I caught them just last night. You're certainly welcome to them."

"Human beings can't eat mice and birds," said Blanchefleur. "They have to cook their food."

"Yes, yes, of course," said Professor Owl. "An inefficient system, I must say. I believe I had—but where did I put it?" He turned around, looking perplexed, then opened the door of a closet under the stairs. He poked his head in, and then tossed out several things, so both Ivan and Blanchefleur had to dodge them. A pith helmet, a butterfly net, and a pair of red flannel underwear for what must have been a very tall man. "Yes, here it is. But you'll have to help me with it."

"It" was a large iron kettle. Ivan helped the owl pull it out of the closet and place it on the long wooden table. He looked into it, not knowing what to expect, but it was empty.

"It's a magic kettle, of course," said Professor Owl. "I seem to remember that it makes soup. You can sleep on the second floor. The third is my study, and I hope you will refrain from disturbing me during daylight hours, when I will be very busy indeed. Now, if you don't mind, I'm going out for a bit of a hunt. I do hope you will be useful to me. My last apprentice was a disappointment." He waddled comically across the floor and up the stairs.

"These scholarly types aren't much for small talk," said Blanchefleur.

"I thought he was going out?" said Ivan.

"He is," said Blanchefleur. "You don't think he's just going to walk out the door, do you? He's an owl. He's going to launch himself from one of the tower windows."

Ivan looked into the kettle again. Still empty. "Do you really think it's magic?" he asked. He had eaten the bread and cheese a long time ago, and his stomach was starting to growl.

"Try some magic words," said Blanchefleur.

"Abracadabra," he said. "Open Sesame." What other magic words had he learned in school? If he remembered correctly, magic had not been a regular part of the curriculum.

"You really are an idiot," said Blanchefleur. She sprang onto the table, then sat next to the kettle. "Dear Kettle," she said. "We've been told of your magical powers in soup-making, and are eager to taste your culinary delights. Will you please make us some soup? Any flavor, your choice, but not onion because his breath is pungent enough already."

From the bottom, the kettle filled with something that bubbled and had a delicious aroma. "There you go," said Blanchefleur. "Magical items have feelings, you know. They need to be asked nicely. Abracadabra indeed!"

"I still need a spoon," said Ivan.

"With all you require for nourishment, I wonder that you're still alive!" said Blanchefleur. "Look in the closet."

In the closet, Ivan did indeed find several wooden spoons, as well as a croquet set, several pairs of boots, and a stuffed alligator.

"Beef stew," he said, tasting what was in the kettle. "Would you like some?"

"I'm quite capable of hunting for myself, thank you," said Blanchefleur. "Don't wait up. I have a feeling that when the Professor said you should be up by dawn, he meant it."

That night, Ivan slept on the second floor of the tower, where he found a bed, a desk, and a large traveling trunk with *Oswald* carved on it. He wondered if Oswald had been the professor's last apprentice, the one who had been such a disappointment. In the middle of the night, he thought he felt Blanchefleur jump on the bed and curl up next to his back. But when he woke up in the morning, she was gone.

IVAN WAS USED to waking up at dawn, so wake up at dawn he did. He found a small bathroom under the stairs, splashed water on his face, got dressed, and went downstairs. Blanchefleur was sitting on the table, staring at the kettle still set on it, with a look of disdain on her face.

"What is that mess?" she asked.

"I think it's pea soup," he said, after looking into the kettle. It smelled inviting, but then anything would have at that hour. Next to the kettle were a wooden bowl and spoon, as well as a napkin. "Did you put these here?" he asked Blanchefleur.

"Why would I do such a stupid thing?" she asked, and turned her back to him. She began licking her fur, as though washing herself were the most important thing in the world.

Ivan shrugged, spooned some of the pea soup into the bowl, and had a plain but filling breakfast. Afterward, he washed the bowl and spoon. As soon as he had finished eating, the kettle had emptied again—evidently, it did not need washing. Then he sat down at the table and pulled the first of Professor Owl's notes toward him.

It was tedious work. First, he would read through the notes, which were written in a cramped, slanting hand. Then, he would try to add a paragraph to the file, as neatly and succinctly as he could. He had never paid much attention in school, and writing did not come easily to him. After the first botched attempt, he learned to compose his paragraphs on the backs of Professor Owl's notes, so when he went to update the entries, he was not fumbling for words. By noon, he had finished additions to the entries on Justice, Rose, Darwin, Theosophy, Venus, Armadillo, Badminton, and Indochina. His lunch was chicken soup with noodles. He thought about having nothing but soup, every morning, noon, and night for an entire year, and longed for a sandwich.

He sat down at the table and picked up the pen, but his back and hand hurt. He put the pen down. The sunlight out the window looked so inviting. Perhaps he should go out and wander around the tower, just for a little while? Where had Blanchefleur gone, anyway? He had not seen her since breakfast. He got up, stretched, and walked out.

It had been his habit, as long as he remembered, to wander around as he wished. That was what he did now, walking around the tower and then away from it, looking idly for Blanchefleur and finding only lizards. He wandered without thinking about where he was going or how long he had been gone. The sun began to sink in the west.

That was when he realized that he had been gone for hours. Well, it would not matter, would it? He could always catch up with any work he did not finish tomorrow. He walked back in the direction of the tower, only becoming lost once. It was dark when he reached it again. He opened the door and walked in.

There were Professor Owl and Blanchefleur. The Professor was perched on the table where Ivan had been sitting earlier that day, scribbling furiously. Blanchefleur was saying, "What did you expect of someone named Idiot? I told you he would be useless."

"Oh, hello, boy," said Professor Owl, looking up. "I noticed that you went out for a walk, so I finished all of the notes for today, except Orion. I'll have that done in just a moment, and then you can sit down for dinner. I don't think I told you that each day's updates need to be filed by the end of the day, or the Encyclopedia will be incomplete. And it has never been incomplete since I started working on it, five hundred years ago."

"I'll do it," said Ivan.

"Do what?" said Blanchefleur. "Go wandering around again?"

"I'll do the update on Orion."

"That's very kind of you," said Professor Owl. "I'm sure you must be tired." But he handed Ivan the pen and hopped a bit away on the table. It was a lopsided hop: Ivan could tell that the owl's right foot was hurting. He sat and finished the update, conscious of Blanchefleur's eyes on him. When he was finished, Professor Owl read it over. "Yes, very nice," he said. "You have a clear and logical mind. Well done, boy."

Ivan looked up, startled. It was the first compliment he ever remembered receiving.

"Well, go on then, have some dinner," said Professor Owl. "And you'll be up at dawn tomorrow?"

"I'll be up at dawn," said Ivan. He knew that the next day, he would not go wandering around, at least until after the entries were finished. He did not want Blanchefleur calling him an idiot again in that tone of voice.

SUMMER TURNED INTO winter. Each day, Ivan sat at the table in the tower, updating the entries for the Encyclopedia of All Knowledge. One day, he realized that he no longer needed to compose the updates on the backs of Professor Owl's notes. He could simply compose them in his head, and then write each update directly onto the file. He had not learned much in school, but he was learning now, about things that seemed useless, such as Sponge Cake, and things that seemed useful, such as Steam Engines, Epic Poetry, and Love. One morning he realized that Professor Owl had left him not only a series of updates, but also the notes for an entry on a star that had been discovered by astronomers the week before. Proudly and carefully, he took a blank file card out of the cabinet, composed a new entry for the Encyclopedia of All Knowledge, and filed the card in its place.

He came to write so well and so quickly that he would finish all of the updates, and any new entries the Professor left him, by early afternoon. After a lunch of soup, for he had never managed to get the kettle to make him anything else, however politely he asked, he would roam around the rocky countryside. Sometimes Blanchefleur would accompany him, and eventually she allowed him to carry her on his shoulder without complaining, although she was never enthusiastic. And she still called him Idiot.

One day, in February although he had lost track of the months, he updated an entry on the Trojan War. He had no idea what it was, since he had not been paying attention that day in school. So after he finished his updates, he asked the Encyclopedia. It opened to the entry on the Trojan War, which began, "It is a truth universally acknowledged that judging a beauty contest between three goddesses causes nothing but trouble." He read on, fascinated. After that day, he would spend several hours reading through whichever entries took his fancy. Each entry he read left him with more questions, and he began to wish that he could stay with Professor Owl, simply reading the entries in the Encyclopedia, forever.

But winter turned into summer, and one day the professor said, "Ivan, it has been a year since you arrived, and the term of your apprenticeship with me is at an end. Thank you for all of the care and attention you have put into your task. As a reward, I will give you one of my feathers—that one right there. Pluck it out gently. *Gently!*"

Ivan held up the feather. It was long and straight, with brown and white stripes.

"Cut the end of it with a penknife and make it into a pen," said Professor Owl. "If you ever want to access the Encyclopedia, just tell the pen what you would like to know, and it will write the entry for you."

"Thank you," said Ivan. "But couldn't I stay—"

"Of course not," said Blanchefleur. "My mother is expecting us. So come on already." And indeed, since it was dawn, Professor Owl was already heading up the stairs, for he had very important things to do during the day. Owls do, you know.

THE CASTLE IN the Forest looked just as Ivan remembered. There were cats tending the gardens, where the roses were once again blooming, as though they had never stopped. Marmalade greeted them at the door and led them to the Lady's solar, where she was sitting at a desk, writing. Her cats-in-waiting were embroidering a tapestry, and one was strumming a lute with her claws, playing a melody Ivan remembered from when he was a child.

"Well?" she said when she looked up. "How did Ivan do, my dear?"

"Well enough," said Blanchefleur. "Are there any mouse pies? We've been walking all day, and I'm hungry."

Really it had been Ivan who had been walking all day. He had carried Blanchefleur most of the way, except when she wanted to drink from a puddle or play with a leaf.

"Wait until the banquet," said the Lady. "It starts in an hour, which will give you enough time to prepare. It's in honor of your return and departure."

"Departure?" said Ivan.

"Yes," said the Lady. "Tomorrow, you will go to the Southern Marshes, to spend a year with my friend, Dame Lizard. She has a large family, and needs help taking care of it. Blanchefleur, you will accompany your cousin."

"But that's not fair!" said Blanchefleur. "I've already spent a year with Ivan Idiot. Why do I have to spend another year with him?"

"Because he is your cousin, and he needs your help," said the Lady. "Now go, the both of you. I don't think you realize quite how dirty you both are." And she was right. From the long journey, even Blanchefleur's white paws were covered with dirt.

As they walked upstairs, Ivan said, "I'm sorry you have to come with me, Blanchefleur. I know you dislike being with me."

"You're not so bad," she said grudgingly. "At least you're warm." So it had been her, sleeping against his back all those nights. Ivan was surprised and pleased at the thought.

That night, the banquet proceeded as it had the year before, except this time Ivan knew what to expect. Several of the female cats asked him to dance, and this time he danced with more skill, never once stepping on a cat paw or tail. He danced several times with Blanchefleur, and she did not seem to dislike it as much as she had last year. Tailcatcher, the striped cat, was there as well. Once, as they were dancing close to one another, Ivan heard a hiss, but when he turned to look at Tailcatcher, the cat was bowing to his partner.

At the end of the evening, as he wearily climbed the stone stairs up to his bedroom, he passed a hallway and heard a murmur of voices. At the end of the hallway stood Tailcatcher and Blanchefleur. He spoke to her and she replied, too low for Ivan to hear what they were saying. Then she turned and walked on down the hallway, her tail held high, exactly the way she walked when she was displeased with him. Ivan was rather glad that Tailcatcher had been rebuffed, whatever he had wanted from her.

As he sank into sleep that night in the curtained bed, he wondered if she would come to curl up against his back. But he fell asleep too quickly to find out.

THE NEXT MORNING, they started for the Southern Marshes. As they traveled south, the forest grew less dense: the trees were sparser, more sunlight fell on the path, and soon Ivan was hot and sweating. At midafternoon, they came to a river, and he was able to swim and cool himself off. Blanchefleur refused to go anywhere near the water.

"I'm not a fish," she said. "Are you quite done? We still have a long way to go."

Ivan splashed around a bit more, then got out and dried himself as best he could. They followed the river south until it was no longer a river but a series of creeks running through low hills covered with willows, alders, and sycamores. Around the creeks grew cattails, and where the water formed into pools, he could see waterlilies starting to bloom. They were constantly crossing water, so Ivan carried Blanchefleur, who did not like to get her paws wet.

"There," she said finally. "That's where we're going." She was pointing at one of the low hills. At first, Ivan did not see the stone house among the trees: it blended in so well with the gray trunks. Ivan walked through a narrow creek (he had long ago given up on keeping his shoes dry) and up the hill to the house. He knocked at the door.

From inside, he heard a crash, then a "Just a moment!" Then another crash and the voice yelling, "Get out of there at once, Number Seven!"

There were more crashes and bangs, and then the door opened, so abruptly that he stepped back, startled. He might have been startled anyway, because who should be standing in front of him but a lizard, who came almost up to his shoulders, in a long brown duster and a feathered hat askew over one ear.

"I'm so glad you're here!" she said. "They've been impossible today. But they are dears, really they are, and the Lady told me that you were a competent nursemaid. You are competent, aren't you?" Without waiting for a reply, she continued, "Oh, it's good to see you again, Blanchefleur. Did you like the shrunken head I sent you from Peru?"

"Not particularly," said the white cat.

"Splendid!" said the lizard. "Now I'll just be off, shall I? My train leaves in half an hour and I don't want to miss it. I'm going to Timbuktu, you know. Train and then boat and train again, then camel caravan. Doesn't that sound fun? Do help me get my suitcases on the bicycle."

The bicycle was in a sort of shed. Ivan helped her tie two suitcases onto a rack with some frayed rope that he hoped would hold all the way to the station.

"Such a handy one, your young man, my dear," said the lizard to Blanchefleur.

"He's not—" said Blanchefleur.

"Kisses to you both! Ta, and I'll see you in a year! If I survive the sands of the Sahara, of course." And then she was off on her bicycle, down a road that ran across the hills, with her hat still askew. As she rode out of sight, Ivan heard a faint cry: "Plenty of spiders, that's what they like! And don't let them stay up too late!"

"Don't let who stay up too late?" asked Ivan.

"Us!" Ivan turned around. There in the doorway stood five—no, six—no, seven lizards that came up to his knees.

"Who are you?" he asked.

"These are her children," said Blanchefleur. "You're supposed to take care of them while she's gone. Don't you know who she is? She's Emilia Lizard, the travel writer. And you're her nursemaid." Blanchefleur seemed amused at the prospect.

"But the Lady said I was supposed to help," said Ivan. "How can I help someone who's on her way to Timbuktu? I don't know anything about taking care of children—or lizards!"

"It's easy," said one of the lizards. "You just let us do anything we want!"

"Eat sweets," said another.

"Stay up late," said yet another.

"Play as long as we like," said either one who had already spoken or another one, it was difficult to tell because they kept weaving in and out of the group, and they all looked alike.

"Please stand still," he said. "You're giving me a headache. And tell me your names."

"We don't have names," said one. "Mother just calls us by numbers, but she always gets us mixed up."

"I'll have to give you names," said Ivan, although he was afraid that he would get them mixed up as well. "Let's at least go in. Blanchefleur and I are tired, and we need to rest."

But once they stepped inside, Ivan found there was no place to rest. All of the furniture in the parlor had been piled in a corner to make a fort.

"If I'm going to take care of you, I need to learn about you," said Ivan. "Let's sit down—" But there was nowhere to sit down. And the lizards, all seven of them, were no longer there. Some were already inside the fort, and the others were about to besiege it.

"Come out!" he said. "Come out, all of you!" But his voice was drowned by the din they were already making. "What in the world am I supposed to do?" he asked Blanchefleur.

She twitched her tail, then said in a low voice, "I think it's the Seige of Jerusalem." Loudly and theatrically, she said, as though to Ivan, "Yes, you're right. The French are so much better at cleaning than the Saracens. I bet the French would clean up this mess lickety split."

Ivan stared at her in astonishment. Then he smiled. "You're wrong, Blanchefleur. The Saracens have a long tradition of cleanliness. In a cleaning contest, the Saracens would certainly win."

"Would not!" said one of the besiegers. "Would too!" came a cry from the fort. And then, in what seemed like a whirlwind of lizards, the fort was disassembled, the sofa and armchairs were put back in their places, and even the cushions were fluffed. In front of Ivan stood a line of seven lizards, asking "Who won, who won?"

"The Saracens, this time," said Blanchefleur. "But really, you know, it's two out of three that counts."

Life in the Lizard household was completely different than it had been in Professor Owl's tower. There were days when Ivan missed the silence and solitude, the opportunity to read and study all day long. But he did not have much time to remember or regret. His days were spent catching insects and spiders for the lizards' breakfast, lunch, snack, and dinner, making sure that they bathed and sunned themselves, that they napped in the afternoon and went to bed on time.

At first, it was difficult to make them pay attention. They were as quick as seven winks, and on their outings they had a tendency to vanish as soon as he turned his back. Ivan was always afraid he was going to lose one. Once, indeed, he had to rescue Number Two from an eagle, and Number Five had to be pulled out of a fox hole. But he found that the hours spent working on the Encyclopedia of All Knowledge stood him in good stead: if he began telling a story, in an instant they would all be seated around him, listening intently. And if he forgot anything, he would ask the pen he had made from Professor Owl's tail feather to write it out for him. Luckily, Dame Lizard had left plenty of paper and ink.

He gave them all names: Ajax, Achilles, Hercules, Perseus, Helen, Medea, Andromache. They were fascinated by the stories of their names, and Medea insisted that she was putting spells on the others, while Hercules would try to lift the heaviest objects he could find. Ivan learned to tell them apart. One had an ear that was slightly crooked, one had a stubby tail, one swayed as she walked. Each night, when he tucked them in and counted the lizard heads— yes, seven heads lay on the pillows—he breathed a sigh of relief that they were still alive.

"How many more days?" he would ask Blanchefleur.

"You don't want to know," she would reply. And then she would go out hunting, while he made himself dinner. Of course he could not eat insects and spiders, or mice like Blanchefleur. On the first night, he looked in the pantry and found a bag of flour, a bag of sugar, some tea, and a tinned ham. He made himself tea and ate part of the tinned ham.

"What in the world shall I do for food?" he asked Blanchefleur.

"What everyone else does. Work for it," she replied. So the next day, he left the lizards in her care for a couple of hours and went into the town that lay along the road Dame Lizard had taken. It was a small town, not much larger than the village he had grown up in. There, he asked if anyone needed firewood chopped, or a field cleared, or any such work. That day, he cleaned out a pigsty. The farmer who hired him found him strong and steady, so he hired him again, to pick vegetables, paint a fence, any odd work that comes up around a farm. He recommended Ivan to others, so there was soon a steady trickle of odd jobs that brought in enough money for him to buy bread and meat. The farmer who had originally hired him gave him vegetables that were too ripe for market.

He could never be gone long, because Blanchfleur would remind him in no uncertain terms that taking care of the lizards was his task, not hers. Whenever he came back, they were clean and fed and doing something orderly, like playing board games.

"Why do they obey you, and not me?" he asked, tired and cross. He had just washed an entire family's laundry.

"Because," she answered.

After dinner, once the lizards had been put to bed, really and finally put to bed, he would sit in the parlor and read the books on the shelves, which were all about travel in distant lands. Among them were the books of Dame Emilia Lizard. They had titles like *Up the Amazon in a Steamboat* and *Across the Himalayas on a Yak.* He found them interesting—Dame Lizard was an acute observer, and he learned about countries and customs that he had not even known existed—but often he could scarcely keep his eyes open because he was so tired. Once Blanchefleur returned from her evening hunt, he would go to sleep in Dame Lizard's room. He could tell it was hers because the walls were covered with photographs of her in front of temples and pyramids, perched on yaks or camels or water buffalos, dressed in native garb. Blanchefleur would curl up against him, no longer pretending not to, and he would fall asleep to her soft rumble.

In winter, all the lizards caught bronchitis. First Andromache started coughing, and then Ajax, until there was an entire household of sick lizards. Since Ivan did not want to leave them, Blanchefleur went into town to find the doctor.

"You're lucky to have caught me," said the doctor when he arrived. "My train leaves in an hour. There's been a dragon attack, and the King has asked all the medical personnel who can be spared to help the victims. He burned an entire village, can you imagine? But I'm sure you've seen the photographs in the *Herald.*"

Ivan had not—they did not get the *Herald*, or any other newspaper, at Dame Lizard's house. He asked where the attack had occurred, and sighed with relief when told it was a fishing village on the coast. His father was not in danger.

"Nothing much I can do here anyway," said the doctor. "Bronchitis has to run its course. Give them tea with honey for the coughs, and tepid baths for the fever. And try to avoid catching it yourself!"

"A dragon attack," said Blanchefleur after the doctor had left. "We haven't had one of those in a century."

But there was little time to think of what might be happening far away. For weeks, Ivan barely slept. He told the lizards stories, took their temperature, made them tea. Once their appetites returned, he found them the juiciest worms under the snow. Slowly, one by one, they began to get better. Medea, the smallest of them and his secret favorite, was sick for longer than the rest, and one night when she was coughing badly, he held her through the night, not knowing what else to do. Sometimes, when he looked as though he might fall asleep standing up, Blanchefleur would say, "Go sleep, Ivan. I'll stay up and watch them. I am nocturnal, you know."

By the time all the lizards were well, the marsh marigolds were blooming, and irises were pushing their sword-like leaves out of the ground. The marshes were filled with the sounds of birds returning from the south: the raucous cacophony of ducks, the songs of thrushes.

Ivan had forgotten how long he had been in the marsh, so he was startled when one morning he heard the front door open and a voice call, "Hello, my dears! I'm home!" And there stood Dame Lizard, with her suitcases strapped to her bicycle, looking just as she had left a year ago, but with a fuschia scarf around her throat.

The lizards rushed around her, calling "Mother, Mother, look how we've grown! We all have names now! And we know about the Trojan War!" She had brought them a set of papier-mâché puppets and necklaces of lapis lazuli. For Blanchefleur, she had brought a hat of crimson felt that she had seen on a dancing monkey in Marakesh.

Blanchefleur said, "Thank you. You shouldn't have."

Once the presents were distributed and the lizards were eating an enormous box of Turkish Delight, she said to Ivan, "Come outside." When they were standing by the house, under the alders, she said, "Ivan, I can see you've taken good care of my children. They are happy and healthy, and that is due to your dedication. Hercules told me how you took care of Medea when she was ill. I want to give you a present too. I brought back a camel whip for you, but I want to give you something that will be of more use, since you don't have a camel. You must raise your arms, then close your eyes and stand as still as possible, no matter how startled you may be."

Ivan closed his eyes, not knowing what to expect.

And then he felt a terrible constriction around his chest, as though his ribcage were being crushed. He opened his eyes, looked down, and gasped.

There, wrapped around his chest, was what looked like a thick green rope. It was Dame Lizard's tail, which had been hidden under her skirt. For a moment, the tail tightened, and then it was no longer attached to her body. She had shed it, as lizards do. Ivan almost fell forward from the relief of being able to breathe.

"I learned that from a Swami in India," she said. "From now on, when you give pain to another, you will feel my tail tightening around you so whatever pain you give, you will also receive. That's called empathy, and the Swami said it was the most important thing anyone can have."

Ivan looked down. He could no longer see the tail, but he could feel it around him, like a band under his shirt. He did not know whether to thank her. The gift, if gift it was, had been so painful that he felt sore and bruised.

After he had said a protracted farewell to all the lizards, hugging them tightly, he and Blanchefleur walked north, along the river. He told her what Dame Lizard had done, lifting his shirt and showing her the mark he had found there, like a tattoo of a green tail around his ribcage.

"Is it truly a gift, or a curse?" he asked Blanchefleur.

"One never knows about gifts until later," said the white cat.

MARMALADE MET THEM at the front door. "I'm so sorry, Miss Blanchefleur," he said, "but your mother is not home. The King has asked her to the castle, to consult about the dragon attack. But she left you a note in the solar."

Blanchfleur read the note to Ivan.

> My dear, Ivan's third apprenticeship is with Captain Wolf in the Northern Mountains. Could you please accompany him and try to keep him from getting killed? Love, Mother

This time, there was no banquet. With the Lady gone, the castle was quiet, as though it were asleep and waiting for her return to wake back up. They ate dinner in the kitchen with Mrs. Pebbles and the ladies-in-waiting, and then went directly to bed. Blanchefleur curled up next to Ivan on the pillow, as usual. It had become their custom.

The next morning, Mrs. Pebbles gave them Ivan's satchel, with clean clothes, including some warmer ones for the mountains, and his horn-handled knife. "Take care of each other," she told them. "Those mountains aren't safe, and I don't know what the Lady is thinking, sending you to the Wolf Guard."

"What is the Wolf Guard?" Ivan asked as they walked down the garden path.

"It's part of the King's army," said Blanchfleur. "It guards the northern borders from trolls. They come down from the mountains and raid the towns. In winter, especially . . ."

"Blanchefleur!" Tailcatcher was standing in front of them. He had stepped out from behind one of the topiaries. "May I have a word with you?" He did not, however, sound as though he were asking permission. Ivan gritted his teeth. He had never spoken to Blanchefleur like that—even if he had wanted to, he would not have dared.

"Yes, and the word is no," said Blanchefleur. She walked right around him, holding her tail high, and Ivan followed her, making a wide circle around the striped cat, who looked as though he might take a swipe at Ivan's shins. He looked back, to see Tailcatcher glaring at them.

"What was that about?" asked Ivan.

"For years now, he's been assuming I would marry him, because he's the best hunter in the castle. He asked me the first time on the night before we left for Professor Owl's house, and then again before we left for Dame Lizard's. This would have been the third time."

"And you keep refusing?" asked Ivan.

"Of course," she said. "He may be the best hunter, but I'm the daughter of the Lady of the Forest and the Man in the Moon. I'm not going to marry a common cat!"

Ivan could not decide how he felt about her response. On the one hand, he was glad she had no intention of marrying Tailcatcher. On the other, wasn't he a common man?

THIS JOURNEY WAS longer and harder than the two before. Once they reached the foothills of the Northern Mountains, they were constantly going up. The air was colder. In late afternoon, Ivan put on a coat that Mrs. Pebbles had insisted on packing for him, and that he had been certain he would not need until winter.

Eventually, there were no more roads or paths, and they simply walked through the forest. Ivan started wondering whether Blanchefleur knew the way, then scolded himself. Of course she did: she was Blanchefleur.

Finally, as the sun was setting, Blanchefleur said, "We're here."

"Where?" asked Ivan. They were standing in a clearing. Around them were tall pines. Ahead of them was what looked like a sheer cliff face, rising higher than the treetops. Above it, he could see the peaks of the mountains, glowing in the light of the setting sun.

Blanchefleur jumped down from his shoulder, walked over to a boulder in the middle of the clearing, and climbed to the top. She said, "Captain, we have arrived."

Out of the shadows of the forest appeared wolves, as silently as though they were shadows themselves—Ivan could not count how many. They were all around, and he suddenly realized that he could die, here in the forest. He imagined their teeth at his throat and turned to run, then realized that he was being an idiot, giving in to an ancient instinct although he could see that

Blanchefleur was not frightened at all. She sat on the dark rock, amid the dark wolves, like a ghost.

"Greetings, Blanchefleur," said one of the wolves, distinguishable from the others because he had only one eye, and a scar running across it from his ear to his muzzle. "I hear that your mother has sent us a new recruit."

"For a year," said Blanchefleur. "Try not to get him killed."

"I make no promises," said the wolf. "What is his name?"

"Ivan," said Blanchefleur.

"Come here, recruit." Ivan walked to the boulder and stood in front of the wolf, as still as he could. He did not want Blanchefleur to see that he was afraid. "You shall call me Captain, and I shall call you Private, and as long as you do exactly as you are told, all shall be well between us. Do you understand?"

"Yes," said Ivan.

The wolf bared his teeth and growled.

"Yes, Captain," said Ivan.

"Good. This is your Company, although we like to think of ourselves as a pack. You are a member of the Wolf Guard, and should be prepared to die for your brothers and sisters of the pack, as they are prepared to die for you. Now come inside."

Ivan wondered where inside might be, but the Captain loped toward the cliff face and vanished behind an outcropping. One by one, the wolves followed him, some stopping to give Ivan a brief sniff. Ivan followed them and realized that the cliff was not sheer after all. Behind a protruding rock was a narrow opening, just large enough for a wolf. He crawled through it and emerged in a large cave. Scattered around the cave, wolves were sitting or lying in groups, speaking together in low voices. They looked up when he entered, but were too polite or uninterested to stare and went back to their conversations, which seemed to be about troll raiding parties they had encountered, wounds they had sustained, and the weather.

"Have you ever fought?" the Captain asked him.

"No, sir," said Ivan.

"That is bad," said the Captain. "Can you move through the forest silently? Can you tell your direction from the sun in the day and the stars at night? Can you sound like an owl to give warning without divulging your presence?"

"Yes, Captain," said Ivan, fairly certain that he could still do those things. And to prove it to himself, he hooted, first like a Eagle Owl, then like a Barn Owl, and finally like one of the Little Owls that used to nest in his father's mill.

"Well, that's something, at least. You can be one of our scouts. Have you eaten?"

"No, sir," said Ivan.

"At the back of the cave are the rabbits we caught this morning," said the Captain. "You may have one of those."

"He is human," said Blanchefleur. "He must cook his food."

"A nuisance, but you may build a small fire, although you will have to collect wood. These caverns extend into the mountain for several miles. Make certain the smoke goes back into the mountain, and not through the entrance."

Skinning a rabbit was messy work, but Ivan butchered it, giving a leg to Blanchefleur and roasting the rest for himself on a stick he sharpened with his knife. It was better than he had expected. That night, he slept beneath his coat on the floor of the cave, surrounded by wolves. He was grateful to have Blanchefleur curled up next to his chest.

The next morning, he began his life in the Wolf Guard.

As a scout, his duty was not to engage the trolls, but to look for signs of them. He would go out with a wolf partner, moving through the forest silently, looking for signs of troll activity: their camps, their tracks, their spoor. The Wolf Guard kept detailed information on the trolls who lived in the mountains. In summer, they seldom came down far enough to threaten the villages on the slopes. But in winter, they would send raiding parties for all the things they could not produce themselves: bread and cheese and beer, fabrics and jewels, sometimes even children they could raise as their own, for troll women do not bear many children. Ivan learned the forest quickly, just as he had at home, and the wolves in his Company, who had initially been politely contemptuous of a human in their midst, came to think of him as a useful member of the pack. He could not smell as well as they could, nor see as well at night, but he could climb trees, and pull splinters out of their paws, and soon he was as good at tracking the trolls as they were. They were always respectful to Blanchefleur. One day, he asked her what she did while he was out with the wolves. "Mind my own business," she said. So he did not ask again.

As for Ivan, being a scout in the Wolf Guard was like finding a home. He had learned so much in Professor Owl's tower, and he had come to love the lizards in his charge, but with the wolves he was back in the forest, where he had spent his childhood. And the wolves themselves were like a family. When Graypaw or Mist, with whom he was most often paired, praised his ability to spot troll tracks, or when the Captain said "Well done, Private," he felt a pride that he had never felt before.

"You know, I don't think I've ever seen you so happy," said Blanchefleur, one winter morning. The snows had come, and he was grateful for the hat and gloves that Mrs. Pebbles had included in his satchel.

"I don't think I ever have been, before," he said. "Not since—" Since his mother had died. Since then, he had always been alone. But now he had a pack. "I think I could stay here for the rest of my life."

"We seldom get what we want," said Blanchefleur. "The world has a use for us, tasks we must fulfill. And we must fulfill them as best we can, finding happiness along the way. But we usually get what we need."

"I've never heard you so solemn before," said Ivan. "You're starting to sound like your mother. But I don't think the world has any tasks for me. I'm no one special, after all."

"Don't be so sure, Ivan Miller," said Blanchefleur.

Suddenly, all the wolves in the cave pricked up their ears.

"The signal!" said the Captain.

And then Ivan heard it too, the long howl that signaled a troll raid, the short howls that indicated which village was being attacked.

"To the village!" shouted the Captain.

"Be careful!" said Blanchefleur, as Ivan sprang up, made sure his knife was in his belt, and ran out of the cave with the wolves. Then they were coursing through the forest, silent shadows against the snow.

They saw the flames and heard the screams before they saw any trolls. The village was a small one, just a group of herding families on the upper slopes. Their houses were simple, made of stone, with turf roofs. But the sheds were of wood, filled with fodder for the sturdy mountain sheep. The trolls had set fire to the fodder, and some of the sheds were burning. The sheep were bleating terribly, and as wolves rushed into the village, the Captain shouted to Ivan, "Open the pens! Let the sheep out—we can herd them back later."

Ivan ran from pen to pen, opening all the gates. Mist ran beside him and if any sheep were reluctant to leave their pens, she herded them out, nipping at their heels.

When they reached the last of the pens, Ivan saw his first troll. She was taller than the tallest man, and twice as large around. She looked like a piece of the mountain that had grown arms and legs. Her mottled skin was gray and green and brown, and she was covered in animal pelts. In her hand, she carried a large club. In front of her, crouched and growling, was Graypaw.

"Come on, cub!" she sneered "I'll teach you how to sit and lie down!"

She lunged at Graypaw, swinging the club clumsily but effectively. The club hit a panicked ram that had been standing behind her, and the next moment, the ram lay dead on the snow.

Mist yipped to let Graypaw know she was behind him. He barked back, and the wolves circled the troll in opposite directions, one attacking from the left and the other from the right.

What could Ivan do? He drew his knife, but that would be no more effective against a troll than a sewing needle. To his right, one of the sheds was on fire, pieces of it falling to the ground as it burned. As Graypaw and Mist circled, keeping away from the club, trying to get under it and bite the troll's ankles, Ivan ran into the burning shed. He wrenched a piece of wood from what had been a gate, but was now in flames, then thrust its end into the fire. The flames licked it, and it caught. A long stick, its end on fire. This was a weapon of sorts, but how was he to use it?

Graypaw and Mist were still circling, and one of them had succeeded in wounding the troll—there was green ichor running down her leg. The troll was paying no attention to Ivan—she was wholly absorbed in fending off the wolves. But the wolves knew he was behind them. They were watching him out of the corners of their eyes, waiting. For what?

Then Ivan gave a short bark, the signal for attack. Both Graypaw and Mist flew at the troll simultaneously. The troll swung about wildly, not certain which to dispatch first. *Now*, thought Ivan, and he lunged forward, not caring that he could be hit by the club, only knowing this was the moment, that he had put his packmates in danger for this opportunity. He thrust the flaming stick toward the troll's face. The troll shrieked—it had gone straight into her left eye. She clutched the eye and fell backward. Without thinking, Ivan drew his knife and plunged it into the troll's heart, or where he thought her heart might be.

A searing pain ran through his chest. It was Dame Lizard's tail, tightening until he could no longer breathe. It loosened again, but he reeled with the shock and pain of it.

"Ivan, are you well?" asked Mist.

"I'm—all right," he said, still breathless. "I'm going to be all right." But he felt sick.

The troll lay on the ground, green ichor spreading across her chest. She was dead. Behind her was a large sack.

"That must be what she was stealing," said Graypaw.

The sack started to wriggle.

"A sheep, perhaps," said Mist.

But when Ivan untied it, he saw a dirty, frightened face, with large gray eyes. A girl.

"You've found my daughter!" A woman was running toward them. With her was the Captain.

"Nadia, my Nadia," she cried.

"Mama!" cried the girl, and scrambling out of the bag, she ran into her mother's arms.

"This is the Mayor of the village," said the Captain. "Most of the trolls have fled, and we were afraid they had taken the girl with them."

"I can't thank you enough," said the woman. "You've done more than rescue my daughter, although that has earned you my gratitude. I recognize this troll—she has been here before. We call her Old Mossy. She is the leader of this tribe, and without her, the tribe will need to choose a new leader by combat. It will not come again this winter. Our village has sustained great damage, but not one of us has died or disappeared, and we can rebuild. How can we reward you for coming to our rescue, Captain?"

"Madame Mayor, we are the Wolf Guard. Your gratitude is our reward," said the Captain.

ON THE WAY back to the cave, Graypaw and Mist walked ahead of Ivan, talking to the Captain in low voices. He wondered if he had done something wrong. Perhaps he should not have told them to attack? After all, they both outranked him. They were both Corporals, while he was only a Private. Perhaps they were telling the Captain about how he had reeled and clutched his chest after the attack. Would he be declared unfit for combat?

When they got back to the cave, Blanchefleur was waiting for him.

"Ivan, I need to speak with you," she said.

"Blanchefleur, I killed a troll! I mean, I helped kill her. I want to tell you about it . . ."

"That's wonderful, Ivan. I'm very proud of you. I am, you know, and not just because of the troll. But it's time for us to leave."

"What do you mean? It's still winter. I haven't been here for a year yet."

"My mother has summoned us. Here is her messenger."

It was Tailcatcher. In his excitement, Ivan had not noticed the striped cat.

"The Lady wishes you to travel to the capital. Immediately," said Tailcatcher.

"But why?" asked Ivan.

"You are summoned," said Tailcatcher, contemptuously. "Is that not enough?"

"If you are summoned, you must go," said the Captain, who had been standing behind him. "But come back to us when you can, Ivan."

Ivan had never felt so miserable in his life. "Can I say goodbye to Mist and Graypaw?"

"Yes, quickly," said the Captain. "And thank them, because on their recommendation, I am promoting you to Corporal. There is also something I wish to give you. Hold out your right hand, Corporal Miller."

Ivan held out his hand.

The Captain lunged at him, seized Ivan's hand in his great mouth, and bit down.

Ivan cried out.

The Captain released him. The wolf's teeth had not broken his skin, but one of his fangs had pierced Ivan's hand between the thumb and forefinger. It was still lodged in his flesh. There was no blood, and as Ivan watched, the fang vanished, leaving only a white fang-shaped scar.

"Why—" he asked.

"That is my gift to you, Corporal. When I was a young corporal like yourself, I saved the life of a witch. In return, she charmed that fang for me. She told me that as long as I had it, whenever I fought, I would defeat my enemy. She also told me that one day, I could pass the charm to another. I asked her how, and she told me I would know when the time came. I am old, Ivan, and this is my last winter with the Wolf Guard. I believe I know why you have been summoned by the Lady. With that charm, whatever battles you have to fight, you should win. Now go. There is a storm coming, and you should be off the mountain before it arrives."

Ivan packed his belongings and made his farewells. Then, he left the cave, following Tailcatcher and Blanchefleur. He looked back once, with tears in his eyes, and felt as though his heart were breaking.

* * *

THE JOURNEY TO the capital would have taken several days, but in the first town they came to, Ivan traded his knife and coat for a horse. It was an old farm horse, but it went faster than he could have on foot with two cats. The cats sat in panniers that had once held potatoes, and Tailcatcher looked very cross indeed. When Ivan asked again why he had been summoned, the cat replied, "That's for the Lady to say," and would say nothing more.

They spent the night in a barn and arrived at the capital the next day.

Ivan had never seen a city so large. The houses had as many as three stories, and there were shops for everything, from ladies' hats and fancy meats to bicycles. On one street he even saw a shiny new motorcar. But where were the people? The shops were closed, the houses shuttered, and the streets empty. Once, he saw a frightened face peering at him out of an alley, before it disappeared into the shadows.

"What happened here?" he asked.

"You'll know soon enough," said Tailcather. "That's where we're going."

"That" was the palace.

Ivan had never seen a building so large. His father's mill could have fit into one of its towers. With a sense of unease, he rode up to the gates.

"State your business!" said a guard who had been crouching in the gatehouse and stood up only long enough to challenge them.

Ivan was about to reply when Blanchefleur poked her head out of the pannier. "I am Blanchefleur. My mother is the Lady of the Forest, and our business is our own."

"You may pass, My Lady," said the guard, hurriedly opening the gates and then hiding again.

They rode up the long avenue, through the palace gardens, which were magnificent, although Ivan thought they were not as interesting as the Lady's gardens with their cat gardeners. They left the horse with an ostler who met them at the palace steps, then hurried off toward the stables. At the top of the steps, they were met by a majordomo who said, "This way, this way." He reminded Ivan of Marmalade.

They followed the majordomo down long hallways with crimson carpets and paintings on the walls in gilded frames. At last, they came to a pair of gilded doors, which opened into the throne room. There was the King, seated on his throne. Ivan could tell he was the King because he wore a crown. To one side of him sat the Lady. To the other sat a girl about Ivan's age, also wearing a crown, and with a scowl on her face. Before the dais stood two men.

"Ivan," said the Lady, "I'm so pleased to see you. I'm afraid we have a problem on our hands. About a year ago, a dragon arrived on the coast. At first, he only attacked the ports and coastal villages, and then only occasionally. I believe he is a young dragon, and lacked confidence in his abilities. But several months ago, he started flying inland, attacking market towns. Last week, he was spotted in the skies over the capital, and several days ago, he landed on the central bank. That's where he is now, holed up in the vault. Dragons like gold, as you know. The King has asked for a dragon slayer, and I'm hoping you'll volunteer."

"What?" said Ivan. "The King has asked for a what?"

"Yes, young man," said the King, looking annoyed that the Lady had spoken first. "We've already tried to send the municipal police after him, only to have the municipal police eaten. The militias were not able to stop him in the towns, but I thought that a trained police force—well, that's neither here nor there. The Lady tells me that a dragon must be slain in the old-fashioned way. I'm a progressive man myself—this entire city should be wired for electricity by next year, assuming it's not destroyed by the dragon. But with a dragon sitting on the monetary supply, I'm willing to try anything. So we've made the usual offer: the hand of my daughter in marriage and the kingdom after I retire, which should be in about a decade, barring ill health. We already have two brave volunteers, Sir Albert Anglethorpe and Oswald the—what did you say it was? the Omnipotent."

Sir Albert, a stocky man with a shock of blonde hair, bowed. He was wearing a suit of armor and looked as though he exercised regularly with kettlebells. Oswald the Omnipotent, a tall, thin, pimply man in a ratty robe, said "How de do."

"And you are?" said the King.

"Corporal Miller," said Ivan. "And I have no idea how to slay a dragon."

"Honesty! I like honesty," said the King. "None of us do either. But you'll figure it out, won't you, Corporal Miller? Because the dragon really must be slain, and I'm at my wits' end. The city evacuated, no money to pay the military—we won't be a proper kingdom if this keeps up."

"I have every confidence in you, Ivan," said the Lady.

"Me too," said Blanchefleur.

Startled, Ivan looked down at the white cat. "May I have something to eat before I go, um, dragon-slaying?" he asked. "We've been traveling all morning."

"Of course," said the King. "Anything you want, my boy. Ask and it will be yours."

"Well then," said Ivan, "I'd like some paper and ink."

Sir Albert had insisted on being fully armed, so he wore a suit of armor and carried a sword and shield. Oswald was still in his ratty robe and carried what he said was a magic wand.

"A witch sold it to me," he told Ivan. "It can transform anything it touches into anything else. She told me it had two transformations left in it. I used the first one to turn a rock into a sack of gold, but I lost the gold in a card game. So when I heard about this dragon, I figured I would use the second transformation to turn him into—I don't know, maybe a frog? And then, I'll be king. They give you all the gold you want, when you're king."

"What about the princess?" asked Ivan.

"Oh, she's pretty enough. Although she looks bad-tempered."

"And do you want to be king too?" Ivan asked Sir Albert.

"What? I don't care about that," he said through the visor of his helmet. "It's the dragon I'm after. I've been the King's champion three years running. I can out-joust and out-fight any man in the kingdom. But can I slay a dragon, eh? That's what I want to know." He bent his arms as though he were flexing his biceps, although they were hidden by his armor.

Ivan had not put on armor, but he had asked for a bow and a quiver of arrows. They seemed inadequate, compared with a sword and a magic wand.

The dragon may have been young, but he was not small. Ivan, Oswald, and Sir Alfred stood in front of the bank building, looking at the damage he had caused. There was a large hole in the side of the building where he had smashed through the stone wall, directly into the vault.

"As the King's champion, I insist that I be allowed to fight the dragon first," said Sir Albert. "Also, I outrank both of you."

"Fine by me," said Oswald.

"All right," said Ivan.

Sir Albert clanked up the front steps and through the main entrance. They heard a roar, and then a crash, as though a file cabinet had fallen over, and then nothing.

After fifteen minutes, Oswald asked, "So how big do you think this dragon is, anyway?"

"About as big as the hole in the side of the building," said Ivan.

"See, the reason I'm asking," said Oswald, "is that the wand has to actually touch whatever I want to transform. Am I going to be able to touch the dragon without being eaten?"

"Probably not," said Ivan. "They breathe fire, you know."

"What about when they're sleeping?" asked Oswald.

"Dragons are very light sleepers," said Ivan. "He would smell you before you got close enough."

"How do you know?"

"It's in the Encyclopedia of All Knowledge."

"Oh, that thing," said Oswald. "You know, I worked on that for a while. Worst job I ever had. The pay was terrible, and I had to eat soup for every meal."

Another half hour passed.

"I don't think Sir Albert is coming out," said Ivan. "You volunteered before me. Would you like to go next?"

"You know, I'm not so sure about going in after all," said Oswald. "I can't very well rule a kingdom if I'm eaten, can I?"

"That might be difficult," said Ivan.

"You go ahead," said Oswald, starting to back away. "I think I'm going to turn another rock into gold coins. That seems like a better idea."

He turned and ran up the street, leaving Ivan alone in front of the bank. Ivan sighed. Well, there was no reason to wait any longer. He might as well go in now.

Instead of going in by the front door, he went in through the hole that the dragon had made in the side of the bank. He walked noiselessly, as he had done in the forest. It was easy to find the dragon: he was lying on a pile of gold coins in the great stone room that had once been the vault. Near the door of the vault, which had been smashed open, Ivan could see a suit of armor and a sword, blackened by flames. He did not want to think about what had happened to Sir Albert.

An arrow would not penetrate the dragon's hide. He knew that, because while he had been eating at the palace, he had asked Professor Owl's tail feather to write out the entire Encyclopedia entry on dragons. He had a plan, and would get only one chance to carry it out. It would depend as much on luck as skill.

But even if it worked, he knew how it would feel, slaying a dragon. He remembered how it had felt, killing the troll. Could he survive the pain? Was there any way to avoid it? He had to try.

He stood in a narrow hallway off the vault. Keeping back in the shadows, he called, "Dragon!"

The dragon lifted his head. "Another dragon slayer? How considerate of the King to send me dessert! Dragon slayer is my favorite delicacy, although the policemen were delicious. I much preferred them to farmers, who taste like dirt and leave grit between your teeth, or fishermen, who are too salty."

"Dragon, you could fly north to the mountains. There are plenty of sheep to eat there."

"Sheep!" said the dragon. "Sheep are dull and stringy compared to the delicious men I've eaten here. Just the other day, I ate a fat baker. He tasted of sugar and cinnamon. There are plenty of teachers and accountants to eat in this city. Why, I might eat the Princess herself! I hear princess is even better than dragon slayer."

The dragon swung his head around, as though trying to locate Ivan. "But you don't smell like a man, dragon slayer," said the dragon. "What are you, and are you good to eat?"

I must still smell like the wolves, thought Ivan.

He stepped out from the hallway and into the vault. "I'm an Enigma, and I'm delicious."

The dragon swung toward the sound of his voice. As his great head came around, Ivan raised his bow and shot an arrow straight up into the dragon's eye.

The dragon screamed in pain and let out a long, fiery breath. He swung his head to and fro. Ivan aimed again, but the dragon was swinging his head too wildly: a second arrow would never hit its mark. Well, now he would find out if the Captain's charm worked. He ran across the floor of the vault, ignoring the dragon's flames, and picked up Sir Albert's sword. It was still warm, but had cooled down enough for him to raise it.

The pain had begun the moment the arrow entered the dragon's eye, but he tried not to pay attention. He did not want to think about how bad it would get. Where was the dragon's neck? It was still swinging wildly, but he brought the sword down just as it swung back toward him. The sword severed the dragon's neck cleanly in two, and his head rolled over the floor.

Ivan screamed from the pain and collapsed. He lay next to the dragon's head, with his eyes closed, unable to rise. Then, he felt something rough and wet on his cheek. He opened his eyes. Blanchefleur was licking him.

"Blanchefleur," he said weakly. "What are you doing here?"

"I followed you, of course," she said.

"But I never saw you."

"Of course not." She sat on the floor next to him as he slowly sat up. "Excellent shot, by the way. They'll call you Ivan Dragonslayer now, you know."

"Oh, I hope not," he said.

"It's inevitable."

THE KING MET him with an embrace that made Ivan uncomfortable. "Welcome home, Ivan Dragonslayer! I shall have my attorney draw up the papers to make you my heir, and here of course is my lovely Alethea, who will become your bride. A royal wedding will attract tourists to the city, which will help with the rebuilding effort."

Princess Alethea crossed her arms and looked out the window. Even from the back, she seemed angry.

"Forgive me, Your Majesty," said Ivan, "but I have no wish to marry the Princess, and I don't think she wants to marry me either. We don't even know each other."

Princess Alethea turned and looked at him in astonishment. "Thank you!" she said. "You're the first person who's made any sense all day. I'm glad you slayed the dragon, but I don't see what that has to do with getting my hand in marriage. I'm not some sort of prize at a village fair."

"And I would not deprive you of a kingdom," said Ivan. "I have no wish to be king."

"Oh, goodness," said Alethea, "neither do I! Ruling is deadly dull. You can have the kingdom and do what you like with it. I'm going to university, to become an astronomer. I've wanted to be an astronomer since I was twelve."

"But . . ." said the King.

"Well then, it's decided, " said the Lady. "Ivan, you'll spend the rest of your apprenticeship here, in the palace, learning matters of state."

"But I want to go back to the wolves," said Ivan. He saw the look on the Lady's face: she was about to say no. He added, hurriedly, "If I can go back, just for the rest of my apprenticeship, I'll come back here and stay as long as you like, learning to be king. I promise."

"All right," said the Lady.

He nodded, gratefully. At least he would have spring in the mountains, with his pack.

IVAN AND BLANCHEFLEUR rode north, not on a farm horse this time, but on a mare from the King's stables. As night fell, they stopped by a stream. The mountains were ahead of them, glowing in the evening light.

"You know, before we left, Tailcatcher asked me again," said Blanchefleur. "He thought that my time with you was done, that I would go back to the Castle in the Forest with my mother. I could have."

"Why didn't you?" asked Ivan.

"Why did you refuse the hand of the Princess Alethea? She was attractive enough."

"Because I didn't want to spend the rest of my life with her," said Ivan. "I want to spend it with you, Blanchefleur."

"Even though I'm a cat?"

"Even though."

She looked at him for a moment, then said, "I'm not always a cat, you know." Suddenly, sitting beside him was a girl with short white hair, wearing a white fur jacket and trousers. She had Blanchefleur's eyes.

"Are you—are you Blanchefleur?" he asked. He stared at her. She was and she was not the white cat.

"Of course I am, idiot," she said. "I think you're going to make a good king. You'll have all the knowledge in the world to guide you, and any pain you cause, you'll have to feel yourself, so you'll be fair and kind. But you'll win all your battles. You'll hate it most of the time and wish you were back with the wolves or in Professor Owl's tower, or even taking care of the lizards. That's why you'll be good."

"And you'll stay with me?" he asked, tentatively reaching over and taking her hand.

"Of course," she said. "Who else is going to take care of you, Ivan?"

Together, they sat and watched the brightness fade from the mountain peaks and night fall over the Wolfwald. When Ivan lay down to sleep, he felt the white cat curl up next to his chest. He smiled into the darkness before slipping away into dreams.

Rapunzel

When she learns her history, when she is told
by the vindictive witch that her mother sold
her for a mess of rampions,

she will cut off her hair, the long gold strands
lying in her hands, effective locking herself
into the tower, alone,

wanting no supernatural chaperone,
no prince to rescue her, wanting nothing
except her own mother,

the one thing she cannot have. Rapunzel will sit
with her shorn hair on a chair at the center of the room,
head bowed in mourning.

The birds will bring her food, she will drink the rain,
the wind in the trees will sing to her again,
but who will comb her hair

until it grows once more in a golden tangle,
long enough to reach the ground, so the girl
can escape her grief and pain?

The Sorceress in the Tower

You're speaking to me, and you don't know, you can't see,
that I'm very far away. Deep in the forest
there is a tower surrounded by a high wall,
and in that tower lives a sorceress. That's who I am.

Within that tower hang tapestries with scenes
of a hunt in which the unicorn spears the hunter,
who has been betrayed by the maiden he was trusting
to catch the magical beast, his intended quarry.
The walls in the library are lined with bookshelves
of rich old oak, filled with books in leather bindings,
some handwritten, some printed, with the titles
stamped in gilt on their spines.

At the top of the tower there is a room with windows
that look out over the surrounding countryside.
Under one is a desk, with a pen and inkwell
that never runs dry. That's where she sits and writes
her spells, and also general correspondence.
The room contains a bed shaped like a swan,
a wardrobe filled with the sorts of dresses a sorceress
would wear, whether she wants to go to a ball
and cast a curse on the prince, or attend a convention
of sorceresses (they meet semi-annually),
or sit at home on Sunday, randomly
doing magic. On one of her bedroom walls hangs a mirror
that will reveal any scene in the past or present
if asked politely (there is an etiquette
in talking to magic mirrors. They're most particular.)

Downstairs are the library filled with books
and a kitchen in which she often eats her breakfast.
It contains an oven that can bake anything
from brownies to an elaborate chocolate cake,
a kettle that is perpetually filled with soup,
French onion, cream of mushroom, tomato bisque,

an icebox that never melts and is never empty,
a pantry that's always stocked. In the kitchen closet
hang a broom that sweeps, a dustpan that carries dust
to the compost heap. Everything runs on magic.
The skillet fries up eggs, and after lunch,
the dishes wash themselves.

Outside the tower, within the surrounding wall,
there is an orchard of fruit trees: apples, pears,
peaches, even cherries and apricots
if the frost doesn't get them, as well as raspberry bushes.
By the kitchen door, an herb garden grows in knots,
both ornamental and fragrant. Vegetables
flourish in rows: tomatoes, aubergines,
cabbages, peas, the various kinds of squash.
In June, the rose arbor will be a riot
of albas and gallicas, damasks and mosses.
On summer mornings, she likes to clip the roses
and bring them inside, put a vase on the library table
so the entire tower is filled with their perfume,
from the kitchen to her bedroom.

The sorceress lives in that tower alone, except
for a cat—who owns whom has not been determined.
They argue, mostly about philosophical subjects.
And an owl who lives in the attic. And the toad
at the bottom of the garden. Sometimes Grimalkin
(the cat) tells her she needs to get out more often,
but sorceresses are generally introverts.
Anyway, she has plenty of company:
the maiden in the tapestry likes to talk,
as does the mirror, when it's in the mood,
and she has her library. Of course the trees
converse with her as she walks through the forest.
The birds call down to ask how she is doing
and the winds greet her by name. So maybe alone
isn't quite the right word.

"Can you pass the salt?" you ask, and I look up, startled,
because it's such a long way back from my tower
to this table, so far to return. Fortunately,
the sorceress also owns a pair of shoes
that can carry her anywhere in an instant. Now,
what were you saying?

Fair Ladies

W hen Rudolf Arnheim heard what his father had done, he kicked the leg of a table that his mother had brought to Malo as part of her dowery. It had been in her family for two hundred years, and had once stood in the palace of King Radomir IV of Sylvania. The leg broke and the table top fell, scattering bits of inlaid wood and ivory over the stone floor.

"Damn!" he said. And then, "Damn him!" as though trying to assign blame elsewhere, although he knew well enough what his mother would say, both about her table and about his father's decision.

"WHAT ARE YOU going to do?" asked Karl, when the three of them were sitting in leather armchairs in the Café Krona.

Rudolf, who was almost but not quite drunk, said, "I'll refuse to see her."

"You'll refuse to obey your father's orders?" said Gustav.

They had been at the university together. Gustav Malev had come to the city from the forests near Gretz. His father's father had been a farmer who, by hoarding his wealth, had purchased enough land to marry the daughter of a local brewer and send his son to the university. The brewing operation had flourished; glasses of dark, bitter Malev beer were drunk from the Caucasus to the Adriatic. Gustav, two generations removed from tilling the soil, still looked like the farmer his grandfather had been. He was large and slow, with red hair that stood up on his head like a boar-bristle brush. In contrast, Karl Reiner was small, thin, with black hair that hung down to his shoulders in the latest Aesthetic fashion. He knew the best places to drink absinthe in Karelstad. His father was a government official, like his father and his father's father before him. Most likely, Karl would be a government official as well.

Rudolf looked at his friends affectionately. How he liked Karl and Gustav! Of course, he would not want to be either of them. "I may not have Karl's brains," he thought, "but I would not be such a weasly-looking fellow for all the prizes and honors of the university," none of which, incidentally, had come to Rudolf. "And while Gustav is as rich as Croesus, and a very good sort of fellow to boot, what was his grandfather?" And he remembered with pride that his grandfather had been a Baron, as his father was a Baron. His father, the Baron. He could not understand his father's preposterous—preposterous—he could not remember the word. Yes, Gustav and Karl were his best friends.

He stood up and stumbled, almost falling on Karl. "Really, you know, I think I'm going to throw up."

Karl paid the bill, while Gustav held him under the arms as they wound their way around the small tables to the front entrance.

"The Pearl," said Karl later, when they were sitting in their rooms. They shared an apartment near the university, on Ordony Street. "I wonder what she's like, after all these years. No one has seen her since before the war. She must be forty, at least."

Rudolf put his head in his hands. He had thrown up twice on his way home, and his head ached.

"Surely your father won't expect you to—take her as a mistress," said Gustav, with the delicacy of a country boy. He still blushed when the women on the street corners called and whistled to him.

"I don't know what he expects," said Rudolf, although his father had made it relatively clear.

"As far as I can tell, Rudi, your entire university education has been a waste of money," his father had said. Rudolf hated to be called Rudi. His father was sitting behind a large mahogany desk and he was standing in front of it, which put him, he felt, in a particularly disadvantageous position. "You have shown absolutely no intellectual aptitude, and no preference for any profession other than that of drunkard. You have made no valuable connections. And now I hear that you have formed a liaison with a young woman who works in a hat shop. You will argue that you are only acting like the men with whom you associate," although Rudolf had been about to do nothing of the sort. "Well, they can afford to waste their time drinking and forming inappropriate alliances. Karl Reiner has already been promised a position at the Ministry of Justice, and Gustav Malev will return home to work in his family's business. But we are not rich, although our family is as old as Sylvania, and on your mother's side descended from King Radomir IV himself." Rudolf thought of all the things he would rather do than listen once again to the history of his family, including being branded with a hot iron and drowned in a horse pond. "I have paid for what has proven to be a very expensive university education, in part because of the dissolute life you have led with your friends. You sicken me—you and your generation. You don't understand the sacrifices we made. When I was in the trenches, all I could think of was Malo, how I was fighting for her and for Sylvania. However, now that you have completed your studies, I expect you to take your place in society. Your future, and the future of Malo, depends on the position you obtain, and on whom you marry. You will immediately give up any relationship you have with this young woman." And then his father had told him about The Pearl.

"I will pay for her apartment and expenses. It will be a heavy burden on my purse, but you must be taken in hand. You must be made to attend to your responsibilities. I would do it myself, but I cannot leave Malo until I know how the wheat is performing. If you paid any attention, you would know how precarious a position we are in, how important it is that you begin to consider more than yourself. She will introduce you to the men you need to know to advance your career, and keep you from forming any unfortunate ties."

The Pearl. She had been one of what a Sylvanian writer of the previous generation had referred to as the *grandes coquettes*, mistresses of great men who had moved through society almost as easily as respectable women because of their beauty and wit. She had been called The Pearl because she had shone so brightly, first in the theater and then in the social world of Karelstad, when Rudolf was still learning to toddle on his nurse's strings. She had been famous for her luminescent beauty, adored by the leading noblemen and government officials of her day and tolerated by their wives. Until, one day, she had disappeared.

Rudolf's relationship with Kati, who did indeed work in a hat shop, was less serious than his father suspected. She had allowed him to go so far and no further, in the hope that someday she would be offered a more legitimate role, and become a Baroness. He would have been eager, if somewhat apprehensive, at the thought of having an official, paid mistress. But not one who must be at least twice his age, and certainly not one chosen by his father.

"How in the world did your father find her?" asked Gustav, but Rudolf had no idea.

THEY HAD BEEN walking for at least an hour, farther and farther away from what Rudolf called civilization, meaning Dobromir, the town closest to Malo, the estate that had been in his father's family for generations. When the roads had ended, they had walked on paths marked by cartwheels, and finally over fields where there were no paths. Now they stopped at the edge of a wood. Rudolf looked down with distaste at the mud on his boots.

"There," said his father.

Rudolf looked up and saw a cottage built of stone, like the cottages of farm laborers but without their neat orderliness or the geraniums that always seemed to grow in pots on their windowsills. This cottage seemed almost deserted, with moss growing on the stones and over the thatched roof. It was surrounded by what was probably supposed to be a garden, but was overrun by weeds, and although it was late summer, the apples on the ancient apple trees by the fence were small and hard. In the garden, a woman was working with a spade. As they approached, she stood up and looked at them. She had a straw hat on her head.

"Wait here," said his father. He opened a gate that was leaning on its hinges and walked into the garden. When he reached the woman, he bowed. Rudolf was astonished. Who, in this godforsaken place, would his father bow to?

Rudolf heard them speaking in low voices. To pass the time, he tried to wipe the mud off his boots on the grass.

His father and the woman both turned and looked at him. Then, his father walked back to where Rudolf stood waiting. "Come," he said, "and keep your mouth shut. I don't want her to think that my son is a fool."

She looked thin, almost malnourished, in a dress that was too large for her and had faded from too many washings. When she lifted her head to look at him and Rudolf could see under the brim of her hat, he saw that her skin was freckled by the sun, with lines at the corners of the eyes and mouth. Her eyes were a strange, light green, almost gray, and they stared at him until he felt compelled to look down. Despite the sunlight in the clearing, he shivered.

"This is your son," she said. "He looks like you, twenty years ago."

"It would, as I have said, be a great favor to me, and I would of course make certain that you had only the finest . . ."

"I have no wish to return to Karelstad, Morek. If I do as you ask, it will not be because I want to live in a fine apartment or wear costly jewels. It will be because once, long ago, when I needed kindness, you were kind. Kinder than you knew."

"And the boy is acceptable?"

"He could be lame and a hunchback, and it would make no difference."

Rudolf felt his face grow hot. He opened his mouth.

"Excellent," said his father. "The keys to the apartment will be waiting for you. Send for him when you're ready."

The woman nodded, then turned back to her weeding.

Rudolf trudged over the fields and along the country roads behind his father, wondering what had just happened.

THE SUMMONS CAME two weeks later. *Meet me at 2:00 p.m. at Agneta's*, said the note. It was written on thick paper, soft, heavy, the color of cream, scented with something not even Karl, who considered himself a connoisseur of women's perfumes, could identify. "It's not jasmine," he said. "Sort of like jasmine mixed with lily, but with something else . . ."

"What do you think she wants?" asked Gustav.

"She's his mistress," said Karl. "What do *you* think she wants?"

"I don't know," said Rudolf. What would he say to her? He imagined her in a straw hat and a faded dress in the middle of Agneta's, with its small tables at which students, artists, and women in the latest fashions from Paris sipped cups of Turkish coffee or ate Hungarian pastries. Suddenly, he felt sorry for her. Karelstad had changed so much since she had last seen it. It had been impoverished but not damaged during the war, and since the divisions of Trianon it had become one of the most fashionable capitals in Europe. She would look, would be, so out of place. He would be kind to her, would not mind his own embarrassment. Perhaps they could come to some sort of agreement. She could live in her apartment and do, well, whatever she wanted, and he would be free of any obligations to her.

He looked at himself in the mirror. He looked rather fine, if he did say so himself. He practiced an expression of sympathy and solicitousness.

* * *

BY THE TIME he was sitting at one of the small tables, he was feeling less sympathetic. How like his father, to embarrass him in front of all these people. He did not know most of them, of course, but sitting next to the door—surely that was General Schrader, whom he had seen once in a parade commemorating Sylvanian liberation from the Ottoman Empire, and he was almost certain that the woman with the ridiculously long feathers in her hat was the wife of someone important. Hadn't he seen her sitting on the platform at his graduation?

General Schrader had risen. There was a woman joining him, a woman so striking that Rudolf could not help staring at her. She was wearing a green dress, a dress of almost poisonous green. A green cowl of the same material framed her face, a pale face with a bright red mouth, so vivid that Rudolf thought, *I've never seen anything so alive.*

But she did not stop at the general's table. Instead, she walked across the room in his direction. At every second or third table she paused. Men rose and bowed, women either turned their heads, refusing to look at her, or kissed her on both cheeks. In her wake, she left whispers, until the café sounded like a forest of falling leaves.

"So nice to see you again, Countess," Rudolf heard her say, and the woman with the feathered hat responded, "Good God! Can it really be you, come back from the dead to steal our husbands? Where did I leave mine? Oh my, I'm going to have a heart attack any minute. My dear, where have you been?"

A long, lean man sitting in a corner rose, kissed her hands, and said, "You'll sit for me again, won't you?"

"That's Friedrich, the painter," said Karl. "I've never seen him talk to anyone since I started coming here four years ago. I'll bet you twenty kroner that she's a film actress from Germany."

"I don't think so," said Gustav. "I think—"

And then she was at their table.

"You must be Rudolf's friends," she said. "It was so nice to meet you. Must you be leaving so soon?"

"Yes, I'm afraid so," said Gustav, hastily rising. "Come on, Karl. I'm sure Rudolf wants some privacy."

And then he was alone with her, or as alone as one can be in Agneta's, with a roomful of people trying, surreptitious, to see whom she was speaking with.

"Hello, Rudolf," she said. "Thank you for being prompt. Could you order me some coffee? And light me a cigarette. I haven't had a cigarette in—it must be twenty years now. I've made a list of the people you'll need to meet. You can tell me which ones you've met already." She waited, looking at him from beneath long black lashes. Her eyes were still green, but somehow they had acquired depth, like a forest pool. "My coffee?"

"Yes, of course," said Rudolf. He gestured for the waiter and suddenly realized that his palms were damp.

* * *

THE PARTY HAD lasted long past midnight. The Crown Prince himself had been there. The guest list had also included the Prime Minister; General Schrader; the countess of the feathered hat, this time in a tiara; the painter Friedrich; the French ambassador; Anita Dak, the principal dancer from the Ballet Russes, which was staging *Copélia* in Karelstad; a professor of mathematics in a shabby coat, invited because he had just been inducted into the National Academy; young men in the government who talked about the situation in Germany between dances; young men in finance who talked about whether the krona was going up or down, seeming not to care which as long as they were buying or selling at the right times; mothers dragging girls who danced with the young men, awkwardly aware of their newly upswept hair and bare shoulders, then went back to giggling in corners of the ballroom. At first Rudolf had felt out of place, intimidated although as the future Baron Arnheim he certainly had a right to be there, should probably have been there all along rather than smoking in cafés with Karl and Gustav. But it did not matter. He was escorting The Pearl.

She walked beside him down the darkened street, her white furs clasped around her. She had not wanted to take a cab. "It's not far," she had said. "I want to see the night, and the moon." It shone above the housetops, swimming among the clouds.

"Here it is," she said. It had been three weeks since he had met her at Agneta's, and he had never yet seen where she lived, the apartment that his father was paying for. He had wanted to, but had not, somehow, dared to ask. He still did not know, exactly, how to talk to her.

"Could I—could I come up?" he asked.

For a moment, she did not answer. Then, "All right," she said.

Her apartment was larger than the one he shared with Karl and Gustav, and luxuriously furnished. He recognized a table, a sofa, even some paintings from Malo, and suddenly realized that his mother must have sent them. His father might have paid for an apartment, but he could never have furnished one.

She turned on a lamp, but the corners of the room remained in shadow. She shone in the darkness like a pale moon.

"You made me dance with every girl at the party, but you wouldn't dance with me," he said.

"That wasn't the point," she said. "How did you like the French ambassador's daughter? Charlotte De Grasse—she's nineteen, charming, and an heiress."

"I want to dance with you," he said.

She looked at him for a moment. He could not tell what she was thinking. Then she went to the gramophone and put on a record: a waltz.

Nervously, he took her in his arms. She was wearing something gray, like cobwebs, and her eyes had become gray as well. A scent enveloped him, the perfume that Karl had been unable to place.

"You're exquisite," he said, then realized how stupid that had sounded.

"Don't fall for me," she said. And then, almost as though he did not know what he was doing, he started to dance with her in his arms, around and around and around.

SHE SAT ON the edge of the bed. In the morning light coming through the windows, her robe was the color of milk. She had washed her face. Once again she looked like the woman that Rudolf had seen near Malo: thin, but now paler and more tired, with blue shadows under her eyes. Older than she had looked last night. It was just after dawn; the birds in the park had been singing for an hour.

"This is who I am, Rudolf," she said. "Beneath the evening gowns and cosmetics. Do you understand?"

He pulled her to him by the lapel of her robe, then slipped it off her shoulder. He kissed her skin there, then on her collarbone and her neck. The scent still clung around her, as though it were not a perfume but an exhalation of her flesh. "I don't care," he said.

"No," she said, sounding sad. "I didn't think you would."

Last night, he had touched her carefully, hungrily. At times he had thought, *She is delicate, I must be very gentle.* At times he had thought, *I would like to devour her.* Her fingers had traveled over him, and he had thought they were like feathers, so soft. At times he had shuddered, thinking, *They are like spiders. She is the one who will devour me.* He had looked down into her eyes and wondered if he would drown, and wanted to drown, and had at times felt, with terror and ecstasy, as though he were drowning and could no longer breathe. Finally, when he lay spent and she kissed him on the mouth, he had thought, *It is like being kissed by a flower.*

He pulled her down beside him and kissed her, insistently.

"Rudolf," she said. "The French ambassador's daughter—"

"Can go to hell," he said. And a part of him noticed, gratified, that this time she touched him as hungrily as he had touched her. Afterward, he lay with his head just beneath her breasts, moving as she breathed, his fingers stroking the skin of her stomach.

"I can't stay," she said. "Soon, I'll have to return to Dobromir. Once you have a position and are engaged, you won't need me anymore, and then I'll go."

He raised himself up on his elbow. "Don't be ridiculous. Why would you want to go back there, to that hovel? And why should I marry anyone? I want to be with you."

"I told you not to fall for me." She sighed. "The first time I came to Karelstad, all I wanted was to dress in silk, wear high heels, smoke cigarettes. Motorcars!

Champagne! The lights of the city at night, so much more exciting than the moon and stars. The theater, and playing a part. It allowed me to be something other than myself. And then the men bringing me flowers, white fox furs, diamonds to wear around my neck, like drops of water turned to stone. Many, many men, Rudolf."

Frowning, he turned his head. "I don't want to hear about them."

She stroked his hair. "But I became sick. Very, very sick. I had to go back, live among the trees, drink water from the stream. If I stay here much longer, I'll become sick again."

"How can you know that?" he said.

He turned to look at her, and saw a tear slide from the corner of her eye. He pulled himself up until he lay beside her and kissed it away. "All right then, I'll come to Malo. I'll live in that hovel of yours, or if you don't want me to, I'll visit every day. At least we can see each other."

She smiled, although her eyes still had the brightness of unshed tears. "Now you're being ridiculous. Don't you realize what Malo is? It's been there, the forest and the fields, for a thousand years. The Barons of Malo have cared for that land, and you must care for it, as your son must care for it after you. If I thought you would abandon Malo, I would leave today, knowing that my time here in Karelstad, with you, had served no purpose. Tell me now, Rudolf. Will you abandon Malo?"

Her smile frightened him. She seemed, suddenly, kind and sad and implacable. "If I don't, how long do we have?"

"I promised your father that I would stay until your wedding day. But you must not delay it; you must not put off taking the position I've found for you. You must not try for more than I can give."

"Damn my father," he said. "All right, then. I'll do as I'm told, like a good boy. And if I'm good, what do I get, now? Today?"

She wrapped her arms around him, and suddenly he felt a constriction in his chest, a sudden stopping of the heart that he had felt only when seeing a serpent in his path or listening to Brahms. He could not breathe again. He wondered why anyone had thought breathing was important.

"You know," said Karl, "I would probably kill you if it would make her look at me."

They were sitting in the park. Karl and Rudolf were smoking cigarettes. Gustav was smoking a pipe.

"How you can stand that foul stench . . ." said Rudolf.

"It's no worse than Karl's French cigarettes," said Gustav. "Good Turkish tobacco, that's what this is."

Rudolf knocked ash off the tip of his cigarette. "Well, it smells like you're smoking manure."

"He doesn't want to stink for The Pearl," said Karl. "Rudolf, I hope you enjoyed my announcement of your probable demise."

"*If* she would look at you, but she won't," said Rudolf. He had spent the night with her. He spent every night with her now, knowing and yet refusing to believe that his time with her was coming to an end. Several months ago, he had shared with Karl and Gustav every detail of his frustratingly slow and not at all certain conquest of Kati. But he had told them nothing about the nights he had spent with The Pearl. Karl had hinted several times that he would like to know more. Gustav had stayed silent.

"Why is that, do you think?" asked Karl. "While your face is pleasant enough, you're not exactly the Crown Prince, and my uncle is a minister. Hell, I may even be a minister myself someday."

"Because she's a Fair Lady," said Gustav.

"A what?" asked Karl.

"My grandmother told me about them, once when I had the measles and had to stay home from school. You really don't know about the Fair Ladies?"

Karl blew cigarette smoke through his nose in a contemptuous sort of way. "Why should I?"

"Because they're dangerous," said Gustav. "They live in the forest, inside trees or at the bottoms of pools, and when they see a woodsman or a hunter, maybe, they beckon to him, and he goes to dance with them. He dances with the Fair Ladies until he's skin and bone, or maybe a hundred years have passed and all his friends and relatives are dead, or he promises to give the Fair Ladies anything they want, even the heart out of his chest or his first male child. I tell you, Fair Ladies are dangerous."

"And imaginary," said Karl.

"Ask my grandmother. One of her nephews was taken away by a Fair Lady. She had him for three days, and when she returned him, there were things missing from his house. All of his mother's clothes, some jewelry that had been sitting on her dresser, phonograph records. He said that had been the price of his return—he had promised them to the Fair Lady."

"Sounds like a thief, not a fairy," said Karl.

"Fairies are imaginary. Fair Ladies are real. How else do you explain the fact that when she comes into the room, you actually, unbelievably, shut up?" Gustav put his pipe to his mouth, inhaled, and blew out a smoke ring. "I think she's getting ready to steal our Rudi away. What do you think she'll want, Rudi? The heart out of your chest?"

"Well, Rudi, what do you think? Is she a Fair Lady?" asked Karl. "You haven't said anything for a while."

"She's found me a job," said Rudolf. "I'm going to be secretary to the Prime Minister."

"Hell!" said Karl. And then, "Bloody hell!"

"And I'm supposed to marry someone named Charlotte. She's the French ambassador's daughter. As soon as I'm married, she says, she's going to go back to Malo." He threw his cigarette on the path and ground it out, savagely, with his boot heel.

HE WASN'T GOING to do it. He wasn't going to marry Charlotte.

He had to tell her. Go to her and say, "Come away with me. If you don't want to stay in Karelstad, we'll go to Berlin or Vienna. I'll work to support us, and if you do get sick—why should you get sick when you're with me? But if you do—I'll find the best doctors to treat you. At Vienna they have the best medical school in Europe. Don't you see that I can't live without you?"

What had Gustav said? That Fair Ladies were dangerous. Well, she had taken the heart out of his chest, all right.

"Be happy, Rudolf," she had said to him. And, "Tomorrow is your wedding day. I will not see you again, after tonight." He had made love to her fiercely, angrily. And when he stood for the last time in the hallway, she had cupped his cheek with her hand, kissed him as tenderly as a mother kisses a child, and said "Goodbye." Then, she had closed the door.

But here he was, standing in the street across from her apartment building. He would cross the street, go up the stairs to her apartment, knock on her door, bang on it if she refused to open, and tell her that he wasn't going to go through with it.

"What are you doing here, young Arnheim?" He felt a hand on his shoulder, and turned to see the painter Friedrich standing beside him. "I passed Szent Benedek's on my way here and saw the wedding guests going in. You don't want to disappoint them, do you? If you run, you can be there in ten minutes. So go already." He waved his hand, as though shooing a fly.

"I can't," said Rudolf. "I have to see her, talk to her."

"To say what, exactly? That you're in love with her, that you want to spend the rest of your life with her? Don't you think she's heard it all before?"

"I don't care. This is different. She loves me too, I know she does."

The painter put his hands in his pockets. He looked down at the pavement, then spoke slowly. "It's possible. She's capable of love, although you wouldn't know it from the stories people tell, sitting around their fires in the winter, in places like Lilafurod and Gretz. I'm going to tell you a story of my own. It will take five minutes, which will give you ten minutes to get there, just in time for the wedding.

"Once upon a time, there were three young men as stupid, if that is possible, as you and your friends. Their names were Péter Andrassyi, Morek Arnheim, and Herman Schrader. Andrassyi was a Count, and he was rich enough to buy himself a mistress, the fabulous Pearl of great price, who had just finished a successful run as Juliet at the National Theater. The famously irascible theater critic Mor Benjamin wrote that no other actress could die as convincingly as she could. She had been sitting for me—I had painted the posters for the play, and I asked her to sit for another project of mine, a small painting of a sylph standing naked by a stream, reflected in the water. Twice a week she would come to my studio, and I would paint her—naked, as I said. Have you ever seen a case of tuberculosis? No? Well, that's what it was like. She just started wasting away. I asked her what was wrong, what she was eating. She said she was well enough, that she didn't want to talk about it. But when she started coughing up blood, or whatever she has in those veins of hers, she told me. Her kind—they don't belong here, and if they stay too long, they sicken and then die. I went to Andrassyi's apartment. I told him about her condition, about what I had seen and what he must have noticed himself. Do you know what he said to me? That I shouldn't stick my nose into what was not my business, that I had always been jealous of him and simply wanted her for my own. He would not let her go, and as long as he wanted her, as long as he told her that he could not live without her, she would not leave Karelstad. I argued with her! How I argued. But she said, 'He loves me. You know what I am, Friedrich. My nature binds me to him, more strongly than any of your legal ties. It isn't in the stories, is it, that we can be so caught?'"

"I thought Gustav was joking," said Rudolf. "Do you mean that she's really—"

"Quiet, pup," said Friedrich. "I only have three more minutes to finish my story. So, I challenged him to a duel. It was stupid—he was an excellent shot and I was a poor one, but I was young and in love with her myself, although in a different way than he was. Artists aren't quite human either, you know. They also love differently. Schrader was his second. Arnheim, your father, was mine. I had no friend of my own to second me, and I knew that your father was an honorable, if intolerably boring, man. We met in the park at dawn, when there would be no observers. Andrassyi should have shot me—I should have died that day, but the luck that rewards all fools was with me, and he missed. I, who had never before hit a target, shot him dead. I was brought before a judge, but what could he do? There were two witnesses to swear that we had agreed on the place, the time, the weapons—Andrassyi had even shot first.

"When I told her, she screamed at me and beat me with her fists. Then, she wept for a long time. And then she went back to Malo. I asked your father to take her—there was no train back then. They went in a carriage and the journey took two days. She wrote to me, once. The letter said only, *Thank you. I am better now.* And there I thought she would stay, until your father decided that his ambitions for you were more important than her life. Why she would agree to come back for a pup like you—"

"Not for me," said Rudolf. "For Malo. She cares about Malo . . ." He felt as though he had been hit by something he could neither understand nor name. The street seemed to be reeling around him.

"Why do you think I'm here?" asked Friedrich. "To take her back. I don't know if she feels about you as she felt about Andrassyi, but I'm fairly certain that if you walk into that apartment, if you tell her that you want her, she will not leave. She values her life, and knows that staying will kill her. But that's what it means, to be what she is—she would stay for you and die."

"I—I love her. I would never hurt her."

"Then let her go. Do you know what love is, young Arnheim? Ordinary, human love. It's when you see another person—see her as she is, not as you would like her to be. Have you seen her?"

Her pallor, these last few days. The dark circles under her eyes. The sharpness of her rib cage under his hands. Rudolf looked up at her window. What was she doing now? Packing, no doubt. She had accomplished what she came for. He thought, *I hope she weeps for me, a little.*

Then, he turned in the direction of Szent Benedek's and began to run.

GUSTAV CAUGHT HIM just as he was about to step through the door to the courtyard.

"Where are you going, so early?"

"Hunting," he said, as though the answer were obvious. He wore his flannel hunting coat and carried a rifle.

"I think I'll go with you," said Gustav.

"You'll ruin your shoes."

"They're more appropriate than boots, for a funeral."

The grass was still wet from the night's rains. They walked over the lawn, away from the house that had stood there for fifteen generations, looking, with its battlements and turrets, like a miniature medieval fortress. They passed the privet maze and rose garden, then the herb garden where bees were already at work among the lavender, and followed the road that led to the old chapel.

"Once," said Gustav, "this forest used to stretch across Sylvania. That's why the Romans called it Sylvania—The Forest. There was plenty of room, then."

"For what?" asked Rudolf.

"For whatever you're hunting."

They walked in silence. The sky was growing brighter, and the birds in the trees were filling with air with a cacophony of song.

"Mary, mother of God!" said Gustav suddenly. He surveyed one of his shoes, which was covered with mud. He had stepped into a puddle.

"I told you," said Rudolf.

"You know what that reminds me of?" asked Gustav. "Karl. He always insisted on wearing his city clothes in the country. You should have seen him when he visited me last year, at Gretz! But I knew that if I stopped to change, you would leave without me. Have you talked to him lately?"

"Karl? We don't talk anymore. He believes in the Reich. He thinks it will unite all of Europe. There will be no more war, he says, when Europe is united. He says we must all be international—under a German flag, of course. I don't believe in peace at that price."

"Well, perhaps he is a realist and we are the romantics, clinging to our old ways, our country houses and the lands our parents have farmed for generations. Perhaps in his new world order there will be no place for us."

"Speak for yourself," said Rudolf. "Any German who comes to Malo will get a bullet through the head, until I run out of bullets. And then they can shoot me. There are worse things than dying as a Sylvanian. My father said that to me before he died. He could barely speak after the stroke—but he was right."

"What about Lotta and the baby?"

"They leave for France next week. My mother will take them. If there's going to be a war, I want them out of it."

They stopped. They had come to the chapel. It had been built of the same gray stone as the house, but was now covered with ivy that was starting to obscure even some of the windows, with their pictures of saints and martyrs. It was surrounded by a graveyard.

"We used to come here on Sunday mornings," said Rudolf. "The family and all the laborers on the estate, worshiping together. Karl would call it positively feudal. But now everyone goes to the church in Dobromir. No one comes here anymore."

Nevertheless, among the gravestones stood a priest, beside a fresh grave, reading the burial rites. Around him stood the mourners, their heads bowed.

"So she died," said Gustav.

"She died," said Rudolf. "I would have taken her to a doctor, but she sent me away. And when I heard that she was sick, here at Malo—I wrote to her twice, but she never answered. I could not go to her without her permission—she would not have wanted that."

"What could a doctor have done?" asked Gustav. "Given her medicine? Who knows what it would have done—to her. Or cut her open, and found—what? Would she have had a heart, like a woman? Or would she have had—what a tree has?"

"He could have done something," said Rudolf.

"I doubt it. How do you save a fairy tale?"

"And so we commit her body to the ground, as ashes return to ashes and dust to dust. The Lord bless her and keep her, the Lord make his face to shine upon her, the Lord give her peace. *Amen*," said the priest. The funeral was over.

The mourners lifted their heads and looked at the two men. Later, when Gustav described it to his wife, sitting by their fire at home in Gretz, he shivered. "It was as though someone had thrown cold water at me. A shock, and then a sensation like water trickling down my back, as long as they continued to look at me. So many of them at once." Girls from the cafés and dance halls of Karelstad, some in silk stockings and fur stoles and hats that perched on their heads like birds that had landed at rakish angles, some in mended gloves and threadbare coats. Girls who acted in films, or modeled for artists, or waited tables until a gentleman friend came along. Slim, pale, glamorous, with dark circles under their eyes.

They walked out of the graveyard, passing the two men. Several nodded at Rudolf as they passed and one of them stopped for a moment, put her hand on his lapel, and said, "You were good to her." Then they walked away along the muddy road in their high heels, whispering together like leaves in a forest.

"Good morning, Baron," said the priest. "Would you like to see the stone? It's exactly as you ordered." They walked over and looked. There was no name on the stone, only the word

Fairest

"I'm surprised, Father," said Gustav.

"Why, because she lies in holy ground? God created the forests before He created Adam. She is His creature, just as you are, my son."

"Then you believe she had a soul?" asked Gustav.

"I wouldn't say that. But I've worked with these—young ladies for many years. We have a mission for them in the city. They go there, like moths to a flame. They can't help themselves. It's something in their nature. The priest that served here before me—your father knew him, Baron, old Father Dominik— told me that once, when the forest was larger than it is now and the cities were smaller, it was not so dangerous for them. A farmer would come upon them and they would force him to dance all night. He would find his way home the next morning, with his shoes worn out and no great harm done, although his wife or sweetheart might be angry. But now the forest is logged by the timber companies, and the cities glow all night with electric lights. They go to Karelstad and the theater managers hire them, or the film directors, and eventually they become sick. It's as though a cancer eats them up inside, draws the life, the brightness, out of them. They die young."

"Did I kill her?" asked Rudolf. It was the first thing he had said since he entered the graveyard. "Did going back a second time make her sick again?"

"I can't tell you that," said the priest.

"But I loved her," he said, as though to himself. "I wonder if that matters."

"It mattered to her," said the priest.

"Father," said Gustav, "what will happen to those girls, if the war comes?"

The priest looked the gravestone for a moment. "I don't know. But you must remember that they've survived. The Romans write of the *puellae albae* who lived in the forests of Sylvania. A thousand years ago, they were here. We're no good for them, with our motor cars, phonographs, electric lights. Tanks won't be any better. Father Dominik thought there were fewer of them, after the last war. But as long as the forest remains, they'll be here. Or so I prefer to believe. And as long as they're here, Sylvania will be here, in some fashion."

The two men walked back along the path, without speaking. Then, "What will you do now?" asked Gustav.

"Have breakfast. Send my wife and son to France. Fight the Germans."

"Sausage and eggs?"

"Do you ever think of anything other than immediate pleasures?"

"Frequently, and I always regret it."

Rudolf Arnheim laughed. A flock of wood doves, startled, flew up into the air, their wings flashing in the light of the risen sun.

Swan Girls

They are so lovely, the wild swan girls:
white wings and absence . . .

1. How to recognize a swan girl.

She will have delicate wrists.
You will be able to circle her wrists
with your hands. No, don't try it:
you don't hold swan girls, not like that.
Any suggestion of captivity sends them flying
off on white swan wings, or on high heels
across a street or continent.

They can't bear to be caught.

No, look at her wrists: skin over bone, with faint
pinpricks where the pinions go.

2. How to catch a swan girl.

Feign lack of interest.
Stare off into the distance, at a tree perhaps
or a beach, or the New York skyline.
Turn to her. Be polite, almost too polite.
Ask a question to which she doesn't know the answer.
(Will it snow tomorrow? What are clouds made of?
How do you say eternity in Norwegian?)

Interest her, and keep her interested,
or she will fly off.

3. How to keep a swan girl.

You can't, not in a house or an apartment,
not in a city, sometimes not even a country.

When she telephones, you will ask, where are you?
When she laughs, it will sound
so far away, and in the background
you will hear waves, or a language you don't understand.

4. How to marry a swan girl.

Steal her coat of feathers.
This part always goes badly.

5. How to lose a swan girl.

Wait. Eventually, she will go somewhere else.
If you hide her coat of feathers, she will leave without it.
Wait, you say, but I thought . . . Oh, those old stories?
You didn't believe those, did you?

She knows where to get another, and anyway
she doesn't need wings to fly.

6. How to mourn a swan girl.

Make a shrine, perhaps on a dresser or small table.
Three swan feathers, a candle, a stone smoothed
by ocean waves. That should do it.

Sit on the sofa. Hold one of the feathers. Cry.
Realize it was inevitable.
Swan girls fly. It's just what they do.
It wasn't you.

7. How to be a swan girl.

There are no rules the sky is infinite
the world is yours laid out in rivers and mountains
like a great quilt pieced by your grandmother.

She is older than they are.

Her hair is white as snow and covers them
her eyes are bright as stars and when she laughs
avalanches.

You take after her.

Swan girl where will you go?
Everywhere you say and then
everywhere else.

The Gentleman

Has the milk gone sour this morning?
Are there tracks upon the floor
where you could have sworn you swept
carefully the night before?
Are the window shutters open?
Did the clock forget to chime?
Could you simply have forgotten
to set the time? Surely not.

Are the chickens agitated?
Could a fox have come last night
and sniffed around their coop,
to put them in a fright?
There's a fox that walks on two legs;
when he comes, the farmyard dog
pricks his ears and sits as silent
as a log. Unfortunately.

Is the horse's mane completely
in a tangle, and its hide
crusted with the mud that splashed
from its hooves during the ride?
That's how you know. The Gentleman
does love his nightly ride. And the maid
milking the cows this morning smiles
mysteriously. Oh, for goodness' sake.

You should do something. Gather
the town together, determine to catch
the malefactor. How many of you
have had your tulips trampled,
your best cow addled, your daughter
suddenly dreamy? But. What
if he were brought to justice,
black boots in the courtroom,
black eyes laughing at you,

at the good wives, industrious,
neat as a pin in their cotton
gowns, making you feel,
well, ridiculous, and somehow flushed,

and worse, what if the cabbages
bolted, and the asparagus flopped,
and the squash were all infested
with worms. You can't trust him.
And worse yet, what if the moon
refused to change, and the leaves
on the trees never caught the fire
of autumn. And it was your fault.

I tell you, my dear:

If the milk was sour this morning,
and the laundry is in knots,
if the geraniums are missing
from their flowerpots,
if the mice have gotten into
the bacon and the cheese,
laugh and let the Gentleman do
as he pleases. I know, what a mess.

But a robin's on the handle
of the shovel, singing softly,
and the clouds are floating overhead.
Admit, the world is mostly
as it ought to be. Tonight the moon
will pull the distant tide,
and the Gentleman will come to take
his nightly ride. With a kiss for you

even if you don't notice.
But my dear,
you do.

Christopher Raven

W HY HAD I come back to Collingswood? That was what I asked myself, standing on the path that led to the main school building, built of gray stone and shadowed by oaks that had stood for a hundred years. I had ridden the cart from the train station, just as I had so many years ago, at the beginning of each term. Then, I had been accompanied by a trunk almost as large as I was, filled with clothes and books. Now I carried only a small suitcase. It contained another walking suit, a dress suitable for dinner, and toiletries. I would only be here for one night. Why had I come back? Because I had been invited to give a speech. Surely that was all.

"Lucy!" It was Millicent Tolliver, walking down the path toward me.

"Hello, Tollie!" I called, then wondered if she would mind the schoolgirl nickname. She looked very much like the schoolgirl she had been, with an untidy blouse and, I could see when she gave me an enthusiastic hug, an inkstain on one cheek. Only the length of her skirt and the bun of hair at the back of her head, which threatened to come down at any moment, marked her as, not a schoolgirl any longer, but one of the teachers. I had wondered how many of the girls I knew would be coming back for Old Girls' Day, but I knew Tollie would be here. Unlike the rest of us, she had remained at Collingswood.

"Eleanor Prescott is here, and you won't believe who else—Mary Davenport." She grabbed my suitcase from me and said, "We're upstairs, in our old room, all four of us."

"Why did they put us up there?" I followed her across the front hall and up the staircase. I remembered it echoing with boots. We used to run down it, almost late for French or geography lessons on the first floor. The school felt so empty, without the noise of girls chattering and whispering, without the smell of cabbage that used to float, like a vague miasma, through the halls. I kept expecting the old sounds, the old smells, but there was only the silence of summer vacation, and beeswax.

But there, at the top of the stairs, was a familiar sight: the portrait of Lord Collingswood in his riding jacket, with a horse and hound at his side, holding a riding whip as though to show who was master. He stared down over his long nose, no doubt shocked by the sight of generations of schoolgirls running through his halls. We had inherited the tradition of calling him Old Nosey.

"Oh, I asked for our old room. When I found out that all of you would be here, I asked Halloway if we could share, and of course she said yes. She was the one who first put us together, remember?"

How well I remembered! The four of us glaring at each other. It was our final year at Collingwood, and we were assigned to room with our mortal enemies. I hated Eleanor Prescott, with her French dresses and stuck-up ways, and despised Mary Davenport for her timidity, her tendency to start every sentence with "Well, I don't really know, but . . ." And I had no use for Millicent Tolliver, who was a scholarship girl like me, but enthusiastically tried to curry favor with Eleanor Prescott and her circle.

Miss Halloway herself greeted us. She was the new headmistress, and was said to have advanced educational ideas. "This will be quite a treat for you, girls," she said. "I've put you in the room Lady Collingswood herself slept in, a hundred years ago. It was used for storage under Miss Temple, but we have so many girls this term that we needed all the available space, and it cleaned up quite beautifully. I even found a portrait of Lady Collingswood while we were inventorying the attic and brought it down for you. You know she was the one who founded Collingswood school. I thought she might inspire you to greater academic achievements." She looked particularly at Eleanor, who preferred outdoor games to studying and cared more about tennis than Latin.

We looked up at Lady Collingswood doubtfully. She had clear, pale skin and auburn ringlets cascading over her shoulders. Her eyes were grayish-blue, and she wore a dress of the same color with lace at the sleeves. She was smiling at the painter and playing with a small dog in her lap. I would not have called her beautiful, exactly. Her face was too particular, too individual, for that. But she looked intelligent, and much nicer than Old Nosey out in the hall.

"She was a patroness of the arts, and painted and wrote poetry herself. Also an excellent gardener—the Lady Collingswood rose is named after her. I found a book on the history of Collingswood in the attic. Perhaps you would like to look at it?"

We murmured politely. We had no interest in the history of Collingswood. Despite our enmity, we all knew what the others were thinking. Wasn't it almost time for tea?

Despite her advanced ideas, Miss Halloway evidently understood schoolgirls and their stomachs. "It will be in my office when you're interested. Tea is in the dining hall in half an hour. Come down when you've finished unpacking. I'll see you there, girls."

"When did you say tea was?" asked Eleanor Prescott. I stepped back, startled. I had been absorbed in memories, but this Eleanor was not the girl I had known. She was Lady Thornton-Smythe, the Terror of the Tories. She looked even more formidable than she had as a schoolgirl, tall and elegant, with elaborate loops of blonde hair. I could see a feathered hat on the bed, and I recognized her dress as a model from Worth. It must have cost a small fortune.

"Lucy!" she said now. "How perfectly lovely to see you." She kissed me on both cheeks. "I give copies of *The Modern Diana* to everyone I know. I tell them it's a perfectly scandalous book, all about free love and professions for women."

"Honestly, at first I was afraid to read it," said Mary Davenport, smiling and giving me a hug. "But it really does have an important message. All about using the talents God gave us." She was as short and plump as she had been, although her cheeks were redder from what she had called, in a letter to me, her "country life." There were gray strands in her hair. She had married her father's curate, who was now the Rev. Charles Beaumont, with a living near York. She had come back to visit "dear old Collingswood" while he attended an ecclesiastical conference in London.

Mary had three children living, and one buried. Eleanor had no children, which she did not seem to regret. "Laws to alleviate the oppression of man—and woman—are my children," she had written me. And Tollie had never married. All this I knew from letters I had received over the years—not many, but we had never entirely lost touch. I suppose what we experienced that last year had bound us together.

I had sent them letters about my own life, my relationship with Louis, his death from tuberculosis, my own efforts to raise little Louie, who had his father's complaint. *The Modern Diana* had sold well enough that I had sent him to a sanatorium in Switzerland, but the money would not last forever. I was grateful that Collingswood had paid for my train ticket and offered me an honorarium for my speech at the Old Girls' Dinner. Would I have come back otherwise?

It was Tollie, of course, who said what the rest of us were thinking but would not say. "I'm so glad we're all here. Now we can talk about Christopher Raven."

TOLLIE DREAMED OF him last, but of course she was the first to say anything.

"Lucy, wake up! I had the strangest dream."

I opened my eyes, then closed them again. "Go away. Can't you see it's still dark?"

"But I dreamed of a man. Have you ever dreamed of a man? With curling black hair and a white blouse—at least, it looked like a blouse, like something a woman would wear. Or a pirate. Maybe he was a pirate? Except that he was saying something—like poetry. I was sitting on the parlor sofa, except it was so much nicer than the sofa we have now, and he bowed to me and kissed my hand!"

"You've dreamed about him too!" said Eleanor, sitting up in bed. "Then I'm going to stop dreaming about him. I don't want to share my dreams with Messy Millie."

"Well, I've been dreaming about him for a week." I said. "So you've been sharing your dream with the both of us. How common is that? And what about Mary? Maybe she's been dreaming about him as well."

Mary, who had just opened her eyes, pulled the blanket over her head.

"Have you been dreaming about him too?" asked Eleanor. "Mary, answer me!"

"Yes," came the muffled answer. "For a week."

"Did he kiss your hand?" asked Tollie.

Mary looked out from under the blanket. Her face was bright red. "No. We were in this room, but it had a big bed in it. And he kissed my shoulder."

"He hasn't kissed me," I said. "He just takes me walking around the garden, and he says things—about my hair and eyes. Poetry, like Tollie said."

"Well, he's kissed me," said Eleanor. "We were in the tower, looking out toward Collington, and he told me that I changed like the moon, or something like that, and he kissed me on the *mouth*."

That day, for the first time, we sat together in the front parlor, which was reserved for the older girls, trying to figure it out.

"Maybe he's a ghost, and we're being haunted," said Mary. Her father was a member of the Society for Psychical Research.

"Don't be ridiculous," said Eleanor. "There's no such thing as a ghost."

"Oh yes, there is," said Tollie. "My aunt Harriet was haunted by my uncle, who had lost a leg at sea. She said the ghost went thump, thump, thump on its wooden leg, up and down the hallways at night."

"Ugh," said Mary. "You're making me shiver!"

"But even if he is a ghost," I said, "whose ghost is he? And why is he haunting the four of us?"

"We don't know that he is," said Eleanor. "Maybe the other girls have had dreams as well, and they're just not talking about it."

So we went around asking the other girls about what they had dreamed the night before. None of them had dreamed of a man with curling black hair, or brown skin that made him look like a foreigner, or black eyes that looked as though they were laughing at you, although one of them had dreamed of her brother who was in India.

No, it was just us four.

We made a pact. Each morning we would compare notes. We would tell each other what we had dreamed, all the details, no matter how embarrassing. And we would try to remember what the man had said, those poetic words that seemed to slip out of our heads on waking, like water.

"HE TOLD ME that my eyes are like bright stars," said Tollie.

"Oh, for goodness's sake," said Eleanor. "Your eyes are like eyes. He told me that my hair was like a fire burning down a forest, except he used different words. And they rhymed with something, but I don't remember what."

"You have to try to remember," I said. "I wish all of you had Mary's memory."

In my notebook, I had written down what we dreamed each night, and the fragments of what we thought must be poetry:

> Eleanor: tower, dark but moonlight
> "the cascade of your gown"
> something about "sweet surrender" and "sweetly die"

Mary: in front of fireplace, kissed neck "like a swan's," "proud and fair"
"luxuriance of your hair"
Tollie: passed in hallway and dropped letter
"hide it in your bosom, sweetheart"
"the moon's a secret lover, as am I"
Lucy: kissed several times, passionately
"elements of love" (but hard to hear, could be "dalliance of love"?)

By this time, we had all been kissed, and we blushed as we told each other. "It was—soft," said Mary. "This is wrong, isn't it? Even if it's just a dream."

"Forceful," said Eleanor. "I don't think he would have stopped if I'd wanted him to. How can it be wrong if it's only a dream?"

"Is that what it's like, when boys kiss?" asked Tollie.

"No, it's nothing like that," said Eleanor, who had boy cousins. "That's disgusting."

"I don't think we're any closer to figuring out who he is," I said. "We know he's a poet, because of what he's saying. I mean, neck proud and fair, and all that. So, if he is a ghost, we need to find out if there were any poets who died at Collingswood."

"There's no such thing as a ghost," said Eleanor.

"What about Mrs. Halloway's book?" asked Tollie.

I was sent to ask Mrs. Halloway for the book, as the one most likely to, as Eleanor said, "read boring stuff."

"Of course, Lucy," she said. "I'm glad you're interested in the history of the school. Some of the other girls, well, they'll graduate and get married. But I think you are capable of doing something different, some sort of intellectual work. I hope you'll think about that. There are so many opportunities for women nowadays that did not exist when I was your age."

"Yes, Miss Halloway," I said, hoping to escape a lecture. Miss Halloway's advanced educational theories, we had discovered, involved teaching girls the subjects boys were usually taught, and she had a tendency to lecture us about the advancement of women. I did not quite escape one, but it was not as long as I had feared. I closed the door of her office with "and you really should think about a university education, Lucy" in my ears.

"And who's going to read that?" asked Eleanor when I brought *The History of Collingswood House, from the Crusades to the Present Day* to our room. The book had been covered with dust, and now I was covered with it as well.

"How many pages is it?" asked Mary.

I had already looked. "Seven hundred ninety-two. And there's no index."

By the way they all looked at me, it was obvious who was going to read *The History of Collingswood House.* It was, of course, going to be me. After all, I was the one who won the prizes in composition, who was at the top of the English class.

I was only on page one hundred fifty-seven the morning Mary woke up gasping. Although we asked and prodded, she would not tell us about her dream.

"I can't," she said. "We were in the bedroom again. He—I just can't."

We were sitting on Eleanor's bed, in our nightgowns, as we did every morning for our conferences.

"What was it like?" I asked. I think we all knew, even then, what had happened. Tollie and I had grown up in villages, near farms and animals. And Eleanor had heard the servants gossip.

"I'm sorry. I really don't think I can talk about it."

"Was it so frightening?" asked Tollie, leaning forward.

"Not frightening. Just—I can't, all right?" And we could get nothing else out of her.

Later that day, I looked with dismay at *The History of Collingswood House*. I could not face another list of who had come to visit Collingswood in the Year of Our Lord blankety blank.

"Look, stupid book," I said. "Just tell me what I want to know, all right?" I closed my eyes and opened the book at random. I looked down at the pages I had opened. There it was:

> In the autumn of 1817, Lord Collingswood invited the poet Christopher Raven, whom he had met in London, to Collingswood House. Lady Collingswood was taken with the handsome youth, who was supposed to look like an English Adonis, although some critics asserted that he wrote like a second-rate Shelley. The Collingswood library, which was extensive, had fallen into a state of disarray, and Lord Collingswood hoped that Raven would catalog it. However, the two men quarreled before the work had gotten underway, and the poet left in the middle of the night to join Shelley and Byron in Switzerland. He was overtaken by the snows, and is supposed to have perished in the Alpine passes. Lady Collingswood, who had a tender heart, particularly for poets, artists, and small dogs, was said to have been inconsolable for weeks.

I had found a poet. And he sounded like the right poet. Adonis had been Greek. He would have had curling black hair, the kind they call hyacinthine.

"I think I found him," I told Eleanor, Mary, and Tollie that afternoon. "His name is Christopher Raven. He was a poet, and I think he was in love with Lady Collingswood. And maybe she was in love with him."

"Why do you think we're dreaming about him?" asked Tollie. "If someone had dreamed about him before, we would have known about it, wouldn't we?

I mean, he would be like the Collingswood ghost or something. It would have been like calling the picture Old Nosey. Everyone would have known."

"Maybe it's because we're in her room," I said. "The book only says that she was taken with him, but I bet all the things he says to us are the things he said to her. I mean, seriously, none of us have a neck like a swan's, do we? And hair like a forest fire—she had red hair. I bet no one else has slept in her room for a hundred years. That's why we're dreaming about him, when no other girls have."

"The question is, what do we do now?" asked Eleanor. "He doesn't scare me, but that dream Mary had—yes, I know you can't talk about it, but we all know what it was about. If we're dreaming about him and Lady Collingswood, where is this going?"

Where indeed. I'll give you this, Christopher Raven. I have known love since those days as a schoolgirl at Collingswood, and you loved her as passionately as any poet loves a woman. There is always some selfishness in such a love, always some inclination to turn your love into poetry. But when you walked with her down the garden paths, when you stood beside her on the tower and looked out over the countryside, when you called her the moon and said you were the tide, following her motions, you loved her as passionately as poets love, who are always thinking of the next line. We experienced it, the four of us—experienced that love when we were only schoolgirls and should have been attending to our lessons. We felt the kisses in the darkness, your hand on her shoulder, your fingers running along her collarbone. We felt you slip off her dress of grayish-blue silk, and experienced what we should not have, a passion we were not ready for.

We changed, in those weeks. We grew languorous, as though we were always walking in a dream. We could not attend to our lessons. Eleanor gave up tennis, and she and Tollie used to sit in our room, talking in whispers about their dreams of the night before. Mary took to praying throughout the day. She told us she was convinced that the dreams were wrong, but like the rest of us, she did not want them to end. She developed dark shadows under her eyes, and sometimes she would jump for no reason, as though she had been frightened by a sound that the rest of us could not hear. And what about me? I was as dreamy as the rest, but my lethargy frightened me, and Mary's condition was a constant source of worry. I felt as though we were all slipping away into some dream land, losing touch with the prosaic world of school.

Finally, Miss Halloway spoke to me. "Lucy," she said, putting a hand on my shoulder as I leaned over a composition book, tracing the letters CR over and over with my pencil, "what is going on with you girls? Yesterday, Millicent almost fell asleep in Latin, and I'm told that Mary is starting to look, and behave, quite odd. Is something happening that I should know about?"

I should have told her then, but how could I bear to lose those kisses, the black eyes looking into mine and whispering words sweeter than I had ever heard before, calling me "goddess" and "love"?

"I think we're staying up too late talking," I told her, and looking at me doubtfully, she left it at that.

And so it might have continued, if Eleanor had not woken up one morning screaming.

"Lord Collingswood killed him!" she cried. "He found them together and hit him with his cane! There was blood everywhere!" And then she began to sob into her hands. I had never imagined that Eleanor Prescott could weep, and the sight sent a shiver down my spine.

The next night it was Tollie, and then me. We all dreamed the discovery, the terrifying blow to the back of the head. We all saw blood pooling on the floorboards. And then nothing—that was where the dreams ended. Only Mary was spared. Perhaps the ghost decided that she had seen enough. Certainly she could not take any more.

This time we were all summoned to Miss Halloway's office. "What in the world is going on with you girls?" she asked. "I've heard reports of moans in the night and screams early in the morning. And you all look as though you haven't slept for the past week."

"Miss Halloway," I told her, "We're being haunted. By a ghost." And then I told her everything.

"Good Lord," she said. "That such things should be going on right under my nose! The idea that you're being haunted is ridiculous. There's no such thing as a ghost, Lucy. However, the atmosphere of the room, together with what you read about Collingswood House, may have prompted these dreams. I will move you out of that room immediately."

We were moved into Miss Halloway's own room, for observation. But the dreams did not stop.

"Blood, and then nothing," said Tollie. "I can't see anything after he falls down. Blood on the floor, and then it's as though everything just goes dark."

"But I can still hear something," said Eleanor. "Like Tollie's uncle: thump, thump, thump."

"Miss Halloway," I said, "Lord Collingswood hit him in the front hall, and then there was this sound, like Eleanor said. I think he dragged the body down the stairs. To the cellar."

"I think it's time to summon a brain specialist," said Miss Halloway.

We all stood looking at her, silently—Mary looked especially reproachful. "Oh, all right, girls," she said. "The cellar it is."

"THERE'S NOTHING DOWN here," said Tollie.

"Oh, for goodness' sake," said Eleanor. "We haven't even checked for a priest's hole yet. Hillingdon has one, and a secret staircase. Of course, some people don't have such things in their houses, but I'm quite familiar with them, I assure you."

For the first time in several weeks, I would have liked to hit Eleanor Prescott, but it was obvious from the shrillness of her voice that she was both excited and afraid. And she was actually doing something useful, walking along each wall and knocking carefully, up and down, listening for anything unusual, or just different. These were the foundations of the house, which went back to Norman times. I knew that from having read *The History of Collingswood House*, at least to page one hundred fifty-seven. They seemed so solid.

But Eleanor said, "Can't you see that the cellar isn't as large as the house?" And she was right.

Of course, Tollie had exaggerated in saying that there was nothing in the cellar. In addition to the usual things one finds in cellars, such as the coalbox and stacks of wood, old brooms, a tin bucket, it was filled with the detritus of a girls' school: broken chairs, a pair of crutches, boxes of sports equipment. There were skis stacked against the wall, and an astonishing number of broken tennis rackets.

"There!" said Eleanor. "Can you hear it?"

And we could. Against one wall stood a tall bookcase that had no doubt once been in the library, but was now water-stained and covered with dust. On the shelves stood boxes containing what looked like onions, but labeled "tulips—early" "late" "rembrandt," pairs of ice skates leaning against one another, and a few books that were too damaged for use even by schoolgirls.

"That's where old Amias keeps his bulbs," said Miss Halloway. "He says this is the perfect place to store them."

"Well, there's a space behind it," said Eleanor. And indeed, we had all heard the echo when she knocked.

"All right, girls," said Miss Halloway. "Let's see what's behind those shelves."

Mary held the lamp while the rest of us helped Miss Halloway stack the books and skates and boxes of tulip bulbs on the floor. "It's going to be heavy," she said. "Should I summon Amias and some of his boys?" We all shook our heads. I think we wanted to see what was behind as quickly—and as privately—as possible. "All right then," she said. "Put your backs into it."

Once, while moving the bookcase, as we were taking a momentary rest, we looked at each other—Tollie, Eleanor, and me. When I saw their white faces, I knew mine must be white as well. The lamplight jumped up and down on the walls, no doubt because Mary's hand was trembling. But Miss Halloway looked grim and determined, and I decided then that I rather admired her, despite her boring lectures. All things considered, it would not be a terrible thing to be like Miss Halloway.

When the bookcase had been moved, slowly and awkwardly, back from the wall, we could see that it had covered an arched opening—through which we saw only darkness.

I will give us the credit to say that we all, including Mary Davenport, stepped through the archway together. It opened into a smaller room, the other side of the cellar, which must once have held wine. There were still wine racks on the walls.

There, in the circle of light cast by the lamp, was the skeleton of a man. We could still see the shreds of his white shirt, the remains of black boots that had long ago been nibbled away by rats. Around his ankle was an iron cuff, linked by a chain to an iron ring in the wall. Just out of his reach was a bowl that might once have held water.

We stood silent. Then Mary, with a sigh, crumpled to the floor. The lamp clattered on the stones without breaking. It lay there, still lit, until Eleanor held it up again to illuminate the remains of Christopher Raven. We stood there for what seemed like an interminable moment. Then we followed Miss Halloway, who carried Mary, up the stairs and into the autumn sunshine of the first floor, which seemed so strange to us, after the lamplight and the cellar. She put Mary on the sofa and brought her around with smelling salts, then gave us each a glass of sherry, which made Tollie cough.

Finally, Miss Halloway said, "What a terrible story."

"Do you think she knew?" asked Tollie. "He must have been down there—"

"Dying," I said. "For days."

"She didn't know," said Eleanor. "I think we dreamed exactly what she saw. She didn't know anything after Lord Collingswood hit him with the cane. I think she fainted, like Mary did."

"She must have thought he was dead," said Tollie.

"And Lord Collingswood must have told everyone that they'd had a fight, and Raven had left for Switzerland," I said.

"But she must have been here doing all sorts of things—getting dressed and walking in the garden, and eating her dinner—while he was dying below!" said Mary. She started to gasp and sob, and Miss Halloway waved the sal volatile under her nose again.

"Last summer, after I was hired as headmistress here," she said, "I read that book Lucy thought was so dull, *The History of Collingswood House*. If you'd read a little farther, girls, you would have known that Lord Collingswood died in 1818, just a year later. He was said to have died of heart problems, but there was a rumor that he might have been poisoned—digitalis, which comes from foxgloves, is toxic in a high enough dose. Lady Collingswood created this school and specified that Lord Collingswood's portrait was to be hung over the main staircase in perpetuity. I wonder, now, if that was her idea of a joke? He's been looking down at schoolgirls swarming through his house for a hundred years."

"What happened to her?" I asked.

"She moved to France. Eventually she became a painter, not a great one but there is a picture of hers in the National Gallery. She particularly liked painting flowers." Miss Halloway was silent for a moment. "We'll have to give him a proper burial," she said. "I think the dreams will stop now."

The dreams did not stop, not as long as we stayed at Collingswood. But they changed character. For the rest of that year, we dreamed that we were with him—sitting by the fire in the parlor, browsing through books in the library and reading lines of poetry to one another, walking through the garden, where the roses were blooming, including the white rose called Lady Collingsgwood. He still murmured lines of poetry to us, we still felt kisses on our hands, even our shoulders, but the dreams no longer had the passion, the urgency, that we should not have experienced and that changed us, permanently. When we left Collingswood, Eleanor for a London season, Mary for her father's parish, where she would teach Sunday School, Tollie for Newnham Teacher's College, and me for Girton, we were no longer the girls who had glared at each other on the first day of term. We were older, we knew more about the joys and pains of the world, and we were friends.

The remains of Christopher Raven were buried in the garden, and a stone was placed over him with the words "Here lies the poet Christopher Raven, lover of Lady Collingswood, 1797–1817" carved on it, followed by a line of his own poetry:

> Let her eyes guide me like bright stars, and bring
> Me to the birthing-place of poetry.

I read some of his poetry later—he had published two books, called *Aurora and Other Poems* and *Poems for the Rights of Man*. He was good, and might have become great if he had lived, although he would never have been a Shelley or Keats. But when I remembered his kisses in the dark, the whispered words, it did not matter. I do not think it mattered to her either. She loved the man, and the poet was part of the man. At least, that is what I think now that I have learned something of love—the love one has for a poet, like my Louis.

"WE CHANGED, ALL of us," I said. "Eleanor became less high and mighty, for example."

"Well!" she said, laughing. "I think I'm still both high and mighty. You should see me destroy those pipsqueak MPs on the question of votes for women! They fear my political dinners."

"And Mary became more pious," I added.

"I suppose that's true," said Mary. "I was frightened for a long time. I thought life might be like that, all passion and darkness. My father's faith was reassuring—it made me feel safe. I think I became more judgmental for a while. I went to London once, while Louis was alive, and never visited you, Lucy. I'm sorry about that. But after my little Charles died, I think I became more accepting of human frailty. I started to realize that God is there too, in the darkness as well as the light."

We stared at her. "When did you get philosophical?" asked Eleanor.

She blushed, the red suffusing her cheeks until she looked like a late apple. "I'm getting older, I guess. As we all are." She turned to me. "And losing what you love—you must have known how Lady Collingswood felt."

"Perhaps a little," I said. "But I don't think Louis is going to haunt anyone. Our love was an ordinary human love. Oh, he wrote me a poem or two, but I'm no Lady Collingswood. I went to visit his wife once, in France. You would think—insane asylum and all that. But it was perfectly ordinary as well, kind nurses looking after her. She had no idea who I was. What Christopher Raven and Lady Collingswood had—it was passion and poetry, and it had to end in violence. Could it have ended any other way? Could you imagine them in a cottage in the country, he chopping wood for the fire, she mending dishtowels?"

"Was he the ghost, or was she?" We looked at Tollie, startled by her question. "I mean, was he the one haunting us? Or was she the one, making us relive her experiences?"

"I've never thought of it like that," I said.

"When I came back to Collingswood, I found something," said Tollie. "It was summer and the school was almost empty. I came in here, and I don't know why exactly, but I looked behind the painting of Lady Collingswood. There was something taped back there."

"What did you find?" I asked. We all leaned forward, curious schoolgirls once more.

"Probably a letter of some sort," said Eleanor.

"No, not a letter," said Tollie. "I'll show you." She walked over to one of the desks that we had used, so many years ago, and lifted a framed picture that had been lying on it. She held it up so we could see.

Mary gasped, and Eleanor said, "That's him. Exactly."

It was just a watercolor of the head and shoulders, but there was the curling black hair, the brown cheeks, the laughing, mischievous eyes. In the bottom right-hand corner was written, in pen, *Adela Collingswood*.

"You can see that she loved him," said Tollie. "If she were the ghost, she would have wanted him buried."

"But she didn't know he was in the cellar," I said. "Listen to me! Here I am talking about the habits of ghosts. For all we know, it was both of them together, reliving their lives through us."

"You changed too," said Eleanor. "You'd been so focused on doing well. But after—that was when you started writing stories."

"She did inspire me in the end," I said. "Just as Miss Halloway wanted."

"But Tollie didn't change," continued Eleanor. "Did you, Tollie? You're the same old Tollie as you were back then. The Tollie who would have looked behind the painting. I would never have thought of that."

"I don't know," said Tollie. "I guess I am the same. Although I think I'm getting lines on my forehead from frowning at students!"

We heard a knock on the door. We had been so immersed in talking about the past that we all jumped.

"Ladies, dinner in half an hour," called Miss Halloway.

"We'd better get dressed," said Mary. "We don't want to be late for dinner."

"Why not?" said Eleanor. "Let them wait for us. After all, we have the guest of honor. They're not going to start the dinner without her. Is that high and mighty enough for you, Lucy?" But she was smiling as she said it.

After that, the conversation turned to dresses. Eleanor lent Tollie the second best dress she had brought, which must have cost as much as my entire wardrobe, although Tollie insisted that her gray merino was perfectly adequate. So even she looked sufficiently ladylike as we walked down the stairs, under the watchful eyes of Old Nosey, to the dining room.

My speech, "The Necessity for the Rights of Women," went well and was generally applauded, with Eleanor giving a loud "Hear, Hear!" The food was better than we had eaten as schoolgirls—no cabbage! But it was strange seeing women, some of whom I remembered, some from other years, sitting around the dining room tables, their faces turned toward me. In some of them, I could see the girls they had once been, like echoes.

It was a relief to be finished, to have fulfilled my duties and be free to go back up the stairs, undress, and lie down on the bed I had slept in so many years ago.

"Maybe you'll all dream of him tonight," said Tollie.

"I certainly hope not," said Eleanor. "Once in a lifetime is enough of Christopher Raven, I think."

THE NEXT MORNING, Mary left early to catch the train, and Eleanor had a meeting with the Fundraising Committee. But I had time before I needed to be at the station, so Tollie and I walked through the garden, smelling the late roses and coming at last to his grave.

"Christopher Raven," I said. "I would not have minded dreaming about him again, just for old times' sake."

"But you didn't?" asked Tollie.

"No, of course not," I said. "But I've been thinking about my next book—my publisher keeps asking whether I'm working on it, and of course I need the money. He wants another *Modern Diana*, but I think I'm going to write about Lady Collingswood. I think I'll call it *Adela; or Free Love*. That ought to shock everyone."

"Lucy, do you think Eleanor's right? Do you think I haven't changed?"

I looked at her carefully. "I think you've changed less than the three of us. Maybe it's because you stayed at Collingswood."

"No, it's not just that. It's something else."

Something in her voice made me say, "Tollie, is everything all right?"

"Yes, of course. It's just that I didn't want to tell the others. I still dream about him."

"What do you mean?" I said.

"I still dream about him, every night. When I found that picture, I had it framed, and then I put it in my room, up on the third floor. And I started dreaming about him again. I thought if the three of you were here, sleeping in her room, under her picture, you would have the dreams too. But it was just me." She paused for a moment, then knelt in front of the grave and traced the letters with her hand. "Maybe because I stayed here. I never married or had a child. I didn't have the sort of life that you and Eleanor and Mary have. And the dreams came back. That's what I have, a new set of students every year— and the dreams. Do you think that's awful?"

"Some of your hair's come down in back. Let me fix it for you." I pinned her bun up again. I looked at her, kneeling there, with both pity and under-standing. After a moment of silence, I said, "No, Tollie. I don't think that's awful at all. I think we have to take love where we can find it. That's what I learned with Louis."

"Thank you," she said, standing again and feeling her hair, carefully. "I never can get it to stay up. You know, you always were my best friend."

"You could have fooled me, the way you mooned after Eleanor Prescott!" I said. But I put my arm around her and kissed her cheek.

Later, as the cart bumped over the drive, I turned back to look at Colling-swood House and waved to her, knowing that I might never see her again, knowing that I would probably never come back. I had a larger world to live in, a world that included grief and loss and loneliness, but also success and companionship. It included the cafés of London, and seeing my name on red leather in bookstore windows, and the Alps. I thought of Louie in Switzerland, coughing his lungs out and looking at me with the most beautiful eyes in the world, his father's eyes. The world I lived in was more difficult, but I would not have traded it for hers.

Sometimes I would think of Tollie in her world of perpetual girlhood, dreaming of Christopher Raven, of poetry and burning kisses in the dark. And sometimes I would wish for the dreams myself. But I had a life to live, a book to write. I would always remember her this way, standing in front of Collingswood House and waving to me, under the ancient oaks.

Ravens

Some men are actually ravens.

Oh, they look like men.
Some of them in suits,
some of them in shirts embroidered
with the names of baseball teams,
some in uniforms, fighting in wars we only see
on television.
But underneath, they are ravens.
Look carefully, and you will find their skins of feathers.

Once, I fell in love with a raven man.
I knew that to keep him I had to take his skin,
his skin of feathers, long and black as night,
like ebony, tarmac, licorice, black holes.
I found it (he had taken it off to play baseball)
and hid it in the attic.

He was mine for seven years.

I had to make promises:
not to hurt ravens, to give our children names
like Sky, and Rain Cloud, and Nest-of-Twigs,
spend one night a week in the bole of an old oak tree
that had been hollowed out by who-knows-what.
I had to eat worms. (Yes, I ate worms.)
You do crazy things for raven men.

In return,
he spent six nights a week in my arms.
His black feathers fell around me.
He gave me three children
(Sky, Rain Cloud, Nest-of-Twigs,
whom we called Twiggy).
And I was happy,
which is more than most people achieve.

You know where this is going.
One day, I threw a stone at a raven.
I was not angry, he was not doing anything in particular.
It is just
that raven men are always lost.
Think of it as destiny,
think of it as inevitable.

I was not tired of our nights together,
with the moon gleaming on his feathers.
No.

Or maybe he found his skin in the attic?
Maybe I had taken his skin and he found it,
and he picked three feathers from it
and touched each of our children,
and they flew away together?
Maybe that's how I lost them?

I don't even remember.

Loving raven men will make you crazy.
In the mornings I see them hurrying to their offices,
the men in suits. And I see them in bars
shouting for their baseball teams, and I see them
on television in wars that have no names,
and I say, that one is a raven man,
and that one, and that one.

Sometimes I stop one and say,
will you send my raven man back to me?
And my raven children?
Some night, when the moon is gleaming,
the way it used to gleam
on long black feathers falling
around my face?

The Fox Wife

I saw you dancing in a glade alone,
feet bare and dressed in nothing but a rag,
your red hair like a fire around your head.
I had to stand and look and keep on looking.

I saw you standing there among the trees,
smelled you before I saw you. First, I thought
you were a hunter. But no, you smelled of earth,
not death. I danced because I saw you looking.

Day after day, I went back to that glade.
And sometimes you were there, and sometimes not.

That was deliberate. I did not want you
to always get what you were coming for.
One day you stepped into the glade and spoke:
"I have been watching you. Can you forgive me?"

I wanted to say more: you burn so brightly,
I wonder that the forest is still standing.
You are more graceful than a flock of doves.
You should be dressed in silk instead of rags.
I am only a farmer, but I love you.

And yet somehow you said all of those things.
At least, I heard them and I followed you
out of the forest and into the farmyard.
The dogs barked, but you would not let them near me.

I did not know why all the dogs were barking.
What was it made you come? Now tell me truly.
Was it the possibility of finding
a home, a husband, not some soggy burrow?

That, I suppose. And then you looked so handsome.
And then there were the dresses, silk as promised.

I could have done worse than a prosperous farmer.

Or better: you would make a splendid lady,
upon your horse and riding by his lordship.

You flatter me. But then, you know I like it.
When I was heavy with our oldest son,
you told me I still looked just like the girl
you first saw dancing in the forest glade.

And so you did. Now dear, be reasonable . . .
Were we not always happiest together,
on rainy afternoons when you sat sewing
and I would read to you from some old book?
Or when we would go walking in the spring
to see the glade you dance in filled with bluebells?
Or when we watched our sons and daughter sleeping,
three heads with hair like fire upon the pillows.
Where are they now? Where are our children, dear?

Down in the burrow, safe from you and yours.

I would not hurt a hair upon their heads.

You hung my sister's pelt upon the door.
You said there had been foxes in the henhouse.
You set those traps and did not think to tell me.

But how was I to know? Be reasonable . . .

Each night, while you lay sleeping, I snuck out.
A thing that was once wild is never tame.
I went to smell the earth, to meet my kind.
I went to see the bright disk of the moon.
You set those traps and caught my sister in one.
And what should I see on the henhouse door
next morning when I went to gather eggs?
Our children are asleep inside this burrow.
Your dogs would tear them up within an instant.

But dear, they're human too, you can't deny that.

Your dogs would. They shall learn the forest paths,

learn how to hunt, how to avoid the hunter.
They shall be cold in winter, wet in storms,
they shall eat mice and rabbits, roam the meadow,
drink from the streams and try to catch the birds.
When they are grown, they'll put on human skins
and go into the town, but I shall warn them
never to fall in love. Not with a human.

Why can't you see that I meant you no harm?
I did not know . . . My dear, won't you forgive me?

I am not tame. I can't be reasoned with,
and there is no forgiveness in the forest.
Either kill me with that gun you carry,
or go.

He went. The birches heard him weeping.

Reynalda

S HE WALKS SLOWLY, because she is tired and the road is rough with mud churned by tractor wheels and then frozen—it is March and spring has not yet come to New England. In the forest she could see the first lilies of the valley starting to push their green stems through last year's oak leaves, but here among the farms nothing is green, nothing is growing, all is stubble. The ice on the road shines in the moonlight.

Wearily she walks on, watching for the familiar stump, the bend in the road that will bring her home. She has been gone a fortnight to visit her parents, who live deep in the forest. She is eager to see her man and the baby who sleeps in his bassinet under a warm blanket. She would not have left, but word came that her mother was ill. She has been a dutiful daughter, nursing her mother back to health, helping her father with the chores, even the hunting, for he is getting old and cannot move as stealthily as he used to.

There—there is the stump! And there is the bend in the road, and there is the path to the farmhouse. She moves more quickly now that the house is in sight. In one of the pastures, she can see white hillocks of sheep sleeping together. She smells their familiar odor. In the other is a draft horse that her man won't sell although the tractor does what it used to. She passes the barn with its two sows grunting in their sleep, the silent chicken coop.

By the time she reaches the front door, she is almost stumbling from tiredness. Without thinking about it, she undergoes the transformation that has become automatic for her when returning here, to her home with him. She thinks of him as her man, although the minister of the Methodist Church refused to marry them, saying, "Frank, you should stick to your own kind." As though she is not good enough for a prosperous farmer—coming from the forest, from a family that lives on what it can hunt and forage. The other farmers and their wives also call him Frank—as does she, when summoning him to dinner.

She does not want to wake him or the baby, so she lifts the latch and pushes the door open as quietly as she can. It's the kitchen door—there is a front door, but it's opened only on formal occasions, for weddings and funerals. It has never been opened since she came to live at the farmhouse. The kitchen is where he comes in with his muddy boots, where she goes out to gather eggs or vegetables from the garden.

She takes off her coat—it is dark, but moonlight is shining through the window, so she does not light a candle. She is about to set it down on the table—she wants to check on the baby before putting it in the closet—when she notices a coat already hanging from the back of a chair. It is red, like hers. It looks like hers. For a moment, because she is so tired, she looks at both coats, wondering if somehow she is simultaneously holding her coat and has already put it on the back of a chair, but how is that possible? She picks up the other coat. They are almost indistinguishable, except the other—yes, there is a scent lingering about it, which she recognizes because who has that particular musky perfume? Her sister.

She puts down her coat and examines the other one. On it, on one side next to the lapel, are two holes that are not buttonholes. She touches them, feels their edges. She lifts the coat to her nose. There is her sister's scent, and . . . yes, another scent. Hard, metallic. And the scent of her man.

She stands there for a moment in the moonlight. A long moment, but it ends, and then she picks up her coat again so she is carrying both of them over her arm. She turns and walks out of the kitchen, down the dark back corridor but she does not need a light. She passes her bedroom, where the man is snoring in his sleep. She passes the baby's room. She goes to the parlor, to her sewing box. Snip snip. Stitch stitch. She cuts and sews her sister's coat until it has a new shape. Then she goes back to the baby's room. He is sleeping so sweetly that she does not want to wake him, but it's impossible to dress him, recumbent like this, so she whispers, "Wake up, sweetheart. Mama's here." He stirs but does not open his eyes, so she shakes him a little. He stretches out his fists, cries out, then looks up at her. What big brown eyes he has! Such a handsome boy. "Put this on," she says. "It's time to get dressed."

She slips the little legs over his legs, she slips the little arms over his arms, so he is completely dressed in the red coat she has sewn him. He looks like a cherry.

"It's time to go, sweetheart," she says. She is already wearing her red coat, so when she picks him up, he seems like a part of her once again, as he was in her belly.

She is out the door and halfway across the farmyard when she hears the cry.

"Reynalda! Reynalda! Where are you going?" It is Frank, standing at the kitchen door in his pajamas.

"You promised!" she yells back. "You promised you would never again!" She puts the baby down on the ground, on his feet and hands, so he can run. As soon as he is free of her arms, he jumps around her ankles with excited yips.

"But it was in the chicken coop! A fox in the chicken coop—it had already killed the hens. What was I supposed to do?"

She spits at him, with all the hatred in her heart, which only an hour ago was love: "*That was my sister.*"

Then, like the baby, she drops down on all fours. She turns toward the forest, makes sure her pup is at her side, and starts to run.

Mr. Fox

When I first fell in love with Mr. Fox, he warned me:
You can't trust me, my dear.
Just when you think I am there,
I am gone, I am nowhere.
Look, I'm wearing a mask. Who does that? Thieves.
By the time the autumn leaves have fallen,
you will mourn my absence.

And yet, I couldn't help it. After all,
he was wearing such a dashing red coat,
like a soldier. He had such a twinkle in his eye.
He danced so nimbly, holding my hands
in paws on which he wore black kid gloves.
His tail ended in a white tuft.
I knew about the others, of course—or at least
I'd heard rumors. I knew he was no innocent.
I knew about the one who had drowned
herself in a river, her muslin gown floating
around her. I knew about the one who had locked
herself away in a convent.

How does one fall out of love with a thief
who has already stolen one's heart?
But I was cautious: I went to his castle in the woods.
Be bold, said the sign above the gate. *Be bold.*
But not too bold. I have never been good
at listening to advice, or taking it.
I was too bold, as usual.

What did I find? First, a pleasant parlor,
with blue silk curtains and rosewood furniture,
perfectly charming. Then, a library
filled with books, from Shakespeare to W.B. Yeats.
A kitchen with no implements more dangerous
than a paring knife, beside a barrel of apples
waiting to be turned into cider.

Bathrooms with modern plumbing, a dining room
that contained a mahogany table large enough
for banquets, but seldom used, judging
by the dust. Where was his secret chamber?
There must be one. On top of a desk in his study,
I'd seen a photograph of the girl who drowned,
beside a vase of lilies, like a memorial.

And there it was, at the end of a carpeted hallway.
I knew what it must lead to, that small door.
It was locked, of course, but I took out my lockpick tools
(if he was a thief, I was another).
It opened easily.

There was no blood on the floor. There were
no dead, dismembered wives hanging from hooks.
Instead, the walls were covered with masks:
fox, badger, mole, boar, weasel,
otter, squirrel, even one that resembled a tree.
All the masks he had worn, presumably.
And on one wall, opposite the window,
which badly needed washing, was a portrait
of an ordinary man with sandy hair
and tired eyes.

I locked the room behind me. At our wedding,
he said, "Are you sure, my dear?" with a toothy grin
that seemed wicked, but was, I thought, a little anxious.
"To marry the dangerous Mr. Fox?" I asked.
"Who knows, you might gobble me up,
but I'll take my chances." He seemed satisfied,
and swung me into a waltz. There's a moral to this story:
ladies, have your own set of lockpick tools. Also,
be bold and wise and cunning,
like a fox.

The Mysterious Miss Tickle

Miss Tickle owns a bookshop on the square
called Antique Books and Oddments, where she sells
old maps, and postcards sent from strange hotels,
and photographs of people you don't know
in black and white, rain-spattered travel guides
to places like Ceylon and Samarkand,
one called *Constantinople on Five Pounds
a Day*, a Sanskrit-English dictionary,
and all the Nancy Drews, including ones
I've never seen in the public library,
like *Death by Henbane*, where Nancy, George, and Bess
become witches, form a coven, and solve a murder.
I think it's one of my favorites. After school,
Miss Tickle lets me sit in the battered armchair
in a corner of the shop, beneath *The Collected
Poems of Sappho*, where I do my homework
or play with her various decks of tarot cards.
She has seven, one for each day of the week.
She's hopeless at multiplication, but her cat,
Ebenezer, is pretty good, so he helps me out.

I've decided that someday I'm going to be like Miss Tickle,
with long black hair all the way down my back,
a cat named after a character from Dickens,
though maybe less talkative than Ebenezer,
who can be annoying, a closetful of skirts
in blue and purple that swirl around my shins,
a coat with the moon and all the constellations
embroidered on its lapels, and sparkly eyeshadow.
Of course my dad, who's an accountant, wants me
to be an accountant too, but I think I'd rather
be a witch or own a bookshop, and Miss Tickle
says I can do all three if I really want to,
that learning math can help you cast better spells.
Hers, she says, are always a little slipshod.

The people in town think Miss Tickle's a little strange.
No one else around here goes out to watch the bats
at twilight, or brings home toads in tupperware
to put in their gardens. She doesn't eat them, whatever
Mr. Nowak, the grocer, says—I think he's joking.
No one else keeps newts in a tank, just tropical fish.
Other people use aspirin, not a willow tincture.
Still, they mostly accept her. I mean, she pays her taxes
like anyone else. Though the kids at school suspect
that she flies overhead on a broomstick on windy nights,
with her black hair whipping around her. Miss Finch, the librarian,
says she's seen her almost crash into the steeple
of the Methodist Church. I'm the only one who knows
that she landed badly that night and sprained her ankle.
She told me the broom was in a bad mood, and threw her.

Sure, I have friends my own age to eat lunch with at school,
but Miss Tickle doesn't seem old, though she isn't young:
somewhere between twenty and two hundred.
Her idea of dinner is chocolate cake, and for fun
she plays checkers with her shadow, who usually beats her,
or concocts natural remedies out of toadstools
(she insists they've never poisoned anyone),
or recites lines from Shakespeare she knows by heart.
Yes, someday I want to be like Miss Tickle, although
my hair isn't long and black, just red and curly,
unfortunately. But I'm working on changing that.
I figure magic works as well as hair dye.
I've asked her to teach me some spells, and I can already
light the tips of my fingers on fire, and wiggle my ears,
and levitate, just a little. But give me time.
She says when I'm old enough, she'll leave me the bookshop,
then she'll retire and go where witches go
(I think it's on the dark side of the moon).

Meanwhile, I'll curl up here in the battered armchair
with a batch of cookies that are only a little burned,
but they're chocolate chip, so it doesn't really matter,
ignoring Ebenezer, and start on a chapter
of the *Philosophical Works* of someone named Hypatia
of Alexandria, which is more interesting
then you would expect, judging from the cover,

while Miss Tickle rings up a customer, then calls
to the back of the bookshop, "Would you like some tea?
I'll put the kettle on, my dear, if you'll join me!"

Lessons with Miss Gray

That summer, we were reporters: intrepid, like Molly McBride of the Charlotte *Observer*, who had ridden an elephant in the Barnum & Bailey circus, and gone up in a balloon at the Chicago World's Fair, and whose stagecoach had been robbed by Black Bart himself. Although she had told him it would make for a better story, Black Bart had refused to take her purse: he would not rob a lady.

We were sitting in the cottage at the bottom of the Beauforts' garden, on the broken furniture that was kept there. Rose, on the green sofa with the torn upholstery, was chewing on her pencil and trying to decide whether her yak, on the journey she was undertaking through the Himalayas, was a noble animal of almost human intelligence, or a surly and unkempt beast that she could barely control. Emma, in an armchair with a sagging seat, was eating gingerbread and writing the society column, in which Ashton had acquired a number of Dukes and Duchesses. Justina, in another armchair, which did not match—but what was Justina doing there at all? She was two years older than we were, and a *Balfour*, of the Balfours who reminded you, as though you had forgotten, that Lord Balfour had been granted all of Balfour County by James I. And Justina was beautiful. We had been startled when she had approached us, in the gymnasium of the Ashton Ladies' Academy, where all of us except Melody went to school, and said, "Are you writing a newspaper? I'd like to help." There she was, sitting in the armchair, which was missing a leg and had to be propped on an apple crate. It leaned sideways like a sinking ship. She was writing in a script that was more elegant than any of ours—Rose's page was covered with crossings out, and Emma's with gingerbread crumbs—about Serenity Sage, who was, at that moment, trapped in the Caliph's garden, surrounded by the scent of roses and aware that at any moment, the Caliph's eunuchs might find her. She would always, afterward, associate the scent of roses with danger. How, Justina wondered, would Serenity escape? How would she get back to Rome, where the Cardinal, who had hired her, was waiting? Beside him, as he sat in a secret chamber beneath the cathedral, were a trunk filled with gold coins and his hostage: her lover, the revolutionary they called The Mask. We did not, of course, insist that everything in our newspaper be true. How boring that would have been. And Melody was sitting on the other end of the sofa, reading the Charlotte *Observer*, trying to imitate the advertising.

"Soap as white as, as—" she said. "As soap."

"As the snows of the Himalayas," said Rose, who had decided that her yak was surly, and the sunlight on the slopes blinding. But surely her guide, who was intrepid, would lead her to the fabled Forbidden Cities.

"As milk," said Emma. "I wish I had milk. Callie's gingerbread is always dry."

"For goodness sake," said Rose. "Can't you think of anything other than food?"

"As the moon, shining over the sullied streets of London," said Melody, in the voice she used to recite poetry in school.

"What do you know about London?" said Emma. "Make it the streets of Ashton."

"I don't think they're particularly sullied," said Rose.

"Not in front of your house, Miss Rose," said Melody, in another voice altogether. Rose kicked her, and Melody kicked back.

"As the paper on which a lover has written his letter," said Justina. Serenity Sage was sailing down the Tiber.

"If he's written the letter, it's not going to be white," said Emma. "Obviously."

And then we were silent, because no one said "obviously" to a Balfour, although Justina had not noticed. The Mask was about to take off his mask.

"I don't understand," said Melody, in yet another voice, which made even Justina look up. "Lessons in witchcraft," she read, "with Miss Emily Gray. Reasonable rates. And it's right here in Ashton."

"Do you think it's serious?" asked Emma. "Do you think she's teaching real witchcraft? Not just the fake stuff, like Magical Seymour at the market in Brickleford, who pulls Indian-head pennies out of your ears?"

"You're getting crumbs everywhere," said Rose, who was suddenly and inexplicably feeling critical. "Why shouldn't it be real? You can't put false advertising in a newspaper. My father told me that."

And suddenly we all knew, except Justina, who was realizing the Cardinal's treachery, that we were no longer reporters. We were witches.

"WHERE DID YOU say she lived?" asked Melody. We were walking down Elm Street, in a part of town that Melody did not know as well as the rest of us.

"There," said Emma. We didn't understand how Emma managed to know everything, at least about Ashton. Although her mother was a whirlpool of gossip: everything there was to know in Ashton made its way inevitably to her. She had more servants than the rest of us: Mrs. Spraight, the housekeeper, as well as the negro servants, Callie, who cooked, and Henry, who was both gardener and groom. Rose's mother made do with a negro housekeeper, Hannah, and Justina, who lived with her grandmother, old Mrs. Balfour, had only Zelia, a French mulatto who didn't sleep in but came during the day to help out. And Melody—well, Melody was Hannah's niece, and she had no servants at all. She lived with her aunt and her cousin Coralie, who taught at the negro school, across the train tracks. We didn't know how she felt about this—we often didn't know what Melody felt, and when we asked, she didn't always answer.

"Don't you think it's unfair that you have to go to that negro school, with only a dusty yard to play in? Don't you think you should be able to go to the Ashton Ladies' Academy, with us? Don't you think—" And her face would shut, like a curtain. So we didn't often ask.

"The white house, with the roses growing on it," said Emma. "It used to be the Randolph house. She was a witch too, Mrs. Randolph, at least that's what I heard. She died, or her daughter died, or somebody, and afterward all the roses turned as red as blood."

"They're pink," said Melody.

"Well, maybe they've faded. I mean, this was a long time ago, right?" Rose looked at the house. The white trim had been freshly painted, and at each window there were lace curtains. "Are we going in, or not?"

"It looks perfectly respectable," said Emma. "Not at all like a witch's house."

"How do you know what a witch's house looks like?" asked Melody.

"Everyone knows what a witch's house looks like," said Rose. "I think you're all scared. That's why you're not going in."

At that, we all walked up the path and to the front door, although Justina had forgotten where we were and had to be pulled. Justina often forgot where we were, or that the rest of us were there at all. Rose raised her hand to the knocker, which was shaped like a frog—the first sign we had seen that a witch might, indeed, be within—waited for a moment, then knocked.

"Good afternoon," said a woman in a gray dress, with white hair. She looked like your grandmother, the one who baked you gingerbread and knitted socks. Or like a schoolteacher, as proper as a handkerchief. Behind her stood a ghost.

THAT SUMMER, WE each had a secret that we were keeping from the others.

Rose's secret was that she wanted to fly. She had books hidden under her bed, books on birds and balloons and gliders, on everything that flew. She read every story that she could find about flight—Icarus, and the Island of Laputa, and the stories of Mr. Verne. There was no reason to keep this a secret—the rest of us would not have particularly cared, although Melody might have said that if God intended us to fly, he would have given us wings. Her aunt had said that to a passing preacher, who had told the negro people to rise up, rise up, as equal children of God. And Justina might have looked even more absent than usual, with the words "away, away" singing through her head. But Rose would have been miserable if she had told: it was the only secret she had, and it gave her days, and especially nights, when she was exploring the surface of the moon, some kind of meaning. And what if her mother found out? Elizabeth Caldwell's lips would thin into an elegant line, and Rose would see in her eyes the distance between their house with its peeling paint, beneath a locust tree that scattered its seedpods over the lawn each spring, and the house where her mother had grown up, in Boston. She would see the distance between herself and the girl who had grown up in that house, in lace dresses, playing the piano or embroidering on silk, a girl who had never been rude or disobedient. Who had never, so far as Rose knew, wanted to climb the Himalayas, or to fly.

Justina's secret was that her grandmother, the respectable Mrs. Balfour who, when she appeared in the Balfour pew at the Episcopal Church, resembled an ageing Queen Victoria, was going mad. Two nights ago, she had emptied the contents of her chamberpot over the mahogany suite in the parlor, spreading them over the antimacassars, over the Aubusson carpet. Justina had washed everything herself, so Zelia would not find out. And Zelia had apparently not found out, although the smell— She still had a bruise where her grandmother had gripped her arm and whispered, "Do you see the Devil, with his hooves like a goat's and his tongue like a lizard's? *I can.*" "Away, away" the words sang through her head, and she imagined herself as Serenity Sage, at the mercy of the Cardinal, but with a curved dagger she had stolen from the Caliph hidden in her garter. Then she would be away, away indeed, sailing across the Mediterranean, with the wind blowing her hair like a golden flag.

Emma's secret was that her mother had locked the pantry. Adeline Beaufort had been a Balfour—Emma was Justina's second or third cousin—and no daughter of hers was going to be *fat*. For two weeks now she had been bribing Callie, with rings, hair ribbons, even the garnet necklace that her father had given her as a birthday present. That morning, she had traded a pair of earrings for gingerbread. Callie was terrified of Mrs. Beaufort. "Lordy, Emma, don't tempt me again! She'll have me whipped, like in the old slave days," she had whispered. But she could not resist fine things, even if she had to keep them under a floorboard, as Emma could not resist her hunger. They were trapped, like a couple of magpies, fearful and desiring.

Melody's secret was that she wanted to go to college. There was a negro college in Atlanta that admitted women, the preacher had told her. So they could be teachers, for the betterment of the negro race. Because white teachers went to college, and why should only negro children be taught by high school graduates—if that? And Melody wanted to better the negro race. Sometimes she wondered if she should be with us at all, instead of with the other girls in her school—perhaps, as her aunt often said, she should stick with her own. But her own filled her with a sense of both loyalty and despair. Why couldn't those girls look beyond Ashton, beyond the boys they would one day marry, and the families they would work for? And there was a streak of pragmatism in this, as in many of her actions, because the rest of us checked books out of the library for her, more books than even we read. She had never been told that colored folk could not enter the library, but colored folk never did, and what if she was told to leave? Then she would know she was not welcome, which was worse than suspecting she would not be. So every morning, after her chores were done and before school, when other girls were still ironing their dresses and curling their hair, she went to the houses of the wealthy negro families, of the Jeffersons, who traded tobacco and were, if the truth were told, the wealthiest family in Ashton, and the Beauforts, whose daughters were, as everyone knew, Emma's fourth or fifth cousins, and cleaned. She put the money she earned, wrapped in an old set of her aunt's drawers, in a hole at the back of her closet. For college.

THE GHOST WAS, of course, a girl, and we all knew her, except Justina. She lived near the railroad tracks, by the abandoned tobacco factory that not even the Jeffersons used anymore, with her father. He was a drunkard. We did not know her name, but we could identify her without it. She was the ghost, the white girl, the albino: white hair, white face, and thin white hands sticking out from the sleeves of a dress that was too short, that she must have outgrown several years ago. Only her eyes, beneath her white eyebrows, had color, and those were a startling blue. Her feet were bare, and dirty.

We knew that we weren't supposed to play with her, because she was poor, and probably an idiot. What else could that lack of coloring mean, but idiocy? There was an asylum in Charlotte—her father should be persuaded to put her there, for her own good. But he was a drunkard, and could even Reverend Hewes persuade a drunkard? He rarely let her out. Look at the girl—did he remember to feed her? She looked like she lived on air. Adeline Beaufort and Elizabeth Caldwell agreed: it would be for her own good. Really a mercy, for such a creature.

"Come inside, girls," said Miss Gray. "But mind you wipe your feet. I won't have dirt in the front hall."

It was certainly respectable. The parlor looked like the Beauforts', but even more filled with what Emma later told us were bibelots or objets d'art: china shepherdesses guarding their china sheep; cranberry-colored vases filled with pink roses and sprays of honeysuckle; and painted boxes, on one of which Justina, who had studied French history that year, recognized Marie Antoinette. And there were cats. We did not notice them, initially—they had a way of being inconspicuous, which Miss Gray later told us was their own magic, a cat magic. But we would blink, and there would be a cat, on the sofa where we were about to sit, or on the mantel where we had just looked. "How they keep from knocking down all those—music boxes and whatnots, I don't know," Emma said afterward. But we didn't say anything then. We didn't know what to say.

"Please sit down, girls." We did so cautiously, trying to keep our knees away from the rickety tables, with their lace doilies and china dogs. Trying to remember that we were in a witch's house. "I've made some lemonade, and Emma will be pleased to hear that I've baked walnut bars, and those cream horns she likes." There was also an angel cake, like a white sponge, and a Devil's

Food cake covered with chocolate frosting, and a jelly roll with strawberry jelly, and meringues. We ate although Melody whispered that one should never, ever eat in a witch's house. The ghost ate too, cutting her slice of angel cake into small pieces with the side of her fork and eating them slowly, one by one.

"Another slice, Melody, Justina, Rose?" We did not wonder how she knew our names. She was a witch. It would have been stranger, wouldn't it, if she hadn't known? We shook our heads, except for Emma, who ate the last of the jelly roll.

"Then it's time to discuss your lessons. Please follow me into the laboratory."

It must have been a kitchen, once, but now the kitchen table was covered with a collection of objects in neat rows and piles: scissors; a mouse in a cage; balls of string, the sort used in gardens to tie up tomatoes; a kitchen scale; feathers, blue and green and yellow; spectacles, most of then cracked; a crystal ball; seashells; the bones of a small alligator, held together with wire; candles of various lengths; butterfly wings; a plait of hair that Rose thought must have come from a horse—she liked horses, because on their backs she felt as though she were flying; some fountain pens; a nest with three speckled eggs; and silver spoons. At least, that's what we remembered afterward, when we tried to make a list. We sat around the table on what must have once been kitchen chairs, with uncomfortable wooden backs, while Miss Gray stood and lectured to us, exactly like Miss Harris in Rhetoric and Elocution.

"Once," said Miss Gray, "witchcraft was seen as a—well, a craft, to be taught by apprenticeship and practiced by intuition. Nowadays, we know that witchcraft is a science. Specific actions will yield specific results. Rose, please don't slouch in your chair. Being a witch should not prevent you from behaving like a lady. Justina, your elbow has disarranged Mortimer, a South American alligator, or the remains thereof. A witch is always respectful, even to inanimate objects. Please pay attention. As I was saying, nowadays witchcraft is regarded as a science, as reliable, for an experienced practitioner, as predicting the weather. It is this science—not the hocus-pocus of those terrible women in *Macbeth*, who are more to be pitied than feared in their delusion—that I propose to teach you. We shall begin tomorrow. Please be prompt—I dislike tardiness."

As we walked down the garden path, away from the Randolph house, Emma said to the ghost, "How did you know about the lessons?"

"My Papa was sleeping under the *Observer*," she said. Her voice was a rusty whisper, as though she had almost forgotten how to use it.

"Here, I don't want this," said Emma, handing her the last cream horn, somewhat crumbled, which she had been keeping in her pocket.

None of us realized until afterward that Miss Gray had never told us what time to come.

* * *

"THE FIRST LESSON," said Miss Gray, "is to see yourselves."

We were looking into mirrors, old mirrors speckled at the edges, in tarnished gold frames—Justina's had a crack across her forehead, and Emma stared into a shaving-glass. Justina thought, "I look like her. My mother looked like her. They say my mother died of influenza, but perhaps she died at the asylum in Charlotte, chained to her bed, clawing at her hair and crying because of the lizards. Perhaps all the Balfours go mad, from marrying each other. Is that why Father left?" Because to the best of her knowledge, her father was in Italy, perhaps in Rome, where Serenity glared out through the bars of her prison, so far beneath the cathedral that no daylight crept between the stones, at the Inquisitor and his men, monks all, but with pistols at their sides. Justina looked into her eyes, large and dark, for signs of madness.

Rose scowled, which did not improve her appearance. What would she have looked like, if she had taken after the Winslows rather than her father? She imagined her mother and her aunt Catherine, who had never married. How daunting it must have been, taking for a moment her father's perspective, to marry that austere delicacy, which could only have come from the City of Winter. In Boston, her mother had told her, it snowed all winter long. Rose imagined it as a city of perpetual silence, where the snow muffled all sounds except for the tinkling of bells, sleigh bells and the bells of churches built from blocks of ice. Within the houses, also built of ice, sat ladies and gentlemen, calm, serene, with noses like icicles, conversing politely—probably about the weather. And none of them were as polite or precise as her mother or her aunt Catherine, the daughters of the Snow Queen. When they drove in their sleigh, drawn by a yak, they wore capes of egret feathers. If she were more like them, more like a Snow Princess, instead of sunburnt and ungainly, would she, Rose wondered, love me then?

Emma imagined herself getting fatter and fatter, her face stretching until she could no longer see herself in the shaving glass. If she suddenly burst, what would happen? She would ooze over Ashton like molasses, covering the streets. Her father would call the men who were harvesting tobacco, call them from the fields to gather her in buckets and then tubs. They would give her to the women, who would spread her over buttered bread, and the children would eat her for breakfast. She shook her head, trying to clear away the horrifying image.

Melody thought, "Lord, let me never wish for whiter skin, or a skinnier nose, or eyes like Emma's, as blue as the summer sky, no matter what."

We did not know what the ghost thought, but as she stared into her mirror, she shook her head, and we understood. Who can look into a mirror without shaking her head? Except Miss Gray.

"No, no, girls," said Miss Gray. "All of the sciences require exact observation, particularly witchcraft. You must learn to see, not what you expect to see, but what is actually *there*. Now look again."

It was Melody who saw first. Of course she had been practicing: Melody always practiced. It was hot even for July—the flowers in all the gardens of Ashton were drooping, except for the flowers in Miss Gray's garden. But in the laboratory it was cool. We were drinking lemonade. We were heartily sick of looking into mirrors.

"Come, girls," said Miss Gray. "I would like you to see what Melody has accomplished." We looked into Melody's mirror: butterflies. Butterflies everywhere, all the colors of sunrise, Swallowtails and Sulfurs, Harvesters and Leafwings, Fritillaries, Emperors, and Blues, like pieces of silk that were suddenly wings—silk from evening gowns that Emma's mother might have worn, or Rose's. "O latest born and loveliest visions far of all Olympus' faded hierarchy! Butterflies are symbols of the soul," said Miss Gray. "And also of poetry. You, Melody, are a poet."

"That's stupid," said Melody.

"But nevertheless true," said Miss Gray.

"It's like—a garden, or a park," said Emma, when she too saw. And we could also see it, a lawn beneath maple trees whose leaves were beginning to turn red and gold. They were spaced at regular intervals along a gravel path, and both lawn and path were covered with leaves that had already fallen. The lawn sloped down to a pond whose surface reflected the branches above. Beside the path stood a bench, whose seat was also covered with leaves. On either side of the bench were stone urns, with lichen growing over them, and further along the path we could see a statue of a woman, partially nude. She was dressed in a stone scarf and bits of moss.

"How boring," said Emma, although the rest of us would have liked to go there, at least for the afternoon, it was so peaceful.

And then, for days, we saw nothing. But finally, in the ghost's mirror, appeared the ghost of a mouse, small and gray, staring at us with black eyes.

"He's hungry," said the ghost. Emma handed her a piece of gingerbread, and she nibbled it gratefully, although we knew that wasn't what she meant. And from then on, we called her Mouse.

"If you'd only apply yourself, Rose, I'm sure you could do it," said Miss Gray, as Miss Osborn, the mathematics teacher, had said at the end of the school year while giving out marks. Rose scowled again, certain that she could not. And it was Justina whom we saw next in her mirror.

"It's only a book," she said. It was a large book, bound in crimson leather with gilding on its spine, and a gilt title on the cover: *Justina*.

"Open it," said Miss Gray.

"How?" But she was already reaching into the mirror, opening the book at random—to a page that began, "And so, Justina opened the book." The rest of the page was blank. "Who writes in it?" asked Justina, as the words "'Who writes in it,' asked Justina" wrote themselves across the page.

"That's enough for now," said Miss Gray as she reached into the mirror and closed the book. "Let's not get ahead of ourselves."

On the day that Rose finally saw herself, the rest of us were grinding bones into powder and putting the powder into jars labeled lizard, bat, frog. Mouse was sewing wings on a taxidermied mouse.

"That's it?" asked Rose, outraged. "I've been practicing all this time for a stupid rosebush? It doesn't even have roses. It's all thorns."

"Wait," said Miss Gray. "It's early yet for roses," although the pink roses—La Reine, she had told us—were blooming over the sides of the Randolph house, and their perfume filled the laboratory.

Sitting in the cottage afterward, we agreed: the first lesson had been disappointing. But we rather liked grinding bones.

ROSE'S HEART SWUNG in her chest like a pendulum when Miss Gray said, "It's time you learned how to fly." She told us to meet in the woods, at the edge of Slater's Pond. Mouse was late; she was almost always late. As we stood waiting for her, Emma whispered, "Do you think we're going to use broomsticks? Witches use broomsticks, right?"

Miss Gray, who had been looking away from us and into the woods, presumably for Mouse, turned and said, "Although Emma seems to have forgotten, I trust the rest of you remember that a lady never whispers. The use of a broomstick, although traditional, arose from historical rather than magical necessity. All that a witch needs to fly is a tree branch—the correct tree branch, carefully trained. It must have fallen, preferably in a storm—we are fortunate, this summer, to have had so many storms—and the tree from which it fell must be compatible with the witch. The principle is a scientific one: a branch, which has evolved to exist high above the earth, waving in the wind, desires to return to that height. Therefore, with the proper encouragement, it has the ability to carry the witch up into the air, which we experience as flying. Historically, witches have disguised their branches as brooms, to hide them from—those authorities who did not understand that witchcraft is a science. It is part of the lamentable history of prejudice against rational thinking. I myself, when I worked with Galileo—Sophia, I'm afraid you're late again."

"I'm sorry," mumbled Mouse, and we walked off into the woods, each separately searching for our branches, with Miss Gray's voice calling instructions and encouragement through the trees.

Justina's branch was a loblolly pine, that only she could ride: it kicked and bucked like an untrained colt. Melody rode a tulip poplar that looked too large for her. It moved like a cart horse, but she said that it was so steady, she always felt safe. Rose found an osage-orange that looked particularly attractive, with its glossy leaves and three dried oranges, now brown, still attached, but they did not agree—she liked to soar over the treetops, and it preferred to navigate through the trees, within a reasonable distance of the ground. When she flew too high, it would prick her with its thorns. So she gave it to Emma, who rode it until the end of summer and afterward asked Henry to carve a walking stick out of it, so she would not forget her flying lessons. Rose finally settled on a winged elm, which she said helped her loop-de-loop, a maneuver only she would try. Mouse took longer than all of us to find her branch: she was scared of flying, we could see that. Finally, Miss Gray gave her a shadbush, which never flew too high and seemed as skittish as she was. Miss Gray herself flew on a sassafras, which never misbehaved. She rode side-saddle, with her back straight and her skirt sweeping out behind her, in a steady canter.

"Straighten your backs," she would say, as we flew, carefully at first and then with increasing confidence, over the pasture beneath Slocumb's Bluff, the highest point in Ashton. "Rose, you look like a hunchback. Melody, you must ride your branch with spirit. Think of yourself as Hippolyta riding her favorite horse to war."

"Who's Hippolyta?" asked Emma, gripping her branch as tightly as she could. She had just avoided an encounter with the rocky side of the bluff. Mouse was the most frightened, but Emma was the most cautious of us.

"Queen of the Amazons," said Melody, attempting to dodge two Monarchs. Since the day she had seen herself in the mirror, butterflies had come to her, wherever she was. They sat on her shoulders, and early one morning, when she was cleaning the mirror in Elspeth Jefferson's bedroom, she saw that they had settled on her hair, like a crown.

That day, none of us were Amazon Queens. Rose was flying close to the side of the bluff and over the Himalayas, in a cloak of egret feathers. She could see the yak she had once ridden, sulking beneath her. She was, for the first time she could remember, perfectly happy. Somewhere among those peaks were the Forbidden Cities. She could see the first of them, the City of Winter, where the Snow Queen ruled in isolated splendor and the Princesses Elizabeth and Caroline rode through the city streets in a sleigh drawn by leopards as white as snow. She flew upward, over the towers of the city, which were shining in the sunlight. And there were the people, serene and splendid, looking up at her, startled to see her flying above them with her cloak of egret feathers streaming out behind her, although they were too polite to shout. But then one and another raised their hands to wave to her, and the bells on their wrists jingled, like sleigh bells.

She raised her hand to wave back, and plunged down the side of the bluff.

"What were you thinking!" said Emma, when Rose was sitting on a boulder at the bottom of the bluff, with her ankle bound up in Miss Gray's scarf.

"I pulled out of it, didn't I?" said Rose.

"But you almost didn't," said Melody. "You really should be more careful."

Rose snorted, and we knew what Miss Gray would say to that. A lady never snorts. But Miss Gray had other problems to take care of.

"Justina!" she called, but Justina wasn't listening. Serenity Sage was floating over the Alps in a balloon. In a castle in Switzerland, The Mask was waiting for her. He had not been captured by the Inquisition after all, and knowing that he was free had given her the resolve to starve herself until she was slender enough to slip through the prison bars, and then up through the darkness of the stone passages under the cathedral. There, through a rosewood fretwork, she had seen the secret rites of the Inquisition, and they had marked her soul forever. But today she was free and flying in the sunlight over the mountains. For three days now, her grandmother had been sick. Zelia had been sitting with her, Zelia had taken care of everything, and the cut on Justina's shoulder was healing, although the paperweight with a view of the Brighton Pavilion would never be the same. Three days, three days of freedom, thought Serenity, watching the mountains below, which looked like a bouquet of white roses.

"Justina!" called Miss Emily. "Are you simply going to float up into the sky? Stop at once."

The loblolly stopped, although Justina almost didn't. She lurched forward and looked around, startled, at Miss Gray.

"I don't want to be an Amazon Queen," said Emma, watching from below, "and I don't want to learn to fly."

"How can you not want to fly?" asked Rose.

"Because I'm not you. How can you never remember to comb your hair?"

Rose ran her fingers through her hair, which did look like it had been in a whirlwind.

"Stop arguing," said Melody. "I'm worried about Mouse."

"She's doing all right," said Rose. What Mouse lacked in courage, she made up for in determination: she was sputtering over the meadow, her thin legs stuck out on either sides of the branch, her body bent forward to make it go faster, her hair falling into her face.

"That's not what I'm worried about," said Melody. "Have you noticed how thin she's getting?"

"You'd be so much better if you practiced," said Rose. "Melody practices. That's why she's the best flyer, after me and Justina."

"I don't think you're so much better than Justina," said Emma.

"You're not listening," said Melody. "I said—" But just then a flock of Painted Ladies rose about her, so thick that she had to brush them away with her hands.

We all learned to fly, although it took longer than we expected, and by the time we could all soar over the bluff—except Emma, who preferred to stay close to the ground—the summer storms had passed. We could feel, in the colder updrafts, the coming of autumn.

Despite what Emma had said, Rose was the best of us, the most accomplished flyer. She had explored the Himalayas, had found each of the Forbidden Cities hidden among their peaks, including the city that was simply a stone maze, the City of Birds, where she had practiced speaking bird language, and the temporary and evanescent City of Clouds.

* * *

AUTUMN WAS COMING, and these were the things we knew: how to, in a mirror or still pond, see Historical Scenes (although we were heartily sick of the Battle of Waterloo and the Death of Cleopatra, which Miss Gray seemed to particularly enjoy); summon various animals, including possums, squirrels, sparrows, and stray dogs; turn small pebbles into gold and turn gold into small pebbles (to which we had lost another pair of Emma's earrings); and speak with birds. We could now speak to the crows that lived in the trees beside the Beauforts' cottage, although they never said anything interesting. It was always about whose daughter was marrying whom, and how that changed the rules of precedence, which were particularly arcane among crows.

We thought of them first, when we decided to do something about Mouse.

"Can't we ask the birds? Maybe they know where she is." Melody sat curled in a corner of the green sofa, like one of Miss Gray's cats. "We haven't seen her for days." But the crows, who told us everything they knew about mice, knew nothing about Mouse.

"Try the mirror," said Justina. "If we can watch the Battle of Waterloo over and over, surely we can see where Mouse has gone." We were startled: since we had learned how to fly, Justina had seemed more distant than ever, and although she still spent mornings with us at the cottage, she always seemed to be somewhere else.

The only mirror in the cottage had once been in the Beauforts' front hall; it was tall and in a gilt frame, the sort of hall mirror that had been fashionable when old Mrs. Balfour and Mrs. Beaufort, Emma's grandmother, had ruled the social world of Ashton, whose front halls had to be widened to accommodate their crinolines. When Adeline Beaufort entered the house after Grandma Beaufort's funeral, she said, "That mirror has to go."

Justina wiped the dust from it with her handkerchief, which turned as gray and furry as a mouse.

"Please," she said, as politely as Miss Gray had taught us, because one should always be polite, even to dead alligators, "show us Mouse."

"Not Cleopatra again!" said Emma. We were sitting around Justina, who sat on the floor in front of the mirror. "You know, I don't think she's beautiful at all. I don't know what Mark Anthony saw in her."

"Please show us America," said Justina. "And nowadays, not in historical times." We were no longer looking at the obelisks of Egypt, but at a group of teepees, with Indians sitting around doing what Indians did, we supposed, when they weren't scalping settlers. We had all learned in school that Indians collected scalps like Rose's mother collected Minton figurines.

"Thank you," said Justina. "But here in Ashton." We saw a city, with buildings three or four stories high and crowds in the streets, milling around the trolleys and their teams of horses. "That's New York," said Melody, and we remembered that she had lived there, once—when her mother was still alive. Then ships in a harbor, their sails raised against the sky, and then Emma's mother, staring into a mirror, so that we started back, almost expecting to see ourselves reflected behind her. She spread Dr. Bronner's Youth Cream over her cheeks and what they call the décolletage, and then slapped herself to raise the circulation. She leaned toward the mirror and touched the skin under her eyes, anxiously.

Emma turned red. "Parents are so stupid."

"Yes, thank you," said Justina patiently, "but we really want to see Mouse. No, that's—what's Miss Gray doing with Zelia?" They were walking in the Balfours' garden, their heads bent together, talking as though they were planning—what?

And there, finally, was Mouse.

We saw at once why Mouse had been missing our lessons with Miss Gray: she was tied up. There was a rope tied around one of her ankles, with a knot as large as the ankle itself.

"It looks like—the dungeons of the Inquisition," said Justina.

"It looks like the old slave house at the Caldwell plantation," said Melody. It had burned during the war, and other than the slave house, only the front steps of the plantation, which were made of stone, remained to mark where it had been.

"It's a good thing we can't smell through the mirror," said Emma. "I bet it stinks."

In the mirror, Mouse was waving her hands as though conducting a church choir. And as she waved, visions rose in the air around her. Trees grew, taller and paler than we had ever seen. Melody later told us they were paper birches—she had found a picture in a library book. Mouse was sitting on what seemed to be moss, but there was a low mist covering her knees like a blanket, and we could only see the ground as the mist shifted and swirled. The birches around her glowed in the light of—was it the sun, as pale as the moon, that shone through the gray clouds? The forest seemed to go on in every direction, and it was wet—leaves dripped, and Mouse's eyelashes were beaded with water-drops. Then a pale woman stepped out from one of the birches—from behind it or within it, we could not tell, and all the pale women stepped out, and they moved in something that was not a dance, but a pattern, and the hems of their dresses, which were made of the thinnest, most translucent bark, made the mist swirl up in strange patterns. Up it went, like smoke, and suddenly the vision was gone. Mouse sat, curled in a corner, with the rope around her ankle.

"I don't think she learned that from Miss Gray," said Emma.

"What are we going to do?" asked Rose. "We have to do something." And we knew that we had to do something, because we felt in the pits of our stomachs what Rose was feeling: a sick despair.

"Rescue her," said Melody. She looked around at the rest of us, and suddenly we realized that we were going to do exactly that, because Melody was the practical one, and if she had suggested it, then it could be done.

"How?" asked Rose. "We don't even know where she is."

"On our branches," said Justina. "Mirror, show us—slowly, show us the roof. Now the street. Look, it's one of the drying sheds by the old tobacco factory. All we need to do is follow the railroad tracks."

"How can we fly on our branches?" asked Emma. "We'll be seen."

"No, we won't," said Justina. She looked at us, waiting for us to understand, and one by one, as though candles were being lit in a dark room, we knew. "Rose, how long has it been since your mother asked where you spend your afternoons? How long has it been since anyone asked any of us, even Melody? Why has Coralie started doing her afternoon chores? And when Emma burned one of her braids, when we were making butterscotch on the Bunsen burner and Miss Gray came in suddenly and startled us, did anyone notice?" No one had. "I don't think anyone has seen what we've been doing all summer. We've become like Miss Gray's cats, invisible until you're about to sit on them. I think we could fly through Brickleford on market day and no one would notice."

So we flew through the streets of Ashton, as high as the roofs of the houses, seeing them from the air for the first time. Ashton seemed smaller, from up there, and each of us thought the same thing—I will leave here one day. Only Emma was sorry to think so.

We landed by the shed that the mirror had shown us. One by one, we dismounted from our branches. Justina—we had not known she could be such a good leader—opened the door. It did look like a dungeon of the Inquisition, and smelled just as Emma had expected—the smell of death and rotting meat. Mouse was sitting in her corner, with her arms around her knees and her head down, crying. She did not look up when we opened the door.

"Mouse," said Rose. "We've come to rescue you." It sounded, we realized, both brave and silly.

Mouse looked up. We had never seen her face so dirty. Each tear seemed to have left behind a streak of dirt. "Why?" she asked.

"Because—" said Emma. "Because you're one of us, now."

We could not untie the knot. It was too large, too tight: the rope must once have been wet and shrunk.

"There's a knife, next to the bowl," said Mouse. "I can't reach it from here, the rope won't let me—I tried and tried."

The smell of rotting meat came from that bowl, and it was covered with flies. When Justina had finished cutting the rope from Mouse's ankle—the rest of us were standing as close as we could to the boarded-up window, where the crookedness of the boards let in chinks of light—she said, "I think I'm going to be sick."

The door banged open. "What do you brats think you're doing here?" It was a man, who brought with him a stench worse than rotting meat—the stench of whiskey.

"The drunkard father," whispered Emma. We all stood still, too frightened to move, and from Mouse came a mouse-like whimper.

"You little bitch," he said. "I know you. You're Judge Beaufort's daughter. You know how many times your father's put me in that prison of his? You goddamned Beauforts, sneering down your noses at anyone who isn't as high and all goddamn mighty as you are. Wait until he sees what I'm going to do with you—I'll whip you like a nigger, until your backside is as raw as—as raw meat."

Emma shrieked, a strangled sort of shriek, and dropped her branch.

"You're not a man but a toad," said Justina.

He stared at her, as though she had suddenly appeared in front of his eyes. "What—"

"No, not a man at all," said Rose. "You're a toad, a nasty toad with skin like leather, and you eat flies."

"You don't live here," said Melody. "You live in the swamp by the Picketts' house, where the water is dark and still."

Somewhere, in some other country, where we were still Justina, Rose, Melody, and Emma, instead of witches, we thought, but we haven't learned transformations yet.

"That's right," said Emma. "Go home, toad. Go back to the swamp where you belong. You don't belong here."

"Sophie," he said, looking at Mouse. "I'm your father, Sophie." He looked at her as though, for once, asking for something, asking with fear in his eyes.

"You know you are, Papa," she said. "You know you're a toad. I've tried to love you, but you haven't changed. You'll always be a toad in your heart."

"Go home, toad," said Justina. "We don't want you here anymore."

"Yes, go back to your swamp," said Melody. "And I hope Jim Pickett catches you one day, and Mrs. Pickett puts you into her supper pot. The Picketts like toad. They say it tastes like chicken."

Mouse's father, the drunkard, hopped out through the door and away, we assumed in the direction of the swamp. We let out a sigh, together, as though we had been holding our breaths all that time.

We made Mouse a bed in the cottage, on the green sofa. Emma said, "Callie won't let me have any more food. Since the revival came, she says she's found religion, and she's got jewels waiting for her in heaven that are more beautiful than earthly trinkets. She's given me back my rings and necklaces." So Rose stole some bread and jam from the cupboard when Hannah wasn't looking, and Mouse ate bread with jam until she was full. Melody gave her a dress, because the rest of us were too big, although Melody didn't have many dresses of her own. Emma brought soap and water so Mouse could wash her face, and combed her hair. Properly combed, it was as fine and flyaway as milkweed. Before we went home to our suppers, Melody read to her from *The Poetical Works of Keats*, which Emma had taken out of the library for her, while the rest of us curled up on the sofa in tired silence.

"Good night," said Mouse, when we were leaving. "Good night, good night." And because she was one of us now, we knew that she was happy.

The next day, Rose and Melody were punished for taking bread and jam without permission and for losing a perfectly good dress, which Hannah had just darned.

"THE NEXT LESSON," said Miss Gray, "is gaining your heart's desire. For which you will need a potion that includes hearts. Today, I want you to go out and find hearts."

"You don't want us to kill squirrels, or something?" said Emma, incredulously.

"Don't be ridiculous," said Miss Gray. "Have you learned nothing at all this summer? The heart is the center, the essence, of a thing. It is what gives a stone gravity, a bird flight. Killing squirrels, indeed!" She looked at us with as much disgust as on the first day, when we had failed to see ourselves in the mirror. It was not fair—Emma had asked the question, and the scorn was addressed to us all. But when had Miss Gray ever been fair?

So out we went, looking for hearts.

This was what we put into our potions. Into Melody's potion, she put all the plays of Shakespeare, with each mention of the word "heart" underlined in red, and each mention of the word "art" as well, even the art in "What art thou that usurp'st this time of night?"; *The Poetical Works of Keats* with each page cut into hearts; and a butterfly that she had found dead on her windowsill, a Red Admiral. With its wings outstretched, it looked like two hearts, one upside down. And we knew that Justina had been right: we were invisible that summer. Otherwise, Emma would have had to spend her pocket money on library fines. Emma put in the double yolk of an egg she had stolen from under the hens, which she insisted resembled a heart; chocolate bonbons that Callie had shaped into hearts; Cocoanut Kisses that we told her had nothing to do with hearts, but she said that she liked them; and hearts cut out of a Velvet Cake, all stolen from a Ladies' Tea that her mother was giving for the Missionary Society. Rose put in a heart-shaped locket that her mother had given her; her mother's rose perfume, which she said was the heart of the rose (the laboratory smelled of it for days); and water from the icebox that she had laboriously chipped into the shape of a heart. Mouse's potion contained a strange collection of nuts and seeds: acorns; beechnuts, butternuts, and black walnuts; the seeds of milkweed and thistle; locust pods; the cones of hemlock and cypress; and red hips from the wild roses that grew by Slocumb's Bluff. "Well," she said, "Miss Gray did say that the heart is the center. You can't get much more centery than seeds, can you?" Justina's collection was the strangest of all: when Miss Gray asked for her ingredients, she handed Miss Gray a mask shaped like a heart on which she had sewn, so that it was completely covered, the feathers of crows. "The crows gave them to me," she told us later, when we asked her where the feathers had come from, "once I explained what they were for. They seemed to know Miss Gray."

"Nicely done," said Miss Gray. "I think Justina's spell will be the strongest, since she has been the most focused among you, although one can't quite call this a potion, can one? But Emma's and Melody's potions will do quite well, and Mouse, I'll help you with yours."

"And mine?" asked Rose. If she had done something wrong, she wanted to know.

"Yours is complicated," said Miss Gray. "We'll have to wait and see."

YEARS LATER, EMMA asked, "Rose, did you ever get your heart's desire?" They were walking in the garden of the house where Emma lived with her husband, the senator. Above them, the maples trees were beginning to turn red and gold. Whenever the wind shook the maple branches, leaves blew down around them.

"That's funny," said Rose, reminding herself not to think of her deadline. This was Emma, whom she hadn't seen in—how long? Her deadline could wait. "I don't think we ever told each other what we wished for. I guess what happened afterward drove it out of our heads."

"I suppose you wanted to fly," said Emma. "I remember—you were obsessed with flying, then."

Rose laughed. "I thought I was so good at keeping it secret!" She stopped and looked out over the lawn, where the shadows of the trees were lengthening. Soon, it would be time to dress for dinner. She worried, again, about her gray merino. Would it do for Emma's party? "No," she said, "I wished that my mother would love me. You remember what she was like, even at the end. What a strange thing to admit, after all these years."

"I wished that I could eat all I wanted and never get fat." Emma absent-mindedly pulled a maple leaf from her hair, which was bobbed in the current fashion.

"Well, you got your wish, at least. There's no one in Washington as elegant as Mrs. Balfour." Rose looked at Emma, from her expensively waved hair to her expensively shod feet, in the new heels. "How do you like being a senator's wife?"

Emma let the leaf fall from her fingers. "Has the interview started already?" Rose laughed again, uncomfortably. Nothing is as uncomfortable, her editor had told her, as the truth. Emma continued, and to Rose her voice sounded bitter, almost accusatory, "So did she ever tell you that she loved you?"

How much easier it was, to answer questions instead of asking them. To pretend, for one afternoon, that she was here only as Emma's guest. "No, she never told me. But she did love me, I think, in her own way. It took me a long time to understand that. It wasn't a way I could have understood, as a child."

"Understanding—that's not much of a spell."

Emma sat on a bench beside the ornamental pond, where ornamental fish, red and gold, were darting beneath the fallen leaves. After a moment, Rose sat beside her. She looked at the patterns made by lichen on the ornamental urns, then at the statue of Melpomene, whose name on the pedestal was almost obscured by moss. She did not know how to respond.

"Have you heard from Melody?" asked Emma.

"Not since last spring," said Rose, grateful that Emma had broken the silence. "I don't think she'll ever come back. It's easier in Paris. She says, you know, there are no signs on the bathrooms. But I've brought you a copy of her latest. It's still in my suitcase. I meant to unpack it, but I must be losing my memory. You'll like it—one of the poems is about being a witch. I think that's what she asked for, to be a poet. It's still hard to imagine: Melody, the studious, the obedient one, in Paris cafés with artists and musicians, and girls who dance in beads! Drinking and—did you know? Smoking!"

Emma picked up a piece of gravel and tossed it into the pond, where it splashed like a fish. The sound was almost startling in the still afternoon. "It broke up the group, didn't it? When she left for college. I miss her."

Rose stared up at the leaves overhead, red and gold against the sky. "I think it was broken before that."

"We all paid a price, didn't we?" asked Emma. "Do you remember the advertisement? Reasonable rates. She never charged us, but I think we all paid a price. You—all those years taking care of your mother while she had cancer, when you could have been, I don't know, going to college, getting married, having a life of your own. Melody—she'll never come home. If she did, she wouldn't be a poet, just another colored woman who has to sit at the back of the theater. And me—"

Emma picked up another piece of gravel, then placed it on the bench beside her. "I can't gain weight, you know. No matter what. I've tried. Such a silly problem, but—I don't think James and I will ever have children."

"Oh, Emma!" said Rose. "I'm so sorry." What did her article matter? Emma had been her best friend, so long ago.

"Well, that's the way of the world," said Emma, her voice still bitter. Then suddenly, surprisingly, because this was Emma after all, she wiped her eyes, carefully so as not to smudge her mascara. "You gain and you lose, with every choice you make. That's the way it's always been. But you—" She turned to Rose and smiled, and suddenly she was the old Emma again. "All those years giving sponge baths and making invalid trays, when you barely stepped off the front porch, and now a reporter! Do you remember when we were reporters? Just before we were witches."

"I don't know if the society pages count," said Rose. "Although I suppose everyone has to start somewhere. If only we had stayed reporters! But come to think of it—I really am losing my memory—I have news for you. I've heard of Justina! A friend of mine, a real reporter, who was in Argentina covering the revolution—they're having another one this year—wrote me about an American woman who had married one of the revolutionaries, a man they call—why do revolutionaries always have these sorts of names?—The Mask. They call her *La Serenidad*, and there's a song about her that they play on the radio. He wrote it down for me, but I don't know Spanish."

"Now isn't that Justina all over?" said Emma, laughing. It was the first time, Rose realized, that she had heard her laugh all afternoon. After a pause, during which they sat in companionable silence, Emma continued, "Did you ever hear—"

"No," said Rose. "You?"

"No."

It grew dim under the maple trees, and the air grew chill. Emma drew her shawl about her shoulders, and Rose put her hands into her jacket pockets. They sat thinking together, as we had so long ago, when we were children— wondering what had happened to Mouse.

EMMA HEARD THE news first, at breakfast. Her mother had just said, "Would you like some butter on your toast? Or maybe some jam? You look so nice and thin in that dress. Is it the one Aunt Otway brought from Raleigh?" when Callie came into the morning room and said, "Judge Beaufort, come quick! There's thieves in Ashton. They've gone and murdered Mrs. Balfour, and they'll murder us too, Lord have mercy on our souls!"

"What?" Emma's father rose from the breakfast table. "Who told you this?"

"Mrs. Balfour's Zelia. She stayed just to tell me, then ran on back to help. She's already called Dr. Bartlett, though she says he won't be able to do anything for Mrs. Balfour, poor woman. Blood all over her, Zelia told me, like she sprung a leak. May she rest in the lap of the Lord."

"That's enough. Tell Henry to get Mr. Caldwell and Reverend Hewes, and meet me there." Then he was out the door.

"You haven't finished your boiled egg," said Adeline Beaufort. "Emma? Emma, where are you?"

We watched the events at the Balfour house, the largest house in Ashton, whose white columns leaned precariously left and right, from the top of a tulip poplar, the three of us—Emma, Rose, and Melody. We had looked for Mouse in the cottage, but she was nowhere to be found.

"I heard it all from Coralie," said Melody. "Henry's her sweetheart—at least, one of them. He said the front door was open, and when they went in, they found Mrs. Balfour lying on the parlor floor, with a bullet through her heart. There was blood all over the carpet, and a whole pile of silver, teaspoons and other things, scattered on the floor beside her. They think she heard the thief, then came down with the pistol that General Balfour had used in the war and found him going through the silver. He must have taken it away from her and shot her with it."

"Gruesome," said Emma. "Look, there's the hearse driving up from Pickett's Funeral Parlor."

"And they found Justina in a corner of the parlor, barely breathing, with marks around her neck. They think she must have come down too, and he must have tried to strangle her and left her for dead." Not even our imaginations could picture the scene. Surely death was for people we did not know?

Emma's father came out, with Dr. Bartlett, Reverend Hewes, and Henry. We knew what they were carrying between them: Mrs. Balfour, draped in a black sheet, leaving the house where so many of her ancestors had died with more decorum.

"If he had the pistol, why didn't he just shoot Justina?" asked Rose. "It seems like a lot of trouble, strangling someone. Do you think they'll let us see her?"

"No," said Emma. "Only Zelia can see her. That's what Papa said—she's just too sick. But why don't we look—" and we knew what she was going to say. Why don't we look in the mirror?

The cottage was surrounded by men from the tobacco fields, who had been summoned to form a posse. "Stay away from here, girls," said Judge Beaufort. "That thief's been sleeping in our cottage—can you believe his nerve? We found a blanket and some food, even some books. We think it may be old Sitgreaves, the one with that idiot girl. He hasn't been seen for a while. But it looks like he slept here last night. This time, we'll send him to the prison in Charlotte, and that girl of his should have gone to the asylum long ago. I'll make sure of it, when I find her. But until we catch him, don't you go walking out by yourselves, do you hear?"

We looked at each other in consternation, because—where was Mouse?

"Miss Gray," said Rose. "Let's go talk to Miss Gray."

The roses had fallen from the La Reine and lay in a heap of pink petals on the grass. The garden seemed unusually still. Not even bees moved among the honeysuckle.

"Something's not right," said Emma.

"Nothing's right today," said Rose. "Who wants to knock?" No one volunteered, so she knocked with the brass frog, which was as polished as always. But no one answered. Instead, the door swung open. It had not been locked.

The Randolph house was empty. The sofa in the parlor, where we had eaten with a witch for the first time, the table in the laboratory where we had sat, learning our lessons, all were gone. Even the cats, which had only been partially there, were wholly absent.

"It was all here yesterday," said Melody. "She was going to show us how to make dreams in an eggshell."

"I found something," said Rose. It was a note, in correct Spencerian script, propped on the mantel. It said:

Dear Emma, Rose, and Melody,
Please stop the milk. Don't forget to practice, and don't worry.

> *Sophia and I will take care of each other.*
> > *Sincerely,*
> > *Emily Gray*

We looked at each other, and finally Melody said what we were all thinking—"How did she know?" Because it was evident: Miss Gray had known what would happen.

We went to Mrs. Balfour's funeral. Even Melody sat in one of the back pews of the Episcopal Church, beside Hannah. The organist played "Lead, Kindly Light." We ignored the sermon and stared at the back of Justina's head, in the Balfour pew close to the chancel, and then at her face as she walked up the aisle behind the coffin. She was paler than we had ever seen her, as though she had become a statue of herself. In the churchyard, she watched her grandmother's coffin being lowered into the ground, and when Reverend Hewes said "Dust to dust," she opened her hand and dust fell down, into the grave, on top of the coffin. Then she placed her hand on her mouth and shrieked.

We found her in the privet grove that had been planted around the grave of Emmeline Balfour, Beloved Wife and Mother. We didn't know what to say.

Justina looked at us with the still, pale face of a statue. She had never looked so beautiful, so like a Balfour. "I shot her," she said. "She tried to strangle me—she said she saw the devil in my eyes. But I had Grandpa's gun, I'd been carrying it in the pocket of my robe for weeks, and I shot her through the heart." Then she half sat and half fell, at the same time, slowly, until she was sitting on the grass, leaning against the gravestone.

"But the masked man—" said Rose.

"And the silver—" said Emma.

"That was Zelia," she said. She looked at her hands as though she did not know what to do with them. "Zelia scattered the silver before she went to get Dr. Hewes. She told me to lie still, and that there'd been a thief. But there was no thief—only me!"

We were silent, then Melody said, "She must have been going mad for a long time. You could have told us."

We heard the privet shake. "Don't you pester her no more," said Zelia. "Allons, ma fille. Your duty here is done." She helped Justina up and put a shawl around her shoulders, then led her away. But just before they left the privet grove, Zelia turned back to us and said, "And don't you forget to stop the milk!"

The next day, as we hid behind an overgrown lilac in the Caldwells' garden, Emma told us that Justina was gone. "To Italy, to find her father, I think. Papa saw her off on the train. Zelia was going with her."

Melody said, "I warned you about eating with witches. First Mouse and then Justina. It's as though they've disappeared off the face of the earth."

"Italy's not off the face of the earth," said Emma.

"It might as well be," said Rose. "And it's all her fault—Miss Gray's. I wish she'd never come to Ashton."

Eventually, when it looked like the thief who had killed Mrs. Balfour, whether or not it was old Sitgreaves, would never be found, we were allowed into the cottage again. The first thing we did was look into the mirror—it was the only mirror we could look in, all three of us, without arousing suspicion. "Show us Justina," we said, and we saw her on the deck of a ship, looking out over the Atlantic, with the wind blowing her hair like a golden flag. But when we said "Show us Mouse and Miss Gray," all we saw was a road through a forest of birches, with a low mist shifting and swirling beneath the light of a pale sun.

We practiced, at first. But Emma's mother decided it was time for her to come out into Ashton society, so she spent hours having dresses made and choosing cakes. Emma said that the latter made up, in chocolate, for the boredom of the former. And Melody said that she had to prepare for school, although she spent most of her time scribbling on bits of paper that she would not show us. Rose practiced the longest, and for the rest of that summer she could fly out of her bedroom window, which she did whenever she was sent to her room for punishment. But eventually we could no longer talk to birds, or turn gold into pebbles, or see the Battle of Waterloo in a mirror. We realized that we would never be witches. So the next summer, we became detectives.

The Witch-Girls

The witch-girls go to school just down the street.
I see them pass each morning with their brooms
and uniforms: black dresses, peaked black hats.
They giggle just like ordinary girls,
except that as they walk, their brindled cats
twine around their ankles. One will stop
and say, "You'll trip me, Malkin," scoldingly.
Then Malkin will look up and answer back,
"Carry me then." The witch-girl will bend down,
scooping the cat into her arms, and perch
him on her shoulder. So the witch-girls pass.

I wish I could be one of them. Alas,
I don't know how to fly on windy nights
or talk to bats, or brew a magic potion.
Although I think I could be good at witching.
I'd learn to curse and never comb my hair.
I'm pretty good at scaring passers-by
by making goblin faces through the window.
I'd trade white cotton dresses for black wool,
no matter how it itched. I'd fly my broom
up to the witches' garden on the moon
where they dance nightly, kicking up their heels
with sylphs and fauns and ghouls. At least I think
that's what they do. I don't think witches go
to bed at nine, or even make their beds
each morning. No. Instead, they marry toads,
or live alone and read old books. They paint
landscapes in Germany, or climb the Alps,
or sit in Paris cafés eating chocolate
for lunch and maybe dinner. They get drunk
on elderberry cordial, speak with bears
on earnest topics like philology.
I wonder what the witch-girls learn in school?
Geometry that helps them walk through walls,
and how to turn a poem into a spell . . .

I wish that I could go to school with them.
I'd giggle and be wicked too, if they
would only let me.

The Witch's Cat

A witch's cat isn't always black.
Mine is an elegant tortoiseshell.
She refuses to come when I call to her,
but as soon as I start reciting a spell,
she'll appear at the top of the stairs,
as though she was never gone at all.

Where does she go when she's not with me?
She won't tell me, however much I ask.
Whether for pleasure or to fulfill
some secretive, inscrutable task
given to her by Mother Night.
She simply says, "You've made a mistake,

Mistress mine. I was always here,"
then looks at me with those yellow eyes,
like two full moons. A witch's cat
isn't always truthful, but she is wise.
She knows where magical plants are found
and when the midsummer sun will rise.

She knows which toads are poisonous
and how to pronounce the ancient words,
whether Latin, Greek, or Sumerian.
She understands the weather's moods,
and knows the way to the hidden glade
where witches meet, in the heart of the woods.

There we catch up on the latest charms,
sharing ingredients and recipes,
then dance until the moon has set,
while Mother Night walks beneath the trees,
a tall, pale woman as old as time,
whose long black hair is filled with stars.

When my cat says, "Mistress, it's time to go,"

she climbs on the back of my broom, and we fly
over the sleeping town below,
through a purple and orange sky,
back home, where I promptly get to work,
while she curls in the armchair and sleeps all day!

A witch's cat is never good,
nor ever entirely bad. She's herself.
Sometimes she'll suddenly walk through walls
or appear on the highest shelf
where I hid the cream and knock it down,
more troublesome than any elf.

But what would I do without her? Who
would translate when I summon a demon,
or frighten mice from the herbs in the pantry,
or watch over my simmering cauldron?
Or keep the loneliness away,
a magic stronger than any potion?

Pip and the Fairies

"**W**HY, YOU'RE PIP!"

She has gotten used to this, since the documentary. She could have refused to be interviewed, she supposes. But it would have seemed—ungrateful, ungracious, particularly after the funeral.

"Susan Lawson," read the obituary, "beloved author of *Pip and the Fairies*, *Pip Meets the Thorn King*, *Pip Makes Three Wishes*, and other Pip books, of ovarian cancer. Ms. Lawson, who was sixty-four, is survived by a daughter, Philippa. In lieu of flowers, donations should be sent to the Susan Lawson Cancer Research Fund." Anne had written that.

"Would you like me to sign something?" she asks.

White hair, reading glasses on a chain around her neck—too old to be a mother. Perhaps a librarian? Let her be a librarian, thinks Philippa. Once, a collector asked her to sign the entire series, from *Pip and the Fairies* to *Pip Says Goodbye*.

"That would be so kind of you. For my granddaughter Emily." A grandmother, holding out *Pip Learns to Fish* and *Under the Hawthorns*. She signs them both "To Emily, may she find her own fairyland. From Philippa Lawson (Pip)."

This is the sort of thing people like: the implication that, despite their minivans and microwaves, if they found the door in the wall, they too could enter fairyland.

"So," the interviewer asked her, smiling indulgently, the way parents smile at their children's beliefs in Santa Claus, "Did you really meet the Thorn King? Do you think you could get me an interview?"

And she answered as he, and the parents who had purchased the boxed set, were expecting. "I'm afraid the Thorn King is a very private person. But I'll mention that you were interested." Being Pip, after all these years. Maintaining the persona.

Her mother never actually called her Pip. It was Pipsqueak, as in, "Go play outside, Pipsqueak. Can't you see Mommy's trying to finish this chapter? Mommy's publisher wants to see something by Friday, and we're a month behind on the rent." When they finally moved away from Payton, they were almost a year behind. Her mother sent Mrs. Payne a check from California, from royalties she had received for the after-school special.

Philippa buys a scone and a cup of coffee. There was no café when she used to come to this bookstore, while her mother shopped at the food co-op down the street, which is now a yoga studio. Mrs. Archer used to let her sit in a corner and read the books. Then she realizes there is no cupholder in the rental car. She drinks the coffee quickly. She's tired, after the long flight from Los Angeles, the long drive from Boston. But not much farther now. Payton has stayed essentially the same, she thinks, despite the yoga studio. She imagines a planning board, a historical society, the long and difficult process of obtaining permits, like in all these New England towns.

As she passes the fire station, the rain begins, not heavy, and intermittent. She turns on the windshield wipers.

There is Sutton's dairy, where her mother bought milk with cream floating on top, before anyone else cared about pesticides in the food chain. She is driving through the country, through farms that have managed to hold on despite the rocky soil. In the distance she sees cows, and once a herd of alpacas. There are patches too rocky for farms, where the road runs between cliffs covered with ivy, and birches, their leaves glistening with rain, spring up from the shallow soil.

Then forest. The rain is heavier, pattering on the leaves overhead. She drives with one hand, holding the scone in the other (her pants are getting covered with crumbs), beneath the oaks and evergreens, thinking about the funeral.

It was not large: her mother's coworkers from the Children's Network, and Anne. It was only after the documentary that people began driving to the cemetery in the hills, leaving hyacinths by the grave. Her fault, she supposes.

The interviewer leaned forward, as though expecting an intimate detail. "How did she come up with Hyacinth? Was the character based on anyone she knew?"

"Oh, hyacinths were my mother's favorite flower."

And letters, even contributions to the Susan Lawson Cancer Research Fund. Everyone, it seems, had read *Pip and the Fairies*. Then the books had gone out of print and been forgotten. But after the funeral and the documentary, everyone suddenly remembered, the way they remembered their childhoods. Suddenly, Susan Lawson was indeed "beloved."

Philippa asked Anne to drive up once a week, to clear away the letters and flowers, to take care of the checks. And she signed over the house. Anne was too old to be a secretary for anyone neater than Susan Lawson had been. In one corner of the living room, Philippa found a pile of hospital bills, covered with dust. She remembers Anne at the funeral, so pale and pinched. It is good, she supposes, that her mother found someone at last. With the house and her social security, Anne will be all right.

Three miles to Payne House. Almost there, then. It had been raining too, on that first day.

"Look," her mother said, pointing as the Beetle swerved erratically. If she looked down, she could see the road through the holes in the floor, where the metal had rusted away. Is that why she has rented one of the new Beetles? Either nostalgia, or an effort to, somehow, rewrite the past. "There's Payne House. It burned down in the 1930s. The Paynes used to own the mills at the edge of town," now converted into condominiums, Mrs. Archer's successor, a woman with graying hair and a pierced nostril, told her, "and one night the millworkers set the stables on fire. They said the Paynes took better care of their horses than of their workers."

"What happened to the horses?" She can see the house from the road, its outer walls burned above the first story, trees growing in some of the rooms. She can see it through both sets of eyes, the young Philippa and the old one. Not really old of course, but—how should she describe it?—tired. She blames the documentary. Remembering all this, the road running through the soaked remains of what was once a garden, its hedges overgrown and a rosebush grow-ing through the front door. She can see it through young eyes, only a few weeks after her father's funeral, the coffin draped with an American flag and the minister saying "fallen in the service of his country" although really it was an accident that could have happened if he had been driving to the grocery store. And old eyes, noticing that the rosebush has spread over the front steps.

As if, driving down this road, she were traveling into the past. She felt this also, sitting beside the hospital bed, holding one pale hand, the skin dry as paper, on which the veins were raised like the roots of an oak tree. Listening to the mother she had not spoken to in years.

"I have to support us now, Pipsqueak. So we're going to live here. Mrs. Payne's going to rent us the housekeeper's cottage, and I'm going to write books."

"What kind of books?"

"Oh, I don't know. I guess I'll have to start writing and see what comes out."

How did it begin? Did she begin it, by telling her mother, over her milk and the oatmeal cookies from the food co-op that tasted like baked sawdust, what she had been doing that day? Or did her mother begin it, by writing the stories? Did she imagine them, Hyacinth, the Thorn King, the Carp in the pond who dreamed, so he said, the future, and the May Queen herself? And, she thinks, pulling into the drive that leads to the housekeeper's cottage, what about Jack Feather? Or did her mother imagine them? And did their imagina-tions bring them into being, or were they always there to be found?

She slams the car door and brushes crumbs from her pants. Here it is, all here, for what it is worth, the housekeeper's cottage, with its three small rooms, and the ruins of Payne House. The rain has almost stopped, although she can feel a drop run down the back of her neck. And, not for the first time, she has doubts.

"One room was my mother's, one was mine, and one was the kitchen, where we took our baths in a plastic tub. We had a toaster oven and a crock pot to make soup, and a small refrigerator, the kind you see in hotels. One day, I remember having soup for breakfast, lunch, and dinner. Of course, when the electricity was turned off, none of them worked. Once, we lived for a week on oatmeal cookies." The interviewer laughed, and she laughed with him. When they moved to California, she went to school. Why doesn't she remember going to school in Payton? She bought lunch every day, meatloaf and mashed potatoes and soggy green beans. Sometimes the principal gave her lunch money. She was happier than when the Thorn King had crowned her with honeysuckle. "Young Pip," he had said, "I pronounce you a Maid of the May. Serve the May Queen well."

That was in *Pip Meets the May Queen*. And then she stops—standing at the edge of the pond—because the time has come to think about what she has done.

What she has done is give up *The Pendletons*, every weekday at two o'clock, Eastern Standard Time, before the afternoon talk shows. She has given up being Jessica Pendleton, the scheming daughter of Bruce Pendleton, whose attractive but troublesome family dominates the social and criminal worlds of Pinehurst.

"How did your mother influence your acting career?"

She did not answer, "By teaching me the importance of money." Last week, even a fan of *The Pendletons* recognized her as Pip.

She has given up the house in the hills, with a pool in the backyard. Given up Edward, but then he gave her up first, for a producer. He wanted, so badly, to do prime time. A cop show or even a sitcom, respectable television. "I hope you understand, Phil," he said. And she did understand, somehow. Has she ever been in love with anyone—except Jack Feather?

What has she gained? She remembers her mother's cold hand pulling her down, so she can hear her whisper, in a voice like sandpaper, "I always knew they were real."

But does she, Philippa, know it? That is why she has come back, why she has bought Payne House from the Payne who inherited it, a Manhattan lawyer with no use for the family estate. Why she is standing here now, by the pond, where the irises are about to bloom. So she can remember.

The moment when, in *Pip and the Fairies*, she trips over something lying on the ground.

> "Oh," said a voice. When Pip looked up she saw a girl, about her own age, in a white dress, with hair as green as grass. "You've found it, and now it's yours, and I'll never be able to return it before he finds out!"
>
> "What is it?" asked Pip, holding up what she had tripped over: a piece of brown leather, rather like a purse.
>
> "It's Jack Feather's Wallet of Dreams, which he doesn't know I've taken. I was just going to look at the dreams— their wings are so lovely in the sunlight—and then return it.

But 'What You Find You May Keep.' That's the law." And the girl wept bitterly into her hands.

"But I don't want it," said Pip. "I'd like to look at the dreams, if they're as nice as you say they are, but I certainly don't want to keep them. Who is Jack Feather, and how can we return his wallet?"

"How considerate you are," said the girl. "Let me kiss you on both cheeks—that's the fairy way. Then you'll be able to walk through the door in the wall, and we'll return the wallet together. You can call me Hyacinth."

Why couldn't she walk through the door by herself? Pip wondered. It seemed an ordinary enough door, opening from one of the overgrown rooms to another. And what was the fairy way? She was just starting to wonder why the girl in the white dress had green hair when Hyacinth opened the door and pulled her through.

On the other side was a country she had never seen before. A forest stretched away into the distance, until it reached a river that shone like a snake in the sunlight, and then again until it reached the mountains.

Standing under the trees at the edge of the forest was a boy, not much taller than she was, in trousers made of gray fur, with a birch-bark hat on his head. As soon as he saw them, he said, "Hyacinth, if you don't give me my Wallet of Dreams in the clap of a hummingbird's wing, I'll turn you into a snail and present you to Mother Hedgehog, who'll stick you into her supper pot!"

—From *Pip and the Fairies*, by Susan Lawson

How CLEARLY THE memories are coming back to her now, of fishing at night with Jack Feather, searching for the Wishing Stone with Hyacinth and Thimble, listening to stories at Mother Hedgehog's house while eating her toadstool omelet. There was always an emphasis on food, perhaps a reflection of the toaster and crock pot that so invariably turned out toast and soup. The May Queen's cake, for example, or Jeremy Toad's cricket cutlets, which neither she nor Hyacinth could bear to eat.

"I hope you like crickets," said Jeremy Toad. Pip and Hyacinth looked at one another in distress. "Eat What You Are Offered," was the Thorn King's law. Would they dare to break it? That was in *Jeremy Toad's Birthday Party*.

She can see, really, where it all came from.

"I think the feud between the Thorn King and the May Queen represented her anger at my father's death. It was an accident, of course. But she blamed him for leaving her, for going to Vietnam. She wanted him to be a conscientious objector. Especially with no money and a daughter to care for. I don't think she ever got over that anger."

"But the Thorn King and the May Queen were reconciled."

"Only by one of Pip's wishes. The other—let me see if I remember. It was a fine wool shawl for Thimble so she would never be cold again."

"Weren't there three? What was the third wish?"

"Oh, that was the one Pip kept for herself. I don't think my mother ever revealed it. Probably something to do with Jack Feather. She—I—was rather in love with him, you know."

The third wish had been about the electricity bill, and it had come true several days later when the advance from the publisher arrived.

Here it is, the room where she found Jack Feather's wallet. Once, in *Pip Meets the Thorn King*, he allowed her to look into it. She saw herself, but considerably older, in a dress that sparkled like stars. Years later, she recognized it as the dress she would wear to the Daytime Emmys.

And now what? Because there is the door, and after all the Carp did tell her, in *Pip Says Goodbye*, "You will come back some day."

But if she opens the door now, will she see the fields behind Payne House, which are mown for hay in September? That is the question around which everything revolves. Has she been a fool, to give up California, and the house with the pool, and a steady paycheck?

"What happened, Pip?" her mother asked her, lying in the hospital bed, her head wrapped in the scarf without which it looked as fragile as an eggshell. "You were such an imaginative child. What made you care so much about money?"

"You did," she wanted to and could not say. And now she has taken that money out of the bank to buy Payne House.

If she opens the door and sees only the unmown fields, it will have been for nothing. No, not nothing. There is Payne House, after all. And her memories. What will she do, now she is no longer Jessica Pendleton? Perhaps she will write, like her mother. There is a certain irony in that.

The rain on the grass begins to soak through her shoes. She should remember not to wear city shoes in the country.

But it's no use standing here. That is, she has always told herself, the difference between her and her mother: she can face facts.

Philippa grasps the doorknob, breathes in once, quickly, and opens the door.

> "I've been waiting forever and a day," said Hyacinth, yawning. She had fallen asleep beneath an oak tree, and while she slept the squirrels who lived in the tree had made her a blanket of leaves.

"I promised I would come back if I could," said Pip, "and now I have."

"I'm as glad as can be," said Hyacinth. "The Thorn King's been so sad since you went away. When I tell him you're back, he'll prepare a feast just for you."

"Will Jack Feather be there?" asked Pip.

"I don't know," said Hyacinth, looking uncomfortable. "He went away to the mountains, and hasn't come back. I didn't want to tell you yet, but—the May Queen's disappeared! Jack Feather went to look for her with Jeremy Toad, and now they've disappeared too."

"Then we'll have to go find them," said Pip.

—From *Pip Returns to Fairyland*, by Philippa Lawson

Tam Lin Remembers the Fairy Queen

She had eyes like apple seeds.

A small, angular face that reminded me
of a fox's mask. Was it a mask she wore
the whole time I was with her?

The thing about fairies is, they're not like us,
material. Indeed, they most resemble
assemblages constructed from our dreams.
Their visible forms are for our benefit.

Sometimes, as we lay together in bed
under a canopy of spider silk,
I would turn and find she had become a tree,
branches for arms, a bird's nest between her legs,
with three blue, speckled eggs. Were they our children?
I'd blink, and she would be a woman again,
yawning and stretching as human women do.
She'd smile at me with a fox's sly, wise smile
as though she had tricked me.

The castle was sometimes made of rough gray stone
covered with moss, sometimes of murky water
with fish swimming in the walls. When we danced, the music
came from viols or the buzz of a hundred bees.
I sat on chairs that were either toadstools or clouds,
and ate from plates that stared back up at me,
blinking iridescent eyes. What did I eat there?
Air? Insects? Salads of delicate herbs?
The bread tasted like ashes.

Sometimes she loved me, and we would ride together
on robins, or was it flowering hawthorn branches
whose thorns would prick my legs through leather trousers?
With her strange retinue: the fairy knights
riding on weasels, the goblin standard-bearers

holding thistle spears. They were always half something else,
with the heads of toads or owls, a bat's black wings.
Everything there was always half something else,
except the fairy women, wholly themselves,
and so luminous you had to look at them
through tinted spectacles. It was the fashion
to sew living butterflies to their shoulders,
so they moved in a halo of colored dust
and panicked flapping.
Awkwardly, at the rear of the procession,
walked a stray cat she had turned into a boy,
who mewed and tried to scratch me.

I was mostly unhappy, but sometimes happy. The problem
is this: I would rather be unhappy in fairyland
than happy elsewhere.

At night, I lie beside a woman who never
turns into a tree, who bears me human children.
And all I can think of is her hard black eyes,
which sometimes looked at me with such disdain,
her small red mouth that never told me the truth
and laughed when I believed her.
That fox's face, which was probably always a mask.

Sometimes I go into the forest alone
and whisper into the hollow knot of an oak:
I'd rather spend an hour in fairyland
than a lifetime elsewhere.
Then I stand in the green silence, with only the cries
of birds, the shush of the oak leaves high above,
and wonder if she's listening.

The Fairies' Gifts

The fairies came to my christening.
They were not invited—my family,
not being royalty, did not know
any fairies personally.
They just showed up, as fairies
do sometimes.

One was older, about four centuries old,
the other was younger, less than a century,
a teenager, in fairy years. She
was the older one's apprentice.
What shall we give the baby? she asked
the older. Fairies always bring gifts,
for better or worse.

They were both dressed
in diaphanous things: thistledown, moonshine,
spider silk, the wishes children make, the vows
made by ardent lovers, fairytale ever-afters,
the wind as it blows through birches.
They both had wings,
like moths.

What do you suggest? asked the older.
The younger recognized this as a test.

Beauty? she said, looking at her mentor
nervously. Grace? Oh, I know. Let her be smart
and good at sums. Or maybe the ability
to play any instrument, carry a tune . . .
The older shook her head.
All those things can be learned, she said.
Let us give her, between us, courage
and the ability to endure.

Snow, Blood, Fur

S HE LOOKS AT herself in the full-length mirror of the bridal salon. She resembles a winter landscape, hills and hollows covered with snow, white
and sparkling. She is the essence of purity, as though all that has ever blown
through her is a chill wind. The veil falls and falls to her feet. She shivers.

"Are you cold, Rosie?" her mother asks.

She shakes her head, but she is cold, or rather she is Cold, a Snow Queen.
If she breathed on the mirror, it would frost.

"Well, you look beautiful. Just beautiful. Nana would have been so proud."

WHEN SHE GETS home, she goes up to her bedroom and opens the closet door. In
one corner, in a wooden toybox she has kept from her childhood, is the wolf skin.
She puts it on, draping it around her shoulders, then steps into the closet, pulls
the door closed behind her, and sits down beside a parade of high-heeled shoes.

It is dark, as dark as she imagines it must have been in the belly of the wolf.

SOMETIMES SHE STILL has nightmares.

She is walking through the forest. Pine needles and oak leaves crunch under her boots. Once in a while, blackberry bushes pull at her dress so she has to
stop and untangle the canes. She is wearing the red cloak her grandmother knit
and felted. In it, she looks like a Swiss girl, demure, flaxen-haired: a Christmas
angel. Her grandmother gave it to her for her sixteenth birthday.

Suddenly, on the path ahead of her is the wolf. Dark fur, slavering red
mouth. Sharp, pricked ears, yellow eyes as wild as undiscovered countries. Or
it is a young man, a hunter by his outfit. He has a tweed cap on his head with
a feather in it, and is carrying a rifle. When he sees her, he bows, although she
cannot tell if he is serious or mocking her.

"Aren't you afraid of the wolf, Mistress Rose? He has been seen in this forest. Perhaps I should escort you, wherever you might be going."

In her basket is a bottle of blackberry cordial, a small cake with currants.
She is taking them to her grandmother, who has rheumatism. She has been
told to beware wolves . . . and young men.

She shakes her head, eyes down. Hurriedly, she passes him, but as she is
about to reach the bend in the path that will take her out of his sight, she turns
back, just once, to look.

The wolf is standing in the middle of the path. Then, he disappears through
the trees, off the path, where she is not allowed to go.

When she reaches her grandmother's house—small, tidy, with green shutters, apples ripening on the crooked tree, bees dancing around the skep—she knocks on the door. Hearing no answer, she opens it. There is no one in the parlor. She puts the cordial and cake in the pantry, leaves the basket on the kitchen table.

"Nana!" she calls. Could her grandmother be asleep?

In the bedroom, which smells of lavender, all she sees on the bed is the young man, naked. She has never seen a naked man before. He is beautiful, and grotesque, and frightening.

"Rosie Red, come to bed," he says. "You see, I have gotten here before you."

She takes off the red cloak.

"ROSIE!" HER MOTHER calls. "The florist is here with the centerpiece. Rosie, where are you?"

She knows what it will look like: lilies and gladiolas, so perfect they seem to be artificial. Scentless.

It is very quiet in the closet. It is very dark. She draws up her knees and puts her arms around them.

WHEN SHE WAKES up, the wolf is lying next to her. Where she lay, the sheets are spotted with blood. He has left his rifle on the chair, beside his discarded clothing.

She rises, still naked. Her father taught her how to use a rifle. One shot, and his body jumps on the bed. He yelps, although she does not know if he has woken up or passed directly from dreams into death. Two shots, and he lies still.

HER FIANCÉ WORKS for an accounting firm.

"Leroy has such a good job," says her mother. "He'll take care of you, Rosie. What more could any woman want?"

When he touches her, she shudders, as though his fingers were made of ice.

THE POLICE SAY she is very brave. Did they not find the remains of her grandmother at the edge of the woods, buried under oak leaves? Mauled—that is the only word. Mauled, gnawed, half-eaten.

They make her sit and drink a glass of blackberry cordial—for the shock, they say.

There is blood on the bed, a great deal of blood. It is the wolf's blood, they say, and she nods.

Later, her mother will bleach the sheets, but whenever she looks at them, she will think there was blood here, and here, and here.

* * *

"Rosie, the cake has arrived!" It has tiers and tiers of vanilla sponge iced with fondant, topped with sugar roses.

She imagines the table downstairs, in the dining room. The cake, the flowers, the gifts on display: Limoges dessert plates, engraved demitasse spoons.

Wearing the wolf skin, she does not have to be herself anymore. She does not have to be Rose. She can be something else entirely: pain, longing, anger. She can be silence if she wants to. She can be the word "no."

And what about Leroy? He is no wolf.

But wolves, she has learned, are not the dangerous ones after all.

This is a fairy tale, so all times are the same time: all times are now. She is always walking down the path, letting the white silk slip fall to her feet, pointing the rifle at the sleeping wolf, telling the story—the only story that makes sense—to the policeman. She is always trying on her wedding dress. It is always the season for blackberries and small red apples. She is always sitting in the darkness, warm and safe. She is always running through the forest, under oaks and pines.

All she wants is the wolf's pelt, made into a cloak. Her mother does not think it is suitable, but her father consults the furrier. The red cloak has grown too small for her; she will wear the fur cloak, so much warmer in winter.

She wears it to visit her grandmother's grave, in the parish churchyard. "Nana," she says to the headstone. "Nana, I'm so sorry."

She is fairly certain that if she wears the white dress, the one that makes her look immaculate, the one she may someday be buried in, drops of blood will appear on the bodice. Then streaks will run down the skirt. It will turn as red as a poppy among the wheat, as a flame on a match.

She rises, opens the closet door, and climbs out the window into the branches of the oak tree, then drops down on all fours and lopes, slowly, knowing that no one is watching, toward the forest.

She only stops once, to howl.

When You Have Lost Yourself

It takes a while to find yourself again
after you lost yourself in the dark forest,
accidentally letting go of your hand,
losing sight of yourself. "Where did she go?"
you ask the owl, the squirrel, the skeptical fox
who looks at you like a philosophy professor
when you have given an answer so obviously wrong
that he can tell you haven't read the textbook.
Unfortunately, there are things no philosophy textbook
will tell you, like how not to lose yourself,
where the paths in the forest go, or what the trees
are whispering as you pass—the oak, the beech,
the alder. Are they talking about you, or
the other you, wherever she is wandering?

It takes a while to find yourself—it takes
looking behind each tree, under each rock,
on the backs of leaves, among the meadow grasses,
asking crickets, chickadees, woodpeckers,
calling up to the distant circling hawk,
who can see the flickering tail of a hare as it runs
across a clearing. Perhaps you have hidden yourself
in his burrow, lined with fur, under an oak tree?
Perhaps you have hidden yourself under the roots
that overhang the stream, and only dragonflies
notice your eyes gleaming in the darkness.
Perhaps you have hidden yourself under the litter
of last year's leaves, or up in the canopy,
which is already turning red with autumn.

And once you have found yourself, what will you do?
I suggest taking yourself back to the cottage
near the clearing, sitting yourself in front of the fire,
making yourself some soup on the ancient stove,
with carrots, potatoes, and beans, flavored with parsley,
then putting yourself to bed and telling yourself

one of the old stories. It is after all
stories that tell us who we are, stories
that remind us where the paths might lead, and how
to talk to foxes so we can ask directions,
how to find the witch at the heart of the forest,
who might, as it turns out, be yourself after all,
stories that tell us what we could become,
stories that guide us home.

The Mermaid's Lament

They are there, they are still there:
eyes eaten long ago, replaced by coral
and therefore more beautiful, transformed.
Jaws grinning as though at a fine jest.
Their ribs, like the ribs of the ship itself, become
homes for small fish, eels, and squid, more welcoming
than in life. Only their bones
remain, furred green with sea moss,
and the rings on their fingers, looser perhaps
than they once were,
and the green floating hair.

They are there, still there, alas,
lying on beds of algae
under the dark wave:
all the loves I could not save.

Conversations with the Sea Witch

I N THE AFTERNOONS, they wheel her out on the balcony overlooking the sea. They place her chair by the balustrade. Once there, the queen dowager waves her hand. "Leave me," she says, in a commanding voice. Then, in the shrill tones of an old woman, "Go away, go away, damn you. I want to be alone."

They, who have been trained almost from birth to obey, leave her, bowing or curtseying as they go. After all, what harm can come to her, an old woman, a cripple? They do not call her that, of course. One does not call a queen dowager such things. But their mothers and fathers called her that long ago, when she was first found half-drowned on the sea shore—the crippled girl.

"A poor crippled girl," they whispered, incredulous, when the prince emerged from her room and told his father, "I'm going to marry her. She saved my life in the storm. She has no name—not as we have names. I'll call her Melusine."

Elsewhere in the castle, the king, her son, is issuing orders, perhaps about defending the northern borders, perhaps just about the education of the young prince, his heir. The queen is walking in the garden with her ladies-in-waiting, gathering roses. The young princess, her granddaughter, has stolen into the garden, where she is playing by the water-lily pool with her golden ball. In a moment, it will fall in. She has always been fascinated by water. She takes after her grandmother—her fingers are webbed. There are delicate membranes between each finger.

In the chapel, the former king, her husband, lies in his grand tomb of black-veined green marble. Next to it is another tomb, where she will someday lie. Now, it is empty like a promise unfulfilled. She knows it is there—she can feel it patiently waiting, and she knows it will not have to wait much longer. After all, did she not exchange five hundred years of life in the sea for one human lifetime? Once she lies beside him, completely surrounded by stone, she will have left the sea permanently at last.

But she is not thinking of that now. She is waiting for company.

She does not have to wait long. Soon after they leave—the servants, who have lives about which she knows nothing, about whom she thinks no more than she would of the white foam on a wave—the sea witch rises.

"Greetings, princess," says the witch. That, at least, is the closest we can get in translation, for she speaks the language of the sea, which is not our language. In the air, it sounds strange and guttural, like the barking of seals.

In the water, it is higher, more melodious, like the song of the sleek gray dolphins that sometimes visit our waters. It carries far.

"Greetings, witch," says the queen dowager. It is obvious, from her tone, that this is an honorific. "How goes it beneath the water?"

And then the sea witch tells her: all is well at court. Her eldest sister is a beloved queen. There have been storms along the southern coast, causing shipwrecks. Which is good—that stretch of the coast was suffering from over-fishing, and this will keep the fishermen away for a while. The whales that were trapped in the main harbor of the capital city have returned to the open sea. When Melusine became queen, it was forbidden to harm a whale, and her son continues that tradition. Her middle sister's second child has recently emerged from his father's pouch. The sea-folk, although mammalian, reproduce like sea-horses: a child, once born, is deposited in the father's pouch and emerges only to suckle its mother's breast until it can fend for itself. The sea is a dangerous place. The sea-folks' children must be strong to survive.

"And how is your throat?" asks the sea witch. "Have you tried the poultice I recommended?" It is made of seaweed, boiled down into a paste.

"Better," says the queen dowager. "But I feel death coming close, witch. Coming on human feet, soft and white and tender."

"May it not come for a few years yet," says the sea witch. She herself will likely live for another hundred years. "Who will I talk to after you are gone?"

The queen dowager laughs—the situation is, after all, ironic. And then she puts her hand to her throat, because it aches.

Two old women—that is what they are. Two old women who have lost the ones they loved, whom the world has left behind. All they have now is these conversations. Do not pity them. They get more enjoyment out of these talks than you imagine.

It was, the queen dowager thinks, a fair bargain: her voice, the voice that produced the beautiful songs of the sea-folk, like dolphins calling to one another, for a pair of human legs. Of course they were useless. A witch can split a long, gray, flexible tail into a pair of legs, pink and bare, but she cannot make them functional. What is inside them will not bear a body's weight. The crippled girl, lying on the sea shore, in love with the prince she had saved from the storm, hoping against hope that somehow she could make her way to him, perhaps by crawling higher among the rocks, knew she might die there, among the pools filled with barnacles and snails. She knew the crabs and seagulls might eat her soft white flesh. The rest of her might dry up in the sun.

Was it luck or some vestige of the sea witch's magic, or true love, which has its own gravitational power, that he was walking on the shore at exactly the right time?

As soon as he saw her, he said, "You're the girl I saw among the waves. The one who rescued me."

She tried to answer—she had lost her song, not her vocal cords—but he could not understand what she was saying, and her voice tired quickly, trying to speak through this new medium. The sea-folk learn to understand human speech, from listening to sailors in their boats and children playing along the shore. They must guard the sea from us, so they learn about us what they can. But we, proud and ignorant, thinking there is no intelligent life but that of the air, do not learn about them, and so only a few of us speak their language. Those who do are often considered mad. They spend their lives gathering things the tide has thrown up, living as they can on the detritus of the sea.

The prince carried her to the castle, put her in the grandest of guest bedrooms, and announced to his mother and father that this was the girl he was going to marry. When asked who she was, this girl with nothing—no clothes, no voice, no name—he said she was the daughter of the sea king himself. When his father asked about her dowry, he said it was safety among the waves. If she were queen, their ships would be safe—at least from the sea-folk, who often sank ships for their cargoes of furniture and figurines, which were to them the finest of trinkets, decorating their underwater caves.

In a seafaring nation, which had made its fortune from trade with distant lands—in spices, printed fabrics, hand-painted porcelain—this dowry was judged to be better than gold or jewels. And it is a fact that the fishing boats of that country had luck with their catches once the prince married the girl he had found among the tidal pools. After their marriage, the old king abdicated in favor of his son. The country had never been so prosperous as under King Cedric and Queen Melusine.

It took a few years, working with speech therapists and vocal coaches, for her to communicate clearly with her subjects, to sound merely foreign rather than outlandish and otherworldly. When she laughed, it still startled the palace staff—it sounded so much like barking. She could never learn to walk—she did not have the internal structure for locomotion on dry land. Sometimes she missed the ease of movement under water. Often in dreams she would be swimming, and she would feel the smooth movement of her tail, the strong forward thrust through water, with pleasure. But she loved the prince, later the king, who treated her with such tenderness, carrying her himself anywhere she wished to go—trying to compensate for the loss of her watery kingdom. She loved her children, with their strange pink feet and tiny toes, kicking and waving in the air as their nappies were changed or they threw tantrums. And we all make difficult choices.

The strangest thing about life on land, she told the sea witch once they started holding these conversations, was reproduction. The monthly cycle of blood, as though she were expelling a red tide. Incubating a child herself instead of depositing it in her mate's pouch, to develop safely in that second womb, coming out only for lactation. She did not understand the concept of a wet nurse. When her children were brought to her for feedings, she laid them beside her and imagined moving through the water, with them swimming alongside, latched to her breast. That is how a child of the sea-folk feeds beneath the waves.

Eventually, she taught them to swim in the palace baths, which dated to Roman times. Her legs could not give her the thrust of her lost gray tail, but with a strong breast stroke, she could pull herself through the water and recapture, for a while, what it had been like to swim through the depths of the sea.

She still swims sometimes. And she makes lace—the most delicate, intricate lace. Her fingers have grown crooked, but this is an ancient art of the sea-folk, which they learn as children: they knot strands made of seaweed, pounded and pulled into long fibers. It is a strong thread that shimmers in sunlight. Into her lace, she weaves patterns of starfish and cuttlefish and stingray. When she is too tired to do either, she reads poetry or stares out the window—the king, her husband, made sure that her bedroom window overlooked the sea. She has had a full life. She could, if she wished, spend every moment remembering it. Her childhood in the palace of her father the sea king, swimming through rooms on whose walls grew coral and anemones, coming up to the surface only to breathe the necessary air, although the sea-folk can hold their breath for hours at a time, then diving down again into her natural element. Hunting and foraging with her sisters through algae forests, for the children of the sea-folk have the freedom of the sea from a young age. Rescuing her prince from the storm after his ship went down, dragging him back to shore on a broken spar through turbulent waves. Going to the sea witch, making the fatal bargain. The years of being a wife, mother, widow.

Once a day she is wheeled out to the balcony. The sea witch comes, rising from the waves, and they speak.

Usually, their conversation follows a familiar pattern. But on this day, the queen dowager asks a question she has never asked before. It has never, before, seemed the right time to ask. "Do you regret your decision?" she asks the sea witch, wondering if she is being rude or too personal. But surely between old friends? After all this time, they must consider themselves that.

The sea witch is silent for a moment, then shakes her head. "No, at least I tried. You were not the only one, you know. I traded for your voice, the hair of another maiden, the soft gray skin of yet another. He would not love me, no matter how I tried to please him. He loved no one but himself."

He lived in the deepest, darkest abyss in those parts, an underwater crevasse that seemed to descend to the center of the earth. None of the sea-folk knew how old he was. Four hundred years? Six hundred? Older yet? He had filled himself with the magic of those dark spaces, and did not seem to age.

"He taught me so much," says the sea witch. "From him, I learned a magic that allowed me to stay under water for days at a time. A magic that raised the waves and created storms. The magic that took your voice. For years, I studied spells and potions under his tutelage. But when I told him that I loved him, he called me a silly guppy, no wiser than an infant, and told me to go away, that I was interrupting his studies. I did not go away—I moved to the edge of the crevasse in which he lived, and there I stayed, living in the cavern in which you found me. I hoped that if he saw my devotion, he would come to love me in time. But it merely irritated him.

"He cared only for knowledge—only for discovering the secrets of that dark abyss and the power it would give him. At first he would go to the surface periodically. But after he drove me out, he began to stay beneath the water for weeks at a time. He told me he no longer needed to breathe air. His eyes grew larger, his once-muscular body thinner. He developed a permanent look of hunger. I do not think he ate, except when krill or small shrimp floated by and he could catch them without interrupting his studies. He became hunched, as though curled up on himself. I did not care. I had not loved him for his beauty, which was considerable, but for his intellect, his desire for knowledge. I thought he might admire those things in me as well, so after my attempts to charm him failed, I studied the darkest of arts, the most potent of potions.

"One day, I perfected a spell that was beyond even his power. It was one he had attempted many times himself: a way of turning our tails into the tentacles of a squid, with the squid's ability to darken the water with its ink. I cast it, triumphant, knowing that he must love me now, or if not love, then at least respect me. At last, feeling the reverberations of that spell in the water, he came to my cavern.

"I thought he would be pleased that I had discovered this secret—that he would praise me and want to learn it from me. But no—he hurled himself at me with the full thrust of his tail and struck me across the face. Then, with his hands, he attempted to strangle me. But you see, I had eight new tentacles that I had not yet learned to control . . ."

The sea witch pauses for a moment, then says, "I tore him limb from limb. I could not even see—the water was dark with my ink. When it cleared, there were pieces of him scattered among the coral. The small fish were already nibbling at his flesh."

Then they are both silent, the queen dowager in her wheeled chair on the balcony, the sea witch floating among the waves, her body half out of water, a woman above, an octopus below.

WHAT ARE WE left with in the end, but old women telling stories? The first old women who told stories were the Fates. What else could they do, sitting in their chairs all day, spinning, measuring, and cutting the threads of our lives? Each thread was also a story, and as they spun it, they told it. They are telling our stories still.

Once upon a time, says Clotho as she spins the thread on her spindle. There was a king with three sons, the youngest of whom was called Dumbling, or the prettiest girl you have ever seen who was born with the feathers of a swan, or a queen who could not bear a child until a white snake told her that she was pregnant. And then, says Lachesis, the lass lived happily with her bear husband until she wanted to see what he looked like at night, or the prince found a castle in the forest inhabited entirely by cats, or the cook was so hungry that she took a spoonful of soup and all the sudden she could understand the language of animals. Finally, says Atropos, the loyal servant chopped off the brown bull's head and there stood the prince he had been searching for, or the maid spun linen so fine that it could fit through the eye of a needle so the Tsar took her back to his palace, or the false princess was put in a barrel filled with nails drawn by two white horses, and did she regret her treachery! They lived happily ever after, or not, and they are feasting still unless they have died in the interval. Every story has a beginning, middle, and end. After that end, there are only old women sitting together in the sunshine.

"And were you happy?" asks the sea witch.

"Very happy," says the queen dowager. "I'm still happy, even when I lie awake at night in a bed that is too large for one shrunken old woman, remembering tenderness that will never come again. Even when I know that soon my body will lie in a dry, dark place. My granddaughter, the youngest, Eglantine— I think someday she will come find you and ask to return to the sea. When she does, I hope you will give her my tail."

She pauses a moment. "And were you happy?" she asks the sea witch, for everyone deserves a little happiness in life, even witches.

The sea witch thinks for a moment. "No, I cannot say that I was. But I learned a great deal. No one in the sea, or perhaps even on land, has the knowledge I do. If I wished to, I could send a storm to destroy all the ships in this harbor, like a boy breaking sticks. Of course I would not do that, out of courtesy to you . . ." She bows to the queen dowager, who bows in return. "But I could, and that is something. Knowledge and power—those count for something when one is old."

"As does the memory of loving and being loved," says the queen dowager.

And then they are silent for a while, enjoying the sunshine and the lapping of waves.

"Well, until tomorrow," says the sea witch, finally. She knows the queen dowager's attendants will be coming soon.

"Of course," says the queen dowager.

The thread is spun, measured, and snipped, whether it be gold or hemp or sea silk. And afterward, the old women sit in the sunshine.

Diamonds and Toads

This fairy tale is a metaphor.

Because it really would be just as uncomfortable
to have diamonds coming out of your mouth as toads:
one hard, sharp, like a mouthful of glass. The other
soft, squishy, making you
disgusted with yourself, because . . . toads!
Ugh. At least the diamonds are valuable,
glittering in the palm of your hand,
although their edges leave your throat aching,
your mouth sore.

The diamonds knock against your teeth.
The toads make your tongue feel coated
as though a snail had crawled across it,
leaving a trail.

Once there were two girls, sisters.
One, whose name was Tabitha,
woke up in a good mood. The sun was shining.
She did not mind the sheep
bleating in the meadow,
although some days she wished
they could be eaten by wolves
so it would be quiet, just for a moment.
Her dress was hanging in the closet,
freshly pressed (her sister had done the ironing
yesterday). Her hair was curling naturally,
rather than tangling in the brush, as usual.
So she sang as she went to the well.
There she met an old woman
who was secretly a witch. (Isn't that how
it always goes?) The woman asked for water
and Tabitha gave it to her,
drawing up the pulley
with a smile and a "Lovely day, isn't it?"

She's the one who got the diamonds.

Her sister, Dolores,
woke up the next day with a headache.
It was raining, and rainy days always did that to her.
They also made her hair frizzy.
Her only clean dress
lay crumpled in the laundry basket, still damp
because Tabitha had forgotten to hang it on the clothesline.
(We can't blame her. She was dealing
with the diamond problem, still lying down
with a hot compress on her throat.)
That morning, the breakfast porridge burned
and the cat had left a half-chewed mouse in the parlor.
Ugh. So Dolores went to the well
in a foul mood
and told the woman to draw up the water herself.
She got the toads.

I told you this tale is a metaphor.
They used the diamonds
to buy more dresses, a carpet for the parlor,
a phonograph, some sturdy shoes,
and books. Quite a lot of books.
Tabitha was able to finish her degree
in library science. Eventually
a prince proposed to Tabitha, but she didn't want
to become his main source of income, better than taxes,
which parliament wouldn't let him raise, so she told him
she wasn't interested.

It was the toads that kept the garden
free of damaging insects: cutworms, leafrollers,
loopers, hornworms, rootminers, the ubiquitous beetles
that chew through rose leaves, leaving them
looking like window panes.
Dolores grew the finest cabbages, tomatoes,
aubergines. Her orchard was the only one
not devastated by a new apple borer.
Her roses were perfection.
From their hips she made a syrup for sore throats,
for which Tabitha was grateful.
She patented it and created a thriving business.

Eventually Dolores married a gentleman
with a very large garden. She's Lady Dolores, now.
Tabitha became a librarian,
so she rarely has to talk:
she can *shush* without triggering the diamonds.
Still, she wears a spectacular brooch
pinned to her sweater, because after all, why not?

Here is the moral: there are circumstances
in which toads are as useful as diamonds.
Or it may be, try not to get out of bed
grumpy, especially when there are witches
around. Or always be nice to old women,
because you never know.
Or maybe Tabitha and Dolores are really
one woman, and some days what comes out of our mouths
is diamonds, and other days, toads.
Which is better? I don't know.
The moral of a fairy tale
is as difficult to figure out as what to do
about cutworms and beetles, or blackspot
on the rose leaves.

Medusa Gets a Haircut

On the one hand, they had been her friends
for so long, whispering
in her ears, telling her stories,
reciting poems, not just the sorts of things
you would expect, Sappho and Hesiod,
but Auden, Eliot, Yeats—they liked the modernists—
and Sylvia Plath, Adrienne Rich—
they were eclectic in their tastes.
Sometimes they had sung to her,
only a little out of tune.

But Perseus never liked them. He said
they were distracting, that she was always listening
to them instead of him. Did she like them
more than she liked him? They were implying
things about him, weren't they?
Anyway, although he loved her
as she was—of course he did, otherwise
why would he be with her, instead of Andromeda—
in a relationship, everyone should be willing
to compromise.

So, she compromised.
Anyway, the pixie cut was in fashion.
Everyone wanted to look like Audrey Hepburn.
She went to a veterinarian—
after all she didn't want to hurt them.
Yes, other women go to a hairdresser,
but what would you do when you have snakes
for hair? He removed them gently,
under topical anesthesia.
She said goodbye to them reluctantly—
they were going to some sort of sanctuary
for abandoned reptiles.

The silence was disconcerting.

No more stories, no more poetry.
No more whispered conversations
as she walked to the grocery store
or down to the seashore. Of course,
no one looked at her strangely anymore
either, although the librarian
at her local branch said, "I kind of miss them"
while checking out her books—
Hesiod, Auden, Plath. She had never
actually read them. She was surprised
to find how much had been lost of Sappho.
The snakes had, of course, known
the lost bits.

But Perseus seemed happy,
for a while. And after all relationships
require compromise, don't they? Until the day
he told her about Andromeda. There was a sea serpent.
He would have to go rescue her,
because of course he would,
as though there weren't other heroes just itching
for a sea serpent fight.

"Let's stay friends," he said.
She sat in front of her mirror, staring at
where the snakes used to be, thinking
that she didn't look much like Audrey Hepburn
after all, just some girl
who once had snakes for hair
and no longer did. Then she noticed something:
small, wriggling.
The thing about hair is,
as your hairdresser will tell you after
you try to cut your own bangs with nail scissors,
it grows back.

The Other Thea

T HEA STARED OUT the train window. Forest, more forest, and then a small town would flash by. And then more forest. She had taken this route many times while she was in school, although then she'd traveled with a large trunk filled with the clothes and books she would need for a semester at Miss Lavender's. This time she had a backpack, with just enough for a day or two. How long would it take? She hadn't really known what to bring. Should she even be going, in the middle of Winter Break?

But she hadn't known what else to do. She checked the text on her phone: *Of course. Always pleased to see you, Thea. Let us know when your train gets in. Love, Emily*

Then a smiling black cat emoji. It was not one of the regular iPhone emojis, but Thea was not surprised that Miss Gray had somehow gotten into her phone. After all, she taught *Magic and Technology*. Thea remembered her standing in front of the classroom: "Manipulating technology is no different from manipulating any other aspect of reality," she had said. And then she had put some complicated equations up on the board. Math was Thea's least favorite part of magic. The poetry part had always come more naturally to her.

And then her text in response: *Arriving Thursday 2 p.m. I'll walk from the station.*

Miss Gray's response was another black cat emoji. It winked at her.

"Next stop, Miss," said the conductor. She looked up, startled. "Aren't you one of Miss Lavender's girls?"

"I was," said Thea. "I graduated last year."

He nodded. "Thought I remembered you, with that ginger hair." He pronounced it *jin-juh*. "If you need help with anything, let me know."

"Thanks," she said, and smiled. It was a weak smile, she knew that. She hadn't been very good at smiling lately.

"Hartfield, Massachusetts!" he called down the train corridor. "Next stop Hartfield!"

Thea put her phone back in her backpack and zipped up her jacket. She made her way to the end of the compartment.

Forest, more forest. And then the first houses of Hartfield, with weather-beaten wooden siding. Suddenly they were in the town center, with its brick dental offices, boutiques, and coffee shops. The train slowed, then pulled into the station. The conductor put a metal bridge over the gap, and Thea walked across it. Here she was again, not for some sort of alumnae event, but because she didn't know where else to go.

From the station, she walked up Main Street, passing several antiques stores, the food co-op, and Booktopia, where students from Miss Lavender's always congregated on Saturdays, ordering cappuccinos and egg or chicken salad sandwiches, reading Sylvia Plath or Margaret Atwood or the latest Kelly Link. Should she stop in for a moment? Maybe . . .

Before she could reconsider, she had stepped inside, and there was Sam at the counter. She had not expected him to be, well, right there.

"Thea," he said, a wide smile spreading over his face. It was accepted wisdom at Miss Lavender's that Sam looked like a frog. Nevertheless, a respectable percentage of the students admitted to having crushes on him, despite or because of his rumpled hair, flannel shirts, and encyclopedic knowledge of literature. He had been a clerk at the bookstore through high school. During Thea's sophomore year he had left for college, but his mother had been diagnosed with cancer, and since his parents were divorced, he had returned to Hartfield to care for her. After her death, he had bought Booktopia with the insurance. As he reminded the town council on a regular basis, every town needed an independent bookstore. Now he was finishing his degree by taking night classes at UMass Amherst. At least that's what it had said on the Booktopia blog, the last time Thea had checked.

"What are you doing back here? Don't you live in Boston now? Wait, I'll make you a cappuccino."

"No, that's OK, they're expecting me. But thanks. Yeah, Boston. I'm starting college next fall. I think. I mean, I am. I just took a gap year, that's all. I figured I'd stop in here for a minute, you know, to check out the writing books." There was a special section right up front, left over from National Novel Writing Month, with everything from *The Elements of Style* to Anne Lamott. "And to see where we used to hang out."

His eyes crinkled up at the corners. "Aren't you a little young to be getting nostalgic? You only graduated six months ago."

"Yeah." Thea laughed uncomfortably. "Way too young. Well, I'd better be going. They're expecting me. Maybe I'll come back . . . for one of those books. I always meant to read John Gardner."

"If you have time, come back and tell me about your life in the big city. I'll give you a sandwich on the house. Or, to be more accurate, on the store."

"Yeah, all right, thanks." She turned, then pushed the door open again. Standing outside in the cold air, she thought, *God, I am such a dork.*

He hadn't changed at all. Of course, people didn't change that much in six months. Except her. She had changed, in ways she didn't understand. That was why she had come back here. She continued up Main Street, then turned down Oak and Maple (seriously, how unimaginative were the people who named streets in small New England towns?). And there, at the edge of town, were the brick main house and buildings of Miss Lavender's. And the familiar sign:

Miss Lavender's School of Witchcraft
Founded 1812

Thea had never seen the grounds looking so deserted. The last time she had been here, she had been graduating, and the town had been filled with students and their parents.

Not hers, of course. Her parents had died when she was a child, and her grandmother had been sick for many years—far too sick to travel, for parents' weekends or even graduation. At those sorts of events, one or another friend's parents had always temporarily adopted her, and she had felt what it would be like to have a family, for a little while.

She walked up to the main house, which held the headmistress's office. She rang the bell and heard it echoing through the building.

"So you're back." She looked around, but saw no one. "Down here, idiot."

She looked down. "Oh, it's you, Cordelia. Hello." The tortoiseshell tabby stared up at her with yellow eyes.

"Hello yourself. I'm not at all surprised to see you again."

Before Thea could ask why, the door opened and there was Mrs. Moth, looking just as she always did, in a respectable wool skirt and cardigan, gray hair a little messy as though she had been running her fingers through it. The image of a headmistress.

"Thea, it's so good to see you," she said. "Do come in. I've just made tea. And you," she said, looking down at the cat. "You could have told us you would be out all night. You know how Lavinia worries."

"I was out on cat business, which is none of your business," said Cordelia. She slipped around Mrs. Moth's ankles and disappeared down the hallway.

"Cats!" said Mrs. Moth, shaking her head. "Come in, my dear. Let's go into the parlor. I've prepared one of the guest rooms for you. I'm afraid everyone's gone for the break—it's just me, Lavinia, and Emily right now. We always give teachers and staff two weeks for the holidays."

Sure enough, when Thea went into the parlor, where Mrs. Moth usually met with prospective students and their parents, there was Miss Lavender sitting on the sofa. Whereas Mrs. Moth was comfortably plump, Lavinia Lavender was thin and angular. She was wearing a soft gray dress, and the white hair escaping from her bun formed a halo around her face. It would have been intimidating, having tea with the founder of the school, but Miss Lavender looked so perfectly harmless. She was so forgetful that she sometimes accidentally walked through walls. It was a good thing that Mrs. Moth had taken over as headmistress, long before any of the alumnae could remember. But older students who had taken her seminar on *Philosophy of Magic* warned younger ones not to underestimate Miss Lavender. How could you be expected to remember the locations of walls when you were contemplating the fundamental structure of reality?

And standing beside the fireplace was Miss Emily Gray. Thea was almost shocked to see that she was wearing leggings and a loose sweater, as though she had just finished doing yoga or something. Her brown hair hung in a neat braid over one shoulder. It made Miss Gray seem almost human, although as soon as she said "Hello, Thea. It's so nice to see you again," Thea mentally panicked at the thought that she might have forgotten to do her homework. Did she look a mess? She was sure that she looked a mess. She took a deep breath.

"Cookies on the table, and I'll bring the tea," said Mrs. Moth, then disappeared down the hall toward the kitchen.

Thea quailed at the thought of having to make small talk with Miss Lavender and Miss Gray, but she should have known better. Witches don't make small talk.

"So what's the matter?" asked Miss Gray, sitting down on the sofa beside Miss Lavender. "You wouldn't have called if there was nothing wrong."

Thea put her backpack down and sat in one of the comfortable armchairs. While she was gathering her thoughts, trying to figure out what to say, Mrs. Moth came in with the tea things.

"Orange Pekoe for Lavinia," she said. "Oolong for Emily, and Earl Gray for me. Thea, I'm guessing you want a chai latte. You'll have to add milk." There was nothing in the cups when she poured out, but out of the teapot came four distinctly different smells and colors of tea. Thea added milk and sugar to her cup, then stirred.

"The thing is, I'm not sure," she said. "You know my grandmother died last summer, just after graduation. Thanks for the wreath, by the way. She would have really liked getting a wreath from the school. That was tough, but at first I was all right. I mean, we were never close or anything. I had to meet with her lawyer, then catalog all her furniture for the auction. I sold almost everything, except Mom's stuff. And then I had to sell the house. After that . . . I was supposed to be at Harvard this fall. But I just couldn't—I don't know, I was so tired. So I deferred for a year, and I rented an apartment in Boston. I figured I'd write . . . you know, start becoming a great writer." She smiled self-deprecatingly, in case they thought she was being too grandiose, although all through school that had been her talent: senior year, to her surprise, she had been chosen editor-in-chief of *The Broomstick*. "But I couldn't do that either. So I've been living in the apartment, doing—nothing, really. Some days I just wander around the city. Some days I don't even get out of my pajamas." Thea put her head down in her hands. "I don't know what's wrong with me."

Miss Gray took a sip of her tea. "When you went through your grandmother's house, did you find your shadow?"

It was the question she'd been dreading. When she'd first arrived at school, Mrs. Moth had sent a letter to her grandmother:

Dear Mrs. Tillinghast,
Thea seems to have forgotten her shadow. Since she will need

*it to participate fully in school activities, could you please send it
as soon as possible?*
>   *With best regards,*
>   *Wilhelmina Moth, Headmistress*

A week later, she had received a reply:

> *Dear Mrs. Moth,*
>   *As Thea may have told you, several years ago Mrs. Tilling-
> hast suffered a stroke. Although she has recovered a great deal,
> she lost some of her long-term memory and fine motor coordina-
> tion, which is why I am writing this letter for her. She says she
> remembers putting Thea's shadow in a box, but doesn't remem-
> ber where she put the box. She says it was a very troublesome
> shadow, and Thea is better off without it. I'm sorry not to be
> more helpful, and please give my love to Thea.*
> >   *Respectfully yours,*
> >   *Anne Featherstone, Mrs. Tillinghast's secretary*

It had happened when she was six. After both of her parents died when
their small plane went down, Thea had been sent to live with her grandmother.
She had hated the gloomy old house, and the gloomy old woman who told her
that her mother should never have married that spendthrift, good-for-nothing
Michael Graves. If she hadn't, she would not be dead now.

One day, after her grandmother had forbidden her from going out into
the garden, she had shouted, "I hate you! You're not my mother. I'm going to
run away and you'll never see me again, you old bitch!" Her grandmother had
ordered the butler to hold her, and with a pair of gardening shears she had cut
off Thea's shadow, *snip snip*. And that was the last Thea had seen of it. By the
time her grandmother sent her to Miss Lavender's, the third generation to attend, she had almost forgotten it wasn't there.

"Most people don't even notice," she had said to Mrs. Moth when first
asked about it. She had just arrived at Miss Lavender's, and was trying to figure
out where her room was, what classes she would be taking, whether she would
fit in or have friends. It was so different from her middle school in Virginia.

"Most people aren't witches," Mrs. Moth had replied. "While you're here,
we'll work around it, but there will be certain kinds of magic you can't do. And
you'll need it eventually."

Sometimes new students had said, "What's wrong with Thea? Why
doesn't she have a shadow?" But at Miss Lavender's one quickly learned that
if one's roommate turned into a wolf at certain times of the month, or was
faintly, almost imperceptibly green, or was missing a shadow, it was considered impolite to remark on it as anything extraordinary.

Before she had left for her grandmother's funeral, Miss Gray had said to her, "Find your shadow, Thea. It's time." Well, she had tried.

"No," she said now, in response to Miss Gray's question. "I looked everywhere," from the attic to the cellar, with Anne and the butler and cook until they were all covered with dust, "but I couldn't find it. I have no idea what happened to it. Do you think that's what's wrong with me?"

"Of course, my dear," said Miss Lavender, speaking for the first time. "You could do without it as a child, but now that you're a grown woman—well, a grown woman needs her shadow. Without it, you're fading."

Fading? She was fading?

"It's part of growing up," said Mrs. Moth. "Children don't need their shadows, strictly speaking—remember Peter Pan. But adults are a different matter. Lavinia's right, without it you'll fade away. It will take some time, but I'm afraid the process has already begun. Eventually even ordinary people—well, not ordinary of course, but not witches—will start to notice. Let's just see if we can find it, shall we? This didn't work the last time we tried—I suspect the box was shielded with a spell of some sort. But since your grandmother's passed away and the box has been lost . . . perhaps, just perhaps, it will work now."

How could she be fading? But Miss Lavender, more than anyone, could see things other people couldn't. In school, it was rumored that she could even see the futures—the multiple possibilities created by each moment.

Mrs. Moth leaned down and blew on Thea's tea. In the teacup, on the milky brown liquid, she saw an image form, in sepia like an old photograph. A castle with strange, twisting spires, and mountains in the distance.

"I've seen that before," she said.

"Of course you have," said Miss Gray. "We went there on an eleventh-grade field trip."

Then it must be . . . "Mother Night's castle. Is that where my shadow went?"

"Yes," said Mrs. Moth. "And I'm afraid you'll need to go find it. You can't do without it much longer. When Lavinia says fading, she doesn't just mean visually. Without it, you'll keep getting more tired. You'll start feeling despondent, as though you'll never accomplish anything. Eventually, it will seem too difficult even to try. One day you might not get up at all."

"But how can I find it?" asked Thea. "Mother Night's castle is in the Other Country. When we went, Miss Gray took us. Can you take me there again?" She looked at Miss Gray.

The teacher shook her head so that her brown braid swung around.

"Thea, my dear," said Mrs. Moth, "you are a graduate of this school. Like any witch, you should be able to find your way to the Other Country. By yourself."

* * *

THE NEXT MORNING, Thea woke to Cordelia patting her nose.

"Stop that," she said, and rolled over. That's right, she was at Miss Lavender's, in a guest bedroom on the second floor of the headmistress's house. Through the window, she could see the dormitory where she had spent six years of her life. It reminded her that Shoshana had sent her a Facebook message a couple of days ago, asking if Thea was all right and complaining about Chem 101. Of her two senior-year suitemates, Shoshana Washington was premed at Brown, and Lily Yu was in China working for a human rights organization. She would start an Asian Literature and Culture major at Stanford in the fall. She kept posting pictures of dumplings and rainy green hills on Instagram. Thea really should keep up with them, but it was hard when she was the only one who had nothing to say. *Binge-watched Netflix and ate ice cream for dinner* didn't make for a very inspiring Facebook post.

"Are you getting up, or do I have to sit on your face?"

She turned back over. "Cordy, how do you get to the Other Country?"

"How do I get there? I'm a cat—I just go. The question is, how do you get there?" All cats knew the way to the Other Country. That was one of the first lessons in *Care and Feeding of a Familiar*. If you couldn't find your cat, it was probably in the Other Country.

Thea scratched the cat behind her ears. "Can't you just take me there?"

"No, I can't take you. A little lower down . . . there. Now under the chin." For a moment, Cordelia actually purred. Then she continued, "You're a thick, clumsy human. You can't go the way cats go. We just slip between things. You need to go through a door."

"I remember!" said Thea. "When we went in eleventh grade, it was through a door. And the door was in this house . . . But I don't remember which one it was. Cordy, can you show me which door goes to the Other Country?"

Cordelia swatted her hand away and looked at her with contempt. "Now you really are being an idiot. After six years in this place, you should at least know how to think like a witch."

Think like a witch? What did the cat mean? Suddenly she remembered a visiting lecturer, an alumna named Dr. Something Patel who taught physics at one of the local universities. She had come to talk to Miss Gray's class about magical physics. Thea remembered her standing in front of the blackboard, chalk in hand, saying . . . how did it go? "One of the most important things I learned in my time at Miss Lavender's, which has served me well as a theoretical physicist, is to think like a witch. If you can't find the answer, a witch would say, you're probably asking the wrong question." Miss Gray had nodded emphatically.

Think like a witch.

"It's not *the* door. It's *a* door. I'm going to take a shower. I'll be ready in ten minutes. Wait for me, okay?"

Cordelia didn't answer. She stretched out in a sunny spot on the coverlet and started to wash herself.

Twenty minutes later, Thea was ready. In her backpack, she had a change of clothes, toiletries zipped into plastic bags, a notebook and pens, a battered copy of *A Wrinkle in Time* that she had been rereading, and half a chocolate bar.

"Are you coming?" she said to Cordelia. "Or did you wake me up this morning just because you felt like it?"

"I'm coming." The cat jumped down from the bed, then looked up at her. "Which door?"

"Kitchen. That way I can grab some breakfast along the way."

Thea walked quietly in case anyone else was still asleep, down the back stairs and to the kitchen. Last night, Mrs. Moth had shown her where everything was kept. "Just make yourself breakfast anytime you like," she had said. Thea found a bagel, then cream cheese to smear on both sides. She put them together to form a sandwich so it would be easier to carry. She put an apple into her backpack. That would have to do.

"All right," she said, holding the bagel in one hand, with the backpack slung over her shoulder. "Let's see if I'm right about how to do this."

She walked to the kitchen door. Standing in front of it, she took the notebook out of her backpack, scribbled a few lines . . . Then she put her hand on the door handle and read,

> "An entrance, entranced,
> you open into the brightness
> of summer and winter dancing,
> white snow on white blossoms,
> in the country of my longing."

Not her best effort, but perhaps it would do. And she did like the pun: entrance, entranced. The trick was to tell the door what it was, what it could become. "The creation speaks two languages," Miss Gray had told them in *Introduction to Magical Rhetoric*. "Poetry and math, which are the same language to anyone who speaks them correctly. You must speak to the creation in its own language, so it understands what you want it to do." Thea took a deep breath, hoping the spell had worked, and opened the door.

It was summer. It is always summer in the Other Country, or rather it is always no season at all: the apple trees are always blossoming, and in leaf, and bearing fruit at the same time. Sometimes it snows, and white flakes settle on the ripening fruit. But today seemed to be a perfect summer day. Thea and Cordelia walked down the sloping green hill toward the castle. Tall grass brushed against Thea's jeans, and the sun was warm enough that she stopped for a moment to take off her jacket and stuff it into her backpack. Beyond the castle was a lake, shining in the sunlight, and beyond the lake were mountains with forested slopes and snowy peaks. It looked like a postcard, or something that had been Photoshopped.

The last time she had been here, Shoshana had squealed in delight and Lily had said, "Seriously, are you making that noise? Because stop." Miss Gray had said, "Come on, girls. We're on a schedule." The castle looked just as Thea remembered—beautiful, but strange. As she and Cordelia walked down the hill and came to the gardens, she could see more clearly the stone towers, some going straight up and covered with small balconies, some spiraling like a narwhal's horn, some curled like a snail's shell. The buttresses, some of them supporting nothing but air, resembled a whale's skeleton. The whole structure was improbable, like a castle out of a dream, and reminded Thea of an Escher print. One of those towers, probably the largest, held the Tapestry Room, where gold spiders with jeweled eyes crawled up and down, weaving the threads of life into an enormous tapestry, whose front no person had ever seen. Her thread was somewhere in there. She wondered what it looked like, which part of the pattern it formed.

"And this," she remembered Miss Gray saying, in a voice like a tour guide's, "is the Library of Lost Books. All the books that are lost in the worlds are kept here. To our left, you will see the extension built specifically after the burning of the Library of Alexandria."

Thea stepped onto a garden path. Cordelia ran ahead and stood by the side of a long stone pool with yellow lotus flowers at its farther edge.

"Something interesting?" asked Thea.

"Fish," said the cat, staring down intently.

Thea sat on a stone bench beside the path and put her backpack next to her. She was starting to feel hot, and the bench was shaded by a linden tree, both blossoming and in leaf. "Anyway, I need a plan, you know," she said.

"Why?" said Cordelia, reaching a paw tentatively into the water.

"Well, because I need to find my shadow, and then I need to take it back with me, and I don't know how to do either of those things, is why." What she really wanted to do was stay here, in the warmth and sunlight, with the sound of bees buzzing in the linden flowers above her. After all, she had no idea how to find her shadow, or what to do after she had found it. She would sit, just for a little while . . . At least it was better than sitting in her apartment, scrolling aimlessly through her Facebook newsfeed.

Cordelia leaned down and patted at the water, then jumped back, shaking her head from side to side.

"That's right, stupid cat!" came a shrill voice. "If you put your head down here, I'll spit at you again!" Thea leaned forward just enough to see an orange head sticking out of the water. One of the fish, looking rather pleased with itself. Thea heard a clucking sound and realized that it was laughing. Then it disappeared back beneath the green surface of the water. Cordelia hastily licked herself all over and then stalked off along the path, as though nothing had happened.

"Hey, where are you going?" Thea called, but the cat did not turn back or answer. She was alone in the still, sunlit garden.

"I want my ball back, and I want it now!"

She turned in the direction of the voice. A girl about her own age was walking toward her, dressed in a bathing suit that looked as though it had come from the 1930s, with a frilled bathing cap on her head. "Where is it, Thea? I swear, if you don't give it to me right now, I'm going to turn you into a toad, or worse!"

Thea stared at her in astonishment. The girl pulled off her bathing cap, and down fell long black hair, with stars tangled in it. "Seriously, I don't know why my mother puts up with you. If I were her, I'd put you back in that box!"

"Lady Morgan?" said Thea, hesitantly. This must be Mother Night's daughter. Was she supposed to curtsey or something? They had not met her on the field trip, but who else would be walking around the castle gardens as though she owned them, talking about her mother? And what was that about a box? "I'm not Thea. I mean, I'm the other Thea. I mean, she's the other Thea—I'm the real one."

"Oh!" said Morgan Morningstar, looking at her with astonishment. "Why, so you are. You're faded around the edges. Well for goodness' sake take her back with you—she's such a pest. You'd think being in a box for twelve years would have calmed her down, but evidently not. Last week, she almost started a fire in the library—there's a reason that fireplace is never used! She and one of those annoying satyrs thought it would be a good place to toast marshmallows. Can you imagine? Now that you're here, you can take her—where are you from, anyway?"

"Miss Lavender's," said Thea. She stood up, but decided not to curtsey. The time had passed for it, anyhow.

"Oh, how nice. Say hello to Emily and Mina and dear old Lavinia for me. You must be one of the students."

I graduated, Thea wanted to tell her, but Morgan had already taken her arm and was pulling her down the path toward the castle. "The problem is finding her. She stole my Seeing Ball, and now she can see me coming and hide. You know a shadow can hide in very small places, and the castle has lots of those. But now that you're here, maybe we can convince Mom to send her back. It's clear that Thea—the other Thea—should go home with you. I mean, look at you . . ."

Thea didn't know how to respond, but she didn't have to. Morgan Morningstar was pulling her through the gardens: between flowering borders, and through a privet maze that Thea would surely have gotten lost in, and over a lawn laid out like a checkerboard, with chamomile forming the white squares. Where had Cordelia gone? Drat all cats. Then they were in the castle courtyard, with its Egyptian and Greek and Indian statues, and through the arched doorway.

The great hall was cool and dim after the sunlit courtyard. Just as she remembered, it had no ceiling: tall pillars ascended up to the blue sky. But the sun was already sinking toward the mountains, so the hall was mostly in shadow. It was empty except for a small group of people at the far end, close to the dais.

"Mom!" Morgan called. "Look who I found by the lotus pool."

Several of the—people?—stepped back. Thea noticed a man with the antlers of a stag, a woman with ivy growing over her head instead of hair, and a woman who looked exactly like Dr. Patel, only what would Dr. Patel be doing here? A pirate, in a black leather coat and tricorne hat, took off his hat and bowed to her. But between them all was Mother Night. Today she looked like her daughter, black hair falling to her feet, a face as pale as the moon, unlined. She could have been Morgan's twin. The last time Thea had seen her, she had looked immensely old, with gray hair that wound around her head like a coronet. She had been sitting on her throne, and Miss Gray had introduced the Miss Lavender's students to her, one by one. They had bobbed awkward curtseys, having learned how to curtsey just the week before. Thea remembered what Miss Gray had told them: "Don't be nervous, but remember that she created the universe." It didn't matter what she looked like at any particular moment. You couldn't mistake Mother Night.

"Mom, this is . . ."

"I know, sweetheart. Hello, Thea. We've been expecting you. How are you feeling?"

"Pretty well, Ma'am," said Thea, doing her best to curtsey, trying to remember how. This time she was sure she should curtsey.

"How do you think she's feeling?" said Morgan. "Look at her. Soon she'll be as transparent as a ghost. I could poke my finger through her, not that I want to. You need to make Thea—I mean shadow Thea—go back with her."

"Your mother doesn't *need* to do anything," said the pirate. But he said it so charmingly, with a grin and a wink at Thea, that she could not help smiling back at him. "I know you're in a bad mood, Morgan . . ."

"Don't you start with me, Raven," said Morgan, still gripping Thea by the arm. "You said the same thing when she stole your cloak of invisibility. You said, 'That shadow has to go.' Remember?"

So this was Raven! The famous, or infamous, Raven . . . Mother Night's consort.

"Stop, both of you," said Mother Night. "I can't make her go, for the simple reason that while she's separated from Thea, she's a person. Like any of you. Like Thea herself. I will not order her to leave here. I'm sorry, my dear," she said to Thea. "You need to figure this out yourself." Which was just what Mrs. Moth had told her. Thea felt sick to her stomach. She had no idea how to find her shadow, much less convince her to . . . what, exactly? She still wasn't sure. And what had Morgan meant—as transparent as a ghost? Was she fading that fast?

"Remember there's a ball tonight," Mother Night continued. "The other Thea will certainly be there—she loves to dance. And now, I have some things to attend to before the ball."

"I'll come with you," said Raven, taking her by the arm. The antlered man and the ivy-haired woman followed them out, as did Dr. Patel before Thea could say hello as a fellow Miss Lavender's alum.

"He always takes her side," said Morgan. "I guess I can't blame him. They've been together for what, a thousand years? But I really wanted Mom to just *do* something for once."

"So where do you think we'll find her?" asked Thea. "The shadow, I mean."

"Oh, Mom's right. She'll be at the ball. She wouldn't miss a party, and I have to admit, she is a good dancer. Come on, we need to find clothes to wear. We can't go to the ball looking like this—at least, you can't."

Thea looked down at her jeans and gray Gap shirt. No, she couldn't. Could Morgan really have put a finger through her? She looked solid enough. Tentatively, she poked herself in the stomach. She felt solid. But both Morgan and Mrs. Moth had talked about her fading at the edges, slowly becoming transparent. She wished she didn't have to worry so much—about herself, and the shadow Thea. She was going to a ball in Mother Night's castle! Shoshana was going to freak out. Even Lily might be impressed. Which reminded her . . .

As she followed Morgan down a series of twisting stone hallways, she took out her iPhone. No reception here, of course, but she could take photos and share them later with Shoshana and Lily in their private Facebook group.

Morgan's room was the entire top of a tower. Out of a large wardrobe, she drew dresses and suits of silk and velvet and lace, tossing them on her bed, which was shaped like a swan with its neck curved to form a backboard, while Thea walked around, looking through all the windows. Below she could see the castle and gardens. In one direction, hills and fields stretched away into the distance, until she could see a darkness that must be the sea. In the other, the lake reflected the setting sun, which was just beginning to touch the tops of the mountains with pink and orange.

"What else is there besides the castle?" asked Thea. "I mean, we only ever visited here. Are there—towns in the Other Country? If I went out there, what would I find?"

"All the stories you ever heard of," said Morgan. "And a whole lot you haven't. What about this?" *This* was a dress of green velvet that looked as though it had come from a museum exhibit or a Hollywood red carpet. "You can wear it with this." The second *this* was a mask of peacock feathers. Morgan rummaged among the clothes she had thrown on the bed.

"What are you going to wear?" asked Thea.

Morgan held up a black leather coat just like Raven's, and put a hat just like his on her head. "With this," she said, holding a mask of black feathers to her face. The smile beneath it was mocking.

"You're still mad at him, aren't you?"

"I just don't like him telling me what to do. He's not my father. And he's, what, as old as civilization itself? That's nothing." Morgan shrugged.

"That's like a moment in time."

"But your mother also said . . ."

"Well yeah, Mom. That's different. But Mom's never stopped me from doing anything I want to. She doesn't, you know—interfere. She knows what's on the front of the tapestry, the fate of every person in every world as it's being woven. Sometimes I wish she would step in and act, especially when you otherworlders are doing something dreadful, like having another war. But she says that's what we're here for—you and me and Emily Gray. We're the ones responsible for changing things. That's why places like Miss Lavender's exist. Come on, it's getting dark. You can get dressed in the bathroom."

When Thea emerged from what turned out to be a surprisingly normal bathroom—but she figured people in Mother Night's castle needed to pee just like everyone else—she looked as though she had stepped out of a painting. Green velvet fell to the floor, covering her red Keds. Morgan's shoes had all been too small for her.

"I suppose you could magic your feet smaller," said Morgan, but at the beginning of junior year Mrs. Moth had told Thea's class, "If I discover that any of you have used magic for such a vain, trivial purpose as changing your physical dimensions, you will come to my office and have a serious talk with me." That had been enough to deter experimentation. Anyway, Thea wanted to feel at least a little like herself, underneath the dress and mask.

Before they left, she took two selfies in the wardrobe mirror: one by herself and one with the Morningstar, in which Morgan held up two fingers in a peace sign. What would Lily and Shoshana think of *that*? And then she followed Morgan back down through the castle corridors, passing what were obviously partygoers because they wore black tie or fantastical robes and gowns. Most of them wore masks, although sometimes she could not tell whether the masks were simply their faces.

In the great hall, it was twilight. The moon hung directly overhead, surrounded by constellations Thea did not recognize. The hall was illuminated by bubbles of light that floated through the air, seemingly wherever they wished. Earlier the hall had been bare stone, but now between the columns grew a forest of slender birch trees, with leaves that shone silver in the light of the floating bubbles. Thea reached up to touch a leaf and found that it was, indeed, made of pliable metal.

Beneath this forest moved the strangest, most fantastical people Thea had ever seen. There was the stag man, with flowers draped over his antlers. A woman with scaled blue skin was talking to what looked like a large owl. Three young girls with pig snouts were slipping in and out between the trees, playing tag. A satyr was bowing to a woman whose dress seemed to be made of butterflies—not just bowing, but asking her to dance, because now the music was starting. The butterflies fluttered as she took his hand. In the center of the hall was a dance floor that looked like a forest glade, with mossy rocks at its edges to sit on. A small stream ran through it, so dancers had to be nimble to avoid stepping in the water.

"I'll take it as a compliment." Thea turned around. There was Raven, looking Morgan up and down critically. "You could be me as a beardless boy, a thousand years ago."

"I don't think I'll be mistaken for you tonight," said Morgan, then burst out laughing. But who could blame her? The dashing pirate of that afternoon now had the head of a fox, with the same expression of sly humor under the tricorne hat. "Are you showing your true face, Monsieur Renard?"

"One of them, at any rate. *Hola*, I hear a sarabande! Shall we dance, Lady Morgan?"

"I'll be back," said Morgan to Thea. "The refreshments table is over against the wall. You'll be all right, right?" Thea barely had time to nod before Morgan was swept away by the fox man. She took off her mask, which felt hot and strange. What was she doing here anyway? Suddenly, she felt lost and alone.

"How are you, my dear?" Thea turned toward the voice—it was Mother Night. She looked completely different than she had that afternoon. Now her skin was dark, almost blue-black, and she had a nimbus of short white curls around her head. She was wearing a silver dress, very simply cut, that could have come from ancient Egypt or a modern fashion magazine.

"I'm all right, I guess," said Thea. But she didn't feel all right. Instead, she felt as though she might throw up.

"You haven't eaten anything since breakfast, not even the apple in your backpack. You forgot about it, didn't you? You have half a chocolate bar in there too, in the front pocket. So of course you're going to feel sick. You need to take better care of yourself."

"I'm not very good at that," said Thea. "Taking care of myself, I mean."

"No, you're not. But you don't have anyone else to do it, so you'll have to get better at it. Why don't you practice right now? Go over to the refreshments table and get yourself some of the fish pie, which is very good. And there's asparagus with hollandaise, and ice cream. But meat and vegetables first! Not just ice cream, you know." Thea nodded. It had been a long time since anyone had told her to eat healthily, and the fact that Mother Night was doing it made her feel like laughing, despite her sense of nausea.

"I'm serious," said Mother Night. She put her hands, cool and dry, on either side of Thea's face. Her eyes were black, with stars in them. For a moment, Thea felt as though she were floating in space. "Try to remember that you're also one of my daughters." And then, with a soft pat on the cheek, of both affection and admonition, Mother Night was gone. Thea shook her head as though to clear it, then walked around the dance floor, weaving between the birch trees and mossy stones, stepping over the stream, to the refreshments table.

She hung the peacock mask over her arm by its ribbons, then took a plate and some cutlery that looked like forks and knives on one end, and birch branches on the other. That must be fish pie—at least the crust was baked in the shape of a fish. She did not like asparagus but took some anyway, as well as some scalloped potatoes. A potato was a vegetable, right?

"What do you think that is?" asked the person ahead of her in line. Suddenly, she realized who she had been standing behind.

"Dr. Patel?" she said. The professor was wearing an ordinary black evening dress, with pearls. "I don't know, it looks sort of like a fern, you know those fiddle-head ferns they sell at the farmer's market, except those aren't usually purple, are they? I'm Thea Graves. I graduated from Miss Lavender's last spring. I think you lectured to one of my classes. On magic and physics?"

"Oh, hello," said Dr. Patel, smiling the way people do when they're trying to remember who you are. "Call me Anita. It's always nice to see a fellow alumna. Have you tried those little cakes? The ones in all different shapes and colors. They have marzipan inside."

Thea took several of the cakes. She did like marzipan. "It's weird seeing someone I know—I mean, sort of know—here in the Other Country. Are you . . . just visiting?"

"Wouldn't that be nice!" said Dr. Patel. "Sometimes I think only students get real vacations. No, I'm afraid that I'm here on business . . . Mother Night's business, of course. And you?"

"Oh, um, yeah. Me too, business."

"Emily used to say, *We are all on Mother Night's business, no matter what we're doing.* I bet she still says that to her students. How is everyone at Miss Lavender's? It's been so long since I visited—Homecoming, I think."

Suddenly, Thea had a vision of Miss Emily Gray, and Dr. Patel, and Morgan Morningstar, all going about Mother Night's business, whatever that might be.

"I'm really just here to find my shadow," she confessed. She didn't want Dr. Patel to think that she was taking too much credit, making her business out to be grander than it was. . .

"Unless it finds you first!"

Thea turned around. There stood a girl, as tall as her, shaped like her, with her red hair. She wore a black catsuit and a mask that looked like a cat's face, with cat ears and whiskers.

"Asparagus? Seriously?"

"What," said Thea.

"Asparagus? You like asparagus?"

"What . . . no. You're her. Me. You're me. You need to go home with me. We're supposed to be together." Could she sound any more inane?

The shadow took off her mask. Even though Thea had been expecting it, when she saw her own face she stepped back into the table and almost knocked over the tray of little cakes.

Dr. Patel was farther down the table now, and there was no one behind her in line. She and the shadow were as alone as they could be, in a ballroom.

"I'm not going anywhere with you," said the shadow. Her face was subtly wrong. Thea wondered why, then realized that for the first time she was looking at herself the way other people saw her, not reflected in a mirror. "Why should I? You put me in a box for twelve years! A shadow in a dark box—I barely existed. But here I'm as real as you are. Probably realer—you look sort of faded around the edges. In fact, why don't you stay here and be my shadow? That would be amusing!"

No, it wouldn't. "First of all, I didn't put you in a box for twelve years. My grandmother did. And second of all . . ."

"Well, you didn't take me out, did you? I'm not going anywhere with you, no way, no how. I just wanted to see you in person. When I saw you in the Seeing Ball with Morgan Boringstar, I thought, *I wonder what she's like.* Well let me tell you, I am *not* impressed. Except for the shoes—I do like the shoes, but that's it. And you can tell Morgan that she should find herself another Seeing Ball, because I'm not giving this one back!"

"Well, well, so you've found Thea, Thea!" The satyr Thea had seen dancing with the butterfly woman put his arms around the shadow. She laughed and yanked his long hair, then kissed him loudly on the mouth.

"Come on, Oryx," she said. "Let's go somewhere interesting. This party's lame!"

He laughed and swung her onto the dance floor. As they capered away, over the stream and across the moonlit room, Thea heard, "I saw you talking to her! Did she have my Seeing Ball?"

"No," said Thea. She turned around. Morgan was a little out of breath, still wearing her mask of black feathers. "She said to tell you that she wasn't giving it back."

"That little . . . When I find her, I'm going to put her back in a box. A sewing box—a cigar box—a match box. Let's see how she likes that!"

"I'm sorry, I need to sit down." How faint her voice sounded! Still clutching her plate, Thea turned away from Morgan and walked as steadily as she could to one of the doors, leaning for a moment against the frame, then down a torch-lit hall until she reached a stone arch through which she could see the garden. She stumbled out into the night and sat on one of the benches, putting her plate on her lap.

She could not eat. The nausea was even stronger than before. Was it because she had encountered her shadow? She looked down at the plate and almost cried out in fear. Its porcelain edges were visible through her hands. She held one hand up in front of her. Through it she could see the moonlit garden, with its topiaries black in the moonlight, its trellises on which white flowers bloomed in the darkness. Through her hand she could see the moon and constellations. Why was she fading so quickly? Mrs. Moth has said it would take time, but here in the Other Country, it was taking no time at all.

She had no idea what to do.

A small voice, her own although it sounded suspiciously like Mother Night's, said *You must take care of yourself.* Step one: fish pie. Step two: scalloped potatoes. Step three: asparagus, ugh. But she ate every stalk.

"Finally you're doing something sensible," said Cordelia. The cat was sitting on the bench beside her, yellow eyes shining in the moonlight. "When you're done, I want to lick your plate. I mean the fish part of it."

"Where have you been all day?" asked Thea, finishing the little marzipan cakes. She did not feel better, exactly. But at least she did not feel quite so hollow.

"On cat business, which is Mother Night's business, of course," said the cat. Thea put her plate on the bench, and Cordelia licked the remains of the fish and potatoes.

"I found my shadow, or she found me, but Cordy, it's hopeless." Thea looked down at her ghostly, almost transparent hands. "She blames me for putting her in that box. She doesn't want anything to do with me, unless I become *her* shadow. And everyone says this is something I have to figure out myself—Mother Night won't help me, and I don't know what to do."

"Well," said the cat, licking her paws and washing her face with them, "you can start by thinking like a witch instead of a whiny twelve-year-old. Remember the day you arrived at Miss Lavender's?"

"I'm not that girl anymore," said Thea. That small, scared girl, scarcely larger than the trunk she had lugged through the airport and then onto the train from Boston. She wasn't like that, was she?

"You could have fooled me."

Think like a witch. No, she wasn't that girl anymore. She was a graduate of Miss Lavender's, and even if she didn't know what to do right now, she would figure it out.

Thea took a deep breath. "Cordy, I bet she's still in the castle. She's the part of me that my grandmother cut away, the bad part. Or, you know, rebellious. Angry. She's teasing us now, showing us that she's smarter, better than we are. She likes doing that. So she's still here."

"Then let's go find her," said the cat.

"She stole Raven's cloak of invisibility. I think that's why Morgan hasn't been able to find her all this time. So we need another way to find her. Can you find her by smell?"

"How would I do that?" said Cordelia, looking at her incredulously. "Do you have any idea how big the castle is? I don't think even the castle itself knows! We could look for years."

"I think I know where to start. She's so confident, but it's all on the surface—she doesn't belong here any more than I do. She's lost, just like me. I think she's been hiding in the Library of Lost Books. That's what I would do, hide among the lost things. I think that's why she was toasting marshmallows in the library fireplace. Of course if she looks in the Seeing Ball, she can see us coming, in which case we're out of luck. But she didn't have it earlier—I would have noticed it on her, in that cat outfit. We have to take the chance that she's too occupied or distracted to check. Anyway, this is the only plan I can think of right now. Will you help me?"

"All right," said Cordelia. "I'll even let you carry me, as long as you don't turn me on my back. I'm not a human infant, you know!"

Thea put the cat over her shoulder. She didn't have time to return her plate and cutlery to the ballroom—hopefully someone would find them. "To a witch, any door is every door." Senator Warren had said that, speaking at her graduation. It was probably supposed to be a metaphor, but metaphorical language was poetry, right? And poetry was magic. She walked back to the stone arch that led into the castle. She stood in front of it, clutching Cordelia, and said,

> "Ghosts of thoughts are lying
> on the shelves, rustling
> like a forest of dry leaves.
> Take me to them."

See? Metaphor—or was that a simile? She was getting better at this. Thea stepped through the archway and into the Library of Lost Books.

The library was dark and silent, illuminated only by the moonlight that came through tall, mullioned windows. It gleamed on row upon row of books with gilt lettering on their spines. She put Cordelia down on the floor.

"All right," she said. "Look for someone who smells like me. I mean smell for. You know what I mean."

Cordelia sniffed the air. Thea could see the shining circles of her eyes. Then she turned away and slunk into the darkness. This could take a while . . . but no, just a minute later Cordelia was back.

"Well, that was easy," she said disdainfully. "She may have gotten all the anger, but you got all the brains. They're asleep, right in front of the fireplace."

Thea followed the cat across the dark, cavernous room to a stone fireplace. On a carpet in front of the fireplace, there was . . . nothing. "Invisibility cloak," she said. "Show me where?"

Cordelia nudged the nothing.

Thea knelt down and felt the air . . . yes, it was fabric, scratchy like wool. She pulled it off. There, on the carpet, asleep and smelling distinctly of wine, were her shadow and Oryx the satyr. One of her arms was flung over his hairy chest.

"What now?" asked Cordelia.

"I don't know." She had been doing the next thing and the next, as they occurred to her. Looking down at her shadow, nestled against the satyr, she did not know what to do.

"Well, that's helpful," said the cat in her most disgusted tone. She sat on the stone floor and wrapped her tail around her paws.

Thea sat down beside her cross-legged, set the peacock mask on the floor, and put her chin in her hands. The green dress, black in the moonlight, puddled around her. How do you join a shadow to yourself after it has been snipped away? That was the question.

"If I could get her to back Miss Lavender's, I could ask Miss Gray to rejoin us—or maybe Mrs. Moth would do it? But I don't know how to get her back there without waking her up. And if I wake her, she'll never agree to go with me." The shadow had made that perfectly clear.

"Do you always wait for someone else to solve your problems?" Cordelia asked, as though posing a theoretical question.

Thea put her hands over her eyes, ashamed of herself. Yes, mostly, up to now she had. Her grandmother, and then the teachers at school. But she wasn't in school anymore, was she? She was an adult now, and adults solved their own problems. So did witches.

"Wait." She opened her eyes. Her hands were still in front of her face, but she could see right through them, to the bookshelves across the room. Both of her hands were completely transparent. Quickly, she put them in her lap, where she couldn't see them. She didn't want to know how much she had faded here, so close to her shadow. "Mrs. Moth said something—if only I could remember."

Cordelia yawned, pointedly.

"That's it!" Suddenly, it had come back to her—the conversation over tea, and a chance remark. "Magic is poetry. At least, poetry plus math. I always hated the math part, but all we need is for one plus one to equal one." Carefully, she leaned forward and turned the shadow over—the other Thea made a sound, but did not wake up. Then she sat back and pulled out one of her long red hairs. "You'll have to be both needle and thread," she said to the red strand.

> "Thread the needle, sharp as pain,
> sew the fabric, strong as grief."

She put the soles of her feet right on the shadow's, her Keds to the soft black leather boots of the catsuit, and began to sew.

> "Join the twain, join them well,
> bind them as a single soul,
> so they cannot be unbound."

Starting at the heel, up the outside and a few extra stitches at the toe, down the inside, knot. Then the other foot.

> "Sewing spell, join them soundly,
> solidly and well."

Once she had knotted the thread again, she stood up. The shadow lay on the floor, just where the moonlight would have cast Thea's shadow. Thea looked down at her hands. She could no longer see through them. They were completely solid.

"Well?" said Cordelia.

"I don't know. I think it worked. I remember being at Miss Lavender's and being in the box. If I'd been in that box, I would have hated me too! I think I do hate me. And my grandmother, and Anne Featherstone, and my parents for dying, and . . . Cordy, what's wrong with my face?"

"You're crying. You humans do that."

Thea could feel tears coursing down her cheeks. Suddenly, she started to sob—loud, heaving sobs that racked her as she leaned forward, hands on her stomach, then fell to her knees. She felt as though she were going to split apart again, this time from anger and grief. She had never felt anything so painful—the wracking sobs continued—no, she had, she remembered now. But it had been long ago, when she was a child. And it all came flooding back—her mother's soft auburn hair, the sensation of riding on her father's shoulders, the day she had been told they would not, no never, come back. She couldn't bear it. She knelt on the cold, hard floor and sobbed.

"You have to get up," said Cordelia. "We have to go home. Look."

Thea looked up. Through her tears, she saw that it was brighter—no longer moonlight, but the soft blue light of early morning, beginning to come through the library windows.

"What's wrong with me, Cordy? Why can't I stop crying?"

"You're both of you now." The cat rubbed up against her, a rare gesture of affection. "Come on. You can do it, you know."

Thea stood up awkwardly and rubbed her hands across her face. They were slick with tears. She didn't want to ruin the green dress by wiping them on it, so she just rubbed them against each other, hoping they would dry. She took a deep breath that hurt her ribs. Her stomach was still queasy and there was an ache in her chest, but somehow she felt stronger than before. As though the world had stopped tilting around her.

"All right, give me a minute."

She knelt beside the satyr and kissed him on one cheek, despite his bad breath, then stroked his hair. "I liked you—a lot. And honestly, you're pretty hot for someone who's half goat." Then she picked up the peacock mask from where she had set it down.

"Can we go home now?" Cordelia yawned a wide cat yawn and blinked her eyes. This time, she seemed genuinely sleepy.

"One more thing. No, two." Thea found the Seeing Ball where she—the shadow—no, she as the shadow—had left it, behind Volume VII of *The Collected Poems of Sappho*. It was confusing, having two sets of memories. Going to school at Miss Lavender's—being in a box for twelve years, like a long, dreamless sleep—attending her grandmother's funeral—finding herself free in Mother Night's Castle—sitting in her Boston apartment, watching anime on YouTube and eating takeout sushi, afraid of everything, college and what the future held for her—capering around the gardens with Oryx, hiding behind the giant chess pieces, teasing the fish. Which were her memories? All of them, she supposed. She felt around the floor next to the satyr—there, the invisibility cloak, with its scratchy wool. She put it over her arm so that her hand looked as though it were floating in the air. Then she hoisted the soft, sleepy cat to her shoulder. Carrying cat and cloak and mask, she walked to the library door.

> "Morning has come, and morning's star has risen:
> her chamber awaits its radiant messenger.
> Take me there."

She stepped through the library door into Morgan's tower.

The Morningstar was, in fact, not there. Putting Cordelia on the bed, where she promptly curled up and fell asleep, Thea changed into her own clothes. Thank goodness she had brought extra. And Mother Night had said something about chocolate . . . yes, there it was, half a bar in the front pocket of her backpack. She broke off a square and put it into her mouth, chewing it quickly, automatically. But it was the best chocolate she had ever tasted—honestly, ever. Dark, sweet, bitter, creamy . . . had she never actually tasted chocolate before? Oh, for goodness' sake, she was starting to cry again, and her nose was starting to run. Hastily folding the green dress before she could get tears or snot on it, she put it on the bed with the peacock mask on top and the invisibility cloak beside it. Then she took the notebook out of her backpack, tore out a sheet of paper, and left a note, with the Seeing Ball on top to weigh it down:

> *Thank you so much for everything! I got my shadow and sewed it back on—very Peter Pan! Invisibility cloak is to the left <———— If you're on Facebook friend me!!! <3 Thea*

She slung her backpack over one shoulder and draped Cordelia over the other—drat the cat, why couldn't she wake up and walk? She had to keep sniffing so her nose wouldn't drip. Somewhere in her backpack she might have a tissue, but she couldn't search for one while holding Cordelia and trying to come up with a poem. It didn't have to be long, right? Just effective.

> "The greatest magic
> brings you home."

She stepped through the tower door into the kitchen of the headmistress's house.

Mrs. Moth was in an apron making breakfast. "Good morning, Thea," she said. "When we didn't see you yesterday, we figured you'd found your way to the Other Country. Why, look at you!" She said it in the tone of an aunt who has not seen you in a while and remarks on how much you've grown. "Emily, Lavinia," she called. "Thea's back! All of her, thank goodness." Then she held out a paper towel for Thea's dripping nose.

"WELL, HOW DO you feel?" asked Miss Gray. Thea had taken a shower and brushed her teeth, examining herself curiously in the mirror. She looked tired, and her eyes were red, and there was a shadow following her around, everywhere she went. She kept seeing it out of the corner of her eye and flinching. She could not get used to it.

"I don't know." She ate the last spoonful of her oatmeal. "Confused. Sad about my parents. Angry about being put in a box. Glad to be here. Any minute now I'm probably going to burst into tears again. Sometimes I feel like kicking things, and sometimes I feel like dancing around the room. Although I haven't actually done either of those things yet."

"Oh, but you will, my dear," said Miss Lavender. "It's very confusing, being all of yourself. You'll find it quite uncomfortable for a while. But you'll get used to it. We all do."

"Coffee, anyone?" asked Mrs. Moth.

"Not for me," said Thea. "I think I'll go to Booktopia for a latte. There was a book on writing I wanted to get—John Gardner." Maybe even the Anne Lamott.

"Good for you," said Miss Gray. "I always liked your pieces in *The Broomstick*, especially that article on Hans Christian Andersen. He really was a charming man, although terribly insecure."

"And Sam's quite attractive," said Mrs. Moth. "Though very young."

"This is about *literature*, not romance," said Miss Gray. "Anyway, you think anyone under a century is young. Have a good time, Thea."

"I'll try," said Thea. Miss Gray had read something of hers and actually liked it! Maybe she could write some poems, or an article. That shouldn't be too hard, right? The novels could come later . . . She smiled at herself, then sniffed again and wiped her nose with the balled-up paper towel.

On the way out, she scratched Cordelia behind the ears. The cat curled up more tightly on the parlor sofa, purring in her sleep. Thea put on her jacket and scarf, then stepped into the cold New England morning, her shadow accompanying her up the path and into the town, toward the bookstore and anywhere else she might want to go.

Mother Night

Last night I went to the house of my mother, Night.
Her house has many doors, some large, some smaller
than a mouse hole. You are welcome at all of them.
Her house has many windows. They shine like stars
in the darkness, and on top of the highest tower
is the moon, like a weathervane.

I knocked and was invited into her parlor.
She asked me what was wrong, although of course,
as usual, she knew without my having to tell her.
"You're tired," she said. "So very tired, my dear."
I simply nodded in answer.
It was true, I had been tired and sick with longing
for things I could not have: a cloak of darkness,
a library of answers, an elixir
that takes away all pain, a talking raven
to be my boon companion.

"You know the rules," she said, pointing at the wall
where these words were written in calligraphy:
You can have anything you already have,
You can be anything you already are.
"How can I have what I don't have?" I asked her.
"How can I be what I am not yet?" She simply
smiled and shook her head.

"Might as well say you cannot dream until
you are asleep, or cannot dance until
the music has started playing, when you know,
it is the dream that draws your eyelids down,
the dance that summons the tune. Are you a child,
to think clocks only run forward?"

I felt like an idiot, as when I was her student
and bungled every lesson with common sense
when it was uncommon sense her teaching called for.

I sat on the parlor sofa, crying in frustration
while she stroked my hair and poured me a cup of tea,
served with her usual mixture
of metaphysics and sympathy.
Why had I come, after all? I was not certain.

"Now think, my dear," she said, "or rather, don't.
I seem to remember thinking never got you
anywhere but Confusion." She was right, of course:
in school that was my regular destination.
I leaned back against a cushion and sipped my tea,
pondering the nature of reality, which resembles
a ball of string tangled by a kitten.

"I'll weave myself a cloak of darkness," I said,
finally. "For the thread,
I'll unravel my own shadow. The library,
I already have; I just need to catalog
the volumes I own correctly." "And the elixir?"
she asked. Her eyes were shining, as they do
when a student of hers is being unusually clever.
"Doesn't exist," I said, "because pain itself
is the elixir of life. Without it, we may
as well be dead." I didn't like that answer.
But after all, we never get everything
we want, not even at Christmas.
"As for the raven, I believe one will come
to me when I'm wise enough for it to talk to.
You know they're most particular."

"You're wiser than you were already," she answered,
patting my head, which was a bit patronizing,
but I didn't mind it, from her.
"You're wrong about the elixir. I'll tell you the secret
of dealing with pain, which is poetry.
It never gets into every nook and cranny;
nevertheless, I think you should write it more often.
As for the raven, I may have one around here
that I can lend until you find your own."

She sent me home with some gingerbread and a bird,
rusty black, eyeing me with suspicion.
Now, it sits in the library, perched on a stack

of books I'm trying to get in the right order
so I can find an answer—to anything, really.
She was right about the poetry.
And I'm weaving my cloak of darkness. Mother Night
isn't the easiest teacher, but her advice
is generally to be relied on.

The Red Shoes

There are days
when I too want to cut off my feet.

Days on which I desire too much, on which I am filled
with longing for what I don't have, and may never.
When I feel that black hole in my chest
(like a manhole missing its cover)
into which things fall: my phone, the alarm clock,
the bulletin board on the wall,
the to-do list on my desk,
all my best intentions, and I think,
who needs feet? Especially
feet in red shoes.

Once you put the red shoes on,
you can never take them off.
I put them on when I was fifteen
and first fell in love,
and first wanted to live
anywhere but where I was living.

I thought, Let me be wild. Let me dance, just a little.
The red shoes never take you anywhere sensible.
They will take you to Paris
when your credit card is maxed out.

That, of course, is when I first wanted to become
a writer. One of the incorrigible.

But sometimes you get tired
of dancing everywhere: down the street,
on the subway.

And you think, I could just take a hatchet to them.
Karen did it, and she's up in heaven
somewhere, where good girls go.

She no longer wants anything.
She stopped writing long ago.

But what about Hans? Because he had a pair as well.
I suspect he's tap-dancing
in the hell writers make for themselves,
red shoes flashing (his had spangles).
He could never give up desire,
no matter how hard he tried.
He was ugly, and therefore wanted everything.
(As we are all ugly, if not outside, then inside,
all ducklings who only occasionally
recognize our swan parentage.)
He tried very hard to be good,
but kept falling in love,
which is a disadvantage.

So here I am, red shoes on (they never come off):
sometimes they are sandals, sometimes rain boots.
And I don't know what to do with them except keep walking,
which is also dancing, because although I may tire,
they don't.

Red as Blood and White as Bone

I AM AN ORPHAN. I was born among these mountains, to a woodcutter and his wife. My mother died in childbirth, and my infant sister died with her. My father felt that he could not keep me, so he sent me to the sisters of St. Margarete, who had a convent farther down the mountain on which we lived, the Karhegy. I was raised by the sisters on brown bread, water, and prayer.

This is a good way to start a fairy tale, is it not?

When I was twelve years old, I was sent to the household of Baron Orso Kalman, whose son was later executed for treason, to train as a servant. I started in the kitchen, scrubbing the pots and pans with a brush, scrubbing the floor on my hands and knees with an even bigger brush. Greta, the German cook, was bad-tempered, as was the first kitchen maid, Agneta. She had come from Karberg, the big city at the bottom of the Karhegy—at least it seemed big, to such a country bumpkin as I was then. I was the second kitchen maid and slept in a small room that was probably a pantry, with a small window high up, on a mattress filled with straw. I bathed twice a week, after Agneta in her bathwater, which had already grown cold. In addition to the plain food we received as servants, I was given the leftovers from the baron's table after Greta and Agneta had picked over them. That is how I first tasted chocolate cake, and sausages, and beer. And I was given two dresses of my very own. Does this not seem like much? It was more than I had received at the convent. I thought I was a lucky girl!

I had been taught to read by the nuns, and my favorite thing to read was a book of fairy tales. Of course the nuns had not given me such a thing. A young man who had once stayed in the convent's guesthouse had given it to me, as a gift. I was ten years old, then. One of my duties was herding the goats. The nuns were famous for a goat's milk cheese, and so many of our chores had to do with the goats, their care and feeding. Several times, I met this man up in the mountain pastures. (I say *man*, but he must have been quite young still, just out of university. To me he seemed dreadfully old.) I was with the goats, he was striding on long legs, with a walking stick in his hand and a straw hat on his head. He always stopped and talked to me, very politely, as he might talk to a young lady of quality.

One day, he said, "You remind me of a princess in disguise, Klara, here among your goats." When I told him that I did not know what he meant, he looked at me in astonishment. "Have you never read any fairy tales?" Of course not. I had read only the Bible and my primer. Before he left the convent, he gave me a book of fairy tales, small but beautifully illustrated. "This is small enough to hide under your mattress," he said. "Do not let the nuns see it, or they will take it from you, thinking it will corrupt you. But it will not. Fairy tales are another kind of Bible, for those who know how to read them."

Years later, I saw his name again in a bookstore window and realized he had become a poet, a famous one. But by then he was dead. He had died in the war, like so many of our young men.

I followed his instructions, hiding the book under my mattress and taking it out only when there was no one to see me. That was difficult at the convent, where I slept in a room with three other girls. It was easier in the baron's house, where I slept alone in a room no one else wanted, not even to store turnips. And the book did indeed become a Bible to me, a surer guide than that other Bible written by God himself, as the nuns had taught. For I knew nothing of Israelites or the building of pyramids or the parting of seas. But I knew about girls who scrubbed floors and grew sooty sleeping near the hearth, and fish who gave you wishes (although I had never been given one), and was not Greta, our cook, an ogress? I'm sure she was. I regarded fairy tales as infallible guides to life, so I did not complain at the hard work I was given, because perhaps someday I would meet an old woman in the forest, and she would tell me that I was a princess in disguise. Perhaps.

The day on which *she* came was a cold, dark day. It had been raining for a week. Water poured down from the sky, as though to drown us all, and it simply did not stop. I was in the kitchen, peeling potatoes. Greta and Agneta were meeting with the housekeeper, Frau Hoffman, about a ball that was to take place in three days' time. It would celebrate the engagement of the baron's son, Vadek, to the daughter of a famous general, who had fought for the Austro-Hungarian emperor in the last war. Prince Radomir himself was staying at the castle. He had been hunting with Vadek Kalman in the forest that covered the Karhegy until what Greta called this unholy rain began. They had been at school together, Agneta told me. I found it hard to believe that a prince would go to school, for they never did in my tales. What need had a prince for schooling, when his purpose in life was to rescue fair maidens from the dragons that guarded them, and fight ogres, and ride on carpets that flew through the air like aeroplanes? I had never in my life seen either a flying carpet or an aeroplane: to me, they were equally mythical modes of transportation.

I had caught a glimpse of the general's daughter when she first arrived the day before, with her father and lady's maid. She was golden-haired, and looked like a porcelain doll under her hat, which Agneta later told me was from Paris. The lady's maid had told Frau Hoffman, who had told Greta, and the news had filtered down even to me. But I thought a Paris hat looked much like any other hat, and I had no interest in a general's daughter. She did not have glass slippers, and I was quite certain she could not spin straw into gold. So what good was she?

I was sitting, as I have said, in the kitchen beside the great stone hearth, peeling potatoes by a fire I was supposed to keep burning so it could later be used for roasting meat. The kitchen was dark, because of the storm outside. I could hear the steady beating of rain on the windows, the crackling of wood in the fire. Suddenly, I heard a *thump, thump, thump* against the door that led out to the kitchen garden. What could it be? For a moment, my mind conjured images out of my book: a witch with a poisoned apple, or Death himself. But then I realized it must be Josef, the under-gardener. He often knocked on that door when he brought peas or asparagus from the garden and made cow-eyes at Agneta.

"A moment," I cried, putting aside the potatoes I had been peeling, leaving the knife in a potato near the top of the basket so I could find it again easily. Then I went to the door.

When I pulled it open, something that had been leaning against it fell inside. At first I could not tell what it was, but it moaned and turned, and I saw that it was a woman in a long black cloak. She lay crumpled on the kitchen floor. Beneath her cloak she was naked: her white legs gleamed in the firelight. Fallen on the ground beside her was a bundle, and I thought: *Beggar woman. She must be sick from hunger.*

Greta, despite her harshness toward me, was often compassionate to the beggar women who came to our door—war widows, most of them. She would give them a hunk of bread or a bowl of soup, perhaps even a scrap of meat. But Greta was not here. I had no authority to feed myself, much less a woman who had wandered here in the cold and wet.

Yet there she lay, and I had to do something.

I leaned down and shook her by the shoulders. She fell back so that her head rolled around, and I could see her face for the first time. That was no cloak she wore, but her own black hair, covering her down to her knees, leaving her white arms exposed. And her white face . . . well. This was a different situation entirely. It was, after all, within my area of expertise, for although I knew nothing at all about war widows, I knew a great deal about lost princesses, and here at last was one. At last something extraordinary was happening in my life. I had waited a long time for this—an acknowledgment that I was part of the story. Not one of the main characters of course, but perhaps one of the supporting characters: the squire who holds the prince's horse, the maid who brushes the princess's hair a hundred times each night. And now a story had landed with a thump on the kitchen floor.

But what does one do with a lost princess when she is lying on the kitchen floor? I could not lift her—I was still a child, and she was a grown woman, although not a large one. She had a delicacy that I thought appropriate to princesses. I could not throw water on her—she was already soaking wet. And any moment Greta or Agneta would return to take charge of my princess, for so I already thought of her. Finally, I resorted to slapping her cheeks until she opened her eyes—they were as deep and dark as forest pools.

"Come with me, Your Highness," I said. "I'll help you hide." She stood, stumbling a few times so that I thought she might fall. But she followed me to the only place I knew to hide her—my own small room.

"Where is . . ." she said. They were the first words she had said to me. She looked around as though searching: frightened, apprehensive. I went back to the kitchen and fetched her bundle, which was also soaked. When I handed it to her, she clutched it to her chest.

"I know what you are," I said.

"What . . . I am? And what is that?" Her voice was low, with an accent. She was not German, like Frau Hoffman, nor French, like Madame Francine, who did the baroness's hair. It was not any accent I had heard in my short life.

"You are a princess in disguise," I said. Her delicate pale face, her large, dark eyes, her graceful movements proclaimed who she was, despite her nakedness. I, who had read the tales, could see the signs. "Have you come for the ball?" *What country did you come from?* I wanted to ask. *Where does your father rule?* But perhaps that would have been rude. Perhaps one did not ask such questions of a princess.

"Yes . . . Yes, of course," she said. "What else would I have come for?"

I gave her my nightgown. It came only to her shins, but otherwise fitted her well enough, she was so slender. I brought her supper—my own supper, it was, but I was too excited to be hungry. She ate chicken off the bone, daintily, as I imagined a princess would. She did not eat the potatoes or cabbage—I supposed they were too common for her. So I finished them myself.

I could hear Greta and Agneta in the kitchen, so I went out to finish peeling the potatoes. Agneta scolded me for allowing the fire to get low. There was still meat to roast for the baron's supper, while Greta made a cream soup and Agneta dressed the cucumber salad. Then there were pots and pans to clean, and the black range to scrub. All the while, I smiled to myself, for I had a princess in my room.

I finished sweeping the ancient stone floor, which dated back to Roman times, while Greta went on about what we would need to prepare for the ball, how many village women she would hire to help with the cooking and baking for that night. And I smiled because I had a secret: my princess was going to the ball, and neither Greta nor Agneta would know.

When I returned to my room, the princess was fast asleep on my bed, under my old wool blanket that was ragged at the edges. I prepared to sleep on the floor, but she opened her eyes and said, "Come, little one," holding the blanket open for me. I crawled in and lay next to her. She was warm, and she curled up around me with her chin against my shoulder. It was the warmest and most comfortable I had ever been. I slept soundly that night.

The next day, I woke to find that she was already up and wearing my other dress.

"Today, you must show me around the castle, Klara," she said. Had she heard Greta or Agneta using my name the night before? The door was not particularly thick. She had not told me her name, and I did not have the temerity to ask for it.

"But if we are caught," I said, "we will be in a great deal of trouble!"

"Then we must not be caught," she said, and smiled. It was a kind smile, but there was also something shy and wild in it that I did not understand. As though the moon had smiled, or a flower.

"All right," I said. I opened the door of my room carefully. It was dawn, and light was just beginning to fall over the stones of the kitchen, the floor and great hearth. Miraculously, the rain had stopped overnight. Greta and Agneta were—where? Greta was probably still snoring in her nightcap, for she did not rise until an hour after me, to prepare breakfast. And Agneta, who also rose at dawn, was probably out fetching eggs and vegetables from Josef. She liked to take her time and smoke a cigarette in the garden. None of the female servants were allowed to smoke in the castle. I had morning chores to do, for there were more potatoes to peel for breakfast, and as soon as Agneta returned, I would need to help her make the mayonnaise.

But when would I find such a good opportunity? The baron and his guests would not be rising for hours, and most of the house servants were not yet awake. Only the lowest of us, the kitchen maids and bootblacks, were required to be up at dawn.

"This way," I said to my princess, and I led her out of the kitchen, into the hallways of the castle, like a great labyrinth. Frightened that I might be caught, and yet thrilled at the risk we were taking, I showed her the front hall, with the Kalman coat of arms hanging from the ceiling, and then the reception room, where paintings of the Kalmans and their horses stared down at us with disapproval. The horses were as disapproving as their masters. I opened the doors to the library, to me the most magical room in the house—two floors of books I would never be allowed to read, with a spiral staircase going up to a balcony that ran around the second floor. We looked out the windows at the garden arranged in parterres, with regular paths and precisely clipped hedges, in the French style.

"Is it not very grand?" I asked.

"Not as grand as my house," she replied. And then I remembered that she was a princess and likely had her own castle, much grander than a baron's.

Finally, I showed her the ballroom, with its ceiling painted like the sky and heathen gods and goddesses in various states of undress looking down at the dancers below.

"This is where you will dance with Prince Radomir," I said.

"Indeed," she replied. "I have seen enough, Klara. Let us return to the kitchen before you get into trouble."

As we scurried back toward the kitchen, down a long hallway, we heard voices coming from one of the rooms. As soon as she heard them, the princess put out her hand so I would stop. Softly, she stepped closer to the door, which was partly open.

Through the opening, I could see what looked like a comfortable parlor. There was a low fire in the hearth, and a man was sprawled on the sofa, with his feet up. I moved a few inches so I could see his face—it was Vadek Kalman.

"We'll miss you in Karelstad," said another man, sitting beyond where I could see him. "I suppose you won't be returning after the wedding?"

Had they gotten up so early? But no, the baron's son was still in evening dress. They had stayed up all night. Drinking, by the smell. Drinking quite a lot.

"And why should I not?" asked Vadek. "I'm going to be married, not into a monastery. I intend to maintain a social life. Can you imagine staying here, in this godforsaken place, while the rest of you are living it up without me? I would die of boredom, Radomir." So he was talking to the prince. I shifted a little, trying to see the prince, for I had not yet managed to catch a glimpse of him. After all, I was only a kitchen maid. What did he look like?

"And if your wife objects? You don't know yet—she might have a temper."

"I don't know a damn thing about her. She hasn't said two words to me since she arrived. She's like a frightened mouse, doing whatever her father the general tells her. Just the same as in Vienna. I tell you, the whole thing was put together by her father and mine. It's supposed to be a grand alliance. Grandalliance. A damn ridiculous word . . ."

I heard the sound of glass breaking, the words "God damn it all," and then laughter. The princess stood perfectly still beside me. She was barely breathing.

"So he thinks there's going to be another war?"

"Well, don't you? It's going to be Germany this time, and Father wants to make sure we have contacts on the right side. The winning side."

"The Reich side, eh?" said the prince. I heard laughter again, and did not understand what was so funny. "I wish my father understood that. He doesn't want to do business with the Germans. Karel agrees with him—you know what a sanctimonious ass my brother can be. You have to, I told him. Or they'll do business with you. And to you."

"Well, if you're going to talk politics, I'm going to bed," said Vadek. "I get enough of it from my father. Looks like the rain's finally stopped. Shall we go for a walk through the woods later today? That other wolf is still out there."

"Are you sure you saw it?"

"Of course I'm sure. It was under the trees, in the shadows. I could swear it was watching you. Anyway, the mayor said two wolves had been spotted in the forest, a hunting pair. They're keeping the children in at night in case it comes close to the village. You know what he said to me when I told him you had shot one of them? *It's bad luck to kill the black wolves of the Karhegy*, he said. I told him he should be grateful, that you had probably saved the life of some miserable village brat. But he just shook his head. Superstitious peasant."

"Next time, remind him that he could be put in prison for criticizing the crown prince. Things will be different in this country when I am king, Vadek. That I can tell you."

Klara heard appreciative laughter.

"And what will you do with the pelt? It's a particularly fine one—the tanner said as much, when he delivered it."

"It will go on the floor of my study, on one side of my desk. Now I need another, for the other side. Yes, let's go after the other wolf—if it exists, as you say."

The princess pulled me away.

I did not like this prince, who joked about killing the black wolves. I was a child of the Karhegy, and had grown up on stories of the wolves, as black as night, that lived nowhere else in Europe. The nuns had told me they belonged to the Devil, who would come after any man that harmed them. But my friend the poet had told me they were an ancient breed, and had lived on the mountain long before the Romans had come or Morek had driven them out, leading his tribesmen on their small, fierce ponies and claiming Sylvania for his own.

Why would my princess want to marry him? But that was the logic of fairy tales: the princess married the prince. Perhaps I should not question it, any more than I would question the will of God.

She led me back down the halls—evidently, she had learned the way better than I knew it myself. I followed her into the kitchen, hoping Greta would still be asleep—but no, there she stood, having gotten up early to prepare a particularly fine breakfast for the future baroness. She was holding a rolling pin in her hand.

"Where in the world have you been, Klara?" she said, frowning. "And who gave you permission to wander away? Look, the potatoes are not yet peeled. I need them to make pancakes, and they still need to be boiled and mashed. Who the devil is this with you?"

I looked over at my princess, frightened and uncertain what to say. But as neatly as you please, she curtseyed and said, "I've come from the village, ma'am. Father Ilvan told me you need help in the kitchen, to prepare for the ball."

Greta looked at her skeptically. I could tell what she was thinking—this small woman with her long, dark hair and accented voice. Was she a Slav? A gypsy? The village priest was known equally for his piety and propensity to trust the most inappropriate people. He was generous to peddlers and thieves alike.

But she nodded and said, "All right, then. Four hands are faster than two. Get those potatoes peeled."

That morning we peeled and boiled and mashed, and whisked eggs until our arms were sore, and blanched almonds. While Greta was busy with Frau Hoffman and Agneta was gossiping with Josef, I asked my princess about her country. Where had she come from? What was it like? She said it was not far, and as beautiful as Sylvania, and yes, they spoke a different language there.

"It is difficult for me to speak your language, little one," she said. We were pounding the almonds for marzipan.

"Do you tell stories there?" I asked her.

"Of course," she said. "Stories are everywhere, and everyone tells them. But our stories may be different from yours. About the Old Woman of the Forest, who grants your heart's desire if you ask her right, and the Fair Ladies who live in trees, and the White Stag, who can lead you astray or lead you home . . ."

I wanted to hear these stories, but then Agneta came in, and we could not talk again about the things that interested me without her or Greta overhearing. By the time our work was done, long after supper, I was so tired that I simply fell into bed with my clothes on. Trying to stay awake although my eyes kept trying to close, I watched my princess draw the bundle she had brought with her out from the corner where I had put it. She untied it, and down came spilling a long black . . . was it a dress? Yes, a dress as black as night, floor-length, obviously a ball gown. It had been tied with its own sleeves. Something that glittered and sparkled fell out of it, onto the floor. I sat up, awake now, wanting to see more clearly.

She turned and showed me what had fallen—a necklace of red beads, each faceted and reflecting the light from the single bare bulb in my room.

"Do you like it?" she asked.

"They are . . . what are they?" I had never seen such jewels, although I had read about fabulous gems in my fairy tale book. The beads were each the size of a hummingbird's egg, and as red as blood. Each looked as though it had a star at its center. She laid the dress on my bed—I reached over and felt it, surreptitiously. It was the softest velvet imaginable. Then she clasped the necklace around her neck. It looked incongruous against the patched dress she was wearing—my second best one.

"Wait, where is . . ." She looked at the floor where the necklace had fallen, then got down on her knees and looked under the bed, then searched again frantically in the folds of the dress. "Ah, there! It was caught in a buttonhole." She held up a large comb, the kind women used to put their hair up in the last century.

"Will you dress my hair, Klara?" she asked. I nodded. While she sat on the edge of my bed, I put her hair up, a little clumsily but the way I had seen the baroness dress her hair, which was also long, not bobbed or shingled. Finally, I put in the comb—it was as white as bone, indeed probably made of bone, ornately carved and with long teeth to catch the hair securely.

"There," I said. "Would you like to look in a mirror?" I held up a discarded shaving glass I had found one morning on the trash heap at the bottom of the garden. I used it sometimes to search my face for any signs of beauty, but I had found none yet. I was always disappointed to find myself an ordinary girl.

She looked at herself from one side, then the other. "Such a strange face," she said. "I cannot get used to it."

"You're very beautiful," I said. And she was, despite the patched dress. Princesses are, even in disguise. That's how you know.

"Thank you, little one. I hope I am beautiful enough," she said, and smiled.

That night, she once again slept curled around me, with her chin on my shoulder. I dreamed that I was wandering through the forest, in the darkness under the trees. I crossed a stream over mossy stones, felt the ferns brushing against my shins and wetting my socks with dew. I found the little red mushrooms that are poisonous to eat, saw the shy, wild deer of the Karhegy, with their spotted fawns. When I woke, my princess was already up and dressed.

"Potatoes," she said. "Your life is an endless field of potatoes, Klara." I nodded and laughed, because it was true.

That day, we helped prepare for the ball. We were joined by Marta, the daughter of the village baker, and Anna, the groom's wife, who had been taking odd jobs since her husband was kicked by one of the baron's horses. He was bedridden until his leg was fully healed, and on half-salary. We candied orange and lemon peels, and pulled pastry until it was as thin as a bedsheet, then folded it so that it lay in leaves, like a book. We soaked cherries in rum, and glazed almonds and walnuts with honey. I licked some off my fingers. Marta showed us how to boil fondant, and even I was permitted to pipe a single icing rose.

All the while, we washed dishes and swept the floor, which quickly became covered with flour. My princess never complained, not once, even though she was obviously not used to such work. She was clumsier at it than I was, and if we had not needed the help, I think Greta would have dismissed her. As it was, she looked at her several times, suspiciously. How could any woman not know how to pull pastry? Unless she was a gypsy and spent her life telling fortunes, traveling in a caravan . . .

There was no time to talk that day, so I could not ask how she would get to the ball. And that night, I fell asleep as soon as my head touched the pillow.

The next day, the day of the ball, we were joined by the two upstairs maids: Katrina, who was from Karberg like Agneta, and her cousin, whose name I have forgotten. They were most superior young women, and would not have set foot in the kitchen except for such a grand occasion. What a bustle there was that day in the normally quiet kitchen! Greta barking orders and Agneta barking them after her, and the chatter of women working, although my princess did not chatter of course, but did her work in silence. We made everything that could not have been made ahead of time, whisking the béchamel, poaching fish, and roasting the pig that would preside in state over the supper room, with a clove-studded orange in its mouth. We sieved broth until it was perfectly clear, molded liver dumplings into various shapes, and blanched asparagus.

Nightfall found us prepared but exhausted. Greta, who had been meeting one last time with Frau Hoffman, scurried in to tell us that the motorcars had started to arrive. I caught a glimpse of them when I went out to ask Josef for some sprigs of mint. Such motorcars! Large and black and growling like dragons as they circled around the stone courtyard, dropping off guests. The men in black tails or military uniforms, the women in evening gowns, glittering, iridescent. How would my princess look among them, in her simple black dress?

At last all the food on the long kitchen table—the aspics and clear soup, the whole trout poached with lemons, the asparagus with its accompanying hollandaise—was borne up to the supper room by footmen. It took two of them to carry the suckling pig. Later would go the cakes and pastries, the chocolates and candied fruit.

"Klara, I need your help," the princess whispered to me. No one was paying attention—Katrina and her cousin had already gone upstairs to help the female guests with their wraps. Marta, Anna, and Agneta were laughing and gossiping among themselves. Greta was off doing something important with Frau Hoffman. "I need to wash and dress," she said. And indeed, she had a smear of buttery flour across one cheek. She looked as much like a kitchen maid as a princess can look, when she had a pale, serious face and eyes as deep as forest pools, and long black hair that kept escaping the braid into which she had put it.

"Of course," I said. "There is a bathroom down the hall, beyond the water closet. No one will be using it tonight."

No one noticed as we slipped out of the kitchen. My princess fetched her dress, and then I showed her the way to the ancient bathroom shared by the female servants, with its metal tub.

"I have no way of heating the water," I said. "Usually Agneta boils a kettle, and I take my bath after her."

"That's all right," she said, smiling. "I have never taken a bath in hot water all my life."

What a strict regimen princesses followed! Never to have taken a bath in hot water . . . not that I had either, strictly speaking. But after Agneta had finished with it, the bathwater was usually still lukewarm.

I gave her one of the thin towels kept in the cupboard, then sat on a stool with my back to the tub, to give her as much privacy as I could while she splashed and bathed.

"I'm finished," she said finally. "How do I look, little one?"

I turned around. She was wearing the black dress, as black as night, out of which her shoulders and neck rose as though she were the moon emerging from a cloud. Her black hair hung down to her waist.

"I'll put it up for you," I said. She sat on the stool, and I recreated the intricate arrangement of the other night, with the white comb to hold it together. She clasped the necklace of red beads around her neck and stood.

There was my princess, as I had always imagined her: as graceful and elegant as a black swan. Suddenly, tears came to my eyes.

"Why are you crying, Klara?" she asked, brushing a tear from my cheek with her thumb.

"Because it's all true," I said.

She kissed me on the forehead, solemnly as though performing a ritual. Then she smiled and said, "Come, let us go to the ballroom."

"I can't go," I said. "I'm just the second kitchen maid, remember? You go . . . you're supposed to go."

She smiled, touched my cheek again, and nodded. I watched as she walked away from me, down the long hallway that led to other parts of the castle, the parts I was not supposed to enter. The white comb gleamed against her black hair.

And then there was washing-up to do.

It was not until several hours later that I could go to my room, lie on my bed exhausted, and think about my princess, dancing with Prince Radomir. I wished I could see her . . . and then I thought, *Wait, what about the gallery?* From the upstairs gallery one could look down through a series of five roundels into the ballroom. I could get up to the second floor using the back stairs. But then I would have to walk along several hallways, where I might meet guests of the baron. I might be caught. I might be sent back to the nuns—in disgrace.

But I wanted to see her dancing with the prince. To see the culmination of the fairy tale in which I had participated.

Before I could take too long to think about it, I sneaked through the kitchen and along the back hallway, to the staircase. Luckily, the second-floor hallways were empty. All the guests seemed to be down below—as I scurried along the gallery, keeping to the walls, I could hear the music and their chatter floating upward. On one side of the gallery were portraits of the Kalmans not important enough to hang in the main rooms. They looked at me as though wondering what in the world I was doing there. Halfway down the other side were the roundels, circular windows through which light shone on the portraits. I looked through the first one. Yes, there she was—easy to pick out, a spot of black in the middle of the room, like the center of a Queen Anne's lace. She was dancing with a man in a military uniform. Was he . . . I would be able to see better from the second window. Yes, the prince, for all the other dancers were giving them space. My princess was dancing with the prince—a waltz, judging by the music. Even I recognized that three-four time. They were turning round and round, with her hand on his shoulder and her red necklace flashing in the light of the chandeliers.

Were those footsteps I heard? I looked down the hall, but they passed—they were headed elsewhere. I put my hand to my heart, which was beating too fast, and took a long breath in relief. I looked back through the window.

My princess and Prince Radomir were gone. The Queen Anne's lace had lost its center.

Perhaps they had gone into the supper room? I waited, but they did not return. And for the first time, I worried about my princess. How would her story end? Surely she would get her happily ever after. I wanted, so much, for the stories to be true.

I waited a little longer, but finally I trudged back along the gallery, tired and despondent. It must have been near midnight, and I had been up since dawn. I was so tired that I must have taken a wrong turn, because suddenly I did not know where I was. I kept walking, knowing that if I just kept walking long enough through the castle hallways, I would eventually end up somewhere familiar. Then, I heard her voice. A door was open—the same door, I suddenly realized, where we had listened two days ago.

She was in that room—why? The door was open several inches. I looked in, carefully. She stood next to the fireplace. Beside her, holding one of her hands, was the prince. She was turned toward him, the red necklace muted in the dim light of a single lamp.

"Closer, and farther, than you can guess," she said, looking at him, with her chin raised proudly.

"Budapest? Perhaps you come from Budapest. Or Prague? Do you come from Prague? Tell me your name. If you tell me your name, I'll wager you I can guess where you come from in three tries. If I do, will I get a kiss?"

"And if you don't?"

"Then you'll get a kiss. That's fair, isn't it?"

He drew her to him, circling her waist with his arm. She put her arm around his neck, so that they stood clasped together. He still held one of her hands. It was a private moment, and I felt that I should go—but I could not. In my short life, I had never been to a play, but I felt as audience members feel, having come to a climactic moment. I held my breath.

"My name is meaningless in your language," she said. He laughed, then leaned down and kissed her on the lips. They stood there by the fireplace, his lips on hers, and I thought, *Yes, this is how a fairy tale should end.*

I sighed, although without making a noise that might disturb them. Then with the arm that had been around his neck, she reached back and took the intricately carved comb out of her hair, so that it tumbled down like nightfall. With a swift motion, she thrust the sharp teeth of the comb into the side of his neck.

The prince threw back his head and screamed, like an animal in the forest. He stumbled back, limbs flailing. There was blood down his uniform, almost black against the red of his jacket. I was so startled that for a moment I did nothing, but then I screamed as well, and those screams—his maddened with pain, mine with fear—echoed down the halls.

In a moment, a footman came running. "Shut up, you," he said when he saw me. But as soon as he looked into the room, his face grew pale, and he began shouting. Soon there were more footmen, and the baron, and the general, and then Father Ilvan. Through it all, my princess stood perfectly still by the fireplace, with the bloody comb in her hand.

When they brought the prince out on a stretcher, I crouched by the wall, but no one was paying attention to me. His head was turned toward me, and I saw his eyes, pale blue. Father Ilvan had not yet closed them.

They led her out, one footman on each side, holding her by the upper arms. She was clutching something. It looked like part of her dress, just as black, but bulkier. She did not look at me, but she was close enough that I could see how calm she was. Like a forest pool—deep and mysterious.

Slowly, I walked back to the kitchen. In my room, I drew up my knees and hugged them, then put my chin on my knees. The images played in my head, over and over, like a broken reel at the cinema: him bending down to kiss her, her hand drawing the comb out of her hair, the sharp, quick thrust. I had no way of understanding them. I had no stories to explain what had happened.

At last I fell asleep, and dreamed those images over and over, all night long.

In the morning, there was breakfast to prepare. As I fried sausages and potatoes, I heard Greta tell Agneta what had happened. She had heard it from Frau Hoffman herself: A foreign spy had infiltrated the castle. At least, she was presumed to be a foreign spy, although no one knew where she came from. Was she Slovakian? Yugoslavian? Bulgarian? Why had she wanted the prince dead?

She would not speak, although she would be made to speak. The baron had already telephoned the Royal Palace, and guards had been dispatched to take her, and the body of the prince, to Karelstad. They would arrive sometime that afternoon. In the meantime, she was locked in the dungeon, which had not held prisoners for a hundred years.

After breakfast, the baron himself came down to question us. The servants had been shown a sketch of a small, pale woman with long black hair, made by Father Ilvan. Katrina had identified her as one of the village women who had helped in the kitchen, in preparation for the ball. Why had she been engaged?

Because Father Ilvan had sent her, said Greta. But Father Ilvan had no knowledge of such a woman. Greta and Agneta were told to pack their bags. What had they been thinking, allowing a strange woman to work in the castle, particularly when the crown prince was present? If they did not leave that day, they would be put in the dungeon as well. And no, they would not be given references. I was too frightened to speak, to tell the baron that I had been the one to let her in. No one paid attention to me—I was too lowly even to blame.

By that afternoon, Marta, the baker's daughter, was the new cook, and I was her kitchen maid. In two days, I had caused the death of the prince and gotten promoted.

"Klara," she said to me, "I have no idea how we are to feed so many people, just the two of us. And Frau Hoffman says the royal guards will be here by dinnertime! Can you imagine?"

Then it was now or never. In an hour or two, I would be too busy preparing dinner, and by nightfall my princess—my spy?—would be gone, taken back to the capital for trial. I was frightened of what I was about to do, but felt that I must do it. In my life, I have often remembered that moment of fear and courage, when I took off my apron and sneaked out the door into the kitchen garden. It was the first moment I chose courage over fear, and I have always made the same choice since.

The castle had, of course, been built in the days before electric lights. Even the dungeon had windows. Once, Josef had shown them to me, when I was picking raspberries for a charlotte russe. Holding back the raspberry canes, he had said, "There, you see, little mouse, is the deep dark dungeon of the castle!" Although as far as I could tell it was just a bare stone room, with metal staples in the walls for chains. From the outside, the windows were set low into the castle wall, but from the inside they were high up in the wall of the dungeon—high enough that a tall man could not reach them. And they were barred.

It was late afternoon. Josef and the gardener's boy who helped him were nowhere in sight. I crawled behind the raspberry canes, getting scratched in the process, and looked through one of the barred windows.

She was there, my princess. Sitting on the stone floor, her black dress pooled around her, black hair hanging down, still clutching something black in her arms. She was staring straight ahead of her, as though simply waiting.

"Princess!" I said, low in case anyone should hear. There must be guards? But I could not see them. The dungeon door was barred as well. There was no way out.

She looked around, then up. "Klara," she said, and smiled. It was a strange, sad smile. She rose and walked over to the window, then stood beneath it, looking up at me, her face pale and tired in the dim light. Then I could see what she had been clutching: a wolf pelt, with the four paws and eyeless head hanging down.

"Why?" I asked. And then, for the first time, I began to cry. Not for Prince Radomir, but for the story. Because it had not been true, because she had allowed me to believe a lie. Because when Greta said she was a foreign spy, suddenly I had seen life as uglier and more ordinary than I had imagined, and the realization had made me sick inside.

"Klara," she said, putting one hand on the wall, as far up as she could reach. It was still several feet below the window. "Little one, don't cry. Listen, I'm going to tell you a story. Once upon a time—that's how your stories start, isn't it? Quietly, so the guards won't hear. They are around the corner, having their dinners. I can smell the meat. Once upon a time, there were two wolves who lived on the Karhegy. They were black wolves, of the tribe that has lived on the mountain since time out of mind. The forest was their home, dark and peaceful and secure. There they lived, there they hoped to someday raise their children. But one day, a prince came with his gun, and he shot one of the wolves, who was carried away by the prince's men for his fine pelt. The other wolf, who was his mate, swore that she would kill the prince."

I listened intently, drying my face with the hem of my skirt.

"So she went to the Old Woman of the Forest and said, 'Grandmother, you make bargains that are hard but fair. I will give you anything for my revenge.' And the Old Woman said, 'You shall have it. But you must give me your beautiful black pelt, and your dangerous white teeth, and the blood that runs in your body. For such a revenge, you must give up everything.' And the wolf agreed. All these things she gave the Old Woman, who fashioned out of them a dress as black as night, and a necklace as red as blood, and a comb as white as bone. The old woman gave them to the wolf and said, 'Now our bargain is complete.' The wolf took the bundle the Old Woman had given her and stumbled out of the forest, for it was difficult walking on only two legs. On a rainy night, she made her way to the castle where the prince was staying. And the rest of the story, you know."

I stared down at her, not knowing what to say. Should I believe it? Or her? Common sense told me that she was lying, that she was a foreign spy and I was a fool. But then, I have never had much common sense. And that, too, has stood me in good stead.

"Klara, put your hand through the bars," she said.

I hesitated, then did as I was told.

She put the pelt down on the floor beside her, carefully as though it were a child, then unclasped the necklace of red beads. "Catch!" she said, and threw it up to me. I caught it—and then I heard boots echoing down the corridor. "Go now!" she said. "They're coming for me." I drew back my hand with the necklace in it and crawled away from the window. The sun was setting. It was time for me to return to the kitchen and prepare dinner. No doubt Marta was already wondering where I was.

When I got back to the kitchen, I learned that the royal guards had arrived. But they were too late—using the metal staples on the walls, my princess had hanged herself by her long black hair.

When I was sixteen, I left the baron's household. By that time, I was as good a cook as Marta could teach me to be. I knew how to prepare the seven courses of a formal dinner, and I was particularly skilled in what Marta did best: pastry. I think my pâte à choux was as good as hers.

In a small suitcase, I packed my clothes, and my fairy tale book, and the necklace that my wolf-princess had given me, which I had kept under my mattress for many years.

Perhaps it was not wise, moving to Karelstad in the middle of the German occupation. But as I have said, I am deficient in common sense—the sense that keeps most people safe and out of trouble. I let bedraggled princesses in out of the rain. I pack my suitcase and move to the capital with only a fortnight's wages and a reference from the baroness. I join the Resistance.

Although I did not know it, the café where I worked was a meeting-place for the Resistance. One of the young men who would come to the café, to drink coffee and read the newspapers, was a member. He had long hair that he did not wash often enough, and eyes of a startling blue, like evening in the mountains. His name was Antal Odon, and he was a descendent of the nineteenth-century poet Amadeo Odon. He would flirt with me, until we became friends. Then he did not flirt with me any longer, but spoke with me solemnly, about Sylvanian poetry and politics. He had been at the university until the Germans came. Then, it no longer seemed worthwhile becoming a literature professor, so he had left. What was he doing with himself now, I asked him?

It was he who first brought me to a meeting of the Resistance, in the cellar of the café where I worked. The owner, a motherly woman named Malina who had given me both a job and a room above the café, told us about Sylvanians who had been taken that week—both Jews and political prisoners. The next day, I went to a jeweler on Morek Stras, with my necklace as red as blood. How much for this? I asked him. Are these beads worth anything?

He looked at them through a small glass, then told me they would be worth more individually. Indeed, in these times, he did not know if he could find a purchaser for the entire necklace. He had never seen such fine rubies in his life.

One by one, he sold them off for me, often to the wives of German officers. Little did they know that they were funding the Resistance. I kept only one of the beads for myself, the smallest. I wear it now on a chain around my neck. So you can see, Grandmother, that my story is true.

As a member of the Resistance, I traveled to France and Belgium and Denmark. I carried messages sewn into my brassiere. No one suspects a young girl, if she wears high heels and red lipstick, and laughs with the German officers, and looks down modestly when they light her cigarette. Once, I even carried a message to a small town in the Swiss mountains, to a man who was introduced to me as Monsieur Reynard. He looked like his father, as far as one can tell from official portraits—one had hung in the nunnery schoolroom. I was told not to curtsey, simply to shake his hand as though he were an ordinary Sylvanian. I did not tell him, *I saw your older brother die. I hope that someday you will once again return to Sylvania, as its king.*

With my friend Antal, I smuggled political refugees out of the country. By then, we were more than friends . . . We hoped someday to be married, when the war was over. But he was caught and tortured. He never revealed names, so you see he died a hero. The man I loved died a hero.

When the war ended and the Russian occupation began, I did not know what to do with myself. I had imagined a life with Antal, and he was dead. But there were free classes at the university, for those who had been peasants, if you could pass the exams. I was no longer a peasant exactly, but I told the examiners that my father had been a woodcutter on the Karhegy, and I passed with high marks, so I was admitted. I threw myself into work and took my degree in three years—in Sylvanian literature, as Antal would have, if he had lived. I thought I would find work in the capital, but the Ministry of Education said

that teachers were needed in Karberg and the surrounding area, so I was sent
here, to a school in the village of Orsolavilag, high in the mountains. There
I teach students whose parents work in the lumber industry, or at one of the
hotels for Russian and Austrian tourists.

When I first returned, I tried to find my father. But I learned that he had
died long ago. He had been cutting wood while drunk, and had struck his own
leg with an axe. The wound had become infected, and so he had died. A simple,
brutal story. So I have no one left in the world. All I have left is my work.

I teach literature and history to the children of Orsolavilag . . . or such
literature and history as I am allowed. We do not teach fairy tales, which the
Ministry of Education thinks are decadent. We teach stories of good Sylvanian
boys and girls who learn to serve the state. In them, there are no frogs who
turn into princes, no princesses going to balls in dresses like the sun, moon,
and stars. No firebirds. There are no black wolves of the Karhegy, or Fair Ladies
who live in trees, or White Stag that will, if you are lost, lead you home. There
is no mention even of you, Grandmother. Can you imagine? No stories about
the Old Woman of the Forest, from whom all the stories come.

Within a generation, those stories will be lost.

So I have come to you, whose bargains are hard but fair. Give me stories.
Give me all the stories of Sylvania, so I can write them down, and so our underground press in Karberg, for which we could all be sent to a prison camp, can
publish them. We will pass them from hand to hand, household to household.
For this, Grandmother, I will give you what my princess gave so long ago:
whatever you ask. I have little left, anyhow. My only possession of value is a
single red bead on a chain, like a drop of blood.

I am a daughter of these mountains, and of the tales. Once, I wanted to
be in the tales themselves. When I was young, I had my part in one—a small
part, but important. When I grew older, I had my part in another kind of
story. But now I want to become a teller of tales. So I will sit here, in your hut
on goose legs, which sways a bit like a boat on the water. Tell me your stories,
Grandmother. I am listening . . .

Girl, Wolf, Woods

There are days on which I am the girl in the woods
in my red cap, jaunty, with my basket, plentiful,
wearing my innocence like a placard.

There are days on which I am the wolf, slavering
for either seedcake or a grandmother,
on which I am a hunger waiting
to be fed, a need, a desire.

There are days on which I am the woods,
silent, impenetrable.

Let me wander from the path, gathering flowers,
for night comes all too soon.

Feed me, for I am starved.
I want wine and cakes and meat. I want
the girl in the red cap and neat
apron. I want to crunch her bones.
I want to lope through darkness.

Let me be still, let me grow and feel
sunlight on my arms, which are also branches.
Let me hear birdsong.

There was a girl with a red cap,
a *chaperon* as they called it in that region,
which was famed for lace-making.
She ventured into the woods. The sun
was shining, but it was cool under the trees.

There, she met a wolf who was hungry
not for herself, but for her pups,
born late in the season, whom she was nursing.
Give me wine, she said, so I may be strong,
give me seedcake, or I will gobble up

your grandmother, and then you.

The girl knelt and said, here is wine,
here is cake, here is meat, a cold chicken leg
wrapped in a napkin, packed in the basket
by my mother, who embroidered this apron
with a row of red hearts.
I was taking it to my grandmother,
who has rheumatism and cannot run far,
but would be tough anyway.
Come, eat. I will share it with you.

The branches above sighed
as the wind passed through them,
and farther down the path, in a cottage
surrounded by lavender and sage,
among which bees were gathering
nectar from the flowers,
her grandmother was snoring.

That is not how the story goes, you insist.
But that is how I prefer to tell it.

In the Snow Queen's Castle

I. Kay

Kay waits in the castle of ice, sitting
at the center of a lake made of ice, surrounded
by the pieces of a puzzle also made of ice—
everything in the Snow Queen's castle is frozen,
everything is blue with cold, including
Kay himself. Although he still has a small fire
around his heart: you can see it through his translucent
blue chest. It has almost flickered out.

He still remembers what she told him when she drove
past in her sleigh drawn by seven white reindeer:
How do you know that you are truly loved?
If I took you now to my castle made of ice,
where the northern lights flicker above my bedroom,
where it is so cold your breath would turn to frost,
would anyone try to rescue you?
Gerda would come, he told her. Gerda loves me.
She would always come, even if she lost her shoes,
even by foot over Finland.

The Snow Queen threw back her head and brittle laughter
broke in the air, falling to the ground like snowflakes,
each perfectly different from every other.
No one is loved like that, my dear. Not even you,
with your blue eyes, so sincere,
your brown hair arching over your forehead
like a pair of swallows' wings.
I'll prove it to you, he said, hitching his sleigh
to hers. A moment later they were flying.

Now he sits on the lake of ice, trying to solve
the puzzle she set him, which is supposed to spell
the word *eternity*, but shattered long ago
into frozen shards, indecipherable.

If you can put it together again, she told him,
I will give you a pair of skates so you can return
to Copenhagen. Which is, he thinks, the only way
he will ever leave the Snow Queen's castle.
He is realizing what a stupid boy he has been
to think anyone loved him so much, even Gerda,
who is no doubt still at home, learning
how to embroider various flowers on linen
from her grandmother.

He knows no one will come
and the fire in his chest, the small bit of fire
that is left around his heart,
will flicker out.

II. Gerda

Damn him, Gerda thinks, standing in the front hall
of the Snow Queen's castle, her feet frostbitten
from walking over Finland.
Perhaps she should never have come, perhaps
she should have left him with that bleached strumpet.
She sighs, then walks forward on aching feet
to rescue the boy with blue eyes and hair
like swallows' wings.

A Country Called Winter

I N WINTER, THE snow comes down as softly as feathers. I have always loved to watch it. It's different, of course, once it's fallen: thick, heavy, difficult to walk through. In Boston, the snow plows come out almost as soon as the first flakes land on the sidewalk. They make narrow paths, and the snow piles up on either side, so when you walk to class, it's between two mountain ridges, like a miniature Switzerland.

That's how Kay described it to me one morning, while we were sitting in my dorm room, drinking Swiss Miss hot chocolate that I had heated up in the microwave I wasn't supposed to have. He had the most charming accent that sounded, to my ear, sort of German and sort of French, and that look foreign students have. They are generally better groomed, their clothes are better proportioned, and they have the latest electronics. They listen to avant garde music and talk about art. Of course that's partly because they are the children of diplomats and businessmen—the ones who can make the choice to come to an expensive American university. Kay was the son of the Danish ambassador, but he had lived in so many countries that when I asked him where he was from, he simply said, "I am European." Once, he even took me to the art museum on a date. Catch an American student doing that!

He was an undergraduate, and I had just started my M.A. I was a little uncomfortable about that. He was only two years younger than me, but at the university, the undergraduate/graduate divide seemed almost unsurmountable. And anyway, I wasn't looking for a boyfriend. I wanted to finish my M.A. year with a high enough grade point average to go directly into the Ph.D. program. All I was planning to think about that year were my classes in American literature: *The Poetry of Emily Dickinson, Emerson and the Transcendentalists, The Novel from World War I to Postmodernism*, and *The Immigrant Experience*, which I was not particularly excited about. I'd lived my own immigrant experience, and didn't want to read about anyone else's.

When I was a little girl, I asked my mother why she had come to the United States, with one suitcase and an infant daughter, leaving behind her parents, her language, everything she had ever known.

"We come from a cold country," she had told me. "Do you know, Vera, in that country the king lives in a palace built of white stone with veins of quartz that resembles ice. The streets are made of ice between snow banks, and there are no automobiles—only sleighs. They used to be pulled by reindeer, but nowadays they are electronic."

360

Vera was not my real name, but my English name, which she had given
me when we landed at Logan airport. It sounded like part of my name in our
native language, which I will transliterate Veriska, although Americans have
difficulty pronouncing it properly. In our language, it means Snow Flower.

I would write it here in our alphabet, but the letters aren't on my computer. My Apple Mackintosh does not yet speak the language of snow.

I WAS SIX years old, just about to start first grade, when we came to America. I
was put in an English immersion program. The school administration had no
choice, really. There was no one in the school, or even the school district, who
spoke our language. We come from a small country, with a difficult language—
agglutinative, and not related to any Indo-European tongue. The alphabet resembles a series of curlicues, like frost on a windowpane. If you're not familiar
with it, you won't know where one letter begins and another ends. Some of
the letters are not letters at all, but ideas, or more properly, modes of thinking.
There is a letter, for example, that stands for memory. If you put it at the beginning of a word, it means something has been remembered. Or, if you add the
letter for negation, that something has been forgotten.

Even the name of our country is difficult to pronounce for English speak-
ers. Instead of spelling it out phonetically, we refer to it by its name in translation: Winter.

There was a small community of my countrymen and women in Boston,
all my mother's age or older. Many of them had fled after the most recent
revolution. The history of my country in the twentieth century is a series of
revolutions and conquests. I asked my mother who would want to conquer the
country she described to me: a series of valleys between high mountains, where
in summer the snow might melt for several months in the lower valleys, to be
replaced by small white flowers that resembled snow, and winter seemed to last
forever. Even in June the blossoming fruit trees might be covered with a layer
of ice. The cold made our small, hard apples sweeter, tastier, than they were
anywhere else. Cabbages and turnips were staples. Most crops were grown in
large greenhouses that protected tender plants from the cold.

Countries in the lower valleys, my mother answered. Before the Second
World War, in warmer regions, our primary export had been a valued com-
modity. In the days before electric refrigeration, everyone wanted ice. Now, of
course, there was tourism: skiers and snowboarders valued our steep slopes, and
mountain climbers came to conquer the high peaks of our mountains.

Because I could not speak English that first year, I could not make friends.
It was a lonely year for me.

Eventually I learned English, but I never quite learned how to be an American child. Perhaps I had come here too late. Or perhaps it was something in
me that caused me to turn inward rather than toward other children, and I
would have been the same even in my native Winter, never quite fitting in

there either. I found my refuge in books, particularly books about this new country I could barely understand. *Little House on the Prairie* seemed to me the most wonderful fairy tale about the great wide west. Jo, Beth, Meg, and Amy March were four princesses growing up in a magical place called Concord, Massachusetts—just close enough to be real and yet far enough away to seem like a land lost in mists. I was in love with Tom Sawyer, and bitterly jealous of Becky Thatcher, for whom he walked on top of a fence. No one had walked on top of a fence for me. I liked those stories better than the stories in the old book from our country that my mother read to me, in which women married white bears and then had to travel to the ends of the earth, climbing mountains of ice in iron shoes, to rescue their bear husbands from frost giants. Why marry a bear in the first place? I wondered. Why not go to a one-room schoolhouse, form settlements, write for magazines as Jo was doing? Tom Sawyer was a trickster, like the fox in our fairy tales, whose pelt was as white as snow. He would sneak into your house and steal your fire, like a ghost. Huck Finn was like one of the ice trolls—uncivilized and uncouth, but somehow fascinating.

Although my mother read me these fairy tales, she did not like to discuss the history of our country. "We have left all that behind," she said. But the woman she hired to stay with me after school while she worked at Boston University as a research librarian told me about the two princes who had founded our country, climbing high in the mountains to establish their territory above the Roman legions who were harrying them below. They had married the daughters of the king of the ice trolls—tall, beautiful women whose eyes were the color of rocks. Their descendants had battled each other a thousand years for the throne. She had taken the American name Anna, and I called her Nana Anna. It was she who helped me retain my native tongue, for my mother rarely spoke in our language. "Why should I?" she said. "We are never going back, and it makes me sad."

When I was in high school, Nana Anna finally succumbed to lung cancer from the small brown cigarettes she was incessantly smoking, hand-rolled from a tobacco flavored with vanilla. After school—I had been admitted to Boston Latin Academy, one of the prestigious public schools that require an examination—I would go to her small apartment in Alston, and eventually her hospital room in Massachusetts General Hospital, to sit with her for hours, doing my homework. One day in the hospital, she motioned me to approach her bed. Closer, closer, she motioned, impatiently. With her small, frail, claw-like hand, she pulled me down by the lapel of my school jacket and whispered, in a voice that was almost gone, the ghost of a voice, "Versika, when it is time, you must go back."

I did not know what she meant, and did not want to distress her by asking. Anyway, I was American now—the previous year, my mother and I had become citizens. I had no desire to go back to Winter. I did not think of it as my native country anymore—did not even remember what it looked like, except in dreams that were probably based on my mother's stories of frost giants and streets paved with ice and quince trees grown in glass houses. I spoke my native language adequately but not well, and rarely practiced it anymore now that Nana Anna was so sick. Somewhere along the way, I had decided to become as American as possible. I wore blue jeans and had a tattoo of falling snowflakes on my left wrist that scandalized my mother, because well-behaved girls did not get tattoos. I read Sylvia Plath.

My mother wanted me to study library science, "Because you like books so much, Vera," she said, "and it's a practical profession." But I told her I wanted to study literature.

"Well, perhaps you can become a teacher," she replied.

THERE WERE ONLY a few people at Nana Anna's funeral—three old men and one young woman who said she was a distant relative. One of the old men came up to my mother and bowed, then spoke with her too rapidly for me to understand what he was saying. But among the words, I recognized one that meant "princess"—literally, "king's daughter." When I asked my mother about it, she said, "Anna was a member of the royal court, a descendant of one of the two families that have, for time out of mind, fought over Winter's throne. In our country, she was lady-in-waiting to the queen. It was her hereditary right."

How strange that this old woman who had taken care of me had been a member of the royal family! Remembering her one-bedroom apartment with its tiny kitchen, I felt sorry for her. She had been meant for palaces made of white stone with veins of quartz.

But I had the SAT to study for. I could not spend too much time thinking about the history of Winter—about which, anyway, I knew only the fragments Nana Anna had told me.

There were boyfriends here and there, in those years—a couple of casual ones in high school and a steady one in college, at Amherst, where I had gotten a full ride—half scholarships, half grants. I even thought we might become engaged, until the day he told me he was in love with a girl I thought was my best friend. Several months later, when he broke up with her and told me that I was the one, had always been the one—that he had just needed to make sure— I had already been admitted to a graduate program. Sorry, I told him. I really don't have time for a relationship right now.

I was right—the M.A. program took all the time and energy I had, that and being an R.A. in an undergraduate dorm. At least it gave me a place to live so I didn't have to stay at home with my mother. I could never have afforded my own apartment in Boston. I settled down to write my semester papers, determined to do as well as I could. That would be my life, I figured—classes during the day, evenings doing research in Mugar Library.

And then I met Kay.

* * *

CALLED WINTER

I HAVE ALWAYS preferred winter, probably because I was born in Winter, in February, when my mother tells me the capital city was encased in ice and the doctor had to come by electric sleigh through a snowstorm. I love to see the first leaves change, love to feel the cold breath of autumn coming. Seasonal allergies have something to do with it. June and July, I live on Claritin. The pollen from all the blossoming trees gives me a terrible headache. But after September comes, it seems as though the air regains a crystalline quality. It feels like clear water, like something hard and soft at the same time—feathers that can cut. Then the leaves turn and fall, like a splendid sunset lying on the sidewalks, and the first snows come, white and fresh, as though the earth is putting on her wedding gown.

Christmas has always been my favorite holiday. In my country, gifts are not brought by Santa Claus. The Lady in the Moon herself comes down from the sky in her silver sleigh, drawn by snow geese that have put on their white plumage for winter. Next to her sits the white fox who eats the moon each month before the Lady renews it again. With the help of all the stars, who look like elves in sparkling tights and dresses, she distributes gifts to children throughout the land. Although my mother had given up many of our native customs, each year she decorated the tree with a moon on top, papier-mâché stars hanging from the branches, felt reindeer, and gingerbread men. We would leave out elderberry wine for the Lady in the Moon and a plate of oat cakes with a wedge of cheese for the geese and fox. The next morning, the oat cakes always had small bites taken out of it, and the cheese was eaten into a crescent shape.

I met Kay during the first snowfall. He bumped into me as I was walking to class, thinking about my paper on the rhetoric of mourning in the poetry of Emily Dickinson. I slipped and fell on the icy sidewalk. "*Undskyld!*" he said, then switched to English. "I'm sorry, how stupid of me—I should have watched where I was going. Let me help you." He took off his right glove and reached down a pale, firm hand. I recognized him from my class on the Transcendentalists, which was a 500-level course for both upper-class undergrads and M.A. students. He was the one who always did the reading and talked about the Transcendentalists as though their ideas mattered for more than the final exam. I had noticed him—he was, after all, tall and blond and very good-looking. He was hard not to notice. But I had thought of him as simply another undergrad.

What made him so much more exciting than other boys I had dated? Well, he was European—more sophisticated, more intellectual. He could talk about postmodern literary theory, although after several beers his utterances became as convoluted as Lacan's. His area was modern European literature. He had been taking courses in the American Studies department simply for a distribution requirement. But he could also be moody, go silent for days at a time, sitting on his dorm room window seat and looking out at the snow. I asked him once if all that theory was good for him.

Still, there was something in me that was attracted to him. His family came
from a small village in Denmark beside a glacier, where the primary industry
was the ski season. Sometimes he seemed like a breath of cold mountain air. We
had been dating for several months and our relationship was going well—he was
going to stay in Boston for Christmas, and I had already told him that he could
come celebrate with me and my mother—when Gerda showed up.

It was after Thanksgiving Break. We were sitting in our Transcendentalism
class, waiting for Professor Feldman (Bob to those of us who were graduate
students, but only in office hours and at departmental cocktail parties) to show
up when in walked a girl—well, a woman, but she was not much older than
me. She was wearing a pair of red boots that came up over her knees, and her
black hair was cut in a Louise Brooks bob. She stood in front of the class and
said, "Hi everyone. I have some bad news—Professor Feldman had a heart attack over the break. We don't know yet when he'll be able to come back to class.
I was his TA last semester, so I'm going to fill in for him. I'm a grad student, so
don't bother calling me professor. You can just call me Gerda. All right, let's see
who did the reading. Pop quiz!"

She was in my department, but I hadn't met her—she had passed her oral
exam over the summer and was already working on her dissertation. After the
class I introduced myself. "Oh, right, Vera," she said. "You and the other M.A.
students don't need to take the final exam. Just turn in a 20-page paper on the
last day of class. Have you written a prospectus already? No? Well, how about
turning it in next Friday?"

Later, Kay told me that she had "Robber Girl" tattooed across her shoulder blades, right where you could see it if she wore a low-cut dress, or maybe a
bathing suit. It was the name of her rock band. Yes, she had a rock band with a
couple of students from the Berklee College of Music—she was the lead singer
and played guitar. They toured during the summer months, doing covers of the
Eurythmics and other 80s groups. I wondered how he knew—when had he
seen her bare back? But it was the sort of information Gerda volunteered freely.
Perhaps she had simply told him during office hours.

That was after the semester was over, of course—after we had picked up
our final papers from her box in the department mailroom. I was relieved to
have gotten an A on the paper and for the semester. Gerda was much too smart
to mess around with the university's sexual harassment policy. No, she just
stood in front of the class in her high red boots, wearing skinny jeans or a short
denim skirt and a black turtleneck, talking about feminism and sexuality in
Emily Dickinson's poems, which was the topic of her doctoral dissertation. "If
Dickinson could have fucked death, she would have," Gerda said once, clearly
not caring what anyone said on her course evaluations.

She was a good teacher, I'll give her that. She found meanings in Dickinson's poems that I had not seen. I had admired them for their artistic and
intellectual engagement. Gerda revealed their incandescence. Kay always paid

particular attention in that class, but then he had paid attention to Professor Feldman as well. It was only later that I realized there was more to it than caring about Dickinson's subtext.

Just before Christmas, he told me that we should take a break, that he had to focus on exams and didn't have time for a relationship. There was no celebration with my mother after all—he insisted that he had to study. By the time I came back to campus in January, he and Gerda were dating.

When I found out from my friend Stephanie, who was a work-study receptionist in the main office and knew all the departmental gossip, I spent a week crying myself to sleep at night, sobbing into my pillow. But Kay didn't know that. I didn't bother asking him for an explanation, and recriminations have never been my style. I have always prided myself on my ability to let things go. After all, I've had plenty of practice. When I was a little girl, I let go of an entire country.

One day, we ran into each other at the new café that had opened at the edge of campus, on Commonwealth Avenue. Blue Moon, it was called—organic, fair trade, locally sourced. There were scones with chia seeds in them, scones with açai berries. Smoothies that combined mango and kale.

"Vera," he said. "I've been meaning to text you—"

"I already know," I said. "About you and Gerda."

"I really like you," he said, as though it were an apology. "Like, really like. But Gerda, I don't know. We're just on the same wavelength."

But Gerda. I suppose at some level, I had known from the moment she walked in with her high red boots. I had simply not wanted to see that he was drifting away from me like snow. Even when she was standing at the front of the class and he was the undergrad challenging her phallic interpretation of Emily Dickinson's "A narrow fellow in the grass"—"Sometimes a snake is just a snake," he would say—there was something between them, a solidarity. You could tell that despite their differences, they lived in the same intellectual and emotional time zone. They synched.

"I hope you're happy with her," I said. "I'm sure she'll be happy with you." Why wouldn't she be? Any disagreements would be smoothed over by his blue Danish eyes, the perfection of his cheekbones.

CHRISTMAS WAS STRANGE that year. Men and women I did not know came to the apartment and talked to my mother in the walk-in closet she used as a sewing room. They spoke in the language of Winter, but so low and rapidly that I could not hear them through the keyhole, although I tried. I particularly wondered about one woman dressed in a long white coat with silver embroidery all over it, wearing a white fur hat.

"Who was that?" I asked my mother.

"That was the Matriarch of the Orthodox Church," she replied. "Her Holiness is the highest religious authority in our country."

"What is she doing here?" I asked. I had heard of the Holy Mother, but only in Nana Anna's stories. Somehow, she had not seemed real to me, any more than the palace made of white stone or the glass houses with their orchards of flowering trees. But this priestess of the Lady Moon was real the way dreams are real—improbable, and yet indisputably sitting in our small living room, drinking my mother's espresso.

"Paying her respects," said my mother. "Vera, I smell something burning. Did you seal the jam pockets properly?"

Of course not. I never sealed the jam pockets properly. My mother always sealed their edges so the jam did not run out into the pan, but somehow I never managed to. The jam always ran out, overflowed the sides of the pan, and dripped down onto the electric burners. My baking was always accompanied by the smell of burnt sugar.

Winter is a cold country. Most of our deserts incorporate jam, dried fruit, or candied nuts—ingredients that can be stored almost indefinitely during the long, cold months. They are made of hearty grains—barley, oats, rye. Into them we mix cinnamon, nutmeg, ginger.

I rushed into the kitchen to rescue the jam pockets, and by the time I came out again, the Matriarch was gone.

But it was more than a matter of strange visitors coming at all hours. My mother seemed agitated, distracted. When I asked her what was wrong, she said only, "I'm getting old," which was patently untrue. Her black hair was touched with gray, and she had lines of laughter and worry around her eyes, but she was as beautiful as ever—still the woman in the only photograph I had of her with my father, at their wedding. She was wearing an elaborate wedding gown, he was in his military uniform.

"What was his rank?" I asked her when I was in high school. I was curious about this man with the fierce mustache, who had died when I was only a child.

"I do not remember," she had answered. It was more likely that she did not want to remember. All I knew was that he had died in one of our innumerable revolutions, defending the king—Nana Anna had told me that.

To be honest, I was glad when Christmas break was over and I could go back to school. At least I could replace worrying about my mother with working on my papers and avoiding Kay. I transferred out of *Elegance and Anxiety: The Age of Wharton and James* when Stephanie told me he was registered for the course.

AND THEN SPRING failed to come. In April, the snow did not melt. The forecasters shrugged as though to say, sometimes that happens in Massachusetts. But in May it did not melt either. The temperature did not get above thirty-two degrees Fahrenheit. When June came and the temperature still hovered around freezing, the Weather Channel started talking about freak cold snaps, global cooling, a new ice age.

By that time, I assumed Kay had gone back to Denmark for the summer break. Of course I was still on campus, studying for my oral exam and R.A.ing for the high school juniors and seniors taking summer courses, trying out college for the first time. Anyway, I lived in Boston—I had nowhere else to go.

But one day, I got a text on my cell phone: *V need to talk to you please K.*

Why? I texted back.

To talk about us.

Well, that wasn't exactly an answer, was it?

What about?

Please??? I'll buy coffee. Blue Moon @ 2?

Fine. What was I going to do, refuse to see him altogether? That would just prove to him that I cared, and I didn't. Well, I did, but I didn't want him to know that. Anyway, it was uncivilized. Only high school girls who had watched too much reality TV behaved like that.

He was waiting for me at a table near the front of the café, with a small cappuccino topped with cinnamon, my favorite. He still had perfect cheekbones, but just above his right cheekbone, at the corner of his eye, was a rectangular bandaid. Had he cut himself shaving? No, it was too high for a shaving cut. Well, I would not ask him about it. I was no longer his girlfriend, after all. Let Gerda do that.

"All right, what is it?" I asked, sitting down. He slid the cappuccino over to me.

"I know I messed up," he said. "I should have told you about Gerda. I'm really sorry—really really sorry. Is there any way we can start over?"

I looked at him, astonished. "Start over like . . . what? Like it never happened? What about Gerda, anyway? Where is she? And what are you doing here? Shouldn't you be in Denmark?"

"That's over," he said. "I broke it off with her. She was—well, she was kind of nuts, and also kind of cruel. It's as though she kept sticking this knife into me—metaphorically, I mean. With the things she would say, telling me she loved me, and then that she didn't want to see me anymore, then calling me the next day and telling me to come over. It's like she wanted to punish me for caring about her. And she was so negative—she would laugh at me for things like my mom sending me cookies from home—I mean the embassy, not home home. She called me sentimental. I don't know where she is now—she said she was going on tour with Robber Girl, and then she just left. The last I heard from her, she was in Austin, Texas. She hasn't texted me since. But honestly, I don't care where she is. Come on, I know I messed up, but I care about you more than I've ever cared about anyone. Please, can we start over?"

I sipped my cappuccino. I didn't know what to say. On the one hand, he had behaved like a complete asshole. On the other hand, he had very blue eyes, with long lashes. He looked at me pleadingly. That bandaid was incongruous on his perfect face.

"I have to think about it," I finally said, putting my coffee cup down and pushing back my chair. I tried to be nonchalant, but I almost tipped it over as I stood up.

"Sure," he said. "I get it, I really do. Take as long as you need to. Like, a week? I'll text you in a week."

"Thanks for the coffee," I said. "I'm going now."

"You'll let me know in a week, right?" he said, looking up at me anxiously. "I think I was scared of how I felt about you. I think that's why I messed up with Gerda."

"A week," I said, making no promises. But I could already feel myself weakening. He looked at me so appealingly, after all, like a child who wanted approval. Would it be so hard to care about him again? Had I ever actually stopped?

I texted Stephanie, to catch up on the departmental gossip. *What happened between Gerda and Kay?*

It only took her a moment to respond. *I heard they had a big fight. He broke up with her, she threw her Norton Anthology of American Literature at him, and it hit a mirror in his dorm room. He got some glass close to his eye. Had to go to the emergency room to get it out plus a couple of stitches. That girl is batshit crazy.*

Why hadn't he told me about that? Probably because he was ashamed of it, of having gotten involved with someone who would pull a stunt like that. And also of being hurt by a girl.

When I don't know what to do about a situation, I ask my mother. Kay was a situation I didn't know what to do about, so I went home.

I sent my mother a text to let her know I was coming, but she didn't answer. Well, she often had her notifications off—if she turned them off by accident, she never knew how to turn them back on again. She was hopeless at technology. It had taken me a year to convince her to give up her flip-phone for something more practical. It was Thursday, which was her weekday off, so she wouldn't be at the library.

"Mom!" I called as I pushed open the front door. "Mom, are you home?"

No answer, but I heard the murmur of voices from the living room. Did she have guests?

I walked from the hall into the living room. My mother was standing by the fireplace that had once been functional in our nineteenth-century brownstone, but was now purely decorative. Around her stood a group of men and women in business suits, with sashes arranged diagonally across their chests. I recognized the light blue and white of Winter's national flag. There was the Matriarch, in her white hat. On either side of her stood a priestess in a white robe with silver collar and cuffs. But most prominent among them was a woman in a red dress, the color of geraniums. In that company, my mother looked plain and small in her black t-shirt and jeans.

"Vera!" she said, as though startled to see me.

The woman in the red dress turned sharply toward me, then looked me up and down.

"Your Royal Highness," she said. She was tall and striking, with short white hair and a sharp nose. I was startled when she made me a deep curtsey. The men and women in sashes bowed or curtseyed, according to whether they were wearing trousers or skirts. The Matriarch and her priestesses remained upright.

"Excuse me?" I said. "I don't understand . . ."

"Vera," said my mother, coming forward. Suddenly, she was the most authoritative person in that room. The transformation took me by surprise—my mother did not often take charge, except in the library. "This is Baroness Hapsenkopf"—at least, that is the closest approximation in English. "She is the prime minister of Winter. When you were a little girl and your father was killed by his younger brother, she helped us escape, or we would surely have been imprisoned by him and his allies. He was not a good ruler—under his management, the country took on a great deal of debt to finance industries that have not made a profit. Now there is inflation, and no money left to repair the roads or educate the children. There is discontent among the people. Three months ago, he was overthrown by the army. The loyalists who helped your father were released from prison, and they have been attempting to form a new government under the Baroness. Now, they would like you, as the only direct descendant in the royal line, to return as ruler."

"But my father—" I said.

"Was Luthorion VII, King of Winter," said Baroness Hapsenkopf. "You will be Veriska II. The first Veriska was a warrior queen who battled against the Ice Trolls. What we need now is not a warrior but an economist, a ruler who can repair roads, fund schools, and create jobs for the people. And the Ice Trolls have long been our allies. I have been approached by the Ice King himself, who has offered his son in marriage to cement an alliance between our nations. You are, of course, under no obligation to accept, but it would be an advantageous match."

For a moment, I could not think of anything to say. It was as though the entire world had suddenly shifted under me, as though reality was not at all what I had thought, but something else altogether. The Baroness and the semicircle of dignitaries from Winter were staring at me, as was my mother—waiting. I had to say something. But what?

"I'm neither a warrior nor an economist," I said, finally. "I'm not qualified to be queen of anything. I mean, I'm just a grad student. The most responsibility I've ever had is being an R.A." This was ridiculous—I had an oral exam to study for, and suddenly I was supposed to rule Winter? Marry an Ice Troll? Fix an economy when I could barely keep track of my credit card balance, even with the banking app? And yet suddenly, a great many things in my life that had perplexed me came into focus, as though I had put on a pair of glasses for the first time. All the pieces of a complicated puzzle were fitting together. They showed me a picture: of Winter, and who my father had been, and why my mother claimed to have forgotten his rank. No wonder Nana Anna had taken such care to teach me the history of my country. A moment ago, the future had stretched before me, shapeless, formless. Now, it took a definite shape, as though flakes of snow had fallen and formed a pattern: a woman made of snow.

"Veriska," said my mother, calling me by my full name for the first time since I was a child. "Your choice has repercussions here as well. You see, the snow has not gone away. It is still cold in Boston. Winter is more than a country—it is also an idea. It exists among the mountains, and also in the imagination. There must be a king or queen of Winter to maintain balance among the seasons."

Okay, I sort of got that. I had been trained to understand metaphors. I mean, it didn't really make sense, but then neither did a lot of other things that were nevertheless real and tangible. Somewhere, there was probably a Summer kingdom as well. But I was still not comfortable with the whole concept. "Why does it have to be a king or queen?" I asked. "Can't you elect a president or something?"

"You may abdicate, if you wish," said the Matriarch in her sonorous voice. "But doing so will plunge our country once again into chaos. There is no other clear heir to the throne, and several claimants in an indirect line who will fight each other to death if given the opportunity."

So a constitutional monarchy it was, then. A republic was clearly not in the cards. "Can I have some time to think?" I asked.

"Of course," replied the Matriarch. She looked at her wristwatch. "We can give you an hour."

One hour to make the most important decision of my life? These people were crazy, the whole situation was crazy. I was about to say that when I saw the Baroness's face. It was carefully neural, but there were dark circles under her eyes and cheekbones.

Nana Anna had told me about the men and women who had been sent to prison—or worse, to labor camps in the mountains—for supporting the last king. She had simply neglected to mention that he was my father. The dignitaries in front of me, with their blue and white sashes, were some of those people.

"All right, one hour," I said. I walked out of the apartment and down to our street of brownstones, then turned and made my way to Commonwealth Avenue. It was the middle of summer, but the people who passed me were still wearing winter coats. I walked around for a while, randomly, then went down to the Charles River and stared at the ice still floating on the surface. It wasn't thick enough to walk on—there was black water underneath. Should I agree to become Winter's queen? I felt completely inadequate to the task.

Suddenly, the ice on the river cracked into large chunks. The chunks had nowhere to go, so they simply lay on top of the water. The cracks made a pattern in the language of Winter: they spelled out *Queen Veriska*. I rubbed my eyes, absolutely certain that I was hallucinating.

"It's not an illusion." Who had said that, in the language of my country?

Next to me stood a woman in a light blue dress, with a white fur collar and cuffs. She was wearing a white fur hat on her gray hair and carrying what I thought was a ruff of the same fur until I realized it was a fox as white as snow. Behind her stood a sleigh carved of white wood with silver runners, to which were harnessed six white geese.

"Lady Moon," I said. I mean, it was obvious who she was—Nana Ana had told me enough stories. Either I was ready to be committed to a mental hospital, or I was having an encounter with a supernatural being.

"Winter needs you," she said. "You see, it is calling to you all the way here in Boston."

"But I don't know how to be a queen." I looked back down at the ice. Now it was spelling out *Come home Queen Veriska*.

"When have you known how to do anything before you did it?" she asked. "Did you know how to swim before you learned at Walden Pond in summer camp? Did you know how to write a paper before your eleventh grade teacher taught you in Honors English? You will learn this as well. Baroness Hapsenkopf will teach you, as will your mother, the Queen Dowager."

It was disconcerting how much Lady Moon knew about me. But then, she was Winter's equivalent to Santa Claus. She probably knew everything.

"This is different," I said. "No one was going to drown if I didn't learn to swim but me. No one else was going to get an F on her paper if I failed. But if I fail as queen . . . Anyway, I don't understand this whole business about balancing the seasons."

"The Snow King or Queen brings winter," she said. "Then as the year turns, the King or Queen of Summer—currently Rudolph IV—brings back warmth and sunlight, banishing the cold and darkness until it is time for winter again. But the two monarchs must coordinate carefully. If Rudi comes while snow is still lying on the ground, it will cause terrible floods. So you must work with him, you must hand off responsibilities, as it were—he has been waiting for months now for the coronation of Winter's queen." I could tell from the tone of her voice that she was being patient, but I had maybe five or ten more minutes of her putting up with my nonsense. At least, that's the way Nana Anna would have said it.

It all sounded—well, a little crazy, and like a lot of responsibility. How in the world was I supposed to do all this?

"Hold out your hand," she said. "Over the ice. Just there—hold it steadily." I had overestimated: by her tone, I had maybe a minute more of her patience. I didn't think she would frown at me the way Nana Anna had. She was much more likely to turn me into a rock, as she had the daughter of Ivor the Ice Troll in fairy tales, and then smash me to smithereens.

I held my hand over the icy river. What was this supposed to do?

The cracks in the ice reformed themselves into the words *What do you wish, O Queen?*

What did I wish? I didn't even know anymore. "I wish winter would end," I said. I did, at least, want that. Let the high school students play Ultimate Frisbee on the university's small patches of green space. Let people eat ice cream while walking down the street in T-shirts.

Your wish is our command, wrote the ice, and then it broke along those cracks. The pieces of ice stood up on end and danced on the choppy black water, then melted. The sun came out from behind the gray clouds. It was not warm, exactly—it was still a winter sun. But it was something.

"I shall tell Rudi that you are on your way," said Lady Moon with a tight-lipped smile, the same smile her fox seemed to have on his face. I could tell that I had sorely tried her patience. "Run along, Veriska. Give Queen Agata my best wishes, and tell the Matriarch that I will be back in Winter for Christmas, as usual."

I walked back to the apartment in a daze. When I entered the living room again, I walked up to Baroness Hapsenkopf and said, "All right, I'll do it. I'll be Veriska II. I mean, you'll have to teach me how, but I'll try."

"What convinced you?" asked the Matriarch, sounding as though she did not particularly approve of me—but I was the only Veriska II she had, so she would have to make the best of it.

"Lady Moon," I said. "She . . . well, we had a talk. I mean, she did most of the talking."

My mother looked at me with astonishment, but the Matriarch nodded as though she were not at all surprised.

"Then it is time to leave," said the Baroness. "There is a helicopter waiting for us on the roof."

Somehow, I had been expecting a sleigh drawn by snow geese, or something equally improbable. But a helicopter would work as well. I turned to go pack, but no, I would not need to pack. There was nothing here I needed, not even my tattered and heavily underlined copy of *The Complete Poems of Emily Dickinson,* and anyway from now on my packing would be done for me. I had more important things to do—a country to save, a balance to restore, if I could just learn how.

"All right," I said. "I'm ready."

A WEEK LATER, I got a text on my cell phone. It was still my old iPhone with an international plan. I was getting 3G even in Winter.

Holy crap it's all over the Daily Free Press you're like a queen. Do I call you majesty or what. Summer finally here.

I was standing in the greenhouse attached to the palace, under the quince trees. I had spent the morning in a meeting with the finance minister, and would spend the afternoon in a meeting with the ambassadors of Sweden, Norway, and Denmark. Should I write back? At least to tell Kay that I was meeting with a representative of his country. Or not—I doubt he was texting me to hear about politics. Why was he texting me? Oh yeah, it was a week after our meeting in the Blue Moon café.

Winter here. In royal palace. Coronation yesterday, so yes, I'm officially queen. Your majesty, ma'am, whatever. ;)

The response came almost as soon as I had written mine.

So no hope of getting back together I guess. Ma'am.

I had to laugh. The gall of him! I still cared about him—I did, didn't I? Despite the whole Gerda incident. But at a royal reception, I had met the crown prince of Trollheim, whose name was Edrik. Trolls are a lot better looking than you would expect. He had really pretty blue eyes, and excellent taste in British rock bands. We had a long discussion of existentialism once we'd escaped from the reception with a handful of canapés. I didn't know if I wanted to marry him, but I wasn't ruling out the possibility. He wasn't sure how he felt about the arranged marriage either, but we'd already decided to spend a weekend skiing together. I'd learned to ski as a child and wasn't sure if I remembered how. But if he had to teach me, that wouldn't be such a bad thing, would it? Anyway, Winter needed an ally against the frost giants. Or maybe I would look into joining NATO?

You can't date me from Boston, I texted back.

What if I came to Winter.

Do you even know how to get here?

Pretty sure there's a Lufthansa flight to Finland. From there I don't know. Reindeer? It could be like a quest. Or like a road trip except with sleighs.

I looked around me at the glass walls of the greenhouse. Inside, it was all trees and leaves and blossoms. Outside, the snow was just starting to melt. At this altitude, summer came late, even in ordinary years. Here I was, the Snow Queen—what I was born to be, at least according to my mother and Baroness Hapsenkopf. I did not feel like much of a queen. However, in the last week, I had met with members of parliament from the three major parties, the heads of various labor unions, the generals who had participated in the recent coup, the Matriarch and her council of priestesses, the director of the Central Bank, and at my insistence, a selection of ordinary citizens chosen by lottery, from university professors to plumbers and seamstresses. I had been interviewed by both major newspapers, all three state television stations, and an online journal called *WW* for Women of Winter.

I did not know if I would make a good queen, but I was starting to see what needed to be done, how to restore the economy of my country. It would take a while, but these things always did. Slowly, Winter would regain its former reputation and independence from the IMF.

All right, I texted. *If you can figure out how to get here, come find me.*

Would Kay make it to my palace of white stone veined with quartz, or get lost along the way among the snows? If he made it, would I choose him or Edrik, who was after all a prince? I didn't know, but today I was the Queen of Winter, and I had more important things to think about.

For a moment, I stood among the quince trees, whose white blossoms looked like snow on the branches and fell like snow to the ground. Outside, a dusting of snow fell from the roof, like blossoms blown by the wind. Then, I turned and walked into my palace, where my future, whatever it was, awaited me.

How to Make It Snow

First you must fall down the well.

At the bottom of the well
is the country at the bottom of the well.
That is its name, the only one it has.
You have two names, either the beautiful girl
or the kind girl, depending
on what day it is.

At the bottom of the well is a green meadow,
just like in the country you came from
but different. For one thing, the cows can speak.
They say, "Scratch our backs, scratch us
under the chin," and you do.

The meadow is filled with poppies
and cornflowers. The air is warm,
and the sun is shining.

"Thank you, beautiful girl," say the cows
and you walk on.

Across the meadow, there is a narrow path
worn by cow hooves. Follow it.

First you come to the oven.
"Take me out, take me out," cries the bread.
"I'm burning up!" You take it out,
a brown wholemeal loaf. Carry it with you
for the birds—they appear later.

Next you come to the apple tree.
"Shake us down, shake us down," cry the apples.
"We're ripe!" So you shake the branches, as though
you were dancing with them.
The apples come tumbling down.
You put three in your pocket.

Now you are at the edge of the forest
and the birds call, "Feed us, feed us!"
You ask the loaf, "May I?"
"This is what I was baked for," says the loaf.

So you scatter breadcrumbs
and the birds come, sparrows and chickadees,
robins and finches and juncos,
and a nuthatch. They perch on your arms
as you feed them. Absentmindedly,
you whistle as they do.

In the forest, a wild sow approaches.
For the first time you are afraid and step back,
but she says, "My little ones are hungry,
and I smell something sweet."
You pull the apples out of your pocket.
"May I?" you ask, and the apples reply,
"This is why we fell."

You kneel while the sow watches protectively,
feeding the apples to her three piglets,
bristle-backed, with tusks just starting to form
but still striped as though someone had marked them
with her fingers. The sow nods and says,
"You are a kind girl." Then, followed by her progeny,
she disappears into the trees.
You continue alone.

It is getting dark. You have passed through the oaks
and now it is all pines. You are walking on needles.
The light is fading when you come to the cottage.
It looks like the cottage out of a fairy tale:
peaked roof like a witch's hat, dark green trim,
small-paned windows through which firelight is flickering.
Someone is waiting for you.

You have nothing left, no bread, no apples.
So you knock.

The woman who answers is old, small,
like a doll made of cornhusks.
"You're hungry," she says,

"and tired. Come in, my dear.
The soup is almost ready."

There is a fire, and a cauldron on the fire,
and a chair by the fire, and a cat in the chair,
and you can smell the soup.

"Come on, then," says the cat, and gets up,
but only to settle again in your lap
once you sit down.

Here are the things you know about the old woman:
she milks the cows, she causes the apples to ripen,
she teaches the birds their songs, she runs her fingers
along the backs of the wild piglets
to put the stripes on them.

Here are the things she knows about you:
everything, also your name.

"What are you called, my dear?" she asks.
"The beautiful girl," you answer. "Or the kind girl."
"No," she says. "From now on, you shall be
she who makes it snow.
Or Holle, for short."

Holle: it suits you.

"Here's what I'd like you to do tomorrow morning.
Sweep the floor and dust the shelves,
wash the curtains and wind the clock,
polish the silver. And when that's done,
shake out my bedspread until the feathers
fly like snowflakes. It's time for winter.
Can you do that?"

You nod. Yes, of course.

That night you sleep under the cat,
in her attic bedroom.

The next morning, you put on an apron she left for you,
then sweep the floor and dust the shelves,

wash the curtains in a metal basin,
wind the clock and polish the silver. Finally,
you stand on the cottage steps under tall pines
and shake out the old woman's bedspread.

Snow falls and falls, until
the forest is silent.

"Well done, my dear." She's wearing a gray wool coat
and carrying a battered suitcase. "Can you do that again
tomorrow morning, and the day after tomorrow?
I need to visit my sisters, and I'm not sure
when I'll be back yet.
It takes a responsible girl, but I've heard good things
about you from the cows, the bread, the apples,
the birds, even the trees. And the cat likes you."

"I'll do my best," you say.
She kisses you on both cheeks, then rises up, up,
through the trees until she is only a speck
in the colorless sky.

You go back into the cottage.
There is a cat to scratch under the chin,
and books with stories you have never read,
and you haven't introduced yourself to the clock yet.

Besides, you like your new name.
It's the right name for a woman
who makes the snow fall.

Snow White Learns Witchcraft

One day she looked into her mother's mirror.
The face looking back was unavoidably old,
with wrinkles around the eyes and mouth. I've smiled
a lot, she thought. Laughed less, and cried a little.
A decent life, considered altogether.

She'd never asked it the fatal question that leads
to a murderous heart and red-hot iron shoes.
But now, being curious, when it scarcely mattered,
she recited *Mirror, mirror,* and asked the question:
Who is the fairest? Would it be her daughter?

No, the mirror told her. Some peasant girl
in a mountain village she'd never even heard of.

Well, let her be fairest. It wasn't so wonderful
being fairest. Sure, you got to marry the prince,
at least if you were royal, or become his mistress
if you weren't, because princes don't marry commoners,
whatever the stories tell you. It meant your mother,
whose skin was soft and smelled of parma violets,
who watched your father with a jealous eye,
might try to eat your heart, metaphorically—
or not. It meant the huntsman sent to kill you
would try to grab and kiss you before you ran
into the darkness of the sheltering forest.

How comfortable it was to live with dwarves
who didn't find her particularly attractive.
Seven brothers to whom she was just a child, and then,
once she grew tall, an ungainly adolescent,
unlike the shy, delicate dwarf women
who lived deep in the forest. She was constantly tripping
over the child-sized furniture they carved
with patterns of hearts and flowers on winter evenings.

She remembers when the peddler woman came
to her door with laces, a comb, and then an apple.
How pretty you are, my dear, the peddler told her.
It was the first time anyone had said
that she was pretty since she left the castle.
She didn't recognize her. And if she had?
Mother? She would have said. Mother, is that you?
How would her mother have answered? Sometimes she wishes
the prince had left her sleeping in the coffin.

He claimed he woke her up with true love's kiss.
The dwarves said actually his footman tripped
and jogged the apple out. She prefers that version.
It feels less burdensome, less like she owes him.

Because she never forgave him for the shoes,
red-hot iron, and her mother dancing in them,
the smell of burning flesh. She still has nightmares.
It wasn't supposed to be fatal, he insisted.
Just teach her a lesson. Give her blisters or boils,
make her repent her actions. No one dies
from dancing in iron shoes. She must have had
some sort of heart condition. And after all,
the woman did try to kill you. She didn't answer.

And so she inherited her mother's mirror,
but never consulted it, knowing too well
the price of coveting beauty. She watched her daughter
grow up, made sure the girl could run and fight,
because princesses need protecting, and sometimes princes
are worse than useless. When her husband died,
she went into mourning, secretly relieved
that it was over: a woman's useful life,
nurturing, procreative. Now, she thinks,
I'll go to the house by the seashore where in summer
we would take the children (really a small castle),
with maybe one servant. There, I will grow old,
wrinkled and whiskered. My hair as white as snow,
my lips thin and bloodless, my skin mottled.

I'll walk along the shore collecting shells,
read all the books I've never had the time for,
and study witchcraft. What should women do

when they grow old and useless? Become witches.
It's the only role you get to write yourself.

I'll learn the words to spells out of old books,
grow poisonous herbs and practice curdling milk,
cast evil eyes. I'll summon a familiar:
black cat or toad. I'll tell my grandchildren
fairy tales in which princesses slay dragons
or wicked fairies live happily ever after.
I'll talk to birds, and they'll talk back to me.
Or snakes—the snakes might be more interesting.

This is the way the story ends, she thinks.
It ends. And then you get to write your own story.

How to Become a Witch-Queen

I. The Coffin

YOU LOOK AT the coffin as it is lowered into the rectangular opening in the cathedral floor. Inside is your husband, the man to whom you have been married for more than twenty years, you've forgotten exactly how many. The man with whom you have three children. The oldest, Gerhardt, will inherit the throne. He will be called Gerhardt IV after his grandfather, who was Gerhardt III or, to his enemies, Gerhardt the Drunkard. His younger brother, Wilhelm, is jealous of him, and you foresee a rivalry, perhaps even a struggle for the throne. They were such lovely little boys, you think, remembering when they wore short pants and played with toy soldiers. What happened to them? They are young men now, beyond your purview, and Gerhardt in particular takes after his father, who was not a bad man, but not a particularly good one either. A typical king of these small kingdoms, which are perpetually at war with one another, obsessed with politics and power. Wilhelm, at least, is an affection-ate son, but you worry that with the privileges of a prince and nothing to do, he will become dissolute, possibly a drunkard like his grandfather. And your daughter Dorothea, who takes after you—well, you worry about her as well. She is still young, only fourteen, but soon she will be old enough for the use to which princesses are usually put—a marriage to cement alliances. You don't want her married off to a prince she barely knows, who may be cruel, or ugly, or just smell bad. Her father would have married her off without a qualm, so you are glad he is dead, although of course you can never say such a thing. The list of things queens cannot say is a long one, and you have not said them for most of your life. His death means your position at court is diminished, but you never cared for pomp and circumstance anyway. If you had been given a choice, you would have stayed in the forest with the dwarves—or the hunts-man. Your father's court taught you that prestige comes at a price. Most are willing to pay it—you, increasingly, are not.

Would Gerhardt force Dorothea to marry? That is the question which has been bothering you since your husband died. He might—she is a pretty girl, although still awkward, as awkward as you were yourself at that age, when the queen your mother asked for your heart and liver and you had to leave the only home you had ever known.

So that is the dilemma in a nutshell. You have no place here anymore, not really. And there is Dorothea to consider. What should you do?

383

As you stand there pondering, with your black handkerchief held up to your dry eyes in mimic grief, the stone that will cover the coffin is put into place. Lying on top of it is an effigy of your husband in armor, looking as handsome as he did in life, with Harald II engraved beneath his feet. He was always an attractive man, even into his forties. Not the sort of man you would expect to die from a heart condition, but here you are, a widow. Across the cathedral, his mistress, who used to be one of your ladies-in-waiting, is sobbing into a friend's shoulder. For him, or because with his death, she has lost her place in the court hierarchy? Gerhardt has never liked her, and will probably send her packing back to her father's damp manor house by the southern marshes. You have absolutely no pity for her. We all make our own beds, and must lie in them.

After the funeral services are over, you return to your rooms in the castle, escorted by your ladies-in-waiting. As you walk down a corridor, you pass the chamber where your own coffin, the one made of glass, is displayed. Visitors are allowed to see it Mondays through Thursdays, from nine in the morning until four in the afternoon, along with other national treasures such as the crown of Gerhardt I, who was crowned by the pope himself, or the emerald necklace of Queen Sofronia, which you wore at your wedding. Someday you may lie in that coffin again—however, you have no intention of dying anytime soon. A plan is coming to you, but will Gerhardt agree? How can you put it to him so that he cannot refuse? You have an idea . . .

"Your Majesty," says Franziska, your lady's maid, who has been waiting for you in your bedroom.

"Yes?" You turn toward her. As you do, you catch a glimpse of yourself in the mirror. For the first time in your life, you are wearing black. It suits you. Your hair is still black at a distance, although up close, with afternoon light coming through the windows, you can see strands of gray. Your face is still youthful, although there are lines under your eyes, of either age or fatigue. You are the same age as your mother when she tried to kill you, and here you are, trying to figure out how to protect your daughter. She is just as pretty as you were at her age, you think loyally, but you know it's not true—how could she be, without the additional charm of magic? Hair as black as night, skin as white as snow, lips as red as blood—those were the words of the enchantment. Other women might be content with dyes and cosmetics, with carmine and lamp black, but your mother must have a daughter as beautiful as herself, created by magic. Of course, when that daughter turned out more beautiful . . . Well, this is no time to go over that old history.

"Yes, Franziska? What is it?"

"The king, Your Majesty. He requests permission to enter."

For a moment you are startled: when has your husband ever asked permission to enter? You expect him to come walking in as usual, but then you remember—he is lying under a stone effigy of himself. It is of course Gerhardt, who is now king, although the coronation will not be until Sunday, in the cathedral.

"Mother," he says, after you have nodded your permission to Franziska. He is stiff and dutiful as always. He has been like this since his days at military school, which affected Wilhelm so differently—if Willi had not been a prince, he would surely have been thrown out for his drunken capers, despite the fact that he was a surprisingly good scholar. Now he is the opposite of his brother—romantic, impulsive, a natural rebel. "I hope you are bearing up under your grief."

"Indeed," you say, offering him your hand to be kissed. "Thank you for your consideration, my son. As you know, I am devastated by the loss of your father, and cannot think how to console myself. After your coronation, where I shall be proud to see you crowned as his successor, I would like to withdraw to the Abbey of St. Winifred, where my mother is buried. I would prefer to mourn in private. Do I have your permission to make such a journey?" It is tiresome to ask permission, but you have had to ask permission from men all your life—your father, your husband. Only in the forest were you free.

"Of course, of course," he says. He looks relieved that you asked—it seems he would rather have you absent from court for a while. A king newly crowned does not want the queen dowager interfering in matters of state.

"And perhaps I shall take Dorothea with me. The nuns will know how to assuage the grief of an emotional girl."

"No doubt," he says. Again he looks relieved to be rid, for a while, of inconvenient females. "I shall need you both here when Prince Ludwig of Hohenstein comes to negotiate the new trade pact for the Five Kingdoms, but until then . . ."

So that's the husband he has chosen for Dorothea! Ludwig of Hohenstein is only ten years older than her, and not particularly ugly—you do not know whether he smells bad—but he is utterly and completely ordinary. A boring man. You do not want her marrying him, unless she herself wants to—if she is to marry dullness, let her choose it herself.

"Of course, Your Majesty," you say. You curtsey, and you can see that although he raises you up and tells you that sort of thing is not necessary, not for his own mother, he is secretly pleased.

When Gerhardt is gone, you smile. That was easier than you anticipated.

"Franziska," you say. "I want you to pack for a long journey. Only black gowns."

"Of course, Your Majesty," says the lady's maid. It makes sense that at this delicate time, the queen dowager cannot be seen out of mourning.

But black, you think, is for more than mourning. It is the appropriate color for a witch.

* * *

II. The Forest

The huntsman's house is exactly where you remember, both too far and not far enough away from the castle.

He looks at you warily, a little anxiously. He has heard, no doubt, of the king's death. Such news travels fast.

He looks different—how could he not? He has a beard now, and there is gray in it, as well as in his hair. He has taken off his green cap with the feather and is standing respectfully, waiting for your command.

You remember the first time you saw him. He was only seventeen, with golden-red hair and the beginnings of a mustache.

"Princess," he said. "The queen your mother commanded that I lead you out into the forest to kill you. She told me to bring back your liver and heart. But I cannot do such a thing. Take my purse—it does not have much in it, but a little is better than nothing. Run and hide, at least until Her Majesty is no longer angry with you—although why she is angry, I cannot imagine. If you follow the road, you will come to a village—there you can perhaps hide yourself as long as necessary. I shall kill a young doe and take its liver and heart back to her instead."

"My mother the queen will not get over that anger." You remember how she looked at you the day you returned from St. Winifred's, where you had been at school for seven years, coming home only for holidays. You remember the look in her eyes when she realized her magic had worked too well, that you were, not just as beautiful as your mother, but more beautiful. You could hear the courtiers whispering it—"More beautiful than the queen herself."

Your father said, when he did not know you were listening, "She's as beautiful as Elfrida—more beautiful, because younger. She'll be easy to marry off."

You looked up at the huntsman then, thinking, *Why should I run? Let him kill me, let us get this over with.* But you decided, perhaps only because it was a sunlit summer day and all the birds were singing in the trees, that you wanted to live. You took the purse, then went up on tiptoes and to his immense surprise, kissed him on the mouth. And then you turned and ran, not down the road, but into the forest.

Years later, after your mother's death and your husband's coronation, you said to the king, "Do you remember the huntsman who spared my life? We should reward him by giving him a position in the castle."

"There is no use for a huntsman in a castle," said King Harald. "But I can make him a gamekeeper in the forest. That is easy enough."

It was not so easy sneaking out of the castle when you were the queen, especially under the watchful eyes of your ladies-in-waiting, but Franziska helped. When you came to the gamekeeper's house for the first time, you knocked gently, then opened the door. You had not seen him in years—now he definitely looked older, but still tall and handsome as he stood up, startled and a little frightened at this apparition.

"Your Majesty!" he said, bowing.

Of course he recognized you, even after all these years. Who else has hair black as night, skin white as snow, lips red as blood?

"None of that, if you please," you told him. "I have come for something you owe me."

"And what is that?" he asked, although you thought he already knew—he was looking at you not like a queen, but like a woman. A wave of relief washed over you—you had hoped, had thought, there was something between you, that you had not imagined it all those years ago. Some small bit of the magic we call attraction or even love, but you had been so young, and not at all certain. And now here it was in his eyes, and in his arms as you claimed back your kiss.

After that day, you visited him as often as possible, which was not often, for what you were doing had two names: adultery and treason. But you could not live your entire life behind castle walls, by the side of the king to whom you were only another affirmation of his prominence. After all, he had married the fairest in the land.

One day you told your lover that you could not come anymore. "Henrik, I am with child. I have taken precautions, but such things are not infallible."

"Is it mine?" he asked, with a painted expression. He had never asked if you still went to the king's bed. He knew that queens have no choice in such a matter.

"It is," you told him. "But it must not be. You understand, do you not, that it must be the king's?"

He had simply nodded. If your child were not the king's, you would be put to death, most likely by decapitation, before it could be born. He knew that as well as you.

After that day, you did not go back to his house in the forest, not once, no matter how your heart and your arms ached in the long nights.

And yet his eyes, as they look at you now, still leaf-green, harbor no resentment.

"Your Majesty," he says.

"Gamekeeper," you say, although you would prefer to address him by his name, but that will come later. "We are riding to the Abbey of St. Winifred, but as you see our retinue is small—myself, my daughter, our maid, and two men-at-arms." He looks up quickly at Dorothea, but her face is hidden by her riding veil. Will he recognize himself in her, when he looks at her later? She has his eyes. "We need a man to tend to our needs—arrange for lodgings, water the horses, things of that sort. Can you do such tasks?"

He smiles. "I serve at your command, My Queen."

"Come then," you say. "We have a spare horse. You shall ride before us, to clear the road through the forest if necessary, or warn of thieves."

You look at Franziska and she gives you a small smile. You know that whatever inn you stop at, she will arrange it so that for the first time in fourteen years, you will spend the night with the man you love.

III. The Cottage

THE DWARVES GREET you as they have always done, each according to his temperament. Trondor shakes his head and says, "So you're back, are you?" but you can see that he's smiling under his beard. Kristof and Olaf embrace you enthusiastically. Anders makes you a courtly bow, Rolf kisses your hand, Nilsen hangs back shyly until you lean down to give him a long hug. But where is Ingar?

"He found himself a wife," says Trondor. "It won't last. It never does."

Once, when you were young, you saw one of the dwarf women. Unlike the sociable dwarf men, they are solitary and live deep in the forest, in small huts or the hollow trunks of trees. This one wore a dress stitched of squirrel skin. She was as small as the men, with long, fair hair caught up in various places with twigs. It looked like a bird's nest.

You saw her only for a moment, speaking with Olaf in the ancient language of dwarves, more melodious than human language. Her voice sounded like wind in the pine branches. She gave him a basket of mushrooms in exchange for some honey, then disappeared under the trees. Trondor explained to you that dwarf women seldom ventured out of the forest. Dwarf marriages are short-lived: the dwarf woman chooses a mate, then allows him to live with her for a time, often until she is with child. But she can stand the company of another only for so long. Eventually, the men return to the company of their brothers, for all male dwarves who shared a home are considered part of one family, although of the seven you lived with, only Kristof and Olaf had the same mother.

You are glad to see them again, these men who took you in and treated you more kindly than your own parents—the mother who tried to kill you, the father who was concerned only with matters of state and died mysteriously while you were with the dwarves, leaving your mother regent. You have seen them only once since the day the prince found you in the glass coffin and took you away to his castle—they were invited to the wedding. When they came up to the dais on which you were sitting, in your gown of white silk with the necklace of Queen Sofronia around your neck, Trondor said, "What is this fairy story they tell of the prince waking you up with true love's kiss?" You could see Prince Harald across the great hall, speaking with his father, already arranging for the coronation and a transfer of power.

"Is that not what happened?" you asked him. You yourself had been doubtful of the official version, as you were doubtful of the prince himself. But he would protect you from your mother, who had almost succeeded in killing you with that apple, and whom you suspected of poisoning your father for his throne.

"Of course not," said Trondor in his gruff voice. "He ordered us to give him the coffin and threatened us with instant death if we did not obey. He had a whole retinue with him, and we didn't have our weapons on us. Then one of the footmen carrying the coffin away stepped into a rabbit hole. The corner he had been carrying fell to the ground, and a piece of apple dislodged from your throat. That's what woke you, child. Kiss of true love indeed! And they call you White-as-Snow, as though you did not have a perfectly good name of your own. Are you happy, Ermengarde?"

"Happy enough," you told him. Of course, that was before your mother appeared at the reception—before the incident of the red hot iron shoes, which you would rather not think about.

"It's good to see you again, child," says Trondor now. Of course you are not a child any longer, but dwarves live for hundreds of years. To him you are still a mere infant. "We heard of the king's death . . ."

"Yes," you say. "I'm going back to my father's castle. I have . . . certain plans. Will you help me, Trondor? You and your brothers? I will need counselors and allies."

"Of course," he says, looking at you through narrowed eyes. You think he already understands what you intend to do. Even when you were a little girl, he understood you better than anyone else. "Shall I bring my axe, Queen Ermengarde? It has not tasted battle for a long time."

"Yes," you say. "I think that would be a good idea."

IV. The Tower

YOU STOP AT the Abbey of St. Winifred only briefly, to talk to the Mother Superior.

"Are you absolutely certain about this, Ermengarde?" she asks as she gives you the key to the tower. You gave it to her after the wedding and murder, for what else was it but a murder? At your own wedding, ordered by your husband. At the time, you asked her to keep it for you as long as necessary. You did not know if you would ever reclaim it from her again. But now here you are.

"Yes, I'm absolutely sure," you say. "And will you bless me, Reverend Mother? You were, in a way, the closest thing I had to a real mother . . ." One who loved you and taught you, for once upon a time the Mother Superior was Sister Margarete, who taught you your catechism and geography in the abbey's long, cold schoolroom.

"Perhaps I was a sort of mother to you," she says, looking at you as acutely as she did thirty years ago. Age has not diminished her strength of will or mental acuity. "But blood is important too, Ermengarde. Her blood flows through your veins, and I worry about what you will do—"

"Don't worry about me," you say. "I will be absolutely fine."

"I'm sure you will—you were always a clever girl, sometimes too clever for your own good. But what about the rest of us?" Nevertheless, she gives you the key, which is after all yours by right of blood. You are, in the end, your mother's daughter. She blesses you, kissing you on your forehead as though you were fourteen again and not a queen.

Before you leave the abbey, you visit your mother's grave, on which is inscribed only *Elfrida* and the dates of her birth and death. She's been dead for more than twenty years, and you still can't decide how you feel about her.

But her tower, too, is yours now. You lead your retinue to your father's castle, which has not been used except as a hunting lodge since the kingdoms were united after your mother's death. That was another thing the iron shoes accomplished. Did your husband force her to dance in them to revenge the way she treated you, as he said, or so he could claim your father's kingdom? Or perhaps both, for that was the way his mind worked, after all.

Since the castle is empty, there is plenty of room for you, Dorothea, Henrik, six dwarves, two men-at-arms, and of course the indispensable Franziska.

The next day, she and Henrik accompany you to the tower. You have already made him the captain of your men-at-arms, and they obey him without question. You selected them because before the kingdoms were united, they served in your father's household. They are older, so they can be spared from Gerhardt's forces, but also they are loyal to you—they still recognize you as their queen.

As for Henrik, he too asked you, lying back on your pillows, one arm around you, one hand stroking your long black hair, for the gray strands do not show by candlelight, "Are you sure, my love, that you want to do this?"

You turned to look at him and said, "Do you think Gerhardt would allow me to live the life I want, or our daughter either? If he found out about us, you and I would be condemned to death, and Dorothea would be imprisoned or exiled. And if he did not find out, things would continue as they are. He would want her to marry Prince Ludwig, and he would want me to remain a queen dowager—silent, respectable, so dessicated that eventually I would dry up and blow away like a leaf in autumn. Believe me, my love, if there were another way for the three of us to have a life together, I would take it. However, I am not only Ermengarde, the woman who loves you, but White-as-Snow. Twenty years ago I became the heroine of a fairy tale, and it spread throughout the land. If Gerhardt announced that I was missing, had perhaps been kidnapped by an equally missing gamekeeper, I would be searched for, watched for, in this kingdom and others. There would be no place for us to hide. So you see, I must use what I have, including the name I was given, the tale that was told about me—I must use these things to write my own story."

He nodded, then pulled you closer and kissed you. Now, he dismounts and takes the horses' reins. Then he waits by the foot of the tower while you and Franziska enter through the wooden door.

The tower is not tall, only two stories of ancient stone with a crenelated turret, surrounded by ancient trees. Once, it was used to store weapons, and a couple of men-at-arms would sleep there on folding cots. Inside, the windows are small—arrow slits more than windows. It is darker inside than you expected.

On the second floor, after you have climbed up the stone staircase that circles the inside of the tower, Franziska raises her lantern.

There are all your mother's magical implements, scattered about as though she had left them just yesterday: the cauldron, the table of alchemical equipment whose purposes you do not yet understand, the shelves of bottles filled with powders and other ingredients—dried eye of newt and toe of frog? Are those the sorts of things witches keep, as housewives keep pickles? The shelves also hold large books in leather covers, presumably filled with formulas and spells.

On the far side of the table is an ornate wooden stand with the mirror whose pronouncements caused so much trouble.

V. The Mirror

How DOES ONE address a magical mirror?

The problem, of course, is that your mother never taught you witchcraft. Would she have, if her spell had not worked so well? If she had not thought of you as a rival? You would have given up your black hair and white skin and red lips without a second thought, simply for a kind word from her.

"Mirror, mirror, I believe, is how she usually started," says Franziska. She too was chosen for her history with your family as well as her loyalty to you—her mother was your mother's maid, her father drove your father's own carriage.

All right, then. "Mirror, mirror."

The mirror, which reflected you a moment ago, grows misty, as though filled with fog, and then the fog swirls as though blown here and there by a wind inside the mirror itself. Out of that fog comes a voice.

"Well, well. Look who's back. Little White-as-Snow, all grown up. Welcome to your mother's chamber of secrets and spells, Ermengarde."

Is it a man's voice? A woman's? You cannot quite tell. It is, undeniably, a cynical, sarcastic voice. It sounds bitter.

"Do you, too, want to know who's the fairest in the land?" it asks.

"Not particularly," you say. "I assume it's not me any longer."

"You're right about that," says the mirror. "You've aged out of that particular position. What is it you want, then?"

"I want you to teach me my mother's magic," you say, trying to see something in the swirling smoke. The mirror has no discernible face. "She once called you her familiar. You would know how to use all these books, this equipment." You gesture around at the contents of the tower.

"And why do you want to learn magic?" asks the mirror, as the fog swirls more quickly. "Do you, too, want to kill your daughter?"

"No, to save her," you say. "I want to become queen—not queen consort, not queen dowager, but queen in my own right. That's the only way I will have some measure of power over her life, and mine."

"I see," says the mirror, sounding surprised. Clearly, it has not expected this. "I will teach you if you do two things."

"And what are they?" you ask, wondering if you will need to sacrifice something, or sign somewhere in blood. You do not relish the thought.

"First, you must pledge yourself to Hecate. That is merely standard procedure. Second, you must allow me to return to my true form."

"Your true form?" You look at the mirror, astonished. "Is this not your true form?" The mirror has been a mirror as long as you have known that your mother was a witch. You remember seeing it on its ornate stand the only time she brought you to this tower, before you were sent away to the Abbey of St. Winifred. She stood you in front of it, showed you your own reflection, and said, "Look, Ermie, at what a pretty girl you are. Someday, you'll look just like me!"

"No," says the mirror. "Your mother ordered me to become a mirror so I could show her whatever she wished to see—chiefly herself. I have been trapped in this form ever since. You are my mistress now. Allow me to return to my true form—simply say the words—and I will teach you."

"All right, then," you say with some trepidation. "Return to your true form." What will you see? A serpent? A dragon? A demon with horns and a forked tail?

The smoke in the mirror swirls faster and faster, until it looks like a gray whirlpool, and suddenly sitting in front of you is not a mirror in a frame but a wolf with fur the color of smoke.

It stares at you with yellow eyes and says, "Thank you, mistress. Shall we begin the first lesson?"

VI. The Cauldron

It takes Gerhardt longer than you expected to realize that you are not at the Abbey of St. Winifred. When his army comes marching over what used to be the border between two kingdoms, you are ready. You have had three months to learn magic from Grimm, which turns out to be the name of your familiar. You hope that you have learned enough.

You stand outside the portcullis of the castle, which is on a hillside. You are dressed all in black, like a widow or a witch. To one side of you stands Henrik, holding his horse's reins, ready to lead the charge on your command. He is now the general of a small but dedicated army of your father's men-at-arms, who have returned to serve you, and the sons they have brought with them, as well as some men from the village who wish to defend White-as-Snow against a distant king they do not trust. Your legend has served you well—they are proud to follow a queen out of a fairy tale. The strongest of them are standing, waiting armed and armored, on either side of the hilltop for the command to attack. The rest are in the castle behind the portcullis, waiting at arrow slits and on turrets, crossbows cocked.

On the other side of you is Grimm, who is sometimes a mirror, sometimes an owl, and sometimes a wisp of smoke. Today he is a great gray wolf surveying the landscape before him. Scattered around you are seven dwarves, for Ingar has returned. His wife is with child. He will likely not see it until it is several years old, and then only if it is male, for the dwarf women keep their girl children in the forest. You think this may be a very good system.

Behind you is Dorothea, dressed in black as well. Two months ago, you told her the truth about her father. To your relief, she kissed you on the cheek and said, "I always blamed myself for not being able to love Papa—I mean King Harald. But now I don't think it was my fault. Perhaps in some way, I could always tell he was not really my father." She is stirring the cauldron, which is set over a fire and has started to bubble fiercely. Franziska is adding the necessary ingredients from baskets and glass bottles. You will need to pay attention to the cauldron in a moment, but right now, you are waiting for a parley.

Three men are riding across the field beneath Gerhardt's standard. Of course Gerhardt would not come himself, but as they ride closer, you see that the man in the middle is Wilhelm, between two men-at-arms. Your younger son is as handsome as always, and you cannot help feeling proud of him, even though he is currently your enemy.

"Hello, Mother," he says when he has dismounted and walked up the hillside toward you. "Hello, Dorothea. It's good to see you again." He waves at his sister. His escorts remain mounted, and behind. "Mother, Gerhardt wants you to know that if you surrender now and return with him, all will be forgiven. If you do not, he will take this castle by force." He glances around the top of the hill, and then up at the castle. "I must say, you don't have a lot of men, unless you're hiding some of them where I can't see. The castle is strong, so you could hold on for a while if you have stores, but eventually Gerhardt would starve you out if he simply waited long enough. I did learn military strategy at school, you know. That and German poetry, which is considerably less useful except when impressing aristocratic young women. Anyway, I hate to agree with anything Gerhardt says—you know what an irritating bore my older brother can be. But I think you'd better surrender. I don't want you or Dorothea to end up in a dungeon."

"Hello, Willi," you say. "You need a haircut. Your hair is falling into your eyes again." You brush it aside affectionately.

"Oh, Mother!" he says, as though exasperated, but he takes your hand and kisses it—son to mother, and to queen. The two of you have always had a good relationship.

"All the arguments you make are sensible ones," you say. "But there's something Gerhardt does not know. You see, I've been practicing witchcraft."

"Have you really?" he asks, a look of interest and admiration in his eyes. "You mean like grandmother?" Then, for the first time, he notices your companions. "Are those dwarves? Are they *the* dwarves, from 'White-as-Snow and the Seven Dwarves'? There are seven of them, aren't there?" He counts. "And is that a wolf?" He looks at Grimm with alarm.

"That is my familiar. You know all witches have one. Sometimes he is a wolf, and sometimes he is something else altogether." You smile at Wilhelm and pat him on the cheek. "Willi, would you like to be king after I defeat Gerhardt's army? I will give you his kingdom and keep this one for my own, but you must conclude a treaty with me, on my terms. Which include pledging fealty."

"Of course, Mother," he says, looking down at you with amusement. "But how do you intend to defeat Gerhardt? He has a real army, whereas you have a rag-tag collection of old men and young boys dressed in armor. Some of it rather old armor, visibly patched. I take it this is your general." He looks at Henrik. "He at least appears competent and well-armed, but one strong man is not enough."

"Watch," you say, smiling. Then you step back toward the cauldron, which Dorothea has brought to a rolling boil. "Grimm," you say, "are you ready? Trondor?"

The wolf and dwarf both nod. Trondor mounts on the back of the gray wolf and raises his battle axe, which is as large as his head.

"All right, then. Franziska, add the final ingredient." She shakes red powder out of a large box labeled, in ornate calligraphy, *Feoderovsky and Sons Magical Supplies*. Powdered dragon's blood is expensive, even if you order it in bulk, but this is too important for inferior ingredients.

The cauldron bubbles, and a gray smoke rises. You intone the magical words, which are in Latin of course—it's a good thing you received an excellent classical education at St. Winifred. Franziska and Dorothea fall back as the first wolf rises from the cauldron, gray and gaunt and snarling.

"Olaf," you say, and the dwarf mounts his wolf. Then Nilsen and Anders, Rolf and Ingar, and finally Kristof. They are armed with axes like Trondor's, or battle maces. They are wearing leather armor. There is a fierce light in their eyes, which surprises you—are these the mild, gentle dwarves who took you in and raised you, when your mother was trying to kill you and your father was oblivious to the situation? You could not have had better parents. And yet, there are tales of dwarf warriors in the history books. They are said to be fiercer than eagles.

"Trondor, lead the way," you tell him. He throws back his head and shouts something in the ancient dwarf language that is no doubt some sort of battle cry. Then Grimm lopes down the hillside and the other wolves follow, with the dwarves mounted on them. Wolves stream out of the cauldron, each with a fierce dwarf warrior on its back. They look like running smoke, through which you can see the glint of weapons in the sunlight. Only the first wolf is real, only the seven dwarves can draw blood—it is mostly illusion, and yet it looks real enough.

"Henrik, it's time," you say. Henrik mounts his horse, then rides to one side of the hilltop and then the other, commanding the men to charge. They move in formation down the hill on either side of the dwarf army, with Henrik and a few mounted men in the rear, the cavalry following the infantry.

Reality and illusion: enchantment held together by force of will, a few magical powders, and words in a dead language. You have only had three months to learn, and you hope to goodness that your plan will succeed. But you have always been clever, as the Mother Superior knows. You have always attended to your lessons. And you are, quite simply, *done*. Done with listening to men who tell you what to do, whether the father who ignored you, or the husband who turned you into a fairy tale, or now a son. You are done with being rescued, done with obedience and gratitude.

Gerhard's forces stand fast for a moment, and then break. You can hear it even from here, his footmen shouting with fear and surprise, stumbling backward from the ghostly wolves and dwarf warriors. They run into the mounted knights behind, who urge them forward until their horses smell wolf and panic under them. Then all of Gerhardt's soldiers are retreating, and it is a great chaos of men and magic, a complete route.

"Well done, Mother," says Wilhelm beside you. "Shall I ride down and deliver the coup de grace? By which I mean telling Gerhardt to surrender. I would not, of course, commit fratricide."

"Yes, I think that would be for the best," you say. "Tell him I'm not going to execute him, just send him into exile."

"Will do," he says, nodding. Then he leaves you on the hillside, alone with Franziska and Dorothea, the cauldron still smoking between you. The three of you, standing there, resemble the three Fates.

"Well done, Your Majesty," says Franziska, whom you intend to make a countess for her service and loyalty. She will have a lady's maid of her own.

"Mother, that was awesome," says Dorothea. "Will you teach me witchcraft?"

"Of course," you say. "After all, you will be the queen of this kingdom after me. It's much easier to be a queen when you're also a witch."

VII. The Apple

"Is that right?" asks Dorothea. She holds up the apple, which is red on one side and white on the other.

"Quite right," you say. "Now, can you make the red side *not* poisonous? It's much more important knowing how not to be poisoned than knowing how to poison people. And harder."

"That was your mother's spell, wasn't it?" says Dorothea. She intones a few words in Latin while passing her hands over a bowl of red liquid that turns milky white, then dips the apple back into it. Her Latin is coming along well, as is her knowledge of various potions and their ingredients. You are proud of that fact that she is as good a student as you were.

Grimm, who is lying at her feet in wolf form, whimpers softly in his dreams. A few days ago you asked him, out of curiosity, "Who is the fairest, anyway? The fairest in the land?"

"At the moment? Anthea, the blacksmith's daughter in Mallor, a village high on the slopes of Mount Gotteringen. She is admired intensely by the goats she's herding. But last week she had the flu, so the fairest was Sister Maria-Josef, cloistered at the nunnery of Saint Edelweis in the port city of South Fardo. You were the fairest for a very long time, if that's any consolation. Usually it changes at least once a month."

You and Dorothea are both in the tower for her daily magic lesson. A week ago you married your true love and were crowned queen. Henrik is now your prince consort. You are no longer dressed in black, but in crimson velvet edged with ermine, which is suitable for a queen as well as a witch. Wilhelm has pledged fealty to you and is establishing his rule over your late husband's kingdom. Gerhardt is in Hohenstein, plotting an invasion with Prince Ludwig, but Ludwig's father, King Frederik IV, also known as the Rotund, is not at all sure that war with a neighboring kingdom is in his best interests and has so far refused them funding. If Gerhardt does manage to raise an army, it will take a while, and by then you will have something even more effective to greet him with than wolves made of smoke. The dwarves have decided to stay with you in the castle, and you are glad to have your seven fathers with you, to counsel and advise. This is the closest you've ever come to having a family.

"Yes, that was her spell," you say. "Her third and final spell. The one that killed me, at least for a while. And now you know the antidote."

Dorothea looks down at the apple for a moment, then says, "Mama, why did you keep letting the peddler woman in? Rolf says they warned you, over and over again, not to let anyone in at all."

"They did," you say. "But you see, she was my mother. Oh, I know she was in disguise, but a child could have seen through that trick. I mean, what sort of peddler woman tries to sell stay laces in the middle of a forest? Who does she expect to sell them to? No, I knew who she was the moment I saw her. I let her in because she was my mother. I had not seen her in so long . . . And I wanted her to lace me up, to comb my hair. I knew there was something wrong with that apple, but the dwarves had saved me twice already. Why not a third time? And I wanted to share it with her, to take a bite right next to the one she had taken. When I woke up in the glass coffin, I realized that I could have died, truly died that time. I married Prince Harald because I thought he could keep me safe. She wouldn't try to kill the queen of a neighboring kingdom, would she? But then Harald invited her to the wedding and had iron shoes heated on a fire . . . I still remember her screams. I never forgave him for that."

You are silent for a while. The only sounds in the tower are Grimm, who is evidently chasing a dream rabbit, and Dorothea munching her apple while she pages through a leather-bound volume of magical botany.

"I'm glad you're not that sort of mother," she says, looking up at you from a page on Agrimony. "When I grow up, I want to be just like you, Mama."

She won't be, of course. She won't have a father who ignores her or a mother who tries to poison her, because Henrik is positively doting and you are not that sort of mother, as Dorothea said. But she won't have a cottage of dwarves to raise her either, although you hope Trondor and the others will teach her some of the things they taught you, about the forest, and kindness, and home. You sincerely hope she won't have a prince to rescue her, because princes are not to be trusted and their services come at a high price. You will teach her to rescue herself, and you hope she will be better, smarter, stronger than you were.

You smile at her across the table, with its bowls of potion, its magical powders, its leather-bound books. Your beautiful, talented Dorothea. This is how you became a witch-queen. She will have to find her own path, as you are certain she shall.

Mirror, Mirror

Each morning, standing barefoot on cold tiles,
I ask you, not who is the fairest in the land—
I'm neither that vain nor ambitious.

But am I as fair as I was
yesterday, or the day before yesterday,
all the yesterdays on which I was younger
than I am today. Those lines that Mother Time,
the indefatigable spider,
is spinning beneath my eyes—have they spread overnight?
Perhaps I should stop smiling so frequently.

Perhaps I should stop frowning, avoid the sun—
already it has painted a few brown spots
on my cheeks and forehead. Or sleep for a hundred years,
which is as effective, they say, as a facelift.

Each morning you say, yes, you are older now.
There are white hairs on either side of your forehead,
looking as though they had been touched by Frost,
whose fingers leave precisely such fine streaks
over the meadow grasses, the windowpanes.
Soon, you will become a winter landscape
crossed by tracks where hare and deer have passed
on their way into the darkness of the forest.
Soon, you will sprout mushrooms.

Wake up, wake up! you say.
You will sleep all too soon—now is the time
to live as though you were going to live forever,
as though winter never comes
and all the fairy tales
were true.

The River's Daughter

She walks into the river
with rocks in her pockets,
and the water closes around her
like the arms of a father
saying hello, my lovely one,
hello. How good to see you,
who have been away so long.

The eddying water
tugs at the hem of her dress,
and the small fish gather
to nibble at her ankles, at her knees,
to nibble at her fingers. They will find
it all edible, soon, except
the carnelian ring by which her sister
will identify her.

Bits of paper
float away, the ink now indecipherable.
Was it a note? Notes for another
novel she might have written, something new
to confound the critics? They will cling
to the reeds, will be used
to line ducks' nests, with the down
from their breasts. The water
rises to her shoulders, lifts her hair.

Come, says the river. I have been waiting
for you so long, my daughter.
Dress yourself in my weeds,
let your hair float in my pools,
take on my attributes: fluidity,
the eternal, elemental flow
for which you always longed.
They are found not in words but water.
You will never find them while you breathe,

not in the world of air.
And she opens her mouth
one final time, saying father,
I am here.

Saint Orsola and the Poet

DO YOU KNOW how Antal Odon became a poet?

In 1846, the year there were riots in King Karel Square, while the university was shut down, he decided to go on a walking tour of the northern mountains. He could not return home, for his father disapproved of his politics, particularly since his sister Katarina had eloped with his best friend, the radical editor Erno Palko. Anyway, half his professors were in prison.

He was sick of life, and still recovering from a bullet he had taken in the shoulder at one of the protests, when the mercenaries brought in by the usurping Regent Stefan Gustavus fired on the crowd. And to top it all off, a young lady he had been very much in love with for the entire month of September, who worked in a fabric and trimmings shop, had decided to marry a man who owned a button factory. "Buttons make money in war or peace," she had told him. "Everyone needs buttons." So, sick at heart, and to be truthful, sick even of himself, he had packed a rucksack and bought a one-way ticket to Karberg, thinking he would spend several weeks in the dark pine forests of the Wolfwald, walking from village to village, inn to inn, drinking at each until his money ran out and he was forced to go home and ask his father for an advance on his allowance—a prospect he regarded with equal distaste and despair.

Until, that is, he got lost in the forest.

He could not imagine how, since he had a very good guide book with fold-out maps, as well as a compass, and the path was, for the most part, clearly marked. But instead of arriving at the small but comfortable inn described in *A Tour of Rural Sylvania* by Otto Wambier, he had somehow arrived at the valley that now lay below him, at the bottom of what seemed to be a twisting, difficult path. It was twilight, and below he could see houses arranged around the twin poles of all villages: the castle and the church. Surely it would have an inn, or someone in need of a few kroner who would rent him a room. But he did not know how he could reach it before night fell.

He spent a few minutes cursing his guidebook, the compass, his sister for marrying that fool Erno, all young women who worked in shops, fathers in general, and the entire revolution. He stopped just before getting to the young king-in-exile. Then he resigned himself to sleeping on the ground, under the pines. At least he had a warm coat.

But as he was looking for a place to lie down that was not too damp, he saw a light between the trees. Following it, he came to a cottage perched almost at the edge of a cliff, with a small garden. Who would want to build a cottage there, so far above the comfort and safety of a village? Yet the cottage was inhabited, because he could see smoke curling up from the stucco chimney, and from somewhere inside a thatched shed he heard what could only be the bleat of a goat. Here at least he could get directions down to the valley. With the confidence of all well-fed young men of moderate fortune and mediocre education, he knocked on the door.

It was opened by an old woman. She was a typical peasant of the region, wearing an embroidered smock. The only unusual thing about her was her extreme age. She was bent over by it, like a birch tree that had grown in a strong wind, and her bony wrists were as thin as branches. Her face was a spiderweb of lines. But she had bright brown eyes, like a curious bird, with which she regarded him as he stood at her door.

"Well?" she said, not rudely, but as though she were otherwise occupied and wanted to know his business.

"God keep and bless you, Ama," he said, using the old Sylvanian word for mother as a sign of respect. "I've lost my way in the forest, and don't know where I am. What is the name of this place?" He sounded quite stupid to himself—he had meant to say something more clever, to make a little speech that would imply he was *not* lost, just in need of some direction.

"I can see that," she said. "Well, come in. I'll give you supper and a bed for the night, and send you on your way in the morning."

He followed her, ducking under the lintel although he was not a particularly tall man—the cottage seemed to have been made for someone her size and no larger. It was rather bare, with only a bed that, during the day, functioned as a sofa, a rocking chair by the ceramic stove, a table covered with an embroidered cloth, and two carved wooden chairs on either side. There were the usual implements of a peasant cottage: a broom in one corner, a spinning wheel, pots and pans hanging from the wall by the stove, baskets arranged along a shelf, and strings of garlic hanging from the rafters. It was spotlessly neat. The walls seemed freshly whitewashed and there were lace curtains at the windows, no doubt made by the inhabitant of the cottage herself. Antal knew how these old women, half blind from age, could nevertheless create the finest, most delicate patterns. His father's old nurse, who still lived in a cottage on the estate, had done the same. The pillows and coverlet on the bed were embroidered with a pattern of flowers—poppies and lilies and more fanciful floral creations he did not recognize. Most importantly, there was a smell coming from a kettle on the stove. Antal breathed it in as though it were the sweetest Parisian perfume.

"I assume you are hungry," said the woman. "Young men usually are."

"Indeed," he said, trying to nod wisely. To say "yes" would sound stupid, to say "no" would be rude and anyway untrue. Whatever she was cooking, it smelled delicious.

She gestured toward the table, inviting him to sit, and ladled some of the soup into a blue ceramic bowl. She handed him a coarse linen napkin and a wooden spoon.

It was so good that he was finished almost before he had started, and he was ashamed of himself for eating so quickly, without waiting for his hostess. But she did not sit down and eat herself. She stood by the stove and refilled his bowl, then cut him a slice of brown bread in which he could taste the pleasant sourness of rye. The second bowl was as good as the first. So was the third. By that time he was finally full, and darkness had fallen outside the windows. The only light in the cottage came from the stove, which still burned brightly.

"Can I pay you for the meal, Ama?" he asked. He would have been more embarrassed if he had not been so tired. He had eaten so quickly, almost slurping the spicy broth.

"What use to me is your money?" she asked. "Tomorrow you can split and stack the wood that stands beside my goatshed, into pieces small enough to fit into the stove. That will be payment enough. Now get yourself to bed and I will answer your question, Antal Odon."

He took off his boots and climbed into the wooden bed. She swept away the specks of dirt he had left on the floor, and as she swept, she began:

"You asked the name of the village below. Once it was named Pinus Maior, after the pine trees, but for a hundred years it has been named Szent Orsola. Do you know why?"

"No, Ama," said Antal. She finished sweeping and sat in the rocking chair. Her voice, or perhaps the dancing firelight on the walls, or perhaps the supper he had just eaten, was making him sleepy. Seated there, with her face in shadow, she seemed almost a part of the mountain that had detached itself to tell him a story. The chair creaked as she began to rock back and forth. This is the story she told him:

ONCE, THERE WAS a Baron in the valley below. His name was Orsoman, and he was as miserly and parsimonious as a shut purse, which his generally was, no matter how deserving a beggar came to his door. He taxed his peasants on the land they worked and the houses they lived in, on the principle that the land and houses belonged to him, so why should they not pay to live and work on his property? There was a mill tax, a tax on livestock sold in the market, a tax on anything forged in the smithy. Everything that was to be found in the valley, the Baron had a tax on, so that the peasants felt as if their very breaths, as they sang hymns in the church, were being taxed.

The Baron's coffers were filled with silver, copper, and even gold, and his dungeons were filled with men who had not paid their taxes. His second most precious possession, after the contents of his treasury, was a daughter, as beautiful as his wife, who had died giving birth. She had come to the valley as a blushing young bride, shy of the dark, stern man her father had arranged for her to marry. Feeling herself unloved and neglected, she soon grew pale and longed for home. She looked forward to having a child, who might be a companion for her, but the last sight she ever saw was that child's red face and bright blue eyes, and the last hand she ever held was a tiny fist. That daughter was now almost old enough to be married, and the Baron has already considered which of the surrounding landowners would make a most advantageous match.

This daughter, named Orsola after the Baron's late mother, had grown up pale and silent in her father's shadow. She had no friends, for she could not play with the peasant children, and there were no girls of her own age and station within a day's ride. Her father could have taken her to visit other noble families, but then he had no friends among them. He could even have taken her to the court of King Karel III, where she would have been presented to Queen Ludmila, but that would have cost money. As she grew older, her bright blue eyes turned as gray as the stones of the castle. Still, she loved her father, or supposed she loved him, for she had known no other parent. She gazed often at a miniature of her mother that had been painted before her wedding, to demonstrate her beauty to her prospective husband. Orsola had seen it on her father's bureau, lying among some papers, and asked for it. He had handed it to her carelessly, without looking at it. Since the original was gone, having performed the one duty he required of her, he had no more use for its likeness. Orsola wondered, often, what it would have been like to have a mother. Would they have walked through the garden together? Would her mother have talked to her, taught her whatever it is that mothers teach—Orsola did not know exactly what. Would her mother have brushed her hair at night? That was the only example of tenderness she could think of, for her nurse had done it every night when she was a child. That nurse had been followed by a succession of grim, efficient governesses, until her father had decided that she was sufficiently knowledgeable for the role she was expected to fulfill in life.

It was Christmas Eve, and Orsola was sitting in her bedchamber, staring out the window at the lights in the village below. If the sun had been visible behind the gray clouds, it would have been low over the mountain. It would be dark soon. She imagined the families gathered around their hearth fires, celebrating the season. They had little to eat, she knew that, for in the last year or two she had come to realize the conditions that prevailed in the valley and the poverty in which most of the villagers lived. She could not fault the Baron for it, for he was her father after all, but she had begun to look at him with a question in her eyes. If you had asked her what that question might be, she would not have been able to tell you. She only knew it was there, particularly when she looked at her mother's miniature. She knew the villagers would have little to share. Nevertheless, they would have each other, and later that night they would file out of their houses and go to the church, where she knew there would be hymns. She had heard their voices carried on the wind the year before.

That afternoon, the Baron had retired directly after dinner, complaining of a pain in his chest. So she was sitting alone in her room, with a shawl wrapped around herself and a book that her governess had given her lying idly on her lap, when she heard a sound. It seemed to come from outside the narrow stone window. She leaned out to see more clearly what had made the noise and spotted something in the orchard, moving erratically among the trees. At first, in the darkness, she could not distinguish what it was, but as it drew nearer she saw a child, a boy dressed in ragged clothes, skipping and darting over the bare, cold ground. He looked up at her and made that sound again—laughter.

"You there!" she called out. "Who are you? What are you doing here? Where is your mother? You should be at home!"

The child just laughed again and skipped away.

This would not do. Surely his mother would be worrying about him. It did not occur to Orsola that the child's father might be worried as well. She had no experience with fathers who worried about the welfare of their children.

She wrapped the shawl more closely around herself, then ran as quickly as she could to the kitchen and opened the door that led out to the herb garden. She was not dressed for the cold, but it would take too long to fetch her cloak, and this little door was the only one she knew how to open herself, for the key hung on a hook next to the door so the cook could reach it when she wanted to make the soup more savory. If Orsola wanted to leave the castle by the large wooden door, barred with iron, at the imposing front entrance, she would have to summon her father's steward, who had the key but would disapprove of her helping a peasant boy. Anyway, surely she could find the child quickly and bring him inside? She could find him a place to sleep that night, and in the morning one of the maids could take him home.

But when she had run through the herb garden to the orchard, he was nowhere to be found.

"Boy!" she called out. "Come here. No, don't turn away!" For he had done just that, turned away from her and run farther under the trees. She had caught just a glimpse of dark hair tangling down to his shoulders and a bright face with mischievous eyes. He was a small, thin boy, the age to be starting school at the schoolhouse in the village.

Orsola thought for a moment of turning back, returning to her warm fire, and letting him find his own way home. But just then she felt the first flakes of snow starting to fall. She looked up at the gray sky. Yes, snowflakes were coming down, not many but definitively, as though they were determined to cover the ground. What if he got lost in the snow?

Pulling her shawl tightly around her shoulders, she ran after him. Her breath was like a ghost floating in front of her. Twice she lost sight of him, but the first time she heard his laughter again, and the second time she saw the prints of his feet in the snowflakes that lay scattered on the ground. They were not gathering yet, but as night fell and it grew colder, they would begin to form little piles, and soon the ground would be white with them.

Finally she caught up with him at the bridge over the stream, a tributary of the river Morek, which wound around the village like a sinuous dragon.

"Child," she said, and ghostly puffs came out of her mouth. "What is your name? Where does your family live? Let me take you home. It's too cold for you to wander about alone, and night is coming. You should be in bed." She was quite cold now, and almost out of breath.

"But I am going home," he said, laughing once again. His laughter was like a bell, higher than the one that rang in the church to mark the times for prayer. "I'm going to Mama."

"Where is she, your mother?" asked Orsola.

He turned and pointed across the bridge, up the mountain.

"But she can't live on the mountain!" said Orsola. Or could she? Perhaps this was a woodcutter's or charcoal burner's boy, or the son of a widow so poor she could not afford a house in the village, but must live in a hut under the pine trees, like some forest animal. Orsola had heard of such poverty, for the priest had mentioned it in church, but she had never seen it herself. She had never been farther away from the castle than this bridge. It had been the limit of her respectable and circumscribed world.

"Anyway, even if she does, you can't go home alone, at night, in this weather. And with bare feet! Here, let me put my boots on you."

He looked at her doubtfully, but allowed her to come close and take first his right foot and then his left, so that she could put her own boots on them. They were a bit loose, for his feet were not as large as hers, but she tied the laces as tightly as she could. When she had put them on, he laughed with delight and skipped away from her over the bridge.

"Come back!" cried Orsola.

"I need to find Mama!" he said again, and turned toward the dark pines that marched up the mountain slope. She sighed and followed him. What else could she do? She could not let a child that age go into the dark forest alone.

The ground was cold and hard under her stockinged feet. She had never walked outside without boots before, even on pleasant days. The pine needles on the path clung to her wool stockings as she followed the boy into the forest. He was always just a little too far ahead of her, but she could hear him whistling or singing songs under his breath. Perhaps he was a simpleton, unaware of the dangers of the forest? All the more reason not to let him wander about the mountain alone at night. He might stray from the path and get lost, or worse—fall into some sort of crevasse or ravine. And there were wolves in the forest.

But he seemed determined to find his mother, so she continued to follow. At least she could make certain that he reached home safely.

When they had been climbing upward a little while, she came to a rocky clearing among the dark pines. Here the snow had started to gather, and it crunched under her feet. Close to the center of the clearing stood a small tree, bare of leaves. To her astonishment, Orsola noticed there was a sound coming from it that sounded distinctly like weeping. The boy was standing beside it, with his hand on its trunk.

"What is it?" asked the boy as she approached. "Why are you crying?"

For a moment, the tree continued to sob. Then it said, although Orsola was not completely clear on how a tree could say anything, "Alas, young master. All the trees are invited to the Midwinter Ball, but I have nothing to wear. The pines have their brown cones, the yews have their red berries, the birches have their white bark. But I have nothing at all. Look, all my leaves have fallen!"

The boy looked at Orsola for a moment, and then back to the tree. "This lady gave me her boots. Perhaps she can give you something, so you can go to the ball."

Give something to a tree so it could attend a ball? What sort of ball did trees attend—how could they dance, rooted in the ground as they were? Even asking the question was absurd, and Orsola laughed at herself, but the boy looked at her so earnestly. What did she have that could adorn a tree? There was only one thing . . .

"Look," she said, opening her shawl and showing him the string of white pearls on which hung a locket with her mother's miniature in it. "I can't give this—you see, it's my own Mama. But your tree is welcome to my pearls."

The little tree shook, although there was no wind. After a moment, Orsola realized it was the tree's way of quivering with excitement. Then it stood perfectly still and stretched out its branches.

Orsola unclasped the string of pearls, put the miniature carefully into her pocket, and strung it over the branches of the little tree. Somehow, it seemed longer than she remembered. It had gone around her neck once, but it formed three strands of shining white beads on the tree's bare branches. "There, you look quite festive now," she said.

"You see?" said the child. "Now you can go to the ball. Come on," he said to Orsola, pulling at her skirt. "Mama is waiting for me."

The little tree seemed to bow, and then its branches swayed so that the string of pearls gleamed in the fading light. Orsola realized it was dancing. Not quite knowing what to do, she made it a curtsey and then turned to follow the boy, who was once again almost out of sight among the pines. She hurried after him.Up and up they went, higher up the mountain and deeper into the forest. Here at least there was no snow, for it could not fall through the thick branches. The needles under her feet were surprisingly soft, like a carpet, and she was not so cold.

She had been trying to catch up to the child, who always seemed just about to slip out of her sight among the pines—she did not want him wandering up here alone, although he seemed to find his way even in the twilight under the trees. So she was startled when she almost stumbled upon him. He was standing with his hands in his pockets, talking to—could it be a fox? A gray fox sitting beside the path, with its tail tucked neatly around its paws.

"But why aren't you going?" asked the child. "All the animals in the forest are going. They have all been invited."

"Look at me, young master," said the fox. "The wolves of the forest have their black pelts, like a night without stars. The stags have their branching horns, like oak trees. The owls have eyes that catch and reflect the moonlight. Even the hedgehogs have needles upon their backs—an uncomfortable form of decoration. But I am only a shadow that slips through the trees, almost invisible. How can I appear in front of your mother like this?"

"Oh, are the animals invited to the ball as well?" asked Orsola. She was a little out of breath. It had been such a strange journey so far that she did not think it extraordinary to address a fox.

The fox looked at her with narrowed eyes. "I smelled you, daughter of the men who carry guns into my forest. I do not know what you are doing here at night, when your kind stay in their dens. But you are with the young master, so I will answer your question. Yes, all the animals are invited to the Midwinter Ball—weasels and badgers and hedgehogs, bears and wolves, and all the birds that have not flown away to warmer places. We have been invited by the Lady herself. But how can I appear before her looking so shabby?"

"I don't have another string of pearls," said Orsola. "But you may take my shawl, if you wish. It was given to me by my old nurse, who spun the wool and dyed it with madder and knit it herself."

The fox did not respond for a moment, as though appraising her offer. Then, it nodded. "I accept your gift."

Orsola took off her shawl and put it around the fox, tying the ends so it would not come loose. The fox walked up and down the path in it, seeming very pleased with itself. Now Orsola was dressed only in the brown linsey-woolsey she had worn to dinner, over a petticoat and stockings. She began to shiver.

"Will I see you at the ball?" asked the fox. It was now turning around and around, first one way and then the other, to admire its new shawl.

"I haven't been invited," she said.

"Why, did the young master himself not go down to fetch you?" said the fox. "Perhaps I misunderstood, but men are not foxes, and I have never understood their ways."

Orsola wanted to ask the child that the tree and fox had called master if they were indeed going to a ball. By this time she was so tired, despite the cold that bit her fingers and toes, and so many strange things had happened, that she half believed she was back in her bedroom, asleep in her chair, and this was all a dream.

But the child was gone again.

"Little boy!" she cried out. "Where are you?"

"Here!" came the call from farther up the path. "You are too slow! We shall be late if you don't hurry!"

She hurried after the sound. Late for what? This ball that the tree and fox had talked about? There—she could see him ahead of her on the path. In a moment she would catch up to him . . .

Just as she reached him, they emerged from the forest, climbing up the path onto a rocky hilltop. It rose from the forest around it like a bald head surmounted here and there by jutting boulders. On the other side, the forest fell away again before rising to the mountain peaks beyond. By this time, the sun had sunk behind the mountains, so Orsola could see only the shadows of the rocks, but suddenly the clouds parted to show the moon, which was almost full. In the moonlight, she could see dark grass growing from crevices and lighter bits of lichen scattered over the stones.

"Mama!" cried the boy.

How could he live here? Orsola saw no cottage, not so much as a shack. There was nothing on that hilltop but rocks and grass. But as she looked around at the darkness, a shape resolved itself out of it. It was a woman in a long cloak, almost as dark as the night. Her face shone pale in the moonlight. Orsola could not tell whether she was young or old, but she walked straight and steadily. She stopped before them and pushed back her hood with pale hands. Out fell her dark hair, down past her waist, almost to her knees. There were stars caught in it, or so it seemed to Orsola. In their light, she could see a little farther over the hilltop.

"Where did you wander off to, my love?" the woman said to the child. "You are too young as yet to go about the forest alone. Wait until you are older, when summer comes."

"Mama, I found a friend," he said.

"I see that." The woman smiled. "I see also that she has been generous with her shawl, her pretty necklace, and even her boots. You must be quite cold, my dear," she said to Orsola. "Here, take my cloak."

She unclasped her cloak at the neck, then took it off and put it around Orsola's shoulders. It was so warm!

"Thank you, Lady," said Orsola, for this must be the lady that the fox had talked about. She was clearly a noblewoman of some sort, although why she was up on this hilltop, or why her son was running around in ragged clothes, Orsola had no idea. Her long, dark dress was quite simple, but her cloak felt like the finest merino, and the stars in her hair shone like diamonds.

"Look!" said the child. He was pointing to the edge of the hilltop. Where there had once only been rocks, there were now trees. Orsola turned around— the entire hilltop was encircled by trees, as though they had just climbed up from the forest. And there, among the trees, shining in the moonlight, was her little tree with its bare branches. From them hung shining pearls, like little moons. Surely those were more pearls than had been on her necklace? Among the trees she saw movement, and she realized there were animals as well—a herd of deer, a family of wild boars, a brown bear, and innumerable smaller creatures, too far away to identify in the darkness. But there among them, like a bright flame, was a fox with russet fur.

Orsola heard a humming sound—a deep, steady drone. Was it coming from the stars? Then it seemed as though the rocks took it up—it rose and fell, echoing from peak to crag to outcropping. And then it seemed as though the trees joined in, higher and more varied, so that the music became a symphony. And highest of all in that composition—for there must be a composer of such music—she heard the howling of wolves. The woman beside her listened intently—perhaps she was the composer? And the child clapped his hands with delight each time wolf howls rose into the night. It was a strange, wild music that seemed to come from the heart of the Wolfwald itself, and Orsola realized that she had arrived at the ball.

When she woke the next morning, she would have a confused recollection of dancing with oaks and alders and hemlocks, of curtseying to a bear and resting on moss with her arm around a doe. She remembered having gone to a great ball, the first of her life, and celebrating all night under the light of an almost-full moon. Her hostess, the woman with stars in her hair, watched the stately dances with a solemn smile and an owl perched on one shoulder, while her son rode around the hilltop on a great black wolf. She still remembered the ringing of his laughter, like bells.

It seemed to her that at one point she had asked the woman, "Lady, what is your name?"

And the lady had said, "I have many names. At the church down in your valley they call me Maria, but the wolves call me one name, and the mountains another, and the stars have their own name for me. I answer to them all."

Finally, as the sky had grown lighter and the sun had risen over the mountains, the music had grown softer, sweeter, until only the dawn seemed to be singing, a single high, bright note. Orsola saw that the hilltop was once again bare, except for the woman and her son. He ran to Orsola and put something into her pocket—the one without the locket in it. But that was the last she remembered before she woke up on the hard ground in front of the kitchen door, wrapped in a cloak of black wool, her stockings torn beyond mending.

She put her hand in her pocket to see what the boy had put there, and she pulled out a star.

"BUT IT WASN'T a star," said the schoolmaster's daughter. "It was an acorn. She planted it in front of the castle, and it grew into an oak tree. You can still see it there. It has grown as high as the top of the tower—the one that has not fallen. There used to be two towers, but now there is only one." Her name was Lilla, and she was very opinionated.

"It was a star in my dream," said Antal. "Or in the old woman's story, I don't remember which. I must have fallen asleep while she was telling it, because when I woke up this morning, she was gone. The fire in the stove had gone out, but there was bread and butter and honey on the table for me. I left her ten kroner and chopped all the wood that I found beside the goat shed. By the time I was done, the sun was high in the sky and she had not come back, so I found the path again and made my way down the mountain. On the bridge I met your daughter, sir." He nodded to the schoolmaster, who was sitting on the other side of the fireplace, in an identical armchair. Lilla was seated on a sort of low tuffet. Idly, he wondered how old she was. Certainly old enough to be out of school. "And now I'm here. I'm most grateful for your hospitality."

"When my father told me that story," said the schoolmaster, whose name was Janko Pal, "it was an egg as white as snow. Saint Orsola put it under one of the hens, until it hatched, and out of it came a white dove that would sit on her shoulder and fly around her head. But who knows the truth of the matter. These sorts of stories are often told of saints."

"But Papa, who could Antal have met in the forest?" asked Lilla.

He was pleased that she was already referring to him by his first name, although Mr. Odon would have been more appropriate—seeing that he was older than her, and a gentleman. She was, indeed, very opinionated for a young woman. But she was also very pretty. "There is no cottage where he described. No one could live so high on the mountain, certainly not an old woman. How could she survive in winter? She would starve to death."

"I saw her as certainly as I see you and your father," said Antal. "I assure you that her cottage was as real and solid as this house."

It was a pleasant house at the edge of the village, although in a rustic style, with white walls and a red tile roof. That morning, after waking up in the old woman's house and chopping her wood, he had come down the mountain with the intent of finding a proper dinner and lodging in the village. He might stay here a few days and then move on. He had his rucksack with a guidebook and change of clothes, money in his wallet, and nowhere in particular to go.

He had been thinking about the events of the night before—meeting the old woman and then falling asleep to her strange story about the Baron's daughter—when he had seen the schoolmaster's daughter. She had been standing on the bridge, looking down into the water, and he had taken the liberty afforded handsome young men of good family to address her. "Pardon me, miss,"—for her dress was that of a lady, not a peasant woman—"can you tell me the name of this village? Is it indeed Szent Orsola?"

She had curtseyed, responded politely, and pointed the way to the inn. But when he had asked her for more information on the region—he was still thinking about that story—she had offered to take him to her father, who was a scholar of local history and folklore.

And now here he was.

"You should ask Lilla to take you there," said Janko Pal. "The castle, that is. She can show it to you—it's in sad disrepair now. I've been trying to raise the funds to turn it into a school, but it's a slow process. The people of these mountains are not rich—we cannot raise taxes on them, even if we could convince them that education is a common good. They want their children to work in the fields or forests, as they did. And the government sends us so little! After all, that money is needed for Austrian mercenaries, to put down the uprisings in the capital." This was said with a shake of his head, in a tone of deep cynicism.

"I was part of that uprising, briefly," said Antal. Would his host blame or praise him? He wondered if he would be dismissed from this pleasant house as a troublemaker. And if so, would he still be able to see Lilla?

Janko Pal regarded him for a moment from under bushy eyebrows. "Well, you're brave enough, although foolish. You young men, thinking you can change the world by waving placards in the streets and staging hunger strikes in prison! By issuing proclamations on the steps of Parliament. If I were still at university, perhaps I would have joined you. But when you marry and settle down, you will find the world is changed through slow, constant work, not sound and fury. Which is what I need to do today, if I am to teach my student tomorrow! One of my teachers has fallen ill—there are only three of us for this entire district, and two are now doing the work of three. Go with Lilla. She will show you the village, and while you are here, you are welcome to stay in my home. I am told the beds at the inn are so hard, only the dead could lie in them comfortably!"

Antal was glad to go with the schoolmaster's daughter, although she did not, in his opinion, show him the respect due to his age and position. He was, after all, two or three years older than her, and a university student! But he was content to follow her through the village as she pointed out its landmarks—the smithy that looked as though it dated back to the days of Saint Orsola, the inn that was almost as old, the schoolhouse where her father taught.

"That is new," she said. "Fifty years ago, the farmers did not think it worthwhile to send their sons, or certainly their daughters, to school. But when King Ludvig, blessed be his memory, declared that every child had to be educated until the age of fourteen, the school building was built—that was when my father and mother came here. Originally they were from Gretz. Unfortunately, the Regent has cut funding so much that the teachers can barely afford paper and ink for the advanced scholars! You should see the state of the roof . . . I went to that school myself, and then to the Convent of the Sacred Heart in Karberg. My father believes in education for women."

Antal nodded and refrained from saying that his own father emphatically did not, although his sister had tormented a series of governesses with her curiosity, finally borrowing his schoolbooks because she said her own were for children.

The village was considerably smaller than the town in which he had grown up, where his father was a man of some importance. Its poverty was shown by the thatched roofs—only a few were tiled like the schoolmaster's house—and the paint peeling off the stuccoed walls. Yet every house had its small garden, with fruit trees on which he could see a few late apples, and the inhabitants they passed seemed friendly enough. At least they greeted Lilla with a smile and a nod, while staring at him with unabashed curiosity. He found himself a little ashamed of his city clothes.

At one end of the village was the church, a simple enough affair with the same white stucco walls as the houses. "The old church burned down in one of the wars, I don't remember which," said Lilla. "Probably against one of the Napoleons, I suppose. Father could tell you which one."

"You're not interested in Sylvanian history?" he asked, with a superior air. Of course, one could not expect women to be interested in subjects like history and politics. Most likely, the Convent of the Sacred Heart would have focused on embroidery and—what else did young ladies learn? From what his sister had told him, her education had focused a great deal on music and making sauces.

"Not in that part of it," she said, shaking her head. "There is a wall in the church that lists the men who died in each of those wars. So many, just from this village! I imagine their wives, their mothers. Perhaps they had children. How did they feel when their fathers did not come home? But look, there is the oak tree I mentioned. You see? It was an acorn, and it grew into that tree."

The oak was magnificent, certainly at least two hundred years old. Antal shaded his eyes to look at it, for the afternoon sun was high in the sky. Behind it was a castle of gray stone, half fallen down.

"Is that Orsola's castle?" he asked.

"It was. Come, I will show you around it. Just be careful walking under the arches. Sometimes a stone falls on a visitor's head and kills him. Otherwise, it's safe enough."

He looked at her, startled, then realized she was laughing at him. As he followed her, he tried to decide whether or not he was offended. Soon, however, curiosity conquered his pride.

"What happened to Orsola, after she woke on the ground near the castle and found a star in her pocket?"

"An acorn. I only know the story my mother told me. She died when I was a child, the year before I went away to school—of a cancer, we later realized. She grew ill so quickly . . . After Christmas, she told us that she did not feel well, and by midsummer, she was gone. I think my father sent me to Karberg partly to get me away from the village and my memories. He thought it would help me forget the last few months of nursing her."

Antal saw tears in her eyes, and realized for the first time that they were hazel, like a mossy pool. They were the most beautiful eyes he had ever seen. "Forgive me for bringing up a painful topic," he said, which seemed inadequate. But what would have been adequate? He felt like a fool.

She gave a quick shake of her head, as though bringing herself back to the present. "Her father wanted Orsola to marry a neighboring baron—a rather nasty old man, but very rich. She refused and said she had climbed up the mountain on Christmas Eve, following the Christ Child, who had taken her to see the Virgin Mary, shining like the moon and crowned with stars. Henceforth, she would dedicate herself to God. The Baron locked her into her room, and there she stayed for three months. He said he would allow her no food until she agreed to marry. Some say the white dove born from the Virgin Mary's egg flew up to Heaven every morning and evening and brought her food—that

SAINT ORSOLA AND THE POET

is the version my father heard. Some say that she fed on prayer. Who knows? Maybe a servant smuggled it into her room. At the end of three months, her father died—he had not been well since the day she went up the mountain. After his funeral, she gave half his gold to the people. With the other half, she founded a convent, here in the castle. It lasted until that Napoleon, whichever he was, burned it to the ground."

Antal looked at her doubtfully. "Do you think it was the Christ Child and the Holy Mother she met on the mountain?" He remembered his dream of the boy riding a black wolf. He had not looked like any picture of the Christ Child that Antal had ever seen.

"Who knows." Lilla shrugged her shoulders and smiled. "But I think Orsola must have been a clever woman. How else could she refuse her father's command to marry? There was no higher authority than a father, in those days—except the king, and God. They say her convent educated women from all over Sylvania, and even other countries. Queen Matilda herself once studied and prayed within these walls. I suppose being an abbess gave Orsola the freedom and power she could not have had in any other way, at that time."

Lilla walked through the ruins, brushing her fingers along the stone walls as though she could feel that other time on their worn surfaces. Antal watched her move between strips of light and shadow where the walls were either standing or fallen. Her hair was dark brown in the shade and a rich golden brown in the sunlight. He could hear the drone of bees among the clover growing through the broken flagstones, and the swish of Lilla's petticoats. She held her skirts up in one hand to keep them from getting dirty, above a pair of slender ankles in neat but muddy boots. He had a feeling that something important was happening, something that would change his life, but he could not have told you what.

"I mentioned that my father collects the folktales of this region. There are stories of a woman—Mother Night, she is called. Some of the stories say she is older than God, but don't tell Father Mikal I mentioned that, or he would be angry with me. Her son is supposed to be the Day Child, who is reborn every year. Father says they represent the cycle of the year, the days shortening in autumn and then lengthening again in spring. Once, perhaps, they were worshipped—before King Karel I converted the tribes to Christianity. But sometimes you still see a sun, the sign of the Day Child, carved into an old post, and there is an oath in these mountains—old women still swear 'by Mother Night.' My father says even now these beliefs are not entirely dead. They are primitive ways of explaining the natural world around us. Orsola's story also explains why the foxes of the Wolfwald are red, and why Winterberry trees grow on the mountains. Although they grow elsewhere in Sylvania as well."

"And what do you believe?" asked Antal.

Suddenly, in the shadow of the old stone walls, she laughed. "I believe we should get back to the house before the church bell rings the Angelus. Anika will be preparing dinner, and I must help her with the *kapustnika*. In your house, no doubt, the servants do all the cooking, but here there is only me and Anika, and as she continually reminds me, she cannot do everything!"

After dinner, sitting in the parlor with Janko Pal, full of the sausages and sauerkraut that Anika had served him over potato dumplings, Antal sighed with contentment. Somewhere in the house, he could hear the banging of pots and pans—no doubt Lilla was helping the housekeeper wash up. He tried to remember the last time he had felt completely at peace. It must have been in his boyhood, before the conflicts with his father, before his military school and the university, before the first time he had fallen in love—with a kitchen maid who had laughed at the absurdity of his declaration, made in the form of a sonnet. He was tired, but his heart felt light, as though it had put down some burden he was not aware it had been carrying.

He looked up to see the schoolmaster staring at him intently, the way schoolmasters do when you have forgotten your Latin declensions.

"Is smoking one of your vices, Antal?"

"No, sir. Not that particular one. But please, go ahead," for Janko Pal had a pipe in his hand.

"I imagine yours are women and politics. I will, thank you. Anika doesn't like it because the stink stays in the curtains, or so she claims. But a man must have some vices, I tell her, to make certain women remain the superior sex! By the way, if she is a little rude to you, don't mind it. She has been like a mother to Lilla, and a young man in the house—well. If her eyes had been daggers at dinner, I would be calling the doctor!" Janko Pal laughed at his own joke and lit his pipe.

Antal laughed politely and uncomfortably. That afternoon, it had started dawning on him that Lilla was a complicated creature, with an inner life of her own. He had never thought of a woman in that way before. He had never, for example, bothered about the inner life of the young lady in the fabric and trimmings shop. It seemed to him that Lilla was not one woman, but maybe two or three, rolled into one. He wondered if he would ever completely understand her. As for politics, he was heartily sick of it at the moment.

"Have you ever considered being a school teacher?"

The question startled him out of his reverie. "Why do you ask, sir?"

Janko Pal drew on his pipe. "I mentioned that I am short one teacher. You've had two years of a university education. You are already more qualified than most candidates who come to these rural schools. The pay is low, the pupils are willing but slow to learn—through no fault of their own. Their parents never attended school. Some of them must be convinced that reading, writing, and arithmetic will make their sons better farmers, their daughters better housewives. Every few years you will find a particularly clever one who can be trained as a teacher. There is no fame or glory in such work, and yet I believe it is a worthwhile, even noble endeavor. What do you say, Antal?"

* * *

THAT NIGHT, ANTAL Odon, the new teacher at the village school of Szent Orsola, looked up at the moon. It seemed to shine into the bedroom so brightly—it
had been almost full when he had slept in the old woman's cottage. Had that
really happened? Or had he spent a night in the forest and dreamed the entire
adventure? Surely not.

He took off his jacket and put it over the armchair in one corner. There
was a lump in the pocket. What could it be? He put in his hand and pulled out
an acorn.

How had that gotten there? It reminded him of Lilla's insistence about the
object in Orsola's pocket. Star, acorn, egg—which had it been? How strange
these old stories were, that lingered in the rural districts. Tomorrow he would
ask Janko Pal if there were other variations. Perhaps he should write down the
version the old woman had told him, so he would not forget. There was a table
in the corner, with a pen and ink. He put the acorn beside the inkwell. He was
tired, but it would not take long. How to begin?

A first line came to him—a line of poetry. He had not written poetry since
the misadventure of the kitchenmaid, and had sworn never to attempt it again.
The line was bad, very bad. He wrote another. It was worse. He crossed it out
with disgust. Well, so much for that—he was no poet, and might as well give up.

Antal undressed for bed and got under the covers. Just when he was warm
and comfortable, another line of poetry came to him. No, he would not listen
to it! He was almost asleep. But he could not get it out of his head. "By Mother
Night!" he said, angry with himself. It made a surprisingly effective oath. He
got out of bed, sat once again at the desk, and started to write.

YEARS LATER, WHEN he was married to Lilla and had begun to make a name
for himself as a poet, he remembered this small incident. *Songs of the Revolution* was still his bestselling book. It had been published under the pseudonym
Amadeo—his despised middle name had come in handy for this purpose—and
had immediately been banned for its criticism of the Regent and his repressive
policies. It had been passed around secretly in leftist intellectual circles. After
Stefan Gustavus was defeated and his Austrian mercenaries were expelled, Erno
Palko had talked him into revealing that the revolutionary Amadeo was none
other than Antal Odon, rural schoolteacher. He was still not sure how he felt
about that. In consequence, he—or rather Amadeo—had been invited to write
an ode for the coronation of King Radomir V.

Antal was preparing lessons in his study, for he would continue to teach
until the success of *Verses from Old Sylvania*, which included the first poem
he had ever written, "Saint Orsola and the Christ Child." He could hear Kiti
and Anika in the garden. What were his daughters playing? Often their games
seemed to him like strange dreams.

"I am the King of the Fairies," Anika would say. "And Kiti is the Bear Princess. We are writing a treaty between our two countries. We are going to have peace between us, after a hundred years of war. But we will need to make war on the trolls. Are you a troll, Papa? Or a bear? You can be a bear. Mama is the Fairy Queen, but we are not married, because you can't marry your own mother. Everyone knows that."

Later he would go visit Janko, who was getting older now but insisted on living alone, since old Anika had died several years ago. Probably he would retire soon, and Antal would become the schoolmaster, a prospect that filled him with dread.

All things considered, he was content with his life. He had a clever wife, whose beauty still made him catch his breath when she stood by a sunlit window and the silver strands in her hair gleamed among the brown. He had two daughters who sometimes mystified him. The younger, Kiti, was quiet and serious, while Anika was even more headstrong than he had been as a child. What would she become, as a young woman? The King had recently announced the creation of a university for women—his father and sister had argued about it, the last time they had all gathered on the estate for his father's birthday. Katarina always seemed to set the old man off—he would rail against that damned radical husband of hers, although as far as Antal could see, Erno had settled into being a respectable member of parliament whose radicalism showed principally in his support for the labor movement. Anyway, he and Kati were happy together, which was what mattered, in the end. What would his own life have been like without Lilla? He shook his head—he could not imagine it. Perhaps Anika would go to that new university and shock her grandfather.

He could hear the girls shouting and laughing below. He really should stop daydreaming and get back to his lesson plans! The multiplication tables would not teach themselves.

He opened the desk to look for a pencil and there, tucked into one corner, was the acorn.

How had it gotten there? Had he simply not noticed it before?

Just then, Lilla came in. "I've brought you some tea and biscuits, my love. Do you know why? Look, I'll put the tray here on the bureau, if you'll remember to pour the tea. Last time, Marta said she found the teapot cold and untouched."

"No, why?" he said, trying to look back at her as she wrapped her arms around him from behind and kissed him in front of one ear.

"Because I'm the best wife in the world. And now I will return to the garden, where I am sometimes Napoleon, and sometimes Liliana, queen of the fairies. It's a bit confusing."

"Lilla, on the day we met, after I told you my dream about Saint Orsola, did you put an acorn in my pocket?"

"No, why in the world would I do such a thing?" She looked at him so innocently that he was tempted to disbelieve her. Were the corners of her mouth twitching with laughter? He could not tell.

"I've had an idea—to turn the old stories your father has been collecting into poems. I would include my poem about Saint Orsola—you remember, the one that was featured in *The Oracle* before it was shut down for publishing subversive literature. Do you think that's silly?"

"Why would it be silly? Never mind, I'll pour the tea myself. I can see your mind is on other things, and you will certainly forget."

"I'm known for writing about serious topics—war, liberty, the rights of the people. And for that damned Coronation Ode! Should I be writing children's stories?"

"Now you are being silly." She placed a cup of tea and a plate of biscuits on the desk beside him. "These are the tales of the folk, the memories of old Sylvania. That's why my father has spent half his life collecting them. Could anything be more important? Other than your tea, of course. Which is already getting cold."

He sipped from the cup, remembering when he had first come to the village.

"You know, I went back the next day, and several days after that, trying to find the old woman's cottage. I never could find it again."

"Of course not," said Lilla. "I'll leave the tray here. Just bring it down when you're done, please. I have to invade Poland *and* make plum jam with Marta this afternoon, so I will be rather busy. To think I have a kitchen maid! How grand we are getting, now that you're a famous poet!"

"Then you believe it was all a dream, meeting that old woman?" Antal tried a biscuit. It was hard, and crumbled when he bit into it—Marta was still learning the finer points of cookery.

"Of course not." Lilla smiled, and he remembered again how he had once lost himself in her hazel eyes. "I believe that the old woman was Saint Orsola herself, come down from Heaven, or wherever she is, to tell you her story. Now, I really must go. If you start writing this book of yours today, don't stay up past dark! You will need spectacles soon, if you keep writing by candlelight."

After she had gone, Antal stared down at the acorn in his hand. Then he took a notebook from out of the desk, dipped his pen in the inkwell, and wrote on the first page, "*Verses from Old Sylvania*, by Amadeo Odon."

The Nightingale and the Rose

Here is the story:

There was a nightingale.
She looked like nothing at all,
a small brown bird
perched in the rose bushes.
You would scarcely have seen her
unless you were looking carefully.

The roses were still blooming
although it was late summer:
they were hybrid perpetuals, bred
from the old French roses
crossed with roses from China
brought back by sailors and diplomats,
in cargoes with blue porcelain
and embroidered silk.

The nightingale did not know this:
she had not migrated so far.

What she knew was her nest in the thicket
by the orchard, with two eggs in it the size
of your thumbnail, speckled brown.

What she knew was the professor's garden:
the elm tree, the fountain in which she bathed,
shaking her feathers. The sundial
that told the time and all the local gossip.
The green lizards sunbathing on the wall,
the tennis lawn, the roses in clipped rows,
already losing their petals,
yellow and pink, pink striped red,
apricot, and cream with a yellow heart.
She knew they cost a great deal, for the professor
had said so, walking in the garden

with the university chancellor,
and the lizards had repeated it.

She knew the student who lived with the professor
in a rented room and sometimes left his books
on the garden bench. She knew he was studying
something called metaphysics.

She knew the professor's daughter,
who walked in the garden and often sang to herself
while cutting flowers—not quite as well
as a nightingale, but one must make allowances.
Anyway, the nightingale thought she was beautiful,
with rich brown hair. But the butterflies
thought she was ugly, so large and human,
always taking away the flowers
so they could be displayed in vases behind glass windows,
and what was the use of that? They were convinced
the flowers belonged to them. After all,
they were the ones who depended on the nectar
for food. They were socialists.

One day as she sat in her nest, the nightingale heard
the student complaining to the lizards, or perhaps to the wall:
She promised to dance with me if I brought her a red rose
to match her dress, but there are no red roses,
only pink streaked with red, or red on the yellow petals.
The lizards scurried along the wall. They did not care
about the student's relationship problems.

But the nightingale was a romantic.
I shall find him a red rose, she thought.

The student was right: there were no red roses,
not anywhere in the professor's garden.
Why do you want a red rose? asked the Boule de Neige.
It was the most beautiful rose in the garden, and knew it.
Its buds were red, but opened into white globes
of fragrance. A white rose means innocence,
a white rose means *I am pure.*

Because the professor's daughter wants it, said the nightingale.
And red roses mean love. That's what she truly wants: proof

that the student loves her. And then perhaps
she will permit herself to love him back. Can you not turn
your petals red? For love
is the best thing in the world. Or what she had seen
of the world, from Denmark to the coast of Africa.
She had migrated once already.

Look how the sun loves the waterdrops
that splash from the fountain,
how the wind loves the top of the elm tree,
how the lizards love their wall. That is how
the student loves the professor's daughter,
I'm sure of it.

There is only one way to turn a white rose red,
said the Boule de Neige. And it is so terrible
that I do not want to mention it.

Tell me, said the nightingale.
I'm not afraid.

You see that rose? My most beautiful rose
at the end of an arching cane. If you perch
on that cane and put your breast against the thorn,
then press on it, so it drinks of your heart's blood,
and you sing—remember that you must sing—
slowly the rose will turn red.

The nightingale chirped
and flitted about in her agitation.
But my heart's blood—will I not die?
She thought of her eggs, her precious eggs,
speckled brown, the size of your thumbnail.
She loved her eggs, as much as the student
loved metaphysics. They had been laid in June,
for she had mated late. In a few days
they would hatch.

That I can't tell you, said the Boule de Neige.
Very likely, but one must take risks for love,
or so I have heard.

I don't know, I don't know, said the nightingale.

Let me return this evening. I must consider
all the options.

The rest of that day, she sat on her eggs.
What if she never came back, and they did not hatch?
What if they hatched and she was not there
when her children called for her? Who would teach them to fly?
It was the male nightingales, after all, who sang at night,
as her mate had sung to her before an owl
had made a meal of him. Who was she
to do this?

And yet she could already imagine
the red rose, the most beautiful of all roses,
that her song would produce.
She felt this task had been given to her.
In all the garden, only she
could sing a red rose into being.

That evening, as the moon climbed the sky,
she left her nest in the thicket and flew to the rose bushes.
She perched on the arching cane with the most beautiful rose
on it, white as snow. I'm ready, she said.
All right, said the Boule de Neige. We shall do this together.

She put her breast on the thorn so it pierced deeply
and sang. She sang all the songs she had learned
since she had hatched from an egg—
songs of courtship, songs of warning, songs about rain,
songs that meant *The cat is coming*.

The lizards said, what is that racket? But the sundial
liked it, and the fountain accompanied her as well as it could,
and the other rose bushes, who knew what was happening,
listened intently: the Variegata de Bologna,
the Reine des Violettes, the Souvenir de la Malmaison,
who claimed descent from Empress Josephine herself.
Even the daisies in the tennis lawn understood
and blushed to be witnessing an event so important.

The student up in his garret bedroom
said, How prettily the nightingale is singing!
as he leafed through his Kant and Hegel.

Only the professor's daughter did not hear it,
for she was practicing at the pianoforte
and anyway the French doors were closed.

All night long the nightingale sang,
and by morning the rose was as red as her heart's blood,
as red as the velvet mantle of a king,
or a ruby worn by an American heiress.
Even the dawn was astonished
and touched it delicately.

But what about the nightingale? She lay
on the rich soil of the rose bed,
her small heart barely beating. Had it been worth it?
She thought it had, she was almost certain.
For during that long night it had come to her
that the rose, despite being beautiful, was beside the point.
For the point—and here she gasped, her beak open
to take a final breath—was the song, and becoming the song.

Before breakfast, the student walked into the garden.
A red rose! And the most magnificent one
he had ever seen. Surely she would dance with him now
at the party the professor was throwing that evening
for his department. There would be a waltz, he was sure of it.
He would hold her tightly around the waist, and she would dance
with him, and maybe kiss him in the conservatory.

Look, he said, showing it to her
over toast and marmalade in the breakfast room.
It will match your dress perfectly.
Oh, she said. But I'm not wearing that dress anymore.

Where had he found the rose? She had asked for a red one
because there were none in the garden. Tonight, she was planning
to slip away during the mazurka, when no one would notice,
and elope with her cousin, whom she had loved since they were children
spending summers together at their grandparents' house in Funen.
Her father had quarreled with his father and forbidden her
to see him, so they had been meeting in secret.
She wore his engagement ring on a chain under her bodice.
Tomorrow they would be married. They were risking
everything—the anger of their fathers, disinheritance.

But at least they would be together.
She did not want the student searching for her at the party,
preventing her escape. Why could he not have fallen
in love with someone else, like the kitchen maid?

Later the student, despondent,
on his way to the university, discovered
that he had inadvertently tucked the rose into his satchel,
not knowing what else to do with it.
With an oath he flung it into the street,
where a cartwheel ran over it
and a horse's hooves trampled it
into the mud. Love is a fool's game,
he thought. Better stick
with what can be learned in books.

That night, after the party was over,
the professor snoring in his nightcap, the student
sprawled on his bed, still in his clothes
(he would have a hangover the next morning),
the professor's daughter in a coach rolling toward Copenhagen,
her head on her cousin's shoulder, the marriage license
tucked safely in his waistcoat pocket, only the kitchen maid
still awake, washing the last of the coffee cups,

Mother Night came walking down the street.
The pear and quince trees in the orchard bowed,
as did the elm. The fountain spit its waters
as hard and high as it could so the drops would sparkle
like fireworks under the moon. The daisies
grew pale—they were very young. The rose bushes,
who were well-bred, bent their canes gracefully.
Even the lizards, despite being diurnal, blinked their eyes
in the moonlight. And the old house itself, which had stood
since before the Reformation, said to her,
Lady, I am not worthy
of this honor.

She smiled and said, I believe you have something here
that was made for me? Ah, yes.
She stooped in the street, on which the mud had dried,
and picked up the rose, crushed, its petals scattered.
then put it into her dark hair, fastening it

with a jeweled pin. There, it blossomed
and its fragrance filled the garden. In that house
all the sleepers, from the professor to the cook,
would have strange dreams.

She stroked the timbers of the house, which creaked with pleasure,
then scratched the lizards under their chins. To the roses,
she nodded, as great ladies nod to each other,
and they nodded back, knowingly. She smiled
at the daisies, who immediately closed up with shyness.
Finally, she lifted the nightingale, lying
stiff and lifeless, then breathed on her, long and slow.
The nightingale gasped and fluttered. When she saw
the face bent over her,
she hid her head beneath her wing.

Such humility, said Mother Night. And in a great artist.
Would you like to sing in my garden at the end of the world?
The nightingale, not knowing what to say,
gave one small trill, but that was enough.

Pardon me, said Mother Night to the wall,
reaching into the thicket and lifting the nightingale's nest,
then putting the nightingale on her speckled eggs. Carrying
the nest in the palm of her hand, she proceeded up the street,
for she had a great deal to do before sunrise.

In Paris she picked up a poet
who had died that day of meningitis
in a hotel room, after being released from prison.
She put him into her pocket, already filled
with all the oddments she had collected that night.
Still carrying the nightingale's nest,
she walked to the end of the world, to her house
of many rooms, some large as the sky,
some small as a mouse hole,
where everything precious is preserved.

If you ever find it—it's not on any map
and you can only go there by invitation—
sit in the garden, just at twilight,
and hear the nightingales. There are three of them.
They are said to be very fine.

Your House

One day, it may be time
to dismantle your house.

Yes, the one you built so carefully
of brick, remembering the third pig
in the fairy tale, to be storm-proof
and wolf-proof, to stand
for a hundred years. The house
you thought you would retire in,
perhaps die in.

But maybe you found rain
falling from the ceilings, wind
whistling around the rooms,
making the fire gutter. Maybe a hunger
you don't understand began
gnawing at your belly. Maybe
the house became a coffin out of which
you are desperate to awaken,
like Snow White out of her glass casket.
Maybe the fairy tale ended wrong,
maybe you were, all along,
in the wrong story.
Maybe the house you thought was yours
was not, after all, the one you
could live in.

So you take it apart, brick by brick.
Take down the chimney, take up
the floorboards. Hopefully
someone else will recycle them.
And you set out on your journey,
the one you did not want to make,
the one that is inevitable,
although over the mountains

426

a storm is brewing,
and the forest, you know,
is filled with wolves.

Acknowledgments

There are so many people to thank for making a collection like this possible that it's impossible to list them all. There are the teachers who taught and encouraged me along the way, the writers who read and commented on these stories in writing groups, the magazine and anthology editors who edited and published them, the copyeditors who caught my mistakes. If I tried to list them (it would be a long, long list), inevitably I would forget to include someone and, in a reversal of the fairy tale, end up cursing myself. So instead I will send them a general heartfelt thanks. Without them, these stories and poems would not exist. I would like to specifically and especially thank Mike and Anita Allen for suggesting and then publishing this collection, as well as Sydney Macias for all of the work she put into it, including her careful and thorough copyedits. I would also like to thank Paula Arwen Owen for the interior illustrations, Brett Massé for his work on the cover design, and Catrin Welz-Stein for allowing us to use her wonderful art, which perfectly captures the spirit of this collection, on the cover. I am grateful to have a publisher like Mythic Delirium Books, which brings such fantastic (in both senses) books into the world. Finally, and as always, I would like to thank my daughter Ophelia, who is simply the best.

Copyright Notices

MATTHEW STEIN PHOTOGRAPHY

Theodora Goss is the World Fantasy, Locus, and Mythopoeic Award-winning author of the Athena Club series of novels, *The Strange Case of the Alchemist's Daughter*, *European Travel for the Monstrous Gentlewoman*, and *The Sinister Mystery of the Mesmerizing Girl*, as well as the two-sided novella *The Thorn and the Blossom*. Her short story and poetry collections include *In the Forest of Forgetting*, *Songs for Ophelia*, and *Snow White Learns Witchcraft*. She has been a finalist for the Nebula, Crawford, and Shirley Jackson Awards, as well as on the Tiptree Award Honor List. Her work has been translated into fifteen languages. She has a PhD in English literature, and teaches literature and writing at Boston University.

Learn more at theodoragoss.com.

CPSIA information can be obtained
at www.ICGtesting.com
Printed in the USA
BVHW040016030223
657748BV00011B/103/J

9 781732 644076